Praise 1

"Yoshimoto's most fully realized work to date . . . Her firm grasp of her characters, her surefooted prose and her wide-eyed exploration of everything from American pop culture to the Japanese language make this one of the most satisfying books of the summer."

—*Time Out New York*

"Yoshimoto knows the remedial potential of a good, old-fashioned narrative . . . Her characters are immersed in a youth culture that owes more than a little to our notoriously shallow, decadent *fin de siècle.* They sleep around, eat street ramen, and listen with pleasure to Nirvana, but their lives are also marred by old-fashioned timeless tragedy. They lose their jobs and marry unsuccessfully; the people they love die before their time . . . Yoshimoto has never been afraid of trauma." —*The Nation*

"An oddly winsome blend of personal psychology and the paranormal overlay the story of a young woman's fight to reclaim herself after twin tragedies . . . The earnest, peripatetic confusion of Sakumi's narrative whisks the reader from one peak moment to another . . . Endearing." —*Library Journal*

"Her most ambitious work to date . . . many scenes crackle with her hot-wired magic . . . Sakumi, the narrator, is enchantingly muddled, sincere, and full of love for her irregular family . . . [Yoshimoto] spins a mesmerizing and haunting tale." —*Booklist*

ALSO BY BANANA YOSHIMOTO

Kitchen

N.P.

Lizard

Asleep

Goodbye Tsugumi

Hardboiled & Hard Luck

BANANA YOSHIMOTO

amrita

Translated from the Japanese by
Russell F. Wasden

Grove Press / New York

Japanese original edition published by KADOKAWA GROUP PUBLISHING CO., LTD., Japan
English translation rights arranged with Banana Yoshimoto through ZIPANGO, S.L.

Published simultaneously in Canada
Printed in the United States of America

First Grove Atlantic hardcover edition: July 1997
First Grove Atlantic paperback edition: September 2018

Library of Congress Cataloging-in-Publication data is available for this title.

ISBN 978-0-8021-2413-5
eISBN 978-0-8021-9049-9

Grove Press
an imprint of Grove Atlantic
154 West 14th Street
New York, NY 10011

Distributed by Publishers Group West

groveatlantic.com

24 25 10 9 8 7 6 5 4 3

amrita

Prologue

I'm what you might call a night person. Generally the sun comes up before I go down for bed, and as a fundamental rule I never open my eyes until early afternoon. Perhaps that's why the day turned out to be an exception among exceptions. That was the day, the day that I'm speaking of now, when the package first arrived from Ryūichirō.

Yes, it was that morning. From out of nowhere my little brother threw my bedroom door open with a bang and eagerly shook me awake.

"Wake up, Saku-chan, wake up! You got a package!"

Dazed, I pulled myself out of bed. "What?" I whispered.

"A package came for you. A big package!" My brother was exuberant, jumping back and forth. I'm sure he'd have pounced all over me if I'd pretended to still be asleep. So with no choice in the matter, I pushed the sleep from my eyes and gathered the strength to make the journey down the stairs. My little brother coiled himself around me and together we descended to the bottom.

Opening the kitchen door, I found my mother at the dining table, munching on a piece of toast. The strong aroma of fresh coffee floated in the air.

"Morning," I said.

"Good morning," my mother replied. Then, with a puzzled look on her face, she asked, "What's the occasion? You're up so early."

"The kid came and got me out of bed. Why isn't he at school, anyway? The little brat."

"I have a fever!" my brother said, plopping himself into a kitchen chair and grabbing at the toast.

"No wonder he's so hyper," I said, realizing for the first time why he was so excited.

"You were the same way when you were a child," my mother remarked. "I remember it like it was yesterday. You'd bounce off the walls, hang from chandeliers, and I'd just shake my head wondering what had gotten into you. As soon as I'd put my hand on your forehead, the reason was clear. You had a fever."

Smiling, I glanced around. "Where's everybody else?"

"They're still sleeping."

"Oh, yeah. I suppose they would be. It's only nine-thirty." I let out a long sigh. I hadn't gone to bed until five o'clock in the morning. Then I'd been shaken out of my dreams, so now my head was spinning.

"Care for some coffee?" my mother asked.

"Ummm," I said, nodding my head. "I'd love some."

I took a seat. Sunlight shone into the kitchen through the front window in a single, straight line. For the first time in a long time the sunlight poured over my body, and I bathed in its warmth for a while. Glancing over, I saw my mother from behind as she stood in front of the counter, working away in the morning kitchen. She looked so small, almost like a teenager playing newlywed in the kitchen.

To tell you the truth, my mother really was quite young. She had me when she was nineteen. Come to think of it, if I were like my mother, I'd already have two kids by now. Scary thought.

"Here you are, coffee. Why don't you have some bread?"

I noticed, however, that even the hand that brought me the coffee was beautiful. You'd never think it was the hand of someone who had managed the affairs of a household for twenty-odd years. I took delight in my mother. I liked her a lot. But I couldn't help being a little suspicious of her too. Somehow she fooled her own destiny, and got away with looking forever young.

~

Wasn't there at least one girl like that in every one of your high school classes? You know, the girl who managed to find a way to drive all the guys crazy; the girl who could be both elegant and voluptuous in a weird sort of way, despite the fact that she wasn't particularly amazing to look at. That was my mother, it seems, when she was younger. On the day of my parents' wedding my mother was nineteen and my father forty. After my younger sister and I were born, our father collapsed from a cerebral thrombosis. And then he died.

My mother remarried six years ago, and it didn't take long for my brother to come along. But my mother and her second husband split up a year ago. Once the perfect union of "father-mother-and-child" vanished, our home became something of a boarding house. Now, aside from me, my mother, and my brother, there were two others living in the house—our cousin Mikiko, and Junko, a childhood friend of my mother who needed a place to stay when she ran into trouble with her husband. Together we formed a family of five.

It was an unusual balance, a home brought together nicely like a women's paradise. But for some reason I found myself attracted to the lifestyle. And since my brother was still quite young, he brought a certain peacefulness to our hearts, almost as if he were the family pet. Because of him our lives became one.

After separating from my stepfather, my mother found something rare—a boyfriend younger than she was. It was obvious, however, that it would take some time before she would ever consider marrying again. But my brother was still small, and there was always the fear of another spoiled marriage. Nonetheless, her boyfriend often showed up at the house, and eventually my brother and he got along. It seemed it would be only a few weeks or maybe a month before he'd be moving in with us too. Then the day of the package rolled around, and the strange balance that we had managed to maintain seemed to be over.

Blood ties seemed unrelated to how we were living.

It was the same way when my stepfather was with us. He was a timid man, gentle and good. When he left, only sad memories remained, like the indescribable melancholy that lingers in a studio apartment once the sole tenant is gone. Heavy air is inescapable, regardless of where you are. It's impossible to get away from.

I suppose that's the reason I believe that as long as there is someone in charge of the household, someone who can maintain order among its members, someone who is clearly mature and established as a person, someone, in other words, like my mother, then eventually all who live under the same roof, despite blood ties or lineage, will at one point become family. Such a simple idea, but one that took a while for me to catch on to.

Oh, and another thing.

If the same people don't spend enough time in a home, even if they are connected by blood, their bonds will slowly fade away like a familiar landscape.

Just like Mayu.

While sipping coffee and nibbling on some walnut bread, I realized that at some point in time my thoughts had turned to my family. Perhaps that had something to do with the morning light and the way it reflected from the table in front of me.

"Okay, Yoshi," my mother said, pushing my brother in the direction of his room. "We've got to get you in bed. Your fever is only going to get worse."

"Wait," I said. "Did I really get a package?"

"Yes. It's over by the front door," my mother replied, looking back as she closed the door. I pulled myself up and made my way to the entrance.

There, shining in sunlight reflected from the plain hardwood floor, was a large cardboard box that looked like a white marble block. At first I thought it might be flowers, but when I bent down and picked it up I discovered how heavy it was. I glanced at the name of the sender: Ryūichirō Yamazaki. The package had been sent from a traditional Japanese inn in Chiba prefecture. He must have been traveling there.

Bursting with curiosity, I ripped the box open right there on the spot. He hadn't sent a letter, just a statue of Nipper, the old RCA Victor mascot, wrapped tightly in clear plastic. Looking at the dog through the bubbles in the plastic I suddenly felt a surge of emotion, and as I unwound the wrapping, the statue seemed to come closer, as if it were coming up through water from the middle of the sea. It was smooth and glossy, tinted with an antique hue. Nipper was leaning forward, his head silently cocked to one side.

"Oh my god," I whispered. "What a darling statue."

There I stood, half dreaming, riveted to the ground. I gazed at the statue for a moment as I placed it back in the box with the crushed plastic. Amid the morning light and the musk of settling dust, Nipper looked as if he were in a winter snow scene, crystal and clear.

Why would Ryūichirō send me the dog? I was clueless. Perhaps he had come across the statue in a secondhand store and couldn't take his eyes off it. Something told me that that was what Nipper was trying to convey. Clearly the statue was trying to tell me something. But what? There had to be a reason, I was sure. Glancing down at the dog, I decided to imitate him. I leaned down and cocked my head to one side, straining my ears to listen.

Just as I imagined, I couldn't hear a thing.

∾

Ryūichirō was the man who became Mayu's lover.

Now Mayu is dead.

About six months ago she was driving her car when it collided with a telephone pole. She died instantly. She'd been drinking, and on top of that she'd downed a bottle of sleeping pills.

Somehow, I never understood why, Mayu had been born with a beautiful face. Everything was perfectly proportioned. My father, mother, and I didn't look like her at all. Not that we were ugly or anything, but Mayu had managed to get away from the looks that the rest of us seemed to have. I suppose I could be polite and say the three of us possessed a "cool" countenance, but then one could easily say we just looked crabby. Nevertheless, Mayu had escaped those features altogether. When she was a child she seemed almost angelic.

Her face kept her from leading an ordinary life. Out of nowhere she was spotted by an agent, and she began to model at a very young age. Before long she was acting, receiving a supporting role in a television drama. By the end she was a full-fledged movie star. Over the course of events, show business became Mayu's home, and it was there that she grew up. She hadn't lived with us for years.

I suppose that's why I was so surprised when I learned that my sister, so busy that we seldom had a chance to see her, was suddenly retiring from acting. They said she had suffered a nervous breakdown. Even during the times when she had managed to come around, she never showed signs of being discontent. I always thought she looked happy.

Apparently the influence of that kind of lifestyle is not good for a young woman growing up. Over the years Mayu had allowed her outward appearance—her face, her hairstyle, clothing, makeup, everything—to turn her into something that a single man would have lascivious thoughts about. A lot of people can go through a life of fame and fortune without letting it go to their heads, but no matter how many get away with such a thing, I know Mayu had never been ready to handle such a lifestyle. Throughout the years Mayu had tried to hide her own weaknesses by putting up one makeshift disguise after another, covering herself with prefabricated pieces of plywood, but in the end all she had really managed to do was make a patched and darned image of herself. The nervous breakdown was her true self crying out to be saved.

When Mayu stopped acting she reexamined her friendships with men as well. By the time she met and moved in with Ryūichirō, she had managed to wipe the slate clean of all her old boyfriends.

Ryūichirō was a writer, and when he first met Mayu he was ghosting scripts for television. Mayu was a fan of his work, and it was always a game between them to see if she could figure out which shows he was writing for. Maybe that's one of the things which brought them so close together.

As a novelist Ryūichirō had written a full-length book three years earlier, but that was all he had had published. Surprisingly enough it became almost a classic for some people, and it still sells silently at the bookstores. It's a serious novel, somewhat abstract, depicting the lives of a group of insensitive young people. Before I met Ryūichirō, Mayu had forced me to read it, and when I finished I was convinced that I never wanted to meet the author. The book scared me. I figured that it had been written by a maniac. However, when I met him he turned out to be a pretty normal guy. I knew the second I laid eyes on him that it must have taken a tremendous amount of concentration, of both time and effort, for someone like Ryūichirō to weave together a novel so thematically dense as his. It takes a special talent for anyone to accomplish such a task.

After Mayu left home she couldn't cope with a regular job, so she lived with Ryūichirō while working part-time. Things stayed that way for so long that eventually my mother and I, even Ryūichirō and Mayu themselves, forgot that they weren't actually married. I hung out at their apartment a lot, and they came over to our house as well. Since I always saw them having such a good time together, it was hard for me to understand why Mayu had foolishly fallen so deeply into drugs and alcohol.

I never would have guessed that a few pills before bed to help sleep at night, or even a little nightcap, would turn into something that extreme. Can an icy cold beer, taken from the refrigerator to be enjoyed with the beautiful sunlight of an afternoon, do such a thing to a person? As I look back, I realize that there was always a feeling, an uncanny sort of feeling, that I had when she was around—a feeling that maybe, just maybe, she was on something. I suppose I never caught on to what she was taking since she always looked so natural.

As I recall the saintlike face of my sister sleeping, her long eyelashes and pale skin, so weak and fragile, I realize Mayu's difficulties started long before she got into the world of entertainment, long before she ever became friends with Ryūichirō.

No one will ever be able to say when it really started, and it was impossible to have known just how far it would go. Within that outer radiance it was really Mayu's heart that was aching. It was slowly being devoured, damaged and defaced like a piece of fruit infested with worms.

"I don't suppose she just took the wrong pills," Ryūichirō said in the hallway of the hospital when Mayu was taken away. By that time the situation was hopeless.

"Maybe," I said. "But she was so young."

I knew it couldn't be that simple, and so did Ryūichirō. My mother, standing next to us listening to the conversation, agreed. We all knew how she had died. It was as plain as something delivered to us by hand, but to have voiced it would have been foolish. We remained silent.

But why? Why Mayu?

Mayu, who was so methodical, separating each pill, putting just the right amount of medicine in her special case before going away on another trip.

Why Mayu?

She was so young, despite all that she had been through over the years. At some point she must have lost sight of the possibilities awaiting her in life. She was like a burning cinder, slowly losing the glowing energy that kept her alive.

Most likely she couldn't have been saved. Most likely she didn't want to be saved.

She was just a figure, an image. But we loved her. When she finally passed away, those thoughts left my heart, traveling beyond the cold plastic couch where we sat and resonating around the hollow white walls of the waiting room, almost as if a voice were screaming out from inside me.

~

My mother cried her eyes red for the next several days, but oddly enough I couldn't bring myself to grieve. Only once did I shed tears over my sister. It happened two or three days after Nipper arrived in the mail. My brother and Mikiko had gone to the video store and picked up the animated *My Neighbor Totoro*. Then they stopped by my room to invite me to watch it with them. As I walked down the hallway, I realized their actions were innocent, there were no bad intentions. No one could have known what would happen. After casually putting a small tray of cookies together and boiling a hot pot of tea, I moved into the living room and sat down around the coffee table with the others.

Five minutes into the video I knew it was not going to be fun.

The movie was about two sisters. The images were familiar, and memories from my past came tumbling in, one after another, like waves rolling up on a beach. The two were together throughout their childhood, but that youthfulness was short-lived. The color and the blissfulness, the light, the wind—everything was imprinted on my mind.

Actually, I wasn't trying to think about my own sister.

When we were kids we would often go with our mother to the mountain highlands, just the three of us. Mayu and I would snuggle up inside the mosquito tents and fall asleep telling ghost stories. Her thin, brown hair; her babylike smell. I didn't want to recall any of those things while watching the video, but the memories hit me anyway, striking me with a tremendous blow. It was as though the world had suddenly turned to darkness.

Of course, I was the only one who'd received that impression.

My brother was completely caught up in the movie. He was silent, his eyes glued to the screen. I glanced over at Mikiko, and it looked like she was writing a school report or something, occasionally stealing a glance at the TV from the corner of her eye. Every now and then one of us would say something to another, but nothing out of the ordinary. Mikiko, for example, piped in, "Saku-chan, don't you think that Shigesato Itoi does a horrible job at voice-overs?"

"Maybe. But don't you think he's perfect as the dad?"

"Yeah," my brother replied. "That's what makes him seem real."

The world around me was slowly changing even though I was watching the same movie, in the same place, talking about the same things. It was like I'd been taken to some unreal, surrealistic space. A strange sensation, indeed. But don't get me wrong, I wasn't brooding. Rather, I'm convinced that I was caught in that strange space precisely because I was there watching the video with my family, not by myself.

When the film was over I got up and headed for the bathroom. The shock that had come over me in watching the movie was already gone, and I opened the door, saying to myself, like I normally would, "What a pleasant movie." Now that I think about it, I realize the first thing I saw was Nipper. There hadn't been room for him upstairs, so I'd given him a home in the bathroom downstairs.

Sitting down, I turned to look at the statue. He seemed to be leaning forward in a painful way, his quiet head cocked to one side. All at once I felt like crying, and before I could see them coming, the tears just started to flow. Altogether the experience lasted only about five minutes, but in that time I'd managed to let go, inasmuch as the world was spinning around me, and I'd lost track of who was who, and what was what. It was the same kind of nauseating feeling you get when you're about to throw up. I held my breath as the tears continued to fall. I wasn't crying for my sister. I wasn't crying for Mayu, painted in thick makeup, so drunk and drugged that in the last days of her life she'd lost the ability to feel joy or anger. I cried for time lost—time lost between sisters everywhere.

As I was leaving the bathroom my brother looked up and smiled. "Saku-chan, you must've had a pretty big dump!"

"Yes, I did," I answered. "Anything wrong with that?"

Mikiko laughed.

I had cried, finally cried. But that was it. I don't recall ever crying again.

Was that the reason Nipper had been there all along?

∾

I met Ryūichirō once on a night sometime in spring. It was not long before he left on his travels. For a while there I'd worked in an office, but then I got in a fight with my boss and was fired. For the time being I picked up a part-time job at an old bar I went to often, working five nights a week.

That was a strange, long night. During its length, the night was rocked by a number of shifts, but somehow it also maintained a special tone, and in the end it left an everlasting impression.

Thinking I'd be late for work, I dashed through the city, headed for the bar. I could have cared less about how I looked. Rain had just let up, and in front of the train station the lights were blurred like the edge of the water on a nighttime beach. The colors ran together in glorious speckled patterns, and even though I was in a hurry, I felt dizzy as I walked through the light.

The streets were filled with the rush of people coming and going, and among them a group of religious fanatics hustled about, trying to stop people with the question, "What is happiness?" I, myself, was stopped several times, but I managed to get them out of my hair by coldly telling them I didn't know. Upon hearing my response, they skillfully backed away, as if I'd pushed a rewind button. Their question, however, lingered in my heart, and after that I hummed a few songs with the word in the lyrics.

But wait, I thought. There's a place in this world with an unreachable image that shines intensely of gold, representing that one thing each of us truly longs for. It's stronger than hope, or light, or all the other things combined. It's that intense. And if someone was to ask me about happiness in front of a train station, I would run away from it and hide. It's something that if I encountered it while drinking, I would feel an intimacy with it. Something just around the corner, ready to be taken in your hand.

So that must be it, I thought to myself. I realized Mayu was greedy when it came to personal happiness. She was self-indulgent, lazy. Her dual nature was obvious and her intentions were destructive and unwieldy. Only one aspect of her was particularly admirable, a gift Mayu possessed that commanded respect and made you forget about everything else.

Her smile.

Mayu's smile had at least a hundred variations, and she knew how to manipulate each one of them. With her smile she could stab a person's heart, even though she never had the intention of doing so, always appearing so innocent. With that smile she wrote off most of her imperfections.

Yet it was a sweet smile. The distance between her curved upper lip and the soft corners of her eyes resembled the distance between clouds when they fade away in the blue sky to let the sun in. It was a natural smile, a smile that would cause some to weep, a pure, bright, healthy smile.

Even in the end—her liver destroyed, all color drained from her face, her skin parched and dry—Mayu still held on to that beautiful smile. But as with everything else, she took it with her to the grave. I should have told her at the time. I could have taken a deep breath, looked away, and forced myself to say it.

When I finally arrived at the bar I saw that there had been no need to hurry. The place was empty. Not a single customer, anywhere. Behind the counter my boss and another waitress were tediously looking through CDs, trying to come up with some music for the night. The bar without music reminded me of the bottom of the ocean, as still and as quiet as death. When I opened my mouth to speak, I heard the echo of my own voice.

"What's up? Where is everybody? It's Friday night."

My manager responded in his normal, happy-go-lucky way. "It's raining. No one wants to go out in this weather."

I donned my apron and joined their sour group. I used to love coming to the bar when I was a customer. The thing I liked best was the lights, or the lack of them. In the dark everything seemed relaxed, carefree. Sometimes it was so dark you could barely see your hand in front of your face. Night would fall, but the bar seemed to wait before turning on any lights. It was kept that dark on purpose, although I'm not sure why. It had charm even with the lights on. All the tables and chairs, each a different size and shape, had been chosen with good taste, even if they were secondhand. The floor reminded me of my classroom in junior high school—a rich mahogany, shining with oil. The interior was various shades of brown, the counter of the bar so comfortable to lean against you could have died. I stood there that night staring vacantly at the bar, thinking about how different the place looked when it was crammed full of people. Just then the front door flew open, banging against the wall.

"Hey!" Ryūichirō cried as he came through the door. We all stopped and looked over to him at once, stunned by the sudden appearance. It was all I could do to pull myself together and greet him.

"Hello."

"Do you guys always freak out when customers arrive?" Ryūichirō said as he moved over to the counter.

"Actually, we had pretty much decided that no one would show up tonight," I replied.

"Wow. Big place," Ryūichirō exclaimed, looking around the bar. "Kind of a waste, don't you think?"

"We've been known to serve more than one customer at a time, you know." I laughed at myself. My manager walked over to me and smiled.

"Take a break until we get more customers," he said.

My manager was in his mid-thirties, and a cool guy to work for. Whenever things around the bar were slow, he would let us listen to our favorite music. I stepped behind the counter and took off my apron, draping it over the edge so that it would be ready if needed. For the rest of the night I was on official "standby." (Of course, all the effort was in vain. We didn't see another customer that entire night.)

I sat down with Ryūichirō, inside the weary atmosphere of the bar, and we began to drink. Someone had set the tape deck to repeat, and the same jazz played over and over, adding to the sullen mood. Over small talk Ryūichirō quickly looked up at me and said, "What do you think about happiness?"

His question took me by surprise, but only for a moment.

"Happiness?" I responded. "Let me guess. You were stopped in the street on your way over here, right?"

"No, why? What are you talking about?"

"Don't we all just throw that word around like it doesn't mean anything anymore? I mean, what is 'happiness,' anyway?" I let out a sigh. Next to me the brown interior of the bar seemed to melt into the window like cold ice, slowly. I watched it for a while. Every so often there are times when I have a clear understanding of my surroundings, and oddly enough, everything was perfectly aligned that night. Even though I was tipsy from my drinks, the comfort I felt with Ryūichirō was not disturbed in the least. The dim interior of the bar and the melody of the piano that came to us methodically like the sound of approaching footsteps also contributed to how I was feeling.

"Actually," Ryūichirō said, responding to my statement, "I think you and your sister threw that word around a lot more than average. In fact, every time the two of you got together 'happiness' seemed to be the only topic of conversation. You'd just put your heads together and twitter away like birds."

"Said just like a writer," I exclaimed.

"It must have something to do with your family. I mean, you're like a family out of a Hollywood movie. There's you, your mother, your brother, your cousin, and, and . . ."

"And my mother's friend."

"Exactly. In a house like that you'd have as many chances to think about 'happiness' as the people you live with. Think about it—at your age you have a brother who is still in kindergarten. That's more than weird."

"What do you mean?" I asked. "It's great having Yoshio around. He makes life fun for all of us, and all of us feel younger with him there. Sure, he keeps us running, but it's wonderful seeing someone grow up right in front of you. I just see him getting bigger."

"Yeah, but the poor kid's surrounded by women three or four times his age. Anyone put in that situation is bound to turn into a freak."

"Maybe. But won't it be great if he grows into a handsome young man? By the time he's in high school . . . I'll be over thirty. I'll throw on sunglasses and wear my high heels, and we'll go out on a date together. I can't wait to make all the younger girls tremble."

"Still doesn't sound very healthy. He'll wind up with some form of an Oedipus complex," Ryūichirō said.

"More than anything, I just like watching him grow up. It would be so fabulous to be a child again. Everything's possible. There isn't a thing in the world that he can't do."

"You're right. Now that I think about it, he still has everything to look forward to: high school, first love, sex, field trips . . ."

"Field trips?"

"Yeah, field trips. When I was in junior high the whole ninth-grade class packed up and went on a field trip. I caught a damn cold and wasn't able to go. I've always wanted to be young again so I could still take that trip."

"You aren't planning on going anywhere in the future?" I asked. I'm not sure why I asked such a question, but I heard myself asking it anyway. I kind of regret it. Something just came floating up from the bottom of my heart and I allowed it to slip from my mouth, as if it were nothing out of the ordinary.

"A trip?" He paused for a moment. "Actually, that sounds kind of nice. I suppose it's possible. I could probably leave anytime." He looked off vacantly, as if he'd heard the word for the first time, relishing how sweet and beautiful it sounded. Then he continued, "And this trip would be different from those I used to take when I was younger. I could upgrade a little—you know, get away from the backpack and youth hostels."

"Trips like that are never healthy anyway, especially when they last for longer than a month." I managed to nod my head, acting like I agreed. Ryūichirō acted as though he had just got a second wind, along with new inspiration. He continued.

"Every now and then jobs come along that take me to different places, like Kyushu or Kansai, right?" He paused. "But that's only to write articles for a cheap travelogue, and then I'm always stuck with an editor or a cameraman. I go on the job with a partner, doing some half-ass job. It'd be totally different if I went out by myself. I could look around, do and see the things I want to, gather information for my writing, and jot down notes about what I'm thinking. After two or three days of that my head would become clear; I'd see things more sensibly. Then I might feel like coming home, or just moving on. It would seem so natural. I don't have any responsibility here. I could pay the rent by stopping at a bank and transferring the money. With my passport as personal ID, I could even head off to foreign countries. I've got savings, so I could just get on a train and go. When that train stops, I'll jump on another, and then another. I'll just keep going from there. By the time I'm ready to go home, I'm sure I'll just feel the excitement boiling up inside of me, like I'm starting a new life. But in the meantime I'd just do my laundry at a hotel, and pick up whatever I needed along the way. I could fax transcripts back to my editor. I'd remember all the places people told me I should visit, and check them out for myself, looking up all festivals in Japan and seeing them with my very own eyes. Boy, the more I think about it, the more possibilities there are. . . ."

He took a deep breath. "When I think about all the great things that could be done on a trip like that, I wonder what's stopping me. Chances are I'll go back at my apartment tonight and just forget about this conversation. Why is that? I mean, I feel like I have to go home, but why?"

I looked up. "Don't you think it has something to do with Mayu? She was always home."

"She's not there now."

"Yes," I said. "You're right."

At that point our conversation sounded like a going-away party for someone long gone, someone who had managed to run far, far away. Even though we were in a place I knew so well, a feeling of uncertainty began to float on the air. I was afraid. It felt painful, that stifled atmosphere. I looked at the counter, hoping to find something or someone who could help the situation, but my manager and coworkers were engaged in their own conversations and it didn't look as if they were about to throw out any jokes to lighten the mood.

Ryūichirō started to speak again. "Mayu was really . . ." He paused. "Well, you know, really a 'trippy' kind of person." It was the first time that night that he had been the one to bring up my sister in our conversation.

I looked at him closely. "*Trippy?* What in the world do you mean by 'trippy'? Is that an adjective writers use to describe someone who likes going on trips?" I laughed.

"Okay, if you'd like, I'll explain Mayu a little bit better." He chuckled to himself for a moment and then began. "Mayu was the type who was professionally blasé. You might say she had a certain 'coolness' about her, and yes, you might even argue that there was something about her unpredictable personality that made her genuine as well. Certainly that's what gave her charm."

Ryūichirō paused to gather his thoughts. "But a 'trip' is a very strange thing. I don't want to say that 'all of life is a journey,' or that Mayu was 'my companion on the journey of life,' but isn't there something odd about people who go out on their own for the first time together? After two or three days of being away, they act like they're on a natural high. Don't you think so?

"On the train headed for home you realize you don't want to leave the people you've been with. You get really cheerful, and everything seems silly, regardless of what you're talking about. You forget what real life is like. Once you're off that train and on your way home, the same thoughts, feelings, and memories all seem to hover in the air around you. The next morning when you wake up and roll over in bed, your eyes open and you can't see anyone. Then the question comes to mind: *What? Where are they?* All of a sudden the apartment feels painfully lonely, right? I suppose the feelings eventually die, or at least they fade away as we get older. In the end we remember how beautiful the experience was, and that's how it stays in our hearts.

"But Mayu was different. There was something about her awkwardness that made a person realize, even if they were with her only once, that they were responsible for her. And in my case it was more than a feeling of wanting to protect her, it had something to do with love. Regardless of the part of me that couldn't keep a job, and regardless of how much Mayu's thoughts had been turned away by the world, nothing could stop me from caring about her. We never talked about the future, or the things we would do together. We never said, 'Let's get married,' or anything like that. There was no future in Mayu, she was just a trip. When I think about it now it scares me." Ryūichirō let out a sigh. "For some reason even I feel trapped in Mayu's immortality."

"That's only because you've seen her movies," I said. "Things would be different if she hadn't been an actress." Ever since Mayu died, this topic had often been on my mind. "I mean, think about it. You have a director, the cast, the staff—and everyone is together for only a brief period of time. They have the same project and goal—the same members of the same cast, right? It doesn't matter what time of day it is—morning, noon, or night—because even when they're tired, they still need to focus. Eventually they begin to cling together, sticking to one another much closer than some lovers, even closer than some families, physically and mentally. They've come together for only one reason, to create a certain scenario. Once the film has been shot, then *bang*—they're out on their own. They go back to their real lives, the only thing left is the footage, and then only what makes it onto film. On the night of the preview, when they finally come back together, each scene must bring a flood of memories—things that happened on the set, and so on. But even if the memories remain, the moment itself is lost forever. To me, a movie is just a small version of life, so it's pointless to think about something that will never happen again. In all likelihood Mayu wasn't addicted to drugs or alcohol at all, she was just caught up in some intense cycle of coming together for a single purpose, and then leaving once it was done. That's what happens to people in show business."

"I see," Ryūichirō said. "But speaking about addictions, don't they say they run in the family? If what they say is true, you're in the hot spot. Someday you'll be just like Mayu." He smiled.

"Not even," I said, a bit taken aback. "I'm not like Mayu. At least not crazy enough to kill myself."

"Maybe you're right. You and Mayu really are different."

I thought deeply about what he had said.

Is it possible to be so general? Was I really the type who would blissfully fade away in her own memories while eating shell-shaped Madeleine cakes dipped in tea? Could you consider my life in that house with all those people nothing more than a journey, or, even worse, a "trip" that would end in an instant? I couldn't answer my questions, even trying would have been dangerous. Thinking about such a thing so deeply would only have brought me closer to Mayu, so I tried to avoid it altogether. Still, it was all so unnerving.

Two o'clock rolled around and the bar closed. Ryūichirō waited as I helped clean up, and together we went outside. The rain had stopped, there wasn't a cloud in the sky. The stars shone brightly. It was a chilly evening, scented with the pale smell of spring, and the sweet night wind seeped into my thin coat, wrapping itself around my body. Saying good-bye to the others as they left the bar, I stood next to Ryūichirō. We were all alone.

"Do you want to grab a taxi?" I asked.

"It's the only way home, right?" he said.

Nodding, I smiled and said, "In that case, would you mind dropping me off?"

"Fine. You're on the way to my apartment anyway. Oh, but wait. I think you might have a book of mine back at your house."

"Book?"

"Yeah, a book. I've been looking for it since yesterday. Lately I've had this craving to read it. I even checked at the bookstore by my place to see if they had it, but they didn't. I'm almost positive that it got stuck with Mayu's stuff, you know? It's called *Flow My Tears, the Policeman Said* by Philip K. Dick. It's just a small paperback, nothing special. But if you've got it, I'd like to pick it up."

"Do you know what it's about?" I asked, surprised by his sudden interest. The night taxis tumbled around the curb, lining up in front of the train station one after another. Rows of stores and houses lining the street had long since fallen into dark shadows. The night was full of the youthfulness of the changing season, and fragrances permeated the air like dozens of new dreams.

Ryūichirō's answer was unexpected. "No, not really," he said. "It's been so long since I read it, and I've read so many other books by the same guy that I've got them all confused. Why? Have you read it?"

"Well, no," I said, shaking my head.

With that Ryūichirō and I jumped into a taxi.

∾

The house was pitch dark. We opened the front door and silently tiptoed up the stairs, straight to my room. I had inherited all Mayu's books until we decided what to do with them, and they were still stacked in four mountains at the end of my bed. Most of them were still in the original paper wrap from the bookstore.

"Hold on. I'm about to launch into a full-scale search through these books," I said, pushing Ryūichirō to one side.

"Do you want some help?"

"No, I'm fine. Just sit over there for a few minutes. I'll find it." I turned back to the books and began to sort through the stacks.

"Can I put on a CD?"

"Sure. My CDs and tapes are all over there. Do you see them? Play anything you'd like."

"Okay," he said. Meanwhile I had begun the tedious task of peeling off each of the book covers, one after another, to see what was hiding underneath. I could hear Ryūichirō rattling through my stacks of tapes and CDs.

Actually, I was quite familiar with the book Ryūichirō had asked about, and I remembered it well. But something inside me just wouldn't let me talk to him about it. A policeman's daughter gets hooked on drugs, taking some kind of weird hallucinogen. She commits a crime, and in the end she dies a pathetic death. That's it, story over. The resemblance between the main character and Mayu was frightening. If Ryūichirō was just pretending not to know what the story was about (later I learned it was quite the opposite), then maybe he just wanted to cry.

I thought for a moment. Isn't it strange how we unconsciously search for something that will make us cry, only when we want to, and only when we're not able to? Just thinking about it is painful.

As I continued to go through the piles, something was trying to tell me that I shouldn't find the novel on purpose, for Ryūichirō's sake, because of the blunt way it deals with the issue. Debating whether or not I actually had the guts to do such a thing, I heard a blast of sound. A crash of chords came together and echoed for a while. In the background I heard hundreds of voices. The music was hard and loud, enough to shake glass and shatter the tonal quality in the resonation.

"What did you put on?" I shouted as my hands continued to work their way through the books. Ryūichirō innocently picked up the empty cassette case and read the label.

"Um . . . It says, 'Omnibus. Live. April 1988.' What is this? A recording from a concert? Wait! I remember this concert. I wanted to go but I got stuck at work. The group split up right after finishing this tour. I love their music!"

Ryūichirō kept talking, but his words stopped entering my mind. I had been taken to a different time and place, some deep emotion causing me to leave, I'm sure of it.

Something had sympathized with me, or else simply read my mind.

The tape continued to play during the brief moments I allowed my mind to wander. My inner voice, the voice too hidden to form words, made my questions grow louder. Why? Out of all of the tapes, why had Ryūichirō found the one that I'd managed to completely forget? Why?

I wondered if I could express my feelings despite the thousands of different choices in my heart. I couldn't stop it; if I stopped him from listening to the tape now I would be cheating him. Maybe it was the book, or the fact that he had discovered the one tape among all the others randomly thrown together, that tape so different from the rest. If this was his heart crying out from the bottom of his soul, then perhaps it was my responsibility to let him listen.

In a confused array of kindness and hatred, perhaps something deeper like melodrama and nonfiction and all the other things that come together in a romantic sort of way, I decided to let him hear the tape. It was a painful decision, like a certain couple turning to heaven and calling out to Mary for protection in their final days.

Amid the noise we finally heard a familiar voice.

"Saku-chan, how do I get this thing to record? Is this okay?"

It was Mayu.

She and Ryūichirō had gotten tickets to the concert, but when Ryūichirō couldn't make it Mayu invited me to go along instead. She asked if I'd bring my Walkman so we could record the concert. I couldn't say no, and before long I was headed off to the concert hall. Two years ago Mayu had been happy—at least happy enough to want to record her favorite music. Out of all my tapes, that was the only one that had even the slightest bit of her speaking.

The two of us were sitting together, right before the concert was about to begin. The house lights went down, and the stage lights came up, glaring. A whisper came over the crowd, and we knew the music was about to start.

"It's fine," I said. "Don't touch it. The red light's on, right?"

"Yeah, it's on. Thanks," Mayu said.

Her voice, that familiar voice. It came through clearly on the tape. The high quality of her voice sounded like something priceless.

"Are you sure the tape is recording?"

"It's fine. Don't touch it."

"I'm just a natural worrier," Mayu said as she bent down, looking closely at the dials. Then she smiled. In the darkness everything was shadowed, but I could see her smile even through the blur. Such a simple smile, but one to surpass even the greatest smile on earth.

"You're a worrywart, just like Mother," I said.

Mayu, still looking down, opened her mouth and said, "Oh, by the way, how is Mom?"

Suddenly there was huge applause. The concert had begun.

"Oh, look. Look!" I said. "It's starting. . . ."

At that point, as if I were having a dream, Mayu looked up at the stage. It was an amazing performance, far better than any she'd given in her movies. Her profile shone in blue and white light, like a quarter moon reflecting solar rays. The contours of her face were clear in the dark. Her wide eyes were distant, as if she were seeing a vision. Stray locks of hair dangled in front of her eyes, strands of silver shimmering in the light. Her small, pointed ears were turned up, clearly showing the need to hear everything around her. . . .

Finally the tape turned to music, and I found myself returning to the present. Ryūichirō turned to me and said, "I can't believe you just made me listen to that."

Looking back, I saw that he was trying hard not to show any emotion. He just sat squinting his eyes, a bitter smile on his face.

"I'm sorry. I didn't know," I said, lying for the second time that night. It wasn't long before things were back to normal, and I turned back to the books to continue my search.

I'm sure that when Ryūichirō returned that night, all alone, his true feelings broke through that coarse exterior.

~

Once I found the book we decided to have a cup of tea together before Ryūichirō went home. Tiptoeing downstairs, we opened the kitchen door. I was shocked to see my mother and Junko sitting together at the dining table. They were drinking beer under the light of a hanging lamp. Getting over my surprise, I asked what they were doing.

"You've been up all this time?" I said.

"Yes," Junko said with a smile. "We've been sitting here talking for hours."

Junko was an old friend of my mother's, but the exact opposite in personality. She was gentle, relaxed, and far too nice. When I saw Junko's face under the light, I recalled dozens of nursery rhymes I had learned as a child.

"We heard someone sneaking up the stairs, and we saw a pair of men's shoes by the front door. We figured if you weren't down in a couple of hours then we'd really have something to tease you about. Now here you are, fifteen minutes later, and the man turns out to be Ryu-chan. Where has the romance gone in our lives?" My mother chuckled to herself. I don't think she could have sounded more motherly. "Why don't you pull up some chairs and help us with this beer?"

With that, we sat down and poured ourselves each a glass. It felt strange, being there with the three of them. Ryūichirō explained why he was there.

"I'm just stopping by to pick up a book," he said. "I wanted to get it before I left on my trip."

"Trip?" my mother asked, well aware that Ryūichirō had lost Mayu as well.

"Yeah, a trip. I haven't decided where I'll go, but I need to get away for a while." He spoke cheerfully (obviously trying to make my mother feel better).

Junko spoke up. "Well, I suppose that every now and then writers like you need to get away by yourselves in order to come up with more things to write about. I can see how a journey like that could give you lots of ideas." She sounded honestly impressed by what he was about to do.

"Well, I suppose you could say that," Ryūichirō replied.

Not wanting to continue the "trip" conversation, I changed the subject. "Actually," I said, "I'm more interested in what's keeping the two of you talking through the wee hours of the morning. There's got to be an interesting story here somewhere. So what's up?"

With a silent smile Junko looked at me and said, "Oh, don't be silly. It doesn't take much to get a couple of old friends to talk their way through the night. We've just had a lot on our minds lately."

Junko was in the middle of a lawsuit against her husband. They had a young daughter between them who was living with her father and stepmother against Junko's wishes. If things had gone Junko's way, her daughter would have been with us. Thrown out of her house without any money, Junko had had nowhere to go. Things between them had gotten even thicker when Junko's husband refused to give up the daughter. My mother knew that if Junko stayed anywhere alone she would just get depressed, so she laid out the welcome mat. All of us, including Ryūichirō, were aware of her situation.

My mother looked excited. "But tonight's conversation turned to romance, and we've dreamed of the perfect man, and how wonderful it would be to find him. It's so silly, two women our age, acting like giddy fifteen-year-olds. We were just joking about it when you two came down the stairs."

"Yes," Junko said, laughing. "Just like our old slumber parties. We haven't changed the topic of conversation in years."

Ryūichirō leaned over, and with a serious tone in his voice, said, "No wonder the two of you have managed to stay so young."

"Oh, stop trying to flatter us," they said, giggling.

So this is the sign of a writer, I thought to myself as I glanced from Ryūichirō to the two middle-aged women laughing happily under the light. Their faces were shiny, different from the way they usually looked during the day. They looked full of hope, as if they had managed to escape time and return to their own youthful vitality.

The middle of the night. Secret conversations. Talking in whispers. Laughing out loud. Two women telling their dreams. Two women growing younger.

And me, situated between them, living with them, now.

What was it? A nice fairy tale? Or a nightmare?

I was in no position to tell.

∾

"Good night," Ryūichirō said, stepping out the door. The three of us followed to bid him farewell.

"Take care."

"Come back soon."

"Good luck."

We all said good-bye, and waved as we watched him go. Ryūichirō was wearing white gloves, and as his hands returned the wave, the gloves appeared like fireflies dancing in the dark.

I wonder how Ryūichirō saw us that night. I wonder if we shone brightly in the doorway, like three flowers swaying in the breeze.

∾

It wasn't long before he left on his trip. I called his apartment to be greeted by a cold message on his answering machine: "I'll be out of town for a while. Please leave a message. *BEEP*."

It was the same number I had called to talk to that metallic-faced Mayu, when she would cheerfully say something like, "Oh, Saku-chan? How nice of you to call!" The more drugs she had taken, the livelier the greeting from the other end of the telephone.

Hospitals. Drugs. Pills you can buy over the counter. Pills you cannot. Alcohol. Liquor shops lined with rows of spirits from different times and places, all ready to be purchased.

When did it happen? When was Mayu finally tamed by the touch of what she allowed into her body? Alcohol looked so delicious when she devoured it. I had brushed whatever she said aside, thinking that her actions were normal. To keep up the front she needed more energy, to get more energy she needed to keep up the front. Drinks would slide down that thin throat so easily, with such perfect timing. Her profile looked so neat as she brought the glass to her mouth.

~

Three days ago a box of apples arrived, the second in a series of deliveries. Arriving home, I threw open the front door, and there was my brother, chewing on an apple. Next to him was a large green crate that looked like it had been dropped heavily on the floor. Inside the box the bright red apples were layered between rows of brown sawdust. They shone brightly. The entryway was full of their fresh, sweet and sour fragrance.

"What's up?" I asked Yoshio, pointing to the box. "Where did that come from?"

"They're apples from up north," my brother said.

Junko and my mother came bounding down the stairs, and Junko was carrying a large basket. "We thought we should brighten up the living room with the apples for a while, so we went upstairs to find this basket. There's so many, it will take a while to eat them."

My mother smiled and said, "Ryūichirō must be in Aomori now."

I thought for a moment and then, without knowing, opened my mouth and said, "Aomori . . ."

~

Ryūichirō is somewhere up north, under an unknown sky, carrying the book I had returned to him. Where will the next package come from? What will it be? Perhaps it will come with the sound of a distant wind, together with the smell of the ocean.

I have an unusual hunch about Ryūichirō. Something tells me that at some point on his trip he's going to send me something more than a crate of goodies. I think he will compose a letter. Why? The answer is simple. Ryūichirō's a writer. His greatest gifts come from pen and paper, and ever since the night we spent together at the bar, the only possible person he could send such a gift would be me.

I'm waiting for something like that to come.

I feel like I'm a child and it's Christmas morning all over again, since his present is something to look forward to, a new reason to open my eyes and look around. Waking up, I'll find a gift all wrapped up in a multicolored ribbon right next to my pillow. The warmth of my room, a cold delivery in winter.

The letter won't be romantic, just a symbol of forgiveness. Among the perfectly formulated words, he'll find a skillful way to answer my questions, and he'll find a reason for losing my sister. His words might resemble a statue of Nipper, or a crate full of apples. Something complex, something that only Ryūichirō would have the talent for weaving.

Once it comes I'm sure I'll feel relieved. I look forward to its arrival.

Chapter 1

I've often heard that if you go through something really intense your perception of the world will change entirely. Every now and then I wonder if things weren't different in my case.

Now I understand. I'm finally at a point where I can recall everything: all twenty-eight years since my birth, every one of the so-called "episodes" of my life as Sakumi Wakabayashi, that strange conglomeration of misfits who came together to form my family, those foods that I liked, those things that I didn't. Every element that had gone into making me who I was gradually made its way back to me, and now I have the power to reflect on all that has happened. It's like remembering a story someone told me in the past.

I can only perceive my past as a story. Nothing more.

In other words, at some point I had lost the power to distinguish what was real, all of those things that had happened in life prior to the accident. I no longer had any way of knowing how I felt about myself and the world. Perhaps I'd felt the same way all along, perhaps not. I really wonder what things were like.

Was my life, all those days and months and years, nothing more than past time, piled up like fallen snow?

How was I ever able come to terms with myself?

Apparently when you do something major like cutting off all your hair, your personality undergoes a transformation as well, because you change the way you act around other people.

. . . or at least that's what I've been told.

Before they performed my surgery, they shaved my head, and in an instant I was bald. By the time winter rolled around my hair had finally grown in, and I was sporting a trendy, short cut.

When I revealed myself to my family and friends, they barked out unanimously, "Saku-chan! We've never seen you with short hair. You look so different, almost like a new person."

Really? I thought, returning their smiles. Later, all alone, I opened the pages of my photo album in secret. Without a doubt, it was me in the pictures—that long hair and radiant smile. All the places I'd visited, all the scenes I'd encountered. I recognized each one of them from somewhere. I remembered . . .

. . . the weather in this picture, and . . .

. . . I had my period when they took that shot, so it was a pain to even stand up, and . . .

. . . and so on.

There was no question about it; it really was me in that album. It couldn't have been anyone else. Still, something refused to ring a bell. A strange sensation, almost as if I had been floating.

Now I want to stand up and give myself, steadfast and determined, a round of applause for maintaining *"me,"* even though I had been thrust into such a strange psychological dilemma.

~

There were quite a few of us at home back then: my mother, me, my little brother Yoshio, who had just entered the fourth grade, and my mother's old friend Junko, who was living with us for a while. My cousin Mikiko, a student at a nearby women's university, was also at home. My father had passed away many years before, and since then my mother had both remarried and divorced. That's why my brother's father was different from mine. Actually, there was another sister between me and Yoshio. Her name was Mayu. She was my younger sister, from my mother's first husband, so we shared the same father. Throughout her early life Mayu worked in the entertainment business, but that didn't last for very long. Eventually she got out of it and moved in with a friend who was a writer. In the end her heart was troubled, and she died—as if she had taken her own life. It all happened quite some time ago.

I used to wait tables five nights a week. Even though I was on the night shift, and we served drinks, there was nothing questionable about the place where I worked—it was just an old bar, the kind everyone's familiar with. My boss, the bartender, was a hippie, so the inside of the bar looked like some kind of campus festival, a decor you see a lot of nowadays. I also did odd jobs around a friend's office every now and again, whenever I found time in the afternoon—secretarial work, mostly. I suppose I was into a lot of things back then.

My father was rich when he died. I have a hunch that at one point I thought a lot about the amount of money he left us, and about the best way to succeed in life while enjoying everything it has to offer. Chances are my feelings were subconscious, but it seems I was preoccupied with those thoughts—always. Now as I look back, I see that I was no prima donna, and I hadn't turned into a rebel, either. I had just reached a strange juncture in life. Nothing more.

Now I'm in love with all that's happened to me. I've really taken a fancy to it. It's enough to make me laugh aloud—I really have no excuse. Simply put, I've come to a point where this is how I perceive my existence, and if possible, I want everyone in the world to feel as wonderfully about it as I do.

∾

I left the bar around three one night, and when I got home my mother was sitting at the kitchen table—bent over and frowning. I always found her in that spot, sitting in that position, whenever she had something to talk to me about. At least that's how it was back when she was about to get remarried. I remember that on the day my stepfather proposed she was sitting at the table in the same way. Even though she was thrilled to be engaged, she pretended to be sober, obviously an act. Ever since Junko had moved in my mother had used her as a sounding board, so it had been a while since I had talked to my mother like that in the kitchen.

Something told me that the topic of conversation that night would be my kid brother. He was acting kind of peculiar lately, which apparently had caused a stir at his elementary school. Ever since Mayu died, the job of raising my brother seemed to fall endlessly on my mother's shoulders. Thinking about that makes me feel bad, because sometimes it seemed like my mother didn't care for the life she'd been given.

Even though we both lived in the same home, in that home where I floated through life without a care in the world, my mother seemed different. It hurt me to see her so troubled.

I asked her if anything was wrong.

The house was deadly quiet, the kitchen plunged in darkness. Only the small lamp hanging over the sink was lit, shimmering with an eerie, incandescent glow. Under that light my mother looked like a black-and-white photograph. I could see the dark shadows that lived inside the tight curves around her eyebrows and lips.

"Sit down here for a minute," she said.

"Okay," I replied. "But how about some coffee?"

Mother nodded and stood up. "Sounds good. I'll make it."

I pulled a chair over and listened as it screeched against the floor. I plunked down in the chair, landing with a thud. Since I was on my feet all night long, I tended to lose all my power the instant I finally sat down. Then the stiffness from my sore back muscles would release and spread over my entire body. I could feel it happening that night.

There's something familiar about warm coffee on a late night. I wonder what it could be. It always makes me think of my childhood,

even though I never drank coffee as a child. Like the morning of the first fallen snow, or a night of a strong typhoon, there is something reminiscent about late-night coffee, every time it makes a visit.

Mother spoke up. "It's about your brother."

"What's wrong?" I asked.

"He says he wants to become a writer."

First I'd heard of such news. "Why would he want to do something like that?" I said. On the whole, my brother was just like other boys his age, a kid who'd like to become a businessman simply for the money, or because of how they're portrayed so fashionably in television dramas. But a writer?

My mother shook her head. "Well, according to Yoshio, God appeared to him in his dreams."

A small gasp of air left my lips. I smiled and said, "Yeah, apparently that's really popular nowadays." My mother was silent, so I continued speaking. "Perhaps you should just leave him alone; after all, he's still just a kid. He doesn't know what he's talking about."

"But that's not the least of it. Everything about him has been strange lately," my mother replied.

"Whatever the problem is, it's probably best just to wait and see what happens, rather than going off and worrying about it so much."

"I suppose he'll grow out of it."

"Besides, what's wrong with him wanting to become a writer?"

"I'm not sure. I just . . . Oh, I don't know. It just gives me a bad feeling."

"Well," I said, "Yoshio's the first boy in this family and none of us really know what to do with him. We'll just have to wait and see."

"First Mayu died, and then you split your head open. Now this." My mother let out a sigh. "When will it end? I'm beginning to think that there'll never be a time without problems. I mean, you should see Yoshio when he writes. I feel like I'm watching somebody possessed when he's scribbling on his manuscript paper."

"Weird," I said. Intuition told me that my mother was the perfect example of a lighthouse that shines so brightly that ships coming in from sea get lost on their way to shore, falling victim to unusual destinies. I figured her special charm sought to change the very energy that it took to keep it alive. She was already aware of that fact, and she was hurt by it. As such, I didn't want to bring it up that night.

"Think of it this way," I replied. "If something were to happen to the family, then we'd be just like Mishima's *A Beautiful Star.* Wouldn't that be great? It would be so much fun." I didn't realize it until later, but to a certain extent my predictions would wind up coming true. My mother laughed.

"Tell you what," I said. "If it means anything, I'll sit down with the little squirt sometime tomorrow and interview him, see what he's really up to."

"Oh, please do. Then you'll see why I'm so worried."

"Is he really acting that unusual?"

"Like a totally different person," my mother said, bobbing her head. When I told her I would talk to Yoshio, her face grew bright—brighter than it had been since the start of our conversation. I was relieved. I'd finally managed to bring her spirits up to a reasonable level.

When you're alone in a dark kitchen in the middle of the night, you're in a place where thoughts come to an eternal standstill. It's not possible to be there for a long time, and it's wrong. It's wrong for mothers, daughters, and wives to be imprisoned there forever. The kitchen is not only a place where we create wonderful borscht, but it's also a breeding ground for malice and kitchen drinkers. It's the region of the home that holds the power to preside over everything.

∾

Only recently have I discovered that humanity, that large, solid body which seems so steadfast and strong, is actually nothing but a soft, flabby object, easily ruined under pressure—like when it's stabbed, or run into.

This thing we call humanity, soft and as fragile as an uncooked egg, manages to survive each day unscathed. Human beings function together and carry on separate lives, each and every one of us. All people—the people that I know, the people that I love—manage to go through life one day at a time, despite the fact that we do it holding weapons that could easily destroy us at any moment. Every day brings a new miracle.

Once I start thinking like this I find it hard to get distracted.

Of course there will always be calamities in this world, and I wonder why they exist. I ask myself that every time someone I know passes away, or I see someone in pain. But then I can't help thinking about the other side of the story as well—the miracle of life that each one of us witnesses every day. Compared to the wonder of daily life, perhaps there isn't a whole lot we can do about the sorrow . . .

. . . or so such thoughts cross my mind, and when that happens I feel like I'm the one who's come to a stop, right in the middle of living.

Be it the universe, be it the people I know. Be it their parents, and those loved by the people I know. Numberless births. Numberless deaths. Limitless numbers that would make you shudder if you could see them. Let me see the numbers now—those numbers close to infinity—as I think through my foggy perception of the world.

∾

My friends refer to that day as "the day she took a fall on the stairs." It was early autumn, the twenty-third of September.

I was in a hurry to get to work. I thought it would be faster to take a shortcut—a route I rarely used. It meant climbing down a stairwell behind the street I normally took, a stairwell that was infamously steep. It's behind my old junior high school, and the broad stone steps were also notorious for getting dangerously slippery during winter. Everyone knew that the stairwell was closed when it snowed.

It must have been the combination of the navy blue twilight, a hue fading away into the darkness of night, and the yellow half-moon hanging midway in the sky that took me away that day. I lost my footing, came down, and smashed my head against the stone.

The impact was so strong I lost consciousness. They had to carry me away to the hospital.

When I came to, I had no idea of what was happening around me. My mind pounded with a strange pain that seemed to drag my head along with it. I reached out to discover my head was covered in bandages, and then I saw myself back on the stairwell, and remembered all the pain and surprise that came along with it.

In front of me was a nice-looking, middle-aged woman. She opened her mouth and addressed me.

"Sakumi."

Since she appeared to be the right age, and since she was standing right there beside me in the hospital, I had the notion that she was, maybe, my mother. At least that's what went through my mind. It was the only reason I could give for her being there. Something about her was oddly familiar, but I couldn't say who she was, or what she was like. The information just wasn't there. She had to be my mother, or someone like her, because she was there with me in my room that day.

Did she look like me? Then it hit me—I couldn't remember my own face.

One thing was certain. If this woman was there, taking care of me like that, it would have been wrong to say something that might offend her. As I lay there troubled, wondering what to say or do, a small flashback trickled into my mind. This woman was at home (But where was home? Which sky was it under? What kind of place was it?) and she was crying. The memory of her tears came back to me, bubbling up from the crystal-clear surface of my pool of memories, as if it were a flashback in a movie, a scene that had been filmed with a filter over the camera lens. My grandfather had died, yes, I was sure of it. You know, tears really do flow one right after another, each grazing your cheek and hitting the ground . . .

. . . or so the memories came back to me.

Then I saw my sister.

I couldn't remember her name, but the likeness of a gorgeous young woman came floating up along with the impression that I had had a sister. The image of her face was so strong that at first I thought she was something I had created in my mind. Then I felt sure it was Mayu, and I watched her from behind as she organized a pile of things that she'd left behind.

A while ago, back when I was living on my own, I went through a rocky breakup with a boyfriend. Talking to my mother over the phone, tears began to fall from my eyes. My mother stopped in the middle of her sentence and said, "My goodness, Sakumi. You're crying."

I surprised her because I rarely cried, even as a child.

Oh, this person standing next to me really was my mother. There was no mistake about it. I couldn't hurt her. The impression echoed over and over in my mind like the chant of a Buddhist *shingon*.

She must have thought that I was still under the anesthesia. I had large, black circles under both of my eyes. But when she saw that I had come to and was glancing up at her through my blurred vision, she began to rejoice.

Eventually everything cleared. I realized that by perceiving myself in one way I would manage to go on living, but if I thought about things another way I would only wear myself down. In a matter of seconds I'd been introduced to "Sakumi," and before long I'd received a crash course on her life until then. Of course my real knowledge was limited to what came to me on a day-to-day basis, and from there on out I was forced to live a haphazard life, a balancing act, so to speak. But what else could I do? I was only certain of so much.

"Mother?"

The word just slipped from my mouth. She nodded her head slowly. It was a nod from the heart, full of hope and excitement. I burst out laughing like a new bride. There I was, a newborn in this world, having just uttered my first word, a warm and pleasant word at that. Yet there was something bleak and dreary about me, as if I were nothing more than a little hooligan pretending to be a new bride. My head pounded, and brought with it a pain so intense that the concept of "mother" seemed to drill itself straight into the part of my brain that had become a thick, very thick, piece of compressed flesh. The sound of that word had simultaneously caused a lump to form somewhere near my heart. What could it have been?

Moving my eyes, I saw that it was the middle of the day in my hospital room, and the bright, shining sky streamed into my room from the outside window. The light reminded me of my own consciousness—bright, blue, and completely empty.

My memory would eventually come back to me, but most of it happened gradually, like the words of a letter written in invisible ink slowly seeping through the lemon juice. Still, the glass wall that came between me and myself, something that should have been clear and lucid, was cloudy and unclear. It was like a waterproof wristwatch that somehow manages to trap a drop of moisture within its mechanism, fogging up the outer glass. Regardless of how hard you shake it, the water doesn't go away. But that's okay. It didn't matter anymore.

~

When I got home from work the next afternoon, I knocked cheerfully on my brother's door. I've often thought that when something this interesting happens at home, the only way to approach it is directly. Hence, the interview.

"Come in." It was Yoshio's voice.

Opening the door and entering the room, I saw my brother sitting at his desk, his shoulders bent over. Looking closer, I could see that he was fervently scribbling tiny characters all over a piece of B5-size manuscript paper.

"I hear you're becoming a writer?" I asked.

"Yeah." My brother nodded, obviously not too concerned with the conversation.

"Do you want to write mysteries like Jiro Akagawa?" I said, recalling that only a few months earlier Yoshio had really been into a number of his books.

"No," my brother said, shaking his head. "Classics like Akutagawa." I could see the seriousness in his eyes. Without warning I felt tired, as if I had had the wind knocked out of me. There was an aura around my brother that hadn't been there before, just like there was something new about me. It pierced straight through my heart.

"What about Mayu's old boyfriend, Ryu-chan? He's considered to be more than a pop writer, you know." I was referring, of course, to the man my sister had lived with when she died, Ryūichirō. He was a writer of cult fiction, the only writer I knew.

"Yeah, I respect him a lot," Yoshio said. "He's a good writer."

Ryūichirō.

I recalled how difficult his book had been, so vague and abstract.

"You mean you read his book and understood it?" I asked.

"No, not really," Yoshio replied. "But when I look at the pages, they give me a good feeling. I suppose I could say the whole book has a nice fragrance about it."

"Hmm . . ." I'd never thought about books that way before. All I knew was his book, in particular, was dark fiction, so dark that I wasn't sure if I would ever know what he was trying to get at.

My brother continued, "When I read it I remembered Mayu."

Now it was clear, and I nodded my head in reply. Her face was the beauty of perfect independence, a galaxy of possibilities. It delicately encompassed everything, all on its own. That's why I was having such an absurdly painful time recalling it. It was natural and straightforward, something like a flower, so moist and sweet it released a soft perfume, just like Yoshio had said.

I love her face—the image of my sister.

Even now I see her in my dreams, smiling.

"Well then, write a good book and let your big sister read it," I said.

"Will do," Yoshio replied. For some reason when I looked at him he seemed more like an adult than a child.

"But I . . ." I stopped for a moment. "I really want you to turn out okay, Yoshio. Even if you become a writer, that still doesn't make you better than the other boys your age. I want you to grow up to be the kind of guy who makes girls go crazy. You know, a good-looking guy who can write well, too. That would be so much better than turning out like those boys with bad manners."

"Gotcha. I'll watch out."

"So tell me," I said. "Why the change? I mean, all of a sudden here you are, acting like an adult, all smart and clever, and you're writing. What's gotten into you? Come on, you can tell me. I promise to keep it a secret from Mom." I grinned as I spoke.

Seriousness returned to his eyes and he said, "Something happened to me—up here." He pointed to his forehead.

"What?"

"They came in a dream, a bunch of gods, saying all sorts of weird things. That's when it happened—I got all changed inside. Now my mind won't stop working. I just think about things, you know, like how strange people are. We eat, poop, and pee, and our hair grows long. There's no way of stopping it. Even though we're only who we are, right this very second, we still bring up the past and worry about the future. It's so weird! And when I think about those things, I figure the only way I'm going to explain how I feel is by writing my thoughts down. Something tells me that if I make up stories about different people in different places, I'll finally get a grip on what I have to say."

I had to be impressed by a discourse like that. "Okay," I said, "I understand, and you have my full support. But I want you to remember something—something that I've dreamed about for a long time: One day when you're in high school, once you've grown big and tall, I see the two of us going downtown to buy a present for your girlfriend. We'll pick out something fancy, and I'll pitch in some money to help you buy it. Then we'll have tea at a nice, chic cafe in one of the department stores where cool grown-ups shop downtown. I know I might be asking a lot, but ever since you were born I've been thinking about how wonderful a date like that will be—ever since that cold day you blew into our house with the fallen snow."

"I'll remember," my brother said.

Relieved, I sat down and picked up a book that was lying next to me on the floor. I glanced at the title: *100 Real-Life Mysteries.*

"What's this?" I asked, holding up the book.

"Oh!" my brother said with excitement. "That's really interesting." His face seemed to finally reflect the child that was in him.

"Huh . . ." I said, flipping through the loose pages. I stopped at one spot and began reading:

A WOMAN WITH TWO MEMORIES

Ever since a freak automobile accident, Mary Hector of Texas has had recollections of a life quite different from her own. This forty-two-year-old housewife lived a tranquil life with her husband, a high school teacher, and their two boys until the day she was hit by an approaching vehicle on the way to pick up her husband from work. The other driver had fallen asleep at the wheel. Although Mary sustained several serious wounds, reports indicate that there was no injury to the brain. Two months after being released from the hospital, she realized that she had a complete set of separate memories, far from what she remembered about her own life as Mary Hector. The second memory came from a young girl who had died of pneumonia at age seventeen in Columbus, Ohio. Her name was Mary Sontag. Since Mary Hector could remember everything from Mary Sontag's mother's name to the name of the high school she had attended, she consulted with her husband over the issue. After doing some research to confirm the validity of Mary's vivid "second recollection," evidence was found that proved a Mary Sontag had existed in Columbus, Ohio. Studies have shown that people with two memories, although extremely rare, do exist. However, Mary's situation remains an exception. The resemblance between the two women might stop at their first names, but that does not explain this extraordinarily unique phenomenon.

"Wow, pretty interesting," I said.

"Don't you think so?" Yoshio replied, sounding like an expert.

Closing the book, I stood up and said good-bye, and headed for my room. I figured it would be okay to leave my little brother alone, since there didn't appear to be anything wrong. It was winter, and the corridor between our rooms was chilly. Every inch of the hallway seemed saturated with the scent of night. The glass window that ran the length of the hallway was pitch black, and I gazed into it, hoping that along with my face it would reflect all I had lost in memory.

~

That night I had a peculiar dream.

I dreamed that I was sitting on a bench, staring across a vast landscape spread out endlessly before me. The sky was frighteningly blue, a blue so thick it looked like a Jell-O mold. I felt like I would be sucked into it at any moment. The color burst up from the horizon, rising endlessly into the heavens, in a gradation clear enough to touch. Nothing could prevent the sky from rising. There was just the dry air, parched earth, and a few buildings popping up here and there, forming a border along the horizon.

I'd never seen this place before, not once in my entire lifetime. It was overwhelming. As I sat on the oak bench examining my surroundings, a dusty wind came up and blew my hair. I glanced over and realized I was not alone. A woman was sitting next to me on the bench. In my dream I recognized her immediately.

Could I be in Texas?

No, it could have been anywhere. Then again, it must have been nowhere. It was a place where heaven and earth come together, a place where one dream unites with another, a place where the sweet, dry wind blows on forever.

I began to speak. "Mary, please share with me your thoughts on memory. Mine has been giving me a lot of trouble lately."

Her eyes were blue, a color that looked like it would melt into the sky. I was despondent, surrounded by too much of the same color. Was it because the color melted two people's lives into one? The sea of our memories, the echoes of the past—that color seemed to have it all.

She glanced up and said in a low voice, "The me that's only me is the only me that I can't remember." She smiled. "Sounds like a child's word game."

I looked at the deeply cut wrinkles in the corners of her eyes.

She continued, "I'm in the kitchen getting dinner ready, or looking at the sunset—that's when it happens. I feel remorse during those everyday moments, when I'm not doing anything in particular. It's like there's a devil in my heart trying to make me feel bad about what happened, you know? Whenever that feeling comes over me, I think to myself that maybe that's something from the other Mary. In other words, it's gone that far—her memories have melted into my own. Of course, a part of me thinks that my own life is just as important as hers—but don't get me wrong: I don't hate her, even though she did get inside me by some bizarre twist of fate."

"But is it possible," I interrupted, "to know if you ever existed without her?" I looked off into the distance, realizing how desperate I had been for someone to talk to. "I know that concerning myself with things like that I'll never make it out on my own, but every so often I just lash out in pain. It hurts, really hurts. I try looking at the stars, or my brother, and everything looks familiar, but at the same time something keeps telling me I'm seeing things differently than before. I feel like I've died and come back to life."

Mary lowered her head, and stayed silent for a while. Finally she glanced over to me with a faint smile. At that point I realized Mary had a much stronger recollection of death than I did, because even though she was sitting with me on the bench, somewhere inside all of her memory she really had passed away. How could she put up with such a thing? It was so frightening. She and I were there without permission, in a world with a landscape too vast for our eyes, not to mention that she'd have to go through the pain of dying all over again.

"Yes, I suppose things like that do happen," Mary said. "And when it happened to me I think I took it much harder than you. But now I see that inside of me there are two spirits viewing the world from my eyes. What could be wrong with that?" She looked away happily.

A drop of water fell from the sky.

"Oh, look," I said. "Rain. Even on a beautiful day like this."

The drop of rain had fallen through the bright rays of the sun from a single white cloud floating against the blue sky. At first I took it for a small fragment of ice, then more raindrops came down, one right after another, landing in our hair—mine black and hers golden yellow. Like something delightful, the rain fell through the warm air, casting a cold shadow around us. The rain was quiet, throwing light across the beautiful scenery like tiny little globes, giving us quick glances of the brilliant sun. Everything looked sweet glittering in the light. Now the world was wet around us, and even though I thought the moisture on my cheeks had fallen from my eyes, when I wiped away the tears I discovered that it was only water from heaven.

"So it's just the four of us now," I said, "the two of you and the two of me, all looking at the sky and the earth and the rain, which fell from a single white cloud."

Mary nodded silently.

I woke up, and for a brief moment longed for the landscape and rain that had shimmered in that sky. It had been a spectacular dream. I don't know why, but it was something to be thankful for.

Yes, I really think so.

Chapter 2

Rain had been pouring since dawn, even though it was the day of a friend's wedding. With no way around it, I pulled myself out of bed at eight in order to get ready. As I stumbled down the hallway plunged in darkness, I heard the pitter-patter of falling water above me. Once I got to the kitchen, I realized I was dressed only in my pajamas, but I figured it was okay since it was Sunday and everyone would still be asleep anyway. When I opened the door, Mikiko was there.

She's my cousin—the one in college.

She must have just gotten home after partying all night with her friends. Sitting with wet hair in front of the foggy kitchen window, she looked as if she'd just taken a shower. Both of her elbows rested on the table, and she appeared tired.

"Well, aren't you up early," she said.

"When did you get in?" I asked.

"Around seven," she replied. "I was just on my way to bed."

I liked the way she looked, particularly her face. Her eyes, mouth, and nose were petite and perfectly aligned. She was the daughter of my mother's youngest sister, and she'd got every one of the facial features that I thought were so wonderful on that side of my family. When I saw her in that light, I couldn't help but find it odd—the way we were related by blood.

I leaned over and flipped on the TV. Wouldn't you know—the weather report was just starting. The newscaster rambled on about the rain. Listening to his words pound from the TV as the rain pelted on the window outside, I felt trapped, as if I were watching a secret television program from deep within the bowels of the earth. It made me think that the rain would continue endlessly, in the same way that I would remain here forever trapped in listless boredom.

"So why are you up?" Mikiko asked.

"Yōko's wedding," I replied.

Mikiko sat up. "Oh, that's right. Yōko. She's marrying Hasegawasan, isn't she?"

"Yeah. They've been in love for a long time."

"Now wait," Mikiko said, thinking for a moment. "Was she working?"

"Uh-huh," I said, nodding my head. "She's a seamstress. That's how she got to make her own wedding dress."

"Wow!" Mikiko exclaimed, obviously impressed.

"She's been in a panic every time I've talked to her on the phone lately, but that shouldn't surprise me, considering she's had to pull a bunch of all-nighters to get that dress done. Still, for a bride-to-be she doesn't sound very happy. Then I heard she ran off to the Moonrider concert last night, the day before her wedding. I guess that's what happens when you date a guy for as long as she dated Hasegawa," I said.

"Sounds like she hasn't changed a bit," Mikiko said. "Yōko's as funny as ever."

Yōko and I'd gone to the same high school. We were in the same class.

There was a time we both liked the same guy, and things weren't very congenial between us back then (because I ended up getting the guy, I suppose). Then there were nights when I would go to her house to sleep over, and we'd end up talking the night away. She kept a large dog with a quirky name inside her room, and she always seemed to be scratching its stomach. Whenever it was time for me to leave, her brother would drive me home. I remembered the exquisite pasta Yōko's mother made with cod roe.

Whenever I'd hang out at her house, she'd be there on the other side of her sewing table, busily making who knew what.

Those slender fingers were talented, really talented. It didn't matter how much she was distressed or upset, or how boring life would be, her hands would be clear and soft, moving as if they held all the magic in the world—enough magic to resolve any situation.They were as white as the marble fingers of Mary, the kind you often see in Western churches.

But Yōko was known for a nasty temper, and whenever she was mad it would show on her sour face. On top of that, whenever she was in her house she would dispense with her contacts and throw on silver-framed glasses. Yet there was something in the way she appeared, that ugly misshapen temperament, that made her look cute. Somewhere inside her, she had a power that seemed to go on forever.

As I sat listlessly examining her, I knew she was happy. But I couldn't bring myself to tell her.

"What was that?" Mikiko said. "I remember hearing something funny about Yōko the other day."

"What?" I asked.

"Oh, some talk about her dating a guy who would get really jealous . . . she said one day while we were having a serious conversation over coffee."

"I know what you're talking about," I said with a giggle. "You mean her story about being a gorilla."

"Yes, that's it," Mikiko said, laughing with me. "Yōko got all serious when she talked about how he controlled her, saying, 'He just wants to shut me up like a big gorilla in a cage!'"

"An obvious problem with the metaphor," I exclaimed.

"Wasn't she confused with the expression 'a pigeon locked up in its coop'?" Mikiko replied. We laughed together for a while.

The memory of that moment, although quite distant from me now, is sweet. My senses were dulled by the falling rain and the weariness throughout my body. Actually, it was probably the first time I felt the two spirits inside me, me and my former self, really coming together.

Still smiling, Mikiko went over to the stove and sparked the heat underneath the teapot. Soon the room filled with the thick scent of jasmine tea.

There's the present, there's the past. And on a certain rainy morning I had the feeling that I went beyond time to find a spot in the continuum just for myself. That was how the tea made me feel at that moment, its sweet, unruffled smell which seemed to sink into everything.

"It's dark outside, isn't it?" I said, looking out the window.

"You could tell me it was three in the morning and I'd believe you," Mikiko answered.

"Isn't there something around here we can eat?" I asked.

"Well, let's see," Mikiko said, searching about. "We've got some cookies, some miso soup, and look, there's even some sweet-and-sour pork from last night."

"Hmm . . ." I said, thinking for a while. "Why don't we take B and C for the main course, and A for dessert."

"Won't you be eating at the reception?" Mikiko asked.

"Yeah, but that doesn't come until after the ceremony, and I'm bound to get hungry before then. Don't you think I should eat something? Let's have breakfast together."

"Well, in that case," she said, pulling out a container covered with plastic wrap from the fridge and throwing it in the microwave. Whenever I see a woman at work in a kitchen, I'm reminded of something. But what? Something sad, something that tugs at me, making me feel pain. It had to be something related to death, and life—the process of living. It just had to be.

"Did you hear about the murder?" Mikiko suddenly asked from behind.

I sat up, startled. "No, what are you talking about?"

"You haven't heard? Yesterday the entire neighborhood was in a row about it." Mikiko talked as she lit the flame under the pot she had filled with miso soup. Her question was so sudden that it sounded like a line from a horror movie, the kind that echoes in the background.

"What do you expect?" I replied. "When I get home everyone's asleep. I never get in on the gossip."

Mikiko looked directly at me. "You know Miyamoto-san down on the corner?"

"Yes."

"People say she murdered someone yesterday."

Air flowed through my lips. I did know her. I often passed her when I walked through the neighborhood. She was attractive, but almost too ordinary. Whenever we passed she greeted me with a pleasant smile and a polite *"Konnichiwa."* I can see her now, wearing the same navy blue sweater with two white stripes on the sleeves that she always wore, the one that looked like tattoos criminals wore back in the days of Edo.

"Why did she do that?" I asked.

Mikiko sat down in front of me, and leaned forward. "They say that she completely flipped out. Lost it. Went nuts. I guess the guy that she was dating suddenly broke things off, so she just stabbed him in the back. You remember her father who died way back when, don't you? President of the town council or something? Anyway, when he kicked the bucket Miyamoto-san stayed in that house, alone with her mother, and she's been there all these years. She even tried to commit suicide after the stabbing, you know, by slitting her own wrists, but her mom came home and found her bleeding in all the mess." Mikiko seemed beside herself.

Without thinking, I started to laugh. "Where did you hear all of this? You sound like one of those tabloid news shows."

Mikiko pursed her lips and said, "Your mother told me!"

"No wonder," I said. Mother loves getting the details of a good story.

Beep. Beep. Beep. The timer on the microwave went off, and I rose to turn it off. I pulled the wrap from the sweet-and-sour pork, and then turned to Mikiko and asked, "So how old was the guy she stabbed?" I paused for a moment and wondered why I'd asked such a funny question, hoping her answer would somehow clarify my intentions.

"Believe it or not, he was only twenty-one. Miyamoto-san's close to forty."

"That's too much," I said.

The table was set, and our little meal ready. We ate in silence, and for a minute my feelings converged with Miyamoto-san. I thought about the few memories I had of her. Ever since I could remember she had lived at the end of the street. Now I realize that Miyamoto-san and I had probably seen things completely differently, even the same street corner. I've always been one to do my own thing.

"You haven't seen her around for a while, have you?" Mikiko asked.

"No," I replied. "You know, you might find this hard to believe, but there was a time when people thought Miyamoto-san was a real beauty in this neighborhood."

"How could she end up this way?"

"It's impossible to second-guess a person's life," I replied.

Miyamoto-san had been for me what the same kind, good-looking neighbor sister was for "Sasae-san" in the old cartoons. Nothing about her made me feel otherwise. Actually, I remembered her in a different way—a young girl grasping the thick arm of her father as they strolled together down the streets in our neighborhood. I'd seen them like that many times before. Even though my own father had already passed away, when I saw Miyamoto-san and her father walking down the street I wondered in my childlike heart if my father wouldn't have done the same with me, had he still been alive. I remembered a time I looked up at my father's chin, without any idea he would leave so quickly, without any idea of what would ever become of Miyamoto-san.

It was so odd.

Mikiko changed the subject.

"Don't rainy days make you remember your childhood?" she asked.

"Yes," I said, smiling at the timeliness of her statement. "I know exactly what you mean." Maybe the sweet pain in my chest had, quite on its own, returned me to a time when I didn't hate the rain.

Mikiko continued, "There's something nostalgic about it all, don't you think?" And with that, an unusual resonance seemed to come from the way she said "nostalgic." I squinted my eyes at its brightness.

~

"Sakumi? You look so different!"

"Oh, really?"

"I had to look twice before I recognized you! I thought you were a relative of the groom."

Feeling awkward, I stood amid those young women with made-over white faces. We were all dressed in fluttering, flowery outfits—quite a contrast to the glittering gold of the reception center. They couldn't get over how different I looked. It was as though they were angels delivering tidings of great joy, and I should have been thankful for what they were saying.

"You really think I've changed?" I asked. They all nodded their heads without changing the expression on their faces. "You mean I've become more beautiful?" I said, joking around.

"No, no, not that," one of them said, making me angry. "Something else about you is different."

"Yes, yes, something else," the others replied. We fell into silence. I looked across the round table into the sparkling faces of old friends that seemed to be full of promise. Their youth and beauty alone seemed to hold the expression of hope. The formal occasion made them feel like strangers, but in a different light I could see that these faces came from a past not nearly as refined as the reception center. I remembered that these were the few I had been close to sometime long ago.

The bride was seated at the head table, radiating a mysterious glow. The groom was staring down at his hands, but he also appeared marvelous. They seemed so funny to me, since I was familiar with the way they normally looked—a complete change from the admirable countenance they wore at the wedding. It reminded me of one of those awful commemorative photographs you get taken when you're on a tour, the kind where everyone's lined up and you have to throw your neck out just so your face can be seen in the picture.

Then I remembered that everything she was wearing had been made by hand. She probably worked on her dress sitting behind that familiar table, with the same, sullen expression on her face. I was impressed for the first time that day.

The reception center became deadly silent. I knew the long introductory speeches were about to begin; once they were over we would stand and raise our glasses to toast the happy couple. My stomach was growling, and my clothes were tight. I lost interest in what was going on around me, and as my mind began to wander it occurred to me that I was trying to recall another episode from the past.

What could it be?

It had something to do with an event in my life so boring I could have died right there on the spot; then again, it could have been a time I could have gone crazy over how much I loved being there.

The memory finally came back to me. I was with these same people. We were in a classroom, and I'd fallen asleep.

As the low drone of an old man's boring speech echoed off the tall ceiling in the reception center, I recalled a certain lazy afternoon in the classroom. The warm room was filled with sunlight, and I'd dozed off. When I woke up, I had no idea where I was or what I was doing. Soon I realized that I was in class and I had blanked out during the lecture. My teacher was rambling on in the same tired voice that he always spoke in. There were no other sounds in the room.

Once I savored that same kind of silence, I remembered. The man's speech at the wedding did it to me, along with the smell of dry wood, the brilliant rays of the sun, the green outside the window, and those people all around me—all who had been with me from childhood. The fresh gust of wind rushing in when it was time for our break. Light bouncing off my pencil case and dancing on the ceiling above me. I knew that when I left that place the elements, everything that came together like tiny miracles, would never come together again. Pondering that thought, I could feel my newfound wisdom wafting around me like the scent of a subtle perfume. That was the impression, just one more brilliant memory that seemed to pierce through my heart.

Before long, dinner was served, and through numerous rounds of champagne, beer, and white wine I became absorbed in the long, flowing train of the bride's dress as it slithered its way across the hardwood floor in front of me. Thousands of tiny beads sparkled amid carefully embroidered stitching. It was exquisite.

There was a rather strange look on the face of the father of the bride. He seemed far from tears, but he didn't seem gloomy either. He simply appeared distant, as if he were watching the proceedings from some faraway place.

Miyamoto-san popped back into my mind. Funny, she really wasn't someone I would have expected to remember on such an occasion.

I no longer had a father. But I wonder what the expression on his face would have been if he had been alive during my concussion and Mayu's death. How would he have reacted? In the end I gave up, because there was no way of ever knowing such a thing. Dead people appear pleasant only in the heart.

My father was different. Sure, he'd been around in my past, but that just made him unreachable. He was clearly so far away we couldn't see him anymore. But I know he was out there, with all the others, waving his hand and smiling.

I couldn't see him, he was simply too far away.

~

After the wedding I went home and crashed on my bed for a while.

By the time I opened my eyes, the rain had stopped and night had fallen. I felt alone in my dark room. During times like this, mysterious things enter my mind. When had the day ended? I felt as if I'd missed saying something important to someone in my dreams.

For a while, lying on my comforter like a fish cast onshore, I looked through my window. I pulled myself up and stumbled to the door. My brother was keeping guard.

"We're having Aunt Junko's mixed rice for dinner tonight," he announced.

"So how's the novel coming? Are you still writing?" I said, rubbing the sleep from my eyes.

"Today I worked on my journal," he replied.

"So what's the topic of the day?" I asked.

"'Things of the Past,'" Yoshio said. "I've been thinking about old stuff all day."

"You mean things that happened a long time ago?"

"Right. I thought about my dad, and about you falling on your head."

"Why?" I said, somewhat surprised.

"Oh, I don't know," Yoshio responded. "Maybe it had something to do with the rain."

I laughed. "For a kid you sure have a lot of keen senses about you." I leaned down and looked into my brother's eyes. "By the way, I thought about the very same things today." My brother's face turned a bashful red. "Let me ask you a question, because lately it's been on my mind. Which me do you like better—the me before my accident, or after?" I wasn't expecting much of an answer, considering how difficult the question was for a boy. Still, I really wanted to know, and something told me Yoshio's answer would be sincere, an answer that wouldn't come directly from my brother, but through him somehow.

"I don't remember what you were like before. I was too little back then."

"Yeah, I suppose you're right," I said, a bit disappointed.

"But now we're always together, Saku-chan."

Just as I'd expected—our thoughts had become one.

It seemed like some kind of information in some outlandish shape, like an electronic wave, had used my brother's juvenile thoughts to reach me, despite my weariness. It didn't matter that we were living under the same roof, there was more to it than that. We were connected—me, my brother, Miyamoto-san, and everyone else. Maybe it had to do with how we were wandering about in the rain, that endless universe of sleep.

"Okay, tell you what. From here on out, you're an adult. Next time you're coming with me to have tea at one of the cool coffee shops downtown."

"All right!" he screamed with excitement.

I said good-bye and made the journey down the stairs.

~

It felt weird, taking such a long nap right before it was time to go to bed. I should have felt like I do when I wake up in the morning after a long night of sleep—tired. Instead, the night was just starting, and my head was completely clear. Perhaps it had something to do with the wedding. Everything had been so wonderful.

Just as Mikiko had been in the kitchen for me that morning, Junko was there that night.

"My goodness, you're just getting up?" she said in her usual kind voice.

"Yes," I said. "Your mixed rice couldn't keep me away."

"Don't worry. There's still plenty left," Junko said.

"Where's my mother?" I asked.

"She's out on a date."

"Oh, is she?" I said.

Junko fixed me a plate. Without thinking, I reached into the bookshelf under the TV and pulled out an album. After my surgery I'd come here often late at night to open the album, all alone, and gaze at the pictures.

It seemed the more I stared at the images, the closer they would feel, but at the same time they seemed so distant. I was desperate and impatient to understand what had happened in the past, the same way a lot of people feel when they go home after spending a long time away from their family.

Looking at the pictures, I saw that the person with my face was able to smile more naturally than I could. My little sister, now no longer with us, reached up to pull on the end of my skirt. It evoked that kind of feeling—the painful feeling of an invisible world reaching out to choke me in a place so distant no one could have saved me, even if they had tried. I had seen the album the same way many times before, but for some reason things were different that night.

I found myself searching for my father.

He died of a cerebral thrombosis. After his stroke he never regained consciousness, he simply breathed his last as we all stood around watching. It might sound strange to talk about it like this, but in the end we were okay with his death. He was a busy man, full of love, but there was also some regret. I suppose that's why I felt so far away from him. Now I have only good memories of my father.

I saw a picture of us in a sandbox, and the smell of the damp air rushed back to me. Next was a picture of my mother, father, sister, and me, all lined up along a beach, shielding our eyes from the glaring sun.

They were the past, nothing had changed over the years, but the colors floating in the pictures seemed to be alive as they pressed forward off the page. I thought of Miyamoto-san who, in all likelihood, was browsing through a photo album that night exactly like I was. Our current situation, covered with distinct images of times long forgotten, floated amid a distant universe—and that's how we resembled each other.

My father's notes scribbled next to the pictures.

Mayu's graffiti littering the page.

Nothing but ghosts, every one of them.

And I, with the album between my legs, silently staring at them.

"Here you are," Junko said, placing a large plate of steaming rice and a bowl of miso soup in front of me. I closed the album.

"Looks great," I said.

Junko smiled. "Well, mixed rice is my specialty."

Junko had lost her home after she cheated on her husband, falling in love with his best friend. She divorced after ending the relationship with the other man. Although she had a daughter, Junko was alone with us in the house. Her daughter was staying with her ex. It was Junko's dream to someday live with her daughter again.

"So you were looking through the album?" Junko asked.

"Yes," I said, taking a break from my rice. "I remembered my father today."

"Oh, really?" Junko said, nodding. "Albums are always depressing, don't you think? Everyone looks so young."

"Of course they do," I said.

"I have dozens of pictures of your mother and me when we were back in our all-girl high school, pictures of us sneaking off and getting drunk, pictures of us waking up on the mornings of our school outings. I feel so odd when I look at those pictures now. I can't help but wonder why I'm here. It doesn't have anything to do with leaving my husband; it was just one of those things in life that suddenly jumped up and took me by surprise. When your mother laughs like she did when we were young, I feel the weight of my past coming back."

"I see what you mean," I said.

Like a flag flapping in the wind, past and present managed to find a way into my mother's countenance—two small boxes that fit snugly inside each other, mixing together brightly.

Hey, look at me. See? I'm still here!

∾

It was an unusual day.

Drifting in and out of sleep, I felt the past peeking in. Or was it the twisted air that seemed to take control over my mind, that atmosphere which came from a murder in the neighborhood? Maybe not.

How many people on earth will die tonight? How many will feel the warmth of tears on their cheeks?

Despite the time, I couldn't bring myself to fall asleep. I'd taken such a late nap, that's why. Finally I made the decision to stop by the neighborhood minimart and pick up a book to read, and before long I was away from the house. It was almost 2 A.M. The shop around the corner stayed open until three—half of it was actually a video-rental shop. I rushed in and grabbed a couple of new books and magazines, then I left the store and headed for home.

The outside air was filled with the stench of dead winter. A premonition that a real chill was about to set in surrounded my body. A clump of dead, withered trees reflected in the sky, casting dim shadows like dried bones all around me. The waning moon shone small and bright in the distance.

Humming, I walked along the sidewalk until I noticed somebody walking in front of me. Not thinking anything of it, I moved aside to let the person pass. Then I saw who it was—Miyamoto-san's mother.

When I saw that look in her eyes, that hard expression brought on by the world as it glowed brightly under the streetlamp, I realized I was in trouble. What would be the right thing to say in such a situation? Ultimately I bid her the usual night greeting, "*Kombanwa.*" It was a simple statement, but it felt strangely complex that night. The elderly woman nodded her head and smiled faintly, no different from the way Miyamoto-san used to respond to my greetings. She reminded me of my mother when Mayu passed away. There was something similar about the stiff way they viewed their surroundings.

We passed without any further exchange of words.

As I looked back, I watched Miyamoto-san's mother walk silently, ever so silently, into the distance. It seems like she didn't even realize I had passed her. Where was she going so late at night? I had no idea. I wondered if she was just going out for a breath of fresh air, trying to get away from the ghosts of the past which wandered through the walls of her home the way they drifted through mine.

A surge of emotion came over me, and amid the shadows of homes and the cat passing by, and the moon, the streetlamp, and darkness, I found myself whispering, "My day started with Miyamoto-san and ended with her."

Rather rude of me to say, but true.

I felt like putting the events of that day away on a disk and saving the file forever.

Yes, it was that kind of feeling.

Chapter 3

My mother's an unusual woman.

Even though I've lived with her for over twenty years, I can't seem to understand her. Her skin's a little dark, her eyes are raised, and her body is small. Mix in a little bit of the actress Kikko Matsuoka and you have it all (although she'd get angry if she heard me say that).

But that's how she is, just a regular, middle-aged woman with nice looks. She worries about things a lot, and quickly becomes hysterical over the smallest things. There are times when she can be extremely decisive in her opinion, and she's not afraid to come right out and say it.

Funny, it's during times like that when my mother always seems to be her best. She makes statements like they're manifestos from god, looking each of us straight in the eye and enunciating each word with invigorating freshness. Her words seem to be filled with unrefined confidence. They never reach insolence, or arrogance, and they aren't weak, either. They just seem to have the marvelous power of a forgiven heart, the one thing she passed on to us daughters as she raised us with loving care.

For example, when I find myself away from my mother for a few weeks, say on a trip overseas, I picture her in my mind as I stand under the distant sky of that foreign country. For some reason, I'm not exactly sure why, I don't see her as gentle, nor do I think of her smiling. She brought me into this world, and then gave birth to Mayu. After losing a husband she got remarried and bore Yoshio. Then she divorced, and Mayu passed away. She's gone through more in that short time than most people experience in a lifetime, but I wouldn't go as far as to say she's upset over how life has treated her. No, she isn't unhappy, and that probably has something to do with the way she looks at the world—that fiery bright red spot in her eye that rests on the brink of rage.

Within her universe, that pitch black twisting nebula belonging only to a woman, there has always been a certain amount of indignation for having been played a puppet of fortune, yet there has also been a sense of pride for having survived the passage through life. Standing on the center of her mandala, like the beautiful goddess Shiva, she gazes out over vast distances.

I can bring to mind that image of her now.

When I get home from my trip to see what she's really like, cackling with laughter and rattling on endlessly about the souvenirs I brought back or the pointless things that happened at home while I was away, I realize she's rather coarse and unrefined. But when I'm back on foreign soil I see her in a different way. There's a region hidden somewhere inside my mother, a place that seems to be out of reach. At least that's how she makes it seem.

I suppose my father felt it. Maybe all the men who have loved my mother have had to go through it too.

~

As I listened to her heels pound against the sidewalk, watching her from behind as she headed straight down the sidewalk, I found my tired head engrossed with thoughts of my mother. My head was still spinning with sleep, but I could see her brown hair propped up from behind as it fluttered and danced in the wind. For the past few days my brother had been playing hooky from school, and now my mother had to face the music. The school had asked her to be there.

The call had come on Thursday.

"What? He hasn't been at school?" my mother asked, her voice a bit out of tune.

The phone rang about two in the afternoon. I was lounging around, having just gotten out of bed, staring vacantly at the TV, when suddenly my eyes grew wide as I listened to the conversation. It didn't take long for me to realize what the call was about.

How stupid can you get? I thought to myself. It would take a complete idiot to skip school so many times that even my mother found out about it. As I listened in and out of my mother's muffled conversation, another memory from the past rose up in my brain. It was back in junior high—the first time I ever skipped school, to go out on a date with a man twice my age. Since the memory of that event really had escaped me, I couldn't even recall the guy's face anymore.

I'd missed school here and there a few days before, but I'd never actually made a plan to ditch school like I did on that day.

We went to the matinee, his hand sticky in mine, and we kissed under the dim lights of the previews of coming attractions. Then we went out into the bright daylight of the city, and drank tea inside the glazed windows of a cafe.

Beautiful tables, slender silver spoons. The soft, lingering scent of lemon from the crystal-clear water. Thick espresso and sweet, rich cake.

I gazed out the window as we talked. Across the street I saw the brightly colored lights of a game center—those neon bulbs that never turn off, even during the day. I heard the blinking and pounding, all the fabulous sounds of fun games inside.

Then I realized that I was still at the age when game centers were more appealing to me than dates with older men.

Even more than the kiss.

Even more than changing clothes in the public bathroom.

∾

The images were vivid, despite my loss of memory. Since I lost so much of my memory, I had trouble distinguishing events from the distant past from something that happened the day before, and every now and then things that happened long ago suddenly came to me as if they had happened yesterday—the air, feelings, and experience.

It was bitterly painful—so painful that I could only think of everything as something that happened in the present, here and now.

I was confused by all the freshness.

Sometimes when I met other people my thoughts were brought together, and within the past we had created together I was able to find myself. It was a relief to have access to that knowledge. That's why it was so hard to see people go. Whenever I was ready to say good-bye to someone, I was overcome by an indescribable angst. I felt like I would go crazy.

Like the other day, for example. I met my old friend for the first time in a while and we talked away a late-afternoon dinner. When I realized that in a few minutes we would bid each other farewell and I would be forced to be alone, I felt myself panic. In the end she took me all the way home.

Precisely at the moment I was about to say, "Well, I guess I'll see you later," I looked out over the city and saw the soaring contours of the buildings glittering along the skyline, the dancing rays of the western sun, and an absurd amount of people passing back and forth in front of the window where we sat. That's when I froze. I couldn't remember where home was or how I was supposed to get there.

Was my memory right? Did I have the correct recollection of my home? What about my job? How many people were in my family? Even though I had just seen them that morning, why did they suddenly seem so far away? I became confused and frightened. Everything was fuzzy, like something I would see in a dream. I felt alone in the world, a single star in the glittering sky.

Everything was removed from me in equal distance. I was standing alone in the world, a feeling that came to me often. Surprisingly, those thoughts would disappear within a few seconds. I suppose I remained unaffected, since it felt like nothing had happened. At that point I would turn and wend my way home.

But leaving her was different. It was like bidding good-bye to a lover. As we parted, tears came rolling from my eyes. Startled, my friend asked me if anything was wrong. Once I explained my situation she agreed to take me home.

"Don't you think you should go by the hospital and get this thing checked out?" she kindly mentioned as we sat eating cheesecake and sipping coffee back at my place. Somewhere in her gentleness I could feel the harshness of reality. I suppose she was right, but there was fear of going to the hospital only to have some kind of sick label slapped on me. I didn't like the sound of that, so I quit thinking about it altogether.

Before the accident I hated turning back. It always seemed so boring.

Now I like myself. Always.

No one in this world is perfectly healthy. My loneliness was an important part of my own little universe, not some pathological disease that needs to be gotten rid of. It's something that was inside me, just like my mother who seems to have had such rotten luck in her life as a mother and a bride.

~

As my mother confirmed the time of her appointment, it occurred to me that she had been asked to report to the principal's office. Rather than stick around to listen to her bicker about the phone call when it was over, I quickly ran out of the house.

The part of town we lived in wasn't all that big, so finding my brother wasn't difficult. Sure enough, Yoshio was at the game center inside the shopping mall in front of the train station. In the darkness I could see his face reflect the display lights. He looked so mature as he fervently pounded on a jewel-based version of Tetris.

I called out, "It's not healthy, going after precious diamonds at such a young age."

My brother jumped back with surprise, and stopped what he was doing. Looking up at me, he said, "Saku-chan, why are you here?"

"A call came from school," I said with a laugh.

The video game bleeped and burped, and my brother's game was over.

My brother reached into his pocket and pulled out his wallet. "I can't help it, sis," he said, "I think they look so pretty." He stared down at a bunch of imaginary brightly colored jewels. "So is Mom mad?"

"I don't know."

"Saku-chan, you're on your way to work, right?"

"Yeah," I said, nodding my head.

Yoshio looked excited. "Take me with you!"

"Not even," I replied. "I'm not going to have Mom mad at both of us."

Yoshio moved in. "But I don't want to go home." It wasn't hard for me to remember what it felt like to be in his shoes. In fact, the sensation was so familiar it made me feel warm, and I realized that raising a child wasn't an easy thing to do—even though I was far from giving birth to one of my own.

"Tell you what," I said. "Right now let's just grab something to eat. How do cabbage pancakes sound?"

"Great!" Yoshio replied.

We left the game center and danced together down the strip mall until we reached a nearby *okonomiyaki* restaurant. The little shop had been there for ages. Reaching out and sliding the foggy glass door open, I discovered the place was empty—not a customer in sight.

"We'll take fried noodles, a pancake with bacon, and one cooked *monja* style. An order of each, please," I said, kicking off my shoes and sitting down on the tatami. Amid the loud clamor of cooking our pancakes and eating them, I told Yoshio that since our mother was so complacent in her old age, all he'd have to do is tell her that he didn't feel well, and he wanted to stay home and rest. I knew my mother—she'd let him.

Yoshio answered by saying, "But I don't feel like ditching class until I'm heading off to school, right along the way."

His argument seemed logical.

Finished with our meal, everything was suddenly quiet. I could vaguely make out the hustle and bustle from the shopping mall outside. The afternoon sun was shining from the window, looking like steel plate from the war.

"I wonder if Mom's upset," Yoshio asked.

"Why should she be?"

"Because I'm so weird," he said.

"What are you talking about? You're just a kid in elementary school," I replied. That was exactly the reason we should be worried, I thought, but I kept it to myself. Turning back to him, I said, "From here on out you're bound to run into a lot of things, one after another, things that you won't be able to talk about with Mom, like girlfriends, booze, smoking, and sex. If she's worried about you now, what's going to happen then? You've just got to do your own thing, and try not to let her get to you. Do you understand?"

It was true. Lately my brother had been acting peculiar. He seemed unbalanced, a drastic change from how he'd acted before. Bathed in the light, he looked withdrawn. His eyebrows were long, and his eyes stood apart—a trait he picked up from his father. Those soft, thin lips were a gift from his mother.

But his outward appearance had nothing to do with how he behaved. There was something else about him that was strange, as if he had suddenly grown up and lost track of his own age. He always looked so tired.

"Saku-chan," Yoshio said, "you're really hard-boiled."

"Why do you say that?"

"Just seems that way."

"Really?"

"Yeah," he said, squirming in his seat. Then he looked up at me and asked, "So what do you think Mom will do?"

"I'm not sure, but you don't want to make her cry," I said. "So give it up for right now. Go home."

~

I left my brother in front of the restaurant, deciding to head straight to work. The afternoon shopping mall seemed to mix with the mood of the setting sun, like a bazaar in some foreign country. Venus shone brightly in the cold, darkened sky. All around me the red-and-white banners proclaiming the sales of the day fluttered wildly in the wind one right after another, hemming both sides of the street.

During the ten minutes that it took to walk to the bus station, I thought about raising children. In our house there were two of us siblings with separate fathers, our ages so far apart. No wonder my mother was so obsessed lately with my brother's abnormality. She's weird too, there's no doubt about it. But in a different sort of way. I really can't put my finger on it.

Memories of her would discreetly creep into my mind.

Those soft, pink nipples . . .

The golden chain peeking out from the whiteness in her collar . . .

Watching her from behind as she plucked her eyebrows in front of her mirror . . .

All of those things. Nothing more.

I didn't see them as a man or a woman does, but as a small child staring up into the eyes of a loved one. I reflected on my feelings for a moment. Were they love, regret, support, or a desire to drag her down? In the middle of the street shimmering with the golden dusk of evening, I suddenly lost my ability to understand.

That light was good; it made me feel homesick.

When I got home from work that night I found a note from my mother on top of the kitchen table. It read:

> Dear Sakumi:
>
> Thank you so much for taking your brother out for cabbage pancakes.
>
> He came straight home.
>
> They (the people at Yoshio's school) want me to go and talk to them tomorrow, so I'm going to bed early tonight.
>
> Good-night.
>
> Mom

More than the thank-you, more than the good-night greeting, the thing about the note that made it more motherlike than anything was her use of the ( ).

~

After my mother had left for the school, I decided to lie down for a morning nap. Suddenly the telephone rang. Thinking in my dreams that someone would pick it up, I stayed in bed for a while longer, but the telephone just continued to ring without anyone answering it. It occurred to me that Junko was at work and Mikiko was in classes. Yoshio had gone to school, and my mother was off to talk to the people in the office. No one was in the house but me.

Pulling myself out of bed, I ran down the hallway and grabbed the receiver.

"Moshi, moshi," said an unknown female voice. "Is Yukiko there?"

My mother's name.

"She's gone right now," I said. "But I'll give her a message when she comes back. Forgive me for asking, but who shall I say called?"

"I'm just someone who knows your mother and, well . . . I'm not even an acquaintance yet, really. My name is Sasaki and I heard through the grapevine that Ms. Yukiko is having trouble with her son. I know of a wonderful counselor and I thought I would pass the information along."

"I see. I'll make sure she gets the message," I said, finding a quick, suitable response. Inside I just hoped she'd hang up. The conversation was quickly becoming tedious.

She must have heard the lack of interest in my voice, because she quickly ended the call by saying, "I would certainly appreciate it."

So many different people in this world, I thought to myself as I set the receiver back on its hook.

~

I've never thought that I was particularly virtuous in any way. I mean, I banged my memory away, I come from a mixed-up family, and there are dozens of other things I could add to the list. That's why I spent a lot of time back then concerned with my own honesty.

I suppose that was the reason I always thought about the meaning of life as well. Moreover, I've never felt comfortable sharing my thoughts on the subject; then again, regardless of how long I try to stay quiet, the next thing I know I'm suddenly babbling what I think to others. Whenever I talk to people about it, it doesn't matter if they agree or not. If we did agree it would be useless. Everything important would just disappear in succession, one thing right after another, starting from one end and moving to the next. In the end they'd be completely gone, only a silhouette remaining. Even then I would feel a certain sense of comfort—or at least that's how I feel about it now.

There are people in this world less righteous than me. Take my friend, for example. Last I heard she's away in a foreign country, no one knows where. But she's strong, cheerful, and seems to be able to get along just about anywhere. Where is she? Under what sky is she making friends now?

She has extraordinary eyes, the kind that send out rays which kill with their brilliance. She had two mothers when she was growing up.

I wonder if that was the reason, or if it had something to do with the energy of her overly peculiar personality. She never felt comfortable in school, always on the brink of a nervous breakdown. For a time she was into the "Great Purification" of Shinto exorcism, psychic networking, and psychoanalytic advice columns, trying them all at least once. I didn't know the details, nor did I care to find out, either. But I was interested in a seminar she enrolled in where a large group of people gathered together to "discover the meaning of life."

"So how was it? What did you do there all that time?" I said, curious to discover why she packed up and came home after the first day of the seminar. I remember our conversation well. We were sitting over dinner and some drinks at a terrace near Tokyo Bay, and in the darkness we could smell the fragrance of the sea. The end of summer, solitary light from the candles on top of our table, her long hair blowing softly in the sea breeze.

"They told us not to discuss things like that," she replied.

"Why?" I asked.

"Because the things that went on in the conference were just for us, not for anyone else. Besides, they told us the seminar would be impossible to describe."

"Okay, let's see if they're right. Tell me what you were up to," I said, smiling at my own ingenuity.

She sat up in her chair. "Well, let's see. First they made us pair up with someone and tell them a 'secret we wouldn't have dared tell anybody.' I got stuck with an old man who looked so nice and calm that I just couldn't bring myself to tell him. I mean, it was like this . . ." She blabbed about the entire course, even confessing the secret that she hadn't ever told anybody.

Amid the comedy of our conversation, I asked her if she had managed to change at all by taking the course.

"So what was the result?" I inquired.

"Well," she said, "recently when I've been late for work and my boss has yelled at me, it hasn't bothered me anymore." Her face remained so serious that I couldn't help but throw back my head and laugh. She hadn't made a change at all. She'd spent millions of yen to come home after one day of the course, not affected in the least. I've known people like her who have been comforted by going to conferences like that. I've also known many people who have been aggravated by them as well. But she was the only one I knew who, in my opinion, went through the experience without seeing the slightest change.

My friend was, without question, inconsistent and absurd, but she made the decision to be that way on her own. She was so strong-willed that she didn't need to be decisive about things in life—the clothes she wore, the way she kept her hair, her job, her likes and dislikes, everything—regardless of how trivial it might have been.

After a while everything just piled up, one on top of another, in the end creating confidence. Watching her shine brilliant in the light, without needing a single bit of help from anyone, that freedom which might not last throughout time, I thought that she was beautiful.

~

My mother arrived home around two o'clock with a deep wrinkle between her eyebrows.

"I'm home," she said, coming into the kitchen and falling into a chair, not even bothering to remove her suit coat. Feeling pity, I poured her a hot cup of tea.

"How did it go?" I asked.

"I don't know what it is, but I don't feel comfortable in stuffy offices," Mother replied. "It's been that way all my life. I just feel so out of place!"

"What about Yoshio?"

"Just as we expected, he's gotten into a lot of trouble at school. He comes and goes, doesn't show up at school on field day, writes in his diary during class, and so on. I was worn out after listening to it all. It's like he's suddenly turned into a demon."

"Mom, do you have to be so frank? That's quite a vivid expression." I laughed.

"Well, he just doesn't get it. You weren't this way, and neither was Mayu."

"Are you sure he's not getting picked on in school?"

"No, I don't think so," she said.

"Hmm."

"They say that a student's home environment shows up in his behavior," my mother stated with a serious look in her eyes. Then she shook her head and laughed. "What a ridiculous comment. He seems to be doing fine in his studies, and his test scores are all above average."

"Then maybe something extrasensory is going on," I said. "Mother, have you ever felt anything like that?"

"What do you mean? Like a sixth sense?"

I nodded.

"Absolutely not. I didn't even feel different the day your father passed away—that's how devoid I am of feeling. How about you?"

"No," I said. "Nothing."

"So it must be coming from somewhere else," she said. "I wonder where."

"You can say that again," I replied.

Had it come from some huge ocean of swimming DNA, or a strange connection of nerve cells somewhere inside my brother's brain?

At that point I remembered the phone conversation, and I turned to my mother and said, "A woman named Sasaki called." I wasn't sure how my mother would react. On one hand she seems to accept advice from strangers, so there was a chance she'd taken matters elsewhere. Then I thought how troublesome it would be if my mother listened to that woman's advice, and we had to drag Yoshio off to some doctor. I continued to tell her about the call, and after a few patient nods of her head, she frowned and tilted her head in doubt. Then she started laughing.

"What has gotten into everybody? Suddenly I have people I've never even met trying to take care of my son!" Strange logic, but easy to understand. "Don't people have better things to do with their time?" My mother stood and went upstairs to change clothes. At that moment I had the impression that she was all right—body and soul. Even though I could only live on the small clues I felt around me ever since my concussion, I was sure my hunch about her was correct.

Another memory from the past trickled in.

I had gone with my friend on the other page (you know, "Ms. I'm late for work and don't care about it") and we had traveled with a third girl to Hong Kong. When my friend was in Japan, she didn't wear any makeup and she always seemed uptight. Taking her out of the country was like taking a fish out of the ocean. She flipped and flopped, splashing water everywhere. I loved the way she acted outside Japan, and I wasn't alone. The third girl who traveled with us loved her like that as well.

Our three beds were lined up in a row in a gorgeous hotel, in a room so high there were no other rooms on top of ours. The night lights were spectacular from our window. My third friend was drinking beer at the table, and I had just come in with my other friend from the sauna. Dressed in bathrobes, we entered the room and toppled over one of the beds.

Yes, I really loved her. We all did. Each one of us was aware of our feelings.

Conversation leaked from our mouths slowly. We talked about this and that—plans for the next day, boyfriends back at home. Out of the blue she came up from behind me and screamed, "Mama!" throwing her arms around me.

A lump formed in my throat, and I playfully threw her off, my emotions rushing away with my laughter. It was a good thing, because if those feelings had remained, I'm not sure what I would have done. Perhaps I would have done things I shouldn't put into words—everything expressly forbidden. Things that I loved, things that brought fear, things that we know need to be protected.

If I'd been a man at that moment and would have had the power to do so, I'd have slept with her. If I'd been an expecting mother at that moment I'd have softly placed both hands on my bulging stomach. Those were the sensations that rushed through me for that split second we hugged each other tightly. My other friend felt the same way, I'm sure.

Remembering my feelings that night, I feel like crying.

The recollection was simply that vivid.

Chapter 4

I was focused on the scene. Everything was so alive I felt bound by it.

At any rate, the sky was blue, looking like it was made of some hard piece of thick clear glass, clean and defined. I gazed at it through the shadows of trees without number. All around me the foliage grew densely, about my same height. Looking closely, I could see that among the shadows of the thin leaves the trees bore a fruit of some kind, berries, I think, since they were hanging in bunches. From the green to the pink, from the red to the black—the colors formed a gradation that seemed to go on forever. I pulled one of the berries from the tree, and felt my teeth sink into it. Its flavor was sour, its fragrance was sweet.

What was it called? I thought bitterly to myself.

I couldn't remember.

Little by little, the sun filtered through the trees until everything shone brightly. A clean breeze blew softly, but I had a difficult time discerning the direction it was coming from.

I closed my eyes. Before long the contrast between the different colors of trees filled with fruit and the thick blue sky floated up in my mind, an image even more brilliant than before, penetrating my entire body.

Oh, how beautiful.

Oh, how refreshing.

While standing with my eyes closed amid this perfect scene, I felt pleasure beyond imagination. It was luxurious. But at that point I heard a rustling sound, and I sensed a presence from behind, like someone was coming up to me. My eyes popped open and I looked around.

The trees were only swaying in the breeze.

~

Waking up, I felt refreshed by the images in my dream. It took me a while before I realized I hadn't really been there. My heart was still pounding over the thought of someone approaching me, and the sensation of the chilly wind.

Maybe that's why I was bursting with energy that morning. Bounding down the stairs, I met Junko as she was getting ready to go off to work.

"Morning!" I yelled.

"Good morning," Junko said with a smile. "There's some French toast and salad in the refrigerator."

"You fixed me breakfast?" I replied.

"No," she said, "your mother made it before she left."

"Oh, really? Where is she now?" I asked.

"She left early, saying something about going shopping in Ginza."

I sat down in one of the kitchen chairs and pushed the TV on with the remote control. Junko pulled an overcoat over her shoulders and started to leave. Then she turned back and said, "Oh, by the way, Yoshio didn't go to school today. He's still upstairs asleep. Perhaps you could go up later and say something to him."

Lately all my brother did was sleep, and he was absent from school more than not. I had the feeling that something inside him was running off track like a train ready to derail. It seemed that more and more things around the house were becoming unusually warped. Perhaps it was all in my mind.

"I don't know what it is," I responded to Junko, "but there's something odd about Yoshio lately."

"You're right, and I don't know how to explain it, either. I've never had a boy of my own, but I have a notion that this sort of thing happens to all of them at some point in time, to a greater or lesser degree, regardless of where they grow up."

"Maybe you're right," I said. "Chances are he'll have snapped back before we know it."

"Looking inside another person's home from the outside, you begin to see problems you never thought existed. Still, everyone in the house seems to go on eating and cleaning and doing all the other household chores, and the days float by without any major obstacles getting in the way. Regardless of how unnatural things might seem, somehow we manage to move on, with secrets left in a family that outsiders don't get to know. Even when trials occur, most families manage to work things out."

I felt heavy as I listened to Junko talk about families with such casualness, knowing full well that she had lost her own. I added to her comment by saying, "And it doesn't matter how screwed up a family might be, as long as there is balance in life, we'll always have a home."

"That's right," Junko said. "But there's something else a home needs along with balance—love."

"Love?" I said, wondering where on earth that had come from.

Junko smiled. "I turn red when I talk about these kinds of things, but I think that all homes are the same. There needs to be a special kind of feeling that allows the family to carry on. I'm not talking about love in the usual sense of the word; I mean, it's something without form—a situation, say, or environment that has a power to keep things under control, you know, the way they should be. It's not something that thrives off others, because it's something that gives. Unless everyone in the home is willing to contribute to the atmosphere, then it's useless—the home becomes a den of starving wolves."

Junko took a deep breath. "In all reality, I was the one who brought an end to my home, but what I did came long after the real beginning. The collapse of my family was something that happened when everyone under our roof suddenly started making demands.

At that point, when I was forced to decide if we would go on or not, I realized what was missing. A lot of people would say that it was compromise, but I know it was different. The thing that was missing, Sakumi, was love, or the power that comes from such a beautiful recollection. If I could have only looked back and seen that we'd shared something special together, if I could have conjured up the past and remembered a time I had enjoyed with my family, then we would have stayed together." Junko became silent.

I think I understood what she meant.

Perhaps her speech sounded like the quaint confession of a tired old woman, but it still felt odd listening to her open up right there in front of me. It seemed as if I'd been witness to the power of destruction.

Junko left for work, and I was the only one downstairs. Sun was shining through the windows and both rooms were filled with warmth. Everything around me was parched, the sensation of lying on a beach. I pulled food from the refrigerator and attacked it greedily. Plopping myself down on the sofa, I realized for the first time that day that I had a hangover.

Oh, where was I . . . I sat thinking to myself, trying to recall the events of the night before. The information came to me slowly like data retrieved from a floppy disk. Then I remembered. I'd gone out drinking with Eiko.

∾

I was working last night at my attractive but dingy bar, which reminded me of an antique shop, when I received a call from an old friend of mine—a friend who, among all of my acquaintances, was by far the most prissy.

Eiko.

"Sakumi, I heard you fell and hit your head, and you were in the hospital for a while. Is that true?" Eiko asked.

I realized it had been months since I had talked to her, even though the minute I heard her voice I felt like I had seen her just a few days before. We made plans to get together after the bar closed down—to meet for a couple of drinks. I went straight from work to the lounge where we had planned to meet, and saw Eiko sitting there. When I realized how long it had been since we'd met, I once again was pulled down by the weight of my past.

She had seen a dramatic change too. She was . . . well, how can I put it?

Gaudy.

Everything about her was a hundred times, no, two hundred times more colorful than I could remember. The moment I laid eyes on her I assumed that she was some kind of bar hostess, and I quickly looked around to see if my friend was anywhere. Then she waved her hand to attract me, and I was shocked to discover it was really her.

The lounge was pretty much empty when I got there. They had only one small lamp turned on in the place. Fumbling my way through the darkness, I saw a clerk dressed in the typically foreign stereotype of a Japanese man in his tight uniform for work; a couple kissing in the corner; a drunken old man asleep at the counter; a loud group of three businessmen; and a hostess waiting around for a customer . . .

. . . or so I thought until I saw that it was Eiko.

Before I could acknowledge her, the bartender raised his arm and shouted from behind the bar, "Well if it isn't blueberry Saku-chan!"

The bar where I worked was called Berries, and for some reason he always seemed to remember me by that and a mixed drink that he made called Blueberry Sour, a house specialty. The sudden outcry in the middle of the dark lounge had taken me by surprise, making me lose my train of thought, and it took me a while to gather my senses. Eiko smiled and waved again in her red lipstick and fingernails. After scanning the room, I confirmed to myself that it really was my friend in the corner smiling. I had an embossed image of her in my mind, and at first it felt weird seeing her there, so near to me now. Unsure if I would recognize her, it wasn't long before her eyes and nose snapped into my mind at tremendous speed to fit the picture in my head—like when I watch quiz shows and the answer to a question pops into my head. Because of her showiness she stood out even more. Somewhere behind that newly formed, thickened image was a softly drawn sketch of the Eiko I fondly remembered.

"Haven't seen you in ages," she said as I sat down beside her.

"So what's with this getup? You look like you've been plugged in," I said.

"Oh, really?" she responded with a smile. "I don't think I've changed at all. But you—Sakumi, you're completely different, and it's not just your short hair, either. Something's totally changed about you."

"You mean I'm more beautiful?" I said, thinking it wouldn't hurt to try again.

"No," she promptly replied, her face as serious as ever. "It has nothing to do with how you look." She thought for a moment. "Let me see . . . could I say you've grown up? No, that doesn't seem right either. Oh, what's that expression—something like, you've come out of your shell?"

"Yeah, people use that a lot nowadays, 'coming out of your shell,'" I responded. One of these days it would be a pleasure to meet her, the old me who walked around for all of those years with my face, that woman with all my memories.

"Well, it really doesn't matter," Eiko said. "Let's have a drink." Just like in the movies, both sides of her lips shone brightly with red, curving to form a perfect bow-shaped smile.

"So you really think I'm a tad bit bright?" she said.

My head bobbed down firmly. "The only people who dress like you are girls fresh out of school, the ones who run off to work in offices. If you dress like that at our age, people will think you're a prostitute," I said.

"Exactly!" Eiko said. "But I can't help it. Every time I go out shopping for clothes, I end up buying something I can wear to work. It's that simple."

I was flabbergasted. "You mean you're a prostitute?"

"Well, no," she replied. "More of a companion, I suppose."

"You mean you quit your other job?" I said, further amazed. Eiko had been one of those who'd gotten a great office job right after college from a connection she'd made through her father. Then she turned around and fell in love with one of her superiors at work—at least that was the last I'd heard.

Once again I realized how many long days and months had passed since I'd come around. Everything seemed so different.

"Yes," Eiko answered. "I gave it up for this." With that Eiko held up her thumb as if she was trying to flag a ride—the symbol for "boyfriend" in Japanese street talk.

"Do your parents know?"

"Of course not!" she screamed. "If they found out I was dating a guy from the office I would be disowned. That's why I decided to quit before they found out. My father's broad-minded enough to see his daughter quit her job. He didn't even say anything to me about it. But sleeping around with my married boss from work would be a completely different story."

"You're still seeing each other?" I asked.

"Yes."

"So you really like him."

"Well." Eiko shuffled in her seat. "I don't think I would go as far as that. Things were that way at first, of course, but now I'm not really sure. I can't really date other guys, but I guess that's okay. I mean, he's mature, and it might sound stupid, but he knows his way around, plus he works. He's got a lot more going for him than most other guys I've dated."

"You're going to fall for him," I said.

"You're right!" Eiko responded with a huge smile. For one reason or another she was the type who enjoyed being babied by a man, someone much older than she was, someone with whom there would be little disagreement and plenty of dates. I could go on and on about the good and the bad in her relationship, but suffice it to say she was happy. There seemed to be a lot of her going around in those days. At first she was chuckling with laughter, the next minute she was breaking down in tears. Maybe it was just her age.

However, there was something in Eiko that reminded me of my old friend, a refined indolence that seemed to overflow inside her.

The large golden loops through her ears, the five-inch pumps. A suit that cut her off at the waist. The kinky perm, a perfect bob that stopped right at her chin. Her fingers—thin and sexy. Her short, fragile body—perfectly equipped.

As far as I knew she was my old friend from school—a friend who was affable, wearing clothes that, although expensive, were still in good taste. She never wore makeup. In her simplicity and strength, she was the type that grew up without knowing any fear. A combination of a perfect upbringing, no need to worry about finances or prestige, that decadent spirit inside her, and the boyfriend twice her age. There was also the way she threw money away, her sweet voice and long eyelashes, her brightly colored clothes, the way she gave in so quickly . . . and so on.

All of those things crossed my mind that night and brought me to an unclouded understanding of the woman sitting in front of me. I tried my hardest not to think about it. I knew that if I remembered how she had lost the balance and purity she had once possessed it would only be a waste of time. Since I couldn't recall details about her before my fall, I decided to stop thinking about it altogether. Grieving would get me nowhere.

"So how are things for you, Sakumi?" Eiko quickly asked. "Why did you hit your head—were you jilted by a lover?"

"No," I said. "I just fell, that's all, but I've really learned a lot. It seems like a whole new world has opened up to me after my accident."

"I'm just glad to see you made it through in one piece. But why didn't you call? I would have gone to see you at the hospital."

"I couldn't remember. I forgot everyone. I don't know why, but for a while there I really was confused about all the things around me," I said.

"Oh, don't take it so lightly." Eiko seemed nervous. "We're talking serious business. Are you all right? Please be normal, Sakumi."

The process would be gradual, but I knew at that point it was time for me to pull together the forgotten events that seemed to govern so much of my life. It was like my eyes had gotten bad, and I needed to compensate with contact lenses—my new attitude toward my trip down the stairs and everything that had happened since.

Although I had undergone something of enormous consequence, it seemed as if I'd just allowed myself to fuse naturally into the slow flow of my sluggish life, which would ultimately end in death. I'd swallowed as much of myself as I could possibly allow. It was frightening.

"It's okay," I said. "There don't appear to be any problems with me now. They still want me back at the hospital to run a few tests, but nothing more has been said."

"When you say you got all 'confused,' did you mean you just forgot everything?" Eiko asked.

"I suppose so. I mean, there were times when I couldn't even recall my own mother's face. It's scary. I have to bundle down and tell myself that it'll be okay to go on living, despite all the things I can't understand. Then I remember things in life I'm grateful for, and slowly my memory comes back to me."

"You just never know what's going to happen, do you," she commented.

"Exactly. You never know," I replied.

Then Eiko leaned in and asked, with such a serious look on her face that it was obvious she was truly curious to know, "What about your boyfriend? Could you remember what he looked like?"

"Now, when it came to him . . ." I decided to open up to her and say things that I hadn't admitted to anybody before. "It would have been fine if it was just my boyfriend. But before I realized what was going on, I was involved with my sister's old flame—this guy that I just ran into every so often."

"You're kidding me!" Eiko said, surprised. "You mean you didn't even remember that he had gone out with your sister?" A recollection of Eiko at my sister's funeral came back to me. She was perfectly aware of his existence. Suddenly our conversation grew more intense.

"Of course I remembered. But, well, you know—I couldn't discern right from wrong because everything was so out of place." As I talked I felt laughter welling up inside me.

"Whatever," Eiko said, giggling herself.

"He's a writer," I said, "and ever since Mayu died he's been away on his trips, so it's not like he's around, anyway. At least that was what I remembered best. The fact that he used to live with my little sister really didn't occur to me until later, although the information was hiding in the back of my head all along."

Eiko listened to me and smiled. Leaning over, she playfully exclaimed, "Are you sure you didn't forget that part on purpose? I think you were attracted to him from the very beginning."

"To be honest, I'm not really sure. Everything else seems reasonably clear," I said.

"You mean you don't know if you like him?"

"Well, I guess it's more like I don't know if I *liked* him—you know, before the accident. I can't say how I felt about him when Mayu died, or when he started traveling. I don't know how I felt about him, or when. It's all such a mystery to me now."

Eiko thought for a moment and said, "Is it possible for a person to be that precise? I mean, can anyone in the world say exactly at what minute and hour they suddenly knew they were in love?"

Even though I tended to be that kind of person, I refrained from arguing with her.

"I have a huge stack of letters from him, and as I read through them, I can't help but see them as love letters. It's probably foolish, though, to think of them that way."

"Why? Don't you like him?" Eiko asked.

"I haven't seen him for so long," I replied. "I don't know if I like him or not."

"Isn't it that way with every man?" The way she asked her questions brought back so many memories I really felt like I had met an old friend. For the first time that night, I felt like saying to her, "It's really been a while since we've talked."

Our thoughts had merged together—so fresh, so bewildering. The energetic way she was able to be so straight-down-the-line about everything, something I had very little of myself. She was pure gallantry.

Out of nowhere, a wave of flashbacks came rushing into my mind, and I realized that despite how she looked that night, there had been a place in my heart for Eiko all along.

"Anyway, my biggest fear is how I responded to his letters," I said. "I can't remember if I answered them or not, and if I did, I can't remember what I wrote—then, or now."

"That's not good," Eiko responded.

"I just couldn't hold on to any of the memories for some reason, and there's no way of confirming the truth."

"So where is this guy?" Eiko asked.

"I ran into him about three days before he went off on a trip to China. No one knows when he's getting back and I haven't talked to him since."

"Any letters?"

"One or two. But he only writes about the trip."

"Won't he be coming back to Japan?"

"I guess he'll come back for a few days when his next book comes out, but even then it will be for one or two days at the most. Last time we met he was only in Japan for a month or two, taking a trip around the country. He showed his face around here for a couple of days; that's when he heard about my accident. I guess it kind of surprised him." I took in a deep breath.

Eiko looked me full in the face. "And that's when it happened?"

I smiled, and nodded my head. "It must have been a real eye-opener for him."

"It sounds like it was a real eye-opener for you, too." Her head leaned back and she started laughing. "Now I'm sure you liked him all along. That's why it was so hard for you when Mayu died—you wanted to forget your feelings, so you found a convenient way to do it."

"Maybe," I said. "But I think my feelings started after Mayu passed away. I've got this hunch that I really didn't care much for Ryūichirō until then."

Eiko patted me on the shoulder. "That's fine. You think of it that way. Sometimes, though, I really think you tend to be too picky." She giggled. I noticed the red that was forming in the corners of her eyes. She was on her third beer, and the flush from the alcohol was beautiful. I gazed at the artistry that had handsomely come together to form the creature in front of me: that image, her voice, and those words.

~

That morning I woke up startled.

"Wow! What in the world just happened to me?" I asked myself. The question rolled over in my mind. Next to me in bed, I could hear the sound sleep of my sister's boyfriend as I watched the morning fog creeping over Tokyo from our room in the Tokyu Hotel. The room was huge, and the window seemed to go on forever. Thin rays of light bounced off the skyscrapers surrounding us.

My memory felt clear for a moment. I was still in a rest period from my surgery, and my doctor had given me strict orders to refrain from alcohol, exercise, and any other strenuous activity—including sex. They had let me out of the hospital because I had agreed to their conditions. Their orders didn't seem to be a problem at the time.

My mother and Junko had gone off a day before to the hot springs to recuperate from the seemingly tedious task of nursing me back to health. My brother and Mikiko had run off to Tokyo Disneyland. I was put in charge of tending the house while I recovered, all alone. Right then the phone rang, and I picked it up. The call was from Ryūichirō.

He gave me the name of the hotel where he was staying, and when I told him about my accident he sounded pretty shocked. Feeling trapped and bored in my house, I told him to wait at the hotel, because I was on my way. Our plan was to meet in the lobby.

Ryūichirō was beyond himself when he saw what must have looked like a monk—me and my stubble. Still, he kindly told me I looked good with short hair, responding with the usual "Sakumi, you've really changed."

He went on to tell me about a time when he opened the refrigerator at a friend's house and saw a large, red, round thing inside. Even though he knew exactly what he was looking at, for a fraction of a second he couldn't remember what it was called. Then it hit him—a watermelon. In order to serve it with fruit punch, someone had meticulously carved away the rind, leaving only the fleshy red inside. I thought it peculiar that he'd go into such detail with his story, but even more than that I found it funny that I hadn't caught on sooner. He was comparing it with me. When I asked him how I'd changed, he'd replied by calling me a watermelon.

Leave it to a writer to come up with such an expression.

What standard do we use to judge others? When we see somebody we know, how do we determine the way that person should act, or the type of person she should be?

Something told me Ryūichirō was different from my vague recollection, but I held back from saying anything to him about it. There was something in the way he carried himself. He had spent so many years out traveling the world, and I received an impression that I was growing closer and closer to him by the minute. His writings, the complexity of his words, those things far from illusion—I understood all of them. I'm not sure if it happened because my mind had cleared in the fall, or if that was the way things had been all along.

After that we went up to his room and had sex together, as if it was the most natural thing in the world. Our actions probably resulted from his starvation for a woman after years of being away, from the freedom I felt in finally going out on my own after months of being in a hospital. Maybe it came from the fact that we had liked each other all along, and we were just waiting for the chance to be together. Or maybe it was due to the changes we had both made since we met, because we really did feel like strangers. Finally there was the simple miracle of it all, and we had to show our thanks to the gods. Everything seemed to be wrapped together nicely over the course of events that long evening.

It was a pleasant night all around.

I hid the fact that it had been only a few days since I had come home from the hospital. I got up the next morning thinking there would be some repercussion from all of the physical activity of the night before, but everything seemed fine. There was nothing wrong with me.

Looking at the clock, I saw it was already noon. "Time for checkout," I said to Ryūichirō as I kicked him out of bed. His head moved around the room and he squinted at me as if he had no idea who I was. I laughed at his expression, since he reminded me of all those things you hear about travelers who get up and realize they don't know where they slept, or who they slept with.

I had a bad feeling as we sat down for breakfast. Ryūichirō decided to extend his stay an extra day, and luckily when we called down to the front desk they told us that the room was empty. We ordered room service, and I was thrilled to discover they had my favorite breakfast in the world: fried-egg sandwiches, juice, bacon, and coffee.

However, as we were eating, I could see our little festival, the party I'd yearned for so long, was about to come to an end.

Ryūichirō would be off on another trip, and certainly I'd catch it from my mother once I got home and she learned of my foolish one-nighter. I figured it would be pointless to pretend that I had only stepped out for a few minutes, since I was sure they'd be home by the time I got there. Would it be worth going to such trouble?

I couldn't even remember if my mother was tolerant of me staying out all night. Once again it occurred to me I had not reached the point of fully understanding my mother. I tried hard not to worry, but I still felt as though I would be thoroughly examined.

More than being anxious, however, I seemed to be floating indifferently back then. Those things that wrapped themselves around me felt keenly distant. I suppose my mind was wandering, because Ryūichirō turned to me and asked if my head was hurting.

"No," I said shaking my head. "How about you? Did you get sick while you were away?"

"Just a cold here and there, but that's about it," he replied.

"Was it hard to get used to traveling?"

"No. I was surprised at how many people there are like me in the world—you know, us nomads." He smiled.

"All of you just move around?" I asked.

"That's right," he said. "What's more, you see people like me coming from every corner on earth. We could go anywhere, right this very minute, and they'd be out there, traveling around. I took off on my journey thinking I would be the only person doing such a crazy thing, and I was shocked by the amount of people I bumped into who were out doing it along with me."

"Is that so," I replied.

"Yeah, it's that simple. Anybody in the world could get away from real life, just like that. All it takes is two or three days of cutting through red tape. Then you just make sure the petty cash stays on hand. There isn't a person around who couldn't go out and have a great time for at least a month or two."

"I suppose you're right, now that you mention it," I agreed. My thoughts were somewhere in the distance.

"Why don't you come along with me sometime? When you get better, that is." Taken aback by the sudden proposal, I asked where we would go.

His response was simple. "Here and there. Who knows?"

"Maybe the day will come," I replied.

We had been together only once, so my feelings for Ryūichirō stopped at the smell of his hair and the sensation of the palms of his hands. Nothing more, and nothing less. Something had told me, however, that he'd never done anything like that to me before.

Then, out of nowhere, he turned to me and said, "I wonder if I'll ever see you again."

What an idiot. I couldn't believe my own ears. Had he really said such a thing? Something tried to tell me that he was only being conscious of what had happened to Mayu. It was his attempt to be courteous and sincere.

I spoke up. "You know, once I . . ." I looked across at the bed where I had slept with Ryūichirō the night before, remembering us doing this and that. The bed was spotted with thin rays of sunlight. "Once I'm with someone I want to see them again, and if I sleep with that person I want to sleep with them again. After two, three, or four times, then I consider it love. I can't do that with someone who only comes around a few times in my life."

"Of course," Ryūichirō said with a grin. "So can I see you tomorrow?"

"I don't think my mother will let me out of the house. In fact, she's going to yell at me when I get home for having gone out last night."

"Is your mother really that strict?"

"Just when her children go out and sleep with someone right after they've had brain surgery," I said.

"Oh, I see."

"Yes," I said. "I'm about to see, too." At that point I let my eyes fall on the basket of breakfast sandwiches and empty plates on the table in front of me. I could feel the familiar seed of desire swelling inside. If he hadn't propositioned me first, I'm sure I would have been the one to bring it up.

"So do you mind if we go at it once more?" he asked without reservation.

I started to laugh.

Within moments we were back in bed.

Yes, it had actually happened.

~

"Weren't we all the same as children?" Eiko asked. "All of us, destined to become beautiful brides in fluffy white dresses!" She giggled to herself. "Where did we go wrong?"

"Isn't that what keeps life interesting?" I replied. "And who knows? Next year you could be somebody's wife. No one knows what will happen."

"Sometimes I think it would be wonderful just to stay the way I am forever, just kick back and space out during the afternoons thinking about all the exciting things that the night will bring, all the naughty things I might take part in." She snickered again.

"Well," I said, "aren't you the happy one."

She squinted her tiny nose and laughed.

Dawn was breaking as we said good-bye. I saw her off by watching her small body disappear into the background, her high heels clapping along, echoing in the early morning city.

My drunkenness, the sunrise, the bright sky, and a friend who was leaving.

If I had died in my fall I would have missed that morning—that splendid sunrise over Tokyo.

~

As I waded through my memories of the night before, my brother appeared from upstairs. He looked unhappy, like he'd just been through a painful, restless night. His face was so pale he reminded me of a corpse. I didn't feel like talking to him, but I asked how he was anyway.

"I'm going back to bed," he said, acting like it was painful just to speak.

"Stay there until you feel better," I said.

He dipped his head in the refrigerator and pulled out some milk. After a few gulps he turned and left the room.

As I thought about how peculiar he was acting, he slid back into my field of vision.

"Saku-chan." This time he didn't seem to be in a bad mood. Rather, it just sounded like he was once again bothered with the need to speak.

"What?"

"That was me coming up from behind. You could've seen me if you'd wanted to, I was just shadowed by the trees."

I strained my ears to listen to what he was saying. "What on earth are you talking about?" I was clueless. I had no idea what he was trying to get at.

"You know, your dream this morning. You were standing in a grove, eating blueberries." He talked as if he didn't want the conversation to continue.

That's it! I thought to myself. That's what those little fruits were called—blueberries!

Relieved to have finally remembered the name of the berries, I listened to my brother's footsteps tediously climb off to bed.

Chapter 5

I sat next to the swimming pool, drained, surrounded by the tepid air.

All around me people were swimming in their own self-denial. Under the faraway roof of the building, swimmers sent up sprays and splashes of water and children shouted with delight at the lower end of the pool. Mikiko pulled herself out and I watched her approach, her bathing suit gleaming.

"God, I'm tired," she said, right as I opened my mouth to say, "You've lost weight."

"Do you really think so?" she asked, a broad grin sliding across her face.

"Really. There's no doubt about it. You're much thinner."

"But according to the scales, I haven't lost a pound."

"Well then, you've simply tightened up," I said.

"Saku-chan, I can see you've lost it in your face."

"Oh, yeah?" I said. Next it was me who was smiling.

"Only one more week to go!" Mikiko replied.

"We can do it."

Mikiko paused. "I think I'll go back in for one more swim after a short break."

"Me, too," I responded. "Then we're out of here."

Standing up, Mikiko strolled over to the drinking fountain and began to have some water. We'd been coming together to the pool every day for almost a month, quite a feat considering I was working and Mikiko was still in school. Still, we found ourselves absorbed in the exercise each day. Swimming was so much fun we could hardly stand it.

Since early spring I'd managed to put on eleven pounds. Actually, more than the eleven pounds, the thing that hit me the hardest was the scale, which tipped, for the first time, at 110 pounds. I was shocked. My body felt so heavy that I began to wonder if it's possible to change the way you think as you change the amount you weigh.

There was someone at home even more serious than I was over the weight issue. Once she had quit her golf circle, Mikiko put on an extra twelve pounds without even thinking about it. Even though she'd always been one to gain weight easily, for a short time all she did was loaf around the house during the day and go out drinking at night. Every time our eyes would meet she would complain about how much she'd gained, and I wasn't pleased with myself, either. It didn't take long for us to realize our sin.

"Saku-chan, we've got to do something about this," Mikiko said to me on the way home from stuffing ourselves with ramen at the traveling neighborhood noodle stand.

"You're right," I said. "It's time we stop eating and go back to being ourselves."

"It's wrong to go on like this," she stated, a look of anger in her eyes.

Smiling, I said, "But street-stall ramen is so delicious. I don't regret eating a bite."

"That's what I thought, too," Mikiko said. "Before we dived in."

Then the inspiration hit me. "Okay, that's it. We're losing weight. A diet is always more fun if you do it with someone else." I'd convinced myself that what I was saying was true. Mikiko agreed.

"So we're going to do it?" she asked.

"So we're going to *do*," I said.

Our plan became clear as we walked: we'd cut out all sweets and hit the pool once a day. Mikiko got excited. "Don't you think this is great, strolling home in the middle of the night, talking about how we're going to lose weight? Just thinking about it gives me goose bumps!" Her body started to tremble. "I really feel alive, right here, right now."

I laughed out loud. "You masochist! Do you really get that much into pain?" Staring up in the sky I saw the beauty of the moon. My body felt heavy, and my head unclear. The silence of the night path, a soft fragrance in the wind.

Then it struck me.

A desire for a drink in the middle of the night is a wicked demon. It separates you from your spirit and independently takes control. All alcohol is the same, along with violence, drugs, and dieting.

Addictions are universal, regardless of their form.

I can't say if they're good or bad, but they survive. Eventually you can't get enough of them. In the end you're either sick or you've lost your grip. One thing or another. Even when you know you've had more than you can take, they creep back like a wave—their shape might have changed, but they clean the shore just the same, rolling back, over and over. Silently, forcefully, back in and back out. Slowly moving away.

Faraway landscapes—beaches in our lives that bring mitigation and fear.

What do we accomplish through addictions?

∾

On the way home from the pool that day, Mikiko started talking. "I think this is working—cutting out food, exercising at the pool."

"You're right," I said. "We're much thinner." I'd weighed myself in the sauna that day and I was already down four pounds.

"So why is it diets never seem to work?" Mikiko asked.

"For one thing," I replied, "a person's weight adjusts to her standard of living. If her body feels like it needs more energy, then it puts on extra pounds. There's no way of getting around it, because it's something she really needs. Fighting natural weight is the hardest thing in the world. But there's something else that has power to do anything, something we call desire, and it really exists—the wish not to eat, to exercise, lose weight. Somewhere inside our brains those desires are spontaneously decided for us, occasionally keeping us from what we really want to do. When you think about it, human beings are really remarkable."

"Yeah, you're right," Mikiko replied. "I couldn't have gone through with this diet by myself. I always end up with some excuse, taking everything so lightly. But going on a diet with you, Saku-chan, has really been a blast. I mean, look, we've made it this far. If I was on my own I'd have dropped out weeks ago. And the best thing about this diet is we've had a great time doing it."

Still absorbed in my own thoughts, I continued. "People aren't machines, and self-denial is real. When things get rough, they seem to last forever. It's the same thing with things like child neurosis or recovery after surgery. By the time you're finally through it you don't know when it all began."

Mikiko was in high spirits, dancing around. "I've had a ball losing weight!" she screamed.

"Yeah," I said, "and if we get fat again, we'll just go on another diet. Gaining weight in a house with four women is not hard to do."

∾

But I didn't make it through the diet unscathed. There was one serious side effect—I couldn't stop swimming.

Mikiko was different. She recovered quickly, taking the time for shopping or for vegging out in front of the TV, and it didn't take long for her to completely blow off the fun times we'd had at the pool. I figured that it wouldn't do me any harm, so I continued to go to the pool whenever I got the chance. It became a problem when I couldn't find a spare minute—particularly on the days I was scheduled to work.

When I swam before going to the bar, I'd wind up dead at the end of the night. It wasn't healthy, but I couldn't help it. I just had to have a swim once a day. Nights before I decided to go to the pool, a craving to be in the water would come over me, so much that it hurt. I was addicted. Now I miss those days when I skipped off to the pool like a madwoman. Tears well up inside me, a desire so strong I could pull my hair out.

I really needed to swim.

At some point I'd lost confidence in my own power of discrimination. It didn't have anything to do with loss of memory. To me, this new revelation was far more frightening.

Maybe it's always been this way with me.

My mother told me that when I was a child I'd get so absorbed in something I'd do it until I passed out, as long as it was something I liked. I can't recall being that way. At first I thought she was talking about someone completely different. My mother laughed when she told me, saying she couldn't understand why her diligent child had turned out like me. I wholeheartedly agreed.

Then again, every now and then I felt like doing something to distraction, the instinct of a wild beast. Whenever those feelings came up, things going far beyond reason, I felt like I was seeing the child inside of me who had long since been forgotten.

Who are you? Yeah, you, out there.

It doesn't matter. Just keep going!

Not wanting to be tricked, I would stop, listen, and wait. Throughout the spell everything shifted around me, but then the wind quickly disappeared. So that was it.

A more enjoyable way of doing things had been with me all along.

~

That day was no exception.

The urge to swim came over me as I lounged around the living room. With no realization of the drama that it caused, the sound of the water, the smell of the chlorine, and an image of the small black mat that ran from the locker room to the pool came floating up in my mind like some familiar image from heaven.

Anxious, I knew that if I didn't quit work that night and go swimming I'd never be at ease with myself. Something so easy, that thing I always did anyway. But this time it was different. My addiction was not aware of the gratification the swimming gave me, it only knew that the joy should not be first in my mind. Genuine interest in something is always more flexible.

As I sat in the parlor thinking of a number of foolish reasons why I should swim, the time just passed by. My brother came into the room. He'd been in bed all day, no talk of going to school, and now he was tiptoeing through the kitchen. Although he hadn't made a sound I could feel his presence, and I swung around, glaring at him from the sofa.

Even my brother's clothes were bizarre.

I'm not talking about a bad color choice, or mismatched socks. Something was simply unbalanced about the overall tone of his wardrobe. A majority of kids with confidence who undergo such madness eventually get over it, or at least reach a point where they can suppress it somehow, but Yoshio was different. I'm sure he was trying to pose as if everything was okay, except we saw right through to his fear, the one thing he didn't want us to discover. I could tell that on the inside my brother was full of despair and disagreement. His feelings expressed something none of us could do anything about. Such a sensitive child, perhaps that's why it was so hard for him to let us in. I didn't feel good about it at all.

I was afraid it was becoming a vicious cycle.

Yoshio gazed at me sprawled out on the couch, and I saw how uptight he looked. He looked me full in the face and said, "Aren't you going to the pool today?" Boy, he knew right where to pour the vinegar. It wasn't a coincidence, my brother finding quick ways to attack me like that. He could read it in my eyes. I suppose it was his way of protecting himself, rather than wanting to talk to me, or bring me good news. It took him only a second to analyze information, and to evade any emotion that might give us a clue. Watching him, I felt wretched.

"I'm sick of the pool," I lied.

Air left my brother's mouth. He curled up his eyes, an attempt to win my favor. A queasy sensation came over me. They were the eyes of a weakling.

"What about you?" I said, returning the question. "Aren't you going to school?"

"No," he said.

"Do you feel sick?"

"Yes," he said. "A little."

There was no question about it. He looked rather pale.

"So you've been asleep all day long?" I asked. "Why don't we take a walk around the neighborhood or something?"

"I don't want to go out," he replied. "I don't feel like getting any more tired than I am."

"What gets you so down?"

"You wouldn't believe me if I told you," he said, plunging his thin fingers deep into his pockets and rocking back and forth, trying to act like he wasn't really there.

What was going on? What gave this kid power to enter my dreams? Chances are I would never know for certain—not now or ever. It was the same as the change that had occurred inside me, like all the things I'd forgotten, things I'd never be able to retrieve.

Shouldn't that have given me all the more reason to feel sympathy for my brother, since we were both so unequal in a world full of equality? How could I get through to this kid, so young and immature? I deliberated for a while.

"Well, what do you want to do?" I asked.

Yoshio's response was sudden. "I want to see my dad."

"Don't be so sure he'll understand what's happening to you any more than the rest of us," I said. "Sure, your father's still alive, so you can see him anytime you feel like it. I'll even take you to his place. But I don't think it's wise to substitute him for someone else who can help you." Maybe it was rude, telling him such a thing, but it was something that had to be said.

My brother looked glum. "I really don't know what to do. I can't go to school, I just get all fidgety."

"There will always be times like that," I said. "They never end. Like when you're home, or when you can't stop thinking about something, or when you're just plain miserable. Even when you get older, they'll still be there, just like when you feel there's nothing you can't do. Good times, bad times—they'll be there as long as we go on living. Nobody decides who gets more or less. Doesn't matter if you're a great kid or not. And no one on earth feels like you deserve more trouble than anybody else. We don't think you're a coward, either. If we did think that, we'd take it back.

"Come on, Yoshio. Let's get you out of here. I can't take you anyplace in the world, but I'm on my way to work, and you're invited to come along if you wish."

My brother came near me with his head down, like a stray puppy with its tail wagging. For the next few minutes he stood next to me and the couch, and we stared blankly at the TV together.

~

Lately my little brother had been telling me secrets that he wouldn't even tell my mother. Whenever he would open up to me like that I hoped I wasn't the only one he was telling, because I felt my mother should know as well. But she didn't seem to be particular about it. I'm sure that inside she was burning with envy, but whenever I approached her she would smile and say, "As long as Yoshio's happy, then it's okay." Such an off-the-wall form of broad-mindedness.

With that in mind, I scribbled out a note to my mother and grabbed my brother by the hand. We were off. As we walked to work I learned that Yoshio hadn't left the house in over a week. He confessed that the air tasted fresh.

When someone's cooped up inside the security of four walls, they begin to assimilate with the very house that they're in—sort of like a piece of furniture. I see a lot of people like that around town. Even though they're outside, when you look at their faces and clothing you see a plastic couch or tacky lampshade. The way they respond to the world, so void of expression, is slow and dim-witted. Seldom do they look a person in the face, as if they've lost contact with themselves as people, lost contact with the wild instincts they were born with.

I prayed the same would not happen to Yoshio.

Mayu had been frustrated with trying to get her hands on something to drink. Yoshio was just kicking his feet about, like everything in the world frightened him. We strolled along the city streets. Night was settling in around us, and the moon hung low, shining brightly in the navy blue sky. In the west a thin sliver of red tried desperately to stay alive.

~

Afraid that people would see I'd brought Yoshio to the bar, a child not even out of elementary school, I made him sit at the far end of the counter all by himself, and that's where he stayed while I worked. Business picked up after a while, so I didn't have much time to be concerned with my brother. With nothing to do, he grabbed a kid's version of *JUMP* magazine and read it silently in the dark, but it wasn't long before he gave up on that. Next he just stared off into space, obviously bored by the wait. When I asked him if he wanted to go home, he just shook his head. In the end I broke down and bought him a Sangria that my boss had put together for him—a house specialty. He gulped it down, licking his lips and saying it was good. By that time I was in a bad mood myself, and most of the customers had left, so I ordered a drink along with him, feeling a bit more cheerful after that.

I don't know if it was because the little guy was drunk, or if it was because he'd sat on the same stool for hours watching people come into and go out of the bar, but as the night grew deeper he seemed to bounce back to life. I recognized the look immediately, because it was the face I was so familiar with.

Isn't a person's face remarkable? I thought to myself. When a person's heart is returned to his soul, his face releases a loving brightness. I was relieved when it happened to Yoshio. At that point I knew that perhaps the swimming pool hadn't been the only influence on me back then. There was also something about a certain family member sitting next to me. After loitering about for so long, it seems only natural that I would wind up on the receiving end. The air was thick with my slothfulness.

I suppose my boss was thinking I was rather unhappy that night, because he told me I could leave at midnight. Maybe his generosity really stemmed from not wanting a kid around. I gladly removed my apron and threw it in the laundry basket.

On the way home Yoshio turned to me and said, "I can't stop hearing voices."

Oh no, here we go, I thought to myself. I knew it would be wrong to hurt his feelings by not listening to what he had to say—or at least that seemed like the type of advice you'd get from a guidebook on raising children. I knew that something would eventually give way and straighten things out inside him, once it came down to that, but for the time being I decided to humor him.

"What are they saying?" I asked.

My brother took a sip from the can of iced tea I'd bought him on the way home, a futile attempt to get him sober. He spoke slowly, as if forming words was troublesome. "Well, I hear lots of different things—whispers, shouts, grumbles, moans. Men talking, women talking—it never ends. Just a big sound of people chatting all at the same time."

"And it's been this way ever since you started writing your novel?" I asked.

"I didn't hear them so much back then," he replied.

"Seems like that could really get old—voices always sounding in your head."

"It's like a drill sergeant shouting out orders, or different kinds of music. Sometimes I see other people's dreams—like yours. It's all right when I'm asleep, because I can usually watch what's going on. But when I'm awake, and the noises are there, I feel like I'm going crazy."

"Of course you do," I said. "How about now, are you hearing things?"

"Just a faint rumble." He stopped and pricked up his ears to listen.

"If I were to take a stab at it, I'd say you've turned into a radio."

"I don't know what it is. All I know is that I haven't been able to talk about this with anybody. Do you believe me, Sakumi?"

"Of course I believe you. . . . But what do they say? Can you give me an example? You say someone's scolding you in your dreams?" I asked.

"No," Yoshio replied, shaking his head. "It's not like that. I guess it's like a prayer chant of an American Indian tribe."

"What do you mean?"

My brother grew deadly serious. "A little while ago when I was walking along the street I heard a low voice resounding in my brain, the same words going over and over. When I listened closely to what was being said, I could understand it, because in the end the mumbles became clear. I heard, *I appear before you as a person, one of the many of your children. I am small and I am weak . . .* and it went on, forever and ever, over and over again. When I got home I grabbed my notebook and wrote it down. I knew that it had to be some kind of prayer. But it was something I'd never heard before, and so I just left it alone. Then one day I was reading some history books in the library and I came across the same words in one of the books I was reading. Turns out it was a burial chant from ancient American Indians. Do you believe me?"

I stood puzzled for a while. "Did you hear them in Japanese?"

"I don't know," he responded. "But I suppose so. I mean, I understood them."

I wasn't sure what to say. This went beyond truth or error, beyond any kind of disease. I felt sorry for my kid brother.

Yoshio spoke up. "At first I thought they wanted me for some kind of mission."

"Mission?" I echoed.

"Yeah, like they wanted me to write down the things I heard. But if I did that I'd be stealing—you know, plagiarism. I got scared, and the more scared I got, the more I could hear voices. . . ."

"They grew louder?" I asked.

My brother nodded, then he started to cry. It wasn't like when he was a small baby crying himself to sleep at night in an innocent, straightforward sort of way. His tears were more like clear crystals falling from his eyes, the kind that bring adults to a standstill.

"Listen," I said, "you're tough. I'm sure your mind is going through some really strange things. For the time being, though, I think you shouldn't worry about things like school for a while."

"Do you think I've gone crazy?" Yoshio asked, a painful look in his eyes.

"Umm . . ." I fought desperately to find the right words, but nothing would come to me. I told him to sit down on the curb, and I went over and leaned against a brick wall.

"I'm tired," he said, slithering up next to me.

"Whatever you do, don't tell Mom what you've told me tonight, and . . ." I paused.

"And what?"

"And I think we should suppose you've become some kind of radio. Now then, what's a radio like?"

"It has all sorts of channels."

"Exactly. Radios have the power to channel in all sorts of different frequencies." I stopped. "Yoshio, you can also turn a radio on and off, whenever you feel like it, with just the flick of a switch. If you could just get to that point, then everything will be okay."

"So what do you suggest?"

Again I was at a loss for words. It sounded so easy when I said it. If he only believed in himself, or gained the confidence to overcome the sounds. But saying those things to him at that moment was exactly like that peaceful afternoon when I told Mikiko how easy it would be to lose weight, munching away on sweet rice crackers. As long as I just let it slip from my lips, it didn't matter how awesome the task really was. But I couldn't tell him to do something that was obviously beyond his power.

On top of that, I reminded myself I was still talking to a child, unable to discern things like that for himself. Even if Mikiko and I were able to go through with our diet we decided on that spring night, it was something that took two of us to accomplish. Otherwise we would have never succeeded.

It was hard to explain.

I was silent. The night was heavy, filtering like oil between the houses and shops standing in rows around us, seemingly filling everything. Every road, sidewalk, and street corner seemed to have meaning that night as the whole town grew silently dark.

Puzzled, I turned to my brother and said, "How about coming with me to the pool?"

Yoshio quickly lifted his head. His eyes popped open as if someone had suddenly said something to him. It occurred to me that since the voices were going off in his head, maybe he was having a harder time seeing them than hearing them.

"Yoshio, what's going on?" I pretended to be calm.

"Saku-chan, do you mind if we go to the shrine?"

"What for?" I asked.

"A flying saucer's coming," Yoshio said. "If it's really there, will you believe me?"

"What do you mean? I haven't doubted a word you've . . ." Before I could finish my sentence I was distracted by the panic in his eyes. I glanced down at his small hands shining softly under the light of the streetlamp, and then over at our shadows cast thinly against the wall.

"Quick! We've got to go," my brother said, pulling himself up.

"Okay. Let's go and see." I rose to my feet. "You're talking about the shrine at the top of the hill, right?"

"Yeah," Yoshio cried. "Come on, we're going to miss it." He took off running as I trotted behind. It was a strange feeling, following my brother in the dark. My heart was pounding with excitement, and the thought crossed my mind that it would be nice if I could always feel this way—almost separated from my own reality.

"Saku-chan, hurry. We've got to move fast!"

The look of anxiety left my brother's eyes as he bounded up the steps in front of the shrine. It also pleased me to see he wasn't acting like a fanatic, either. Examining his face from the side of the road, his expression glimmered in the darkness like the content look of Buddhist *jizoh,* the guardian deities of children.

After rushing through the large red gates, I glanced back from the pebble road in the courtyard of the shrine to see that the roadway and houses we had passed were nothing more than faraway silhouettes against an enormous night sky. A cargo truck blared off into the darkness, its rumble echoing like a melody.

By the time we reached the top, both of us were panting. Gazing about, I saw we were surrounded by dark trees. It was almost painful—standing amid the thick green aroma filtering from the trees into the air.

The sky reflected softly off the scattered lights of the city below. Everything seemed peaceful.

"Okay, wise guy," I said with a chuckle, "show me your UFO."

Just then, between neon that created a cutout picture of the dark city below and the line that cut the city from the sky, right at the spot that seemed to stab my eye, an illuminated trail, looking like white condensation, sailed through the sky. It was a sudden flash—seemingly splitting the sky's hemisphere in two—jumping from left to right.

The flying saucer stopped right above the foliage in front of us and paused for a split second. The stop had been so elegant it was unlike anything I've ever seen on earth. Then it burst into flames and was gone.

Without question it was the most brilliant sight I'd ever seen. If I had to make a comparison, I'd say it was like a child seeing light at the end of her mother's womb for the first time, a light so pure, full of genuine beauty, a brilliance that would never be repeated. I longed to see it again.

All at once I felt exhausted.

Additional words were unnecessary; it had been the simple whiteness of a light I'd dreamed of seeing forever.

"Wow!" I screamed, every inch of me shaking. "Wow! Wow! Wow!"

"Pretty amazing, huh?" Yoshio exclaimed.

"Because of you, my brother, I saw a terrific thing tonight. Thank you!"

But compared to my frenzy, Yoshio seemed reserved.

"What's wrong?" I asked.

He spoke softly. "See? I told you. Sakumi, what's happening to me?"

"You mean you aren't happy?" I bellowed.

"It doesn't have to do with happiness," he said with a worried look in his eyes.

Feeling sorry, I glanced down and said, "I see." Even though Yoshio had been there to witness something so bright and wonderful, he could hardly share my excitement. I didn't want him to quibble, or tell him it had all been a lie. I simply wanted him to be surprised and moved by the wonderful spectacle of that night. But at that point I was too tired to do anything about it.

"Okay. Let's give it a rest for a while. Don't worry, we'll do something for you, but right now let's go home. Yoshio, I'm glad I came with you tonight."

My brother nodded, and a faint grin crept over his lips.

Wishing there was something I could do or say, I pulled him close to my side and together we found our way home.

Chapter 6

Spring rolled around.

The outside air grew warmer with the same speed it took me to stop wearing my heavy coats, and blossoms burst out of the cherry trees in our garden, one right after the other. From my upstairs window I viewed a perfect blend of pink and green, and it thrilled me to see the colors multiplying.

A letter arrived from Ryūichirō.

Dear Sakumi:

How are you?

Right now I'm in Shanghai. Don't ask me why.

China is a great place. Just lots of people.

I plan to return to Japan (sometime this year). I think I might publish another book.

I'm a bit worried about whether you will see me or not.

Still, I look forward to the day when we meet.

Sometimes when I see a pretty landscape I think of how nice it would be to show it to you. I get homesick for Japan and wish I could be with you.

Everything here seems so big. You would die laughing if you saw how large the statues of Buddha are in this country.

I'll write again soon.

Love,
Ryūichirō

Sometimes I had a hard time believing he was really a writer. His letters seemed to be full of such choppy, little sentences. Still, they had a direct way of reminding me how pleasant the author was.

Like a robot's memory circuit that has gone haywire . . .

Or an illustration of the ugly duckling . . .

When I opened my eyes after the fall, Ryūichirō's face came to mind but as I looked at everything with a whole new perspective, I had no idea of what was going on around me. Alone in an unfamiliar world, the first thing to cut through my heart was the warm touch of his skin. I was frightened by sights and sounds all around me; I didn't know how it would feel to be with a man.

I was in love with my new memory.

I'm sure if I saw him I'd break into tears.

As I pondered over what it was like to be with him, those wonderful parts about Ryūichirō flooded into my brain, and I felt a sharp discomfort in my chest. His talent for writing. His good behavior. The coolness of his actions, his magnanimity. The shape of his hands. The soft echo in his voice . . . and so on.

Then I recalled the bad things, and it hurt to breathe when I thought about how much of me hated him. That crafty way he made it through life. The cowardliness of asking me to travel with him. The cruelty he showed over losing Mayu. Even the clever way he was able to decide when to see me by returning to Japan, with no intention of hanging around for very long . . . and so on.

Each and every little thing about Ryūichirō came back to me so clearly, things that never bothered me about others, with an amplitude as large as the heart of the vector that viewed him in that light. People are full of pain. When an imperfect person attempts to accept the imperfections of other people, the result is always painful, because individual storms that find their way into our hearts survive in different places. Sometimes we tend to focus on images that appear to be strangely alive.

As people we narrowly get by with our lives each day, energy from our soft, delicate actions appearing like cherry blossoms, only once, and only for a short while. Eventually petals fall to the ground. The sun beats down, wind stirs about, and I stand petrified, unable to move, astonished by the sweet color of the blue sky that flows through the dancing petals of pink tumbling gently about me. The trees above sway softly in the breeze.

It happens only once and then it's over. But I eternally melt into that instant.

Wonderful! Bravo!

. . . to that one simple moment.

~

My brother seemed to improve right before me, despite an occasional reemergence of a few of his old grim expressions. But maybe because we'd seen the UFO and had proof of his premonitions, or maybe because he now had me to talk to, whatever the reason, Yoshio seemed more relaxed, and I felt better, too. It was as though my brother had made the decision to step out on his own, now that he knew he couldn't just cling to me and constantly ask for my advice. I was impressed, even if he was my brother. But with so many great things about him, I really hoped he'd turn out okay. It didn't matter if he wound up a thief, pervert, or philanderer. None of those things mattered, as long as he grew up to be a man with a good heart.

Nevertheless, I couldn't bring myself to feel positive about the things taking place inside him. Just because he'd reached a comfort zone with himself didn't mean we'd found a solution to his problem. At some point the awful times were bound to return, and Yoshio would be put through the trial and depression that came along with it.

What could I do? I often asked myself when I was alone. There just had to be something, I was sure.

Why is it people feel they've got to do something for others, even when there's nothing in their power? An ocean is an ocean, nothing more. It draws near and pushes back, violent at times, and so forth. I want to go through life in the same way that the presence of an ocean evokes myriad feelings and emotions, just by being there—arousing disappointment, comfort, and fear.

My presence, just being there, drawing near and pushing away.

Still, the desire to do something for my brother wouldn't leave.

I'd already lost one sister to a slow death, right in front of my eyes. So at least one thing was clear. If someone in this world decides to take her own life, the determination of others to try to stop her from going through with it is exactly the same as their inability to do so.

Perhaps that's what made me struggle.

~

Those thoughts flowed through my mind at the time my mother announced to the family that she had made plans to travel to Paris with her boyfriend.

"It's only for a couple of weeks," she casually mentioned as we sat at the dinner table one Sunday night. Oddly enough, all five of us were eating at the same time, a rare thing around our house.

I made a sly remark about how nice it must feel to be so rich and free to just get up and run off like that.

Junko was the first to doubt. "How will the food be? Doesn't it rain a lot in France this time of year? Are you sure you'll be safe?"

"It really doesn't matter," my mother replied. "We're going because we both have it off. It will just be a break, a perfect way to rest our minds and our bodies." She sounded more defensive than usual. My mother's boyfriend was working full-time at the same small travel agency where my mother put in a few hours each week. He was a lot younger than she was, and from the sound of things, busy. Since it was the peak travel season, it only seemed natural that they would have been swamped in the office, and it was obvious my mother had been tired lately. Thus, the need for a break.

"I think it sounds wonderful," Mikiko said, relating a story of a friend who had just come home from France. "She says funerals are really colorful there. She jumped into a procession thinking she was off to a festival, but then she realized what the line was really for."

We laughed for a minute, but Yoshio was silent, not saying a word.

Although we were pleased with the idea of my mother's trip, we couldn't help but notice the unusual way my brother was acting. Junko turned to him and said, "How do you feel about your mother going away for a few weeks?"

He sat with his mouth closed. It didn't take long for the atmosphere in the kitchen to turn sour. My mother smiled gently and said, "Don't worry, I'll bring you back something nice."

I liked the way my mother came up with things her children could never object to, and I liked it even more when she smiled, letting her feelings shine through. But I guess that didn't do it for my brother.

As though our house had gone up in flames, he started to wail.

We sat dazed at my brother's outburst. It was such a peculiar cry, I felt like I was looking at a man who'd lived his life only to realize that he was a failure. Say, for example, a man loses his job on the same day he turns forty, then gets home to discover his wife is cheating on him. Maybe he wouldn't even cry as intensely as my brother did that night. Yoshio pulled on his hair and banged his head against the table, whining like he was trying to rid himself of all that went on in his mind.

I knew that I had to be calm myself before I could do anything for my brother, so for a few seconds I focused my eyes on the cowlick in his hair. My mother had already started talking amid the flurry.

"Everything will be fine," she said. "I'll only be gone for two weeks. I'm going with, well, you know—the man who always comes over to visit. You don't mind if I spend some time alone with him, right? It's not like I'm trying to run away and leave you."

"NO!" my brother screamed. "THAT HAS NOTHING TO DO WITH IT!"

"What do you mean?" my mother asked.

"The plane . . . ," my brother stammered. "The plane is going to crash." His voice was inside out, and he looked as if he had the chills, since his shoulders quivered as he sat shriveled away in his chair. "You just can't get on that plane."

Maybe he was right. Considering what had happened the night before, I had to agree with my brother's premonition.

"Saku-chan." Yoshio turned to me. "Say something. Tell her she can't get on that plane."

Thinking for a moment I said, "Mother, why don't you reconsider, just for the time being. I mean, look, this could be a bad sign. Yoshio seems to know a lot about this sort of thing. Who knows? It might be for real." I turned back to my brother. "When will it happen—on the way there or back? Which one?"

"The way there," he said. "No doubt about it." He spoke with confidence, as if he was prophesying the occurrence of some dreadful event. I felt troubled.

"See, Mother," I said. "Now, if it was the return flight, then things would be different. You could go to Paris and have a great time, and just give up on whatever happened next. This way you're never going to get off the ground."

"How about scheduling a flight later in the day?" Mikiko piped in. "That way everyone will be happy. That will take care of the danger, now won't it, Yoshi-chan."

"I don't know," he said. "All I see is her going down in a plane. That's all."

"Oh," Mikiko replied. "That means even if Aunt Yukiko changes her flight it would still be the same—the airplane will still go down." Now Mikiko sounded scared.

We'd taken my brother's side, as if out of nowhere our entire conversation had changed to support his plight. Mikiko brought over a large pot of hot tea and poured us each a cup, and we sipped away in silence. I had no way of knowing how it would turn out.

Finally Junko broke the silence. "Consider changing the day." She had always been extremely superstitious. "How about going later, like sometime next month?"

Yoshio nodded, and I could tell that the idea pleased him, the little lord at our table.

That's when it happened. My mother threw down her cup and saucer, and they landed with a clatter. She pounded her fist on the table and said, "What in the hell do you people think you are saying? Now is the only time we can take a vacation! Do any of you realize how hard it is to take this much time off work? My boyfriend is a really busy man. What will happen if I cancel our plans and the plane makes it safely to Paris? Who will be responsible then? Who will be the one to blame?" She continued to scream for a while. All of us were taken aback by her eruption. "We've bought the tickets, and we're ready to go. That's it. Case closed. I'm getting on that plane even if it goes down."

"Seriously?" I said. "Even if it kills you?"

"Exactly." My mother nodded her head. "Even if it kills me. I've made my decision, and I'm going. If the plane crashes and I burst into a million pieces, you can just blame it on me. Say 'It was all her fault, that idiot who wouldn't listen to advice.' Carve it on my tombstone for all I care. I'm sorry, but that's life. Laugh about it when I'm gone." My mother picked up her cup of tea and took a sip. Her face was shining brightly.

Once again my brother burst into tears, thrashing violently in his chair. Mikiko and Junko pulled him away and dragged him up the stairs.

Letting out a sigh, my mother turned back to me and said, "What do you think?"

I thought for a moment and said, "I think you've got a fifty-fifty chance."

"Of what?" she asked.

"Of that little outburst being for real. Yoshio really was seeing something in his mind, or maybe it was just a young boy afraid of a mother who would leave him for a man and Paris."

"Maybe it's just a phase," my mother replied.

"But it's all so forlorn," I said.

"Really?" she asked. "But how do *you* feel, Sakumi?"

"About what?"

"About a mother who'd run off on vacation with a man while her son's at home, unable to go to school." Her eyes grew wide as she spoke, the eyes of a mother full of honesty.

"Actually," I said, "I think it's fine."

"Are you sure?"

"Of course," I replied. "Listen, it would be a lot better for both you and Yoshio if you didn't give up a chance like this for him. I mean, it's never healthy to postpone something this much fun for the sake of another person. We've each got to live a life full of happiness and beauty. In the end you'll both benefit from it, I'm sure."

"Well, then, it's decided," my mother said. "I'm going."

"Even if the plane goes down?" I repeated myself.

"Yes, even if the plane goes down. The decision's been made. I've lived all these years and I really don't feel like changing the course of my life now. It might sound like I'm blowing things out of proportion, but that's exactly how I feel." Then my mother began to chuckle. "And besides, I don't have the slightest fear that that plane will crash."

~

A week passed.

The dinner the night before my mother was scheduled to board the plane was so solemn it felt like the Last Supper. To make matters worse, my brother refused to leave his room. My mother went up and tried to persuade him to come out, giving him as much comfort as possible, but he still refused to budge from his bed. He just sniffled every few seconds, on and off, looking like he was in pain. He seemed to still have respect for our mother, even though she hadn't canceled her flight out of Tokyo: one more reason my brother impressed me.

Her plans were not so precarious that they'd normally take a person to the brink of death, and according to my mother a trip to Paris was simply something that had been pulling at her heart-strings for a while. We were well aware of that by now.

That night, when I crawled between my covers, I could hear my brother's sobs from the next room. A cooing sound from my mother's soft voice also came through the thin walls into the darkness, even though I couldn't make out what she was saying.

The two sounds combined to create the ceaseless chant of a Buddhist sutra.

Somewhere amid that discord, the morning sun managed to slip its way through the window, filling the four corners of my bed. Thoughts began to flow through my mind with a resolute clarity, mixed in particles of light and darkness, taking the following shape:

I know what my brother says is true; I know this more than any other person in the house, more than my mother, more than my brother himself. If I were to try and get her to stop now, she just might do it. Then my mother would be saved. But if she decided not to go, and the plane arrived safely in Paris, then everyone in the house would stop believing in my brother, and he'd get labeled the boy who cried wolf. That would only increase the shock of everything going on right now, reducing his chances for recovery. I don't want to stop her, because I myself don't believe that the plane will go down. I am fond of my mother, I love everything about her. She made the decision to go on this journey herself, and she doesn't need to receive advice from anyone else. How many times has she saved us children through strong will and resilience? On top of that, I don't want my brother to think he can always get his own way. However . . . if my mother dies and I realize I didn't stop her, even when I had the chance, I will not feel regret.

Would it be wrong for me to stand in her way?

. . . I really don't know.

Thoughts like that kept turning in my head, and I remembered how wrong it is to try to predict the future. With half of me desperate for rest, I stayed in bed for a while, but I wasn't getting much sleep. It was the shallowest kind of repose.

Eventually I came to, and with a deep breath, opened each eye. Soon I grew accustomed to the thin darkness of the room.

Far from having a good night's rest, I found myself falling in and out of twisted dreams—silently, ever so silently. A sensation of fluttering through the darkness, the fresh dance of a tumbling snowflake.

I'm small, not much bigger than my brother is now, and I'm standing under a cherry tree. I remember planting the tree with my father—he made me do most of the work. Looking up, I see small patches of pink poking through the young leaves. I don't know why, but Mayu has already passed away. I wish I could see her, even though I know she's gone.

The door of the house opens, and my mother comes out carrying a baby. I see that it's Yoshio. My mother's young, and she's wearing a white sweater so bright that it strains my eyes, reminding me of the color most people wear as they lie dead in their coffins.

I start to feel nervous. My mother doesn't say a thing. Yoshio's also quiet—I can't hear him sniveling. My mother approaches me silently, slowly, in the brightness of the light.

I figure it must be time for lunch, or she's coming to tell me to put on a hat. Maybe she wants me to stay home because she needs to go shopping.

She laughs quietly.

I'm going to Paris so I need you to take care of this child.

Paris? I think to myself. Mother laughs and hands Yoshio over to me. He is warm, and extremely heavy.

* * *

With my heart still pounding, I opened my eyes. It was right before dawn, and everything around me was a rich blue. The same thought kept running over and over in my mind as I stayed in bed.

You won't regret this. You won't regret this.

It was a sorry chant, like an orphan crying helplessly in the night. No wonder I found it hard to sleep that night.

~

The next morning everything was somber. Only my mother rushed around as if nothing were the matter, diverting her thoughts from the rest of us, who plainly showed signs of fear. I watched her dish up a plate of fried eggs and scarf them down.

My brother never came out of his room. Junko asked my mother if she needed a ride to Narita Airport, but she shook her head with her mouth still full of eggs. Swallowing, she said not to bother. Her boyfriend was on his way to get her.

I tried to remember that my mother wasn't a child. She was a grown woman, and her actions were her own, despite the indulgence of her children. Then I remembered how I had reacted to my sentimentalism the day before.

My mother's body remained rigid as she munched on a piece of toast, overflowing in her own self-esteem—hardly the way I would have expected one to act right before she marched off to death. She was just happy to be taking a break, regardless of form. It was written plainly in her eyes, even though there was also something that said this trip had already been more troublesome than she'd previously imagined. Just like I'd read my mother's mind in the past, I knew she was ready to rest. She would bother with problems when they happened, not before. Her hair was glimmering in front of the light, the mark above her eyebrows clearly trying to tell us something.

Tossing on her sunglasses, she turned to us and said, "Well, I'll see you all later." Then, with her carry-on luggage in hand, she made her way to the front door and we followed. Suddenly we heard a huge bang from upstairs, and I knew my brother had thrown his door open. Before long he came tumbling down the stairs, his eyes swollen red with tears. He must have had something to say.

Without opening my mouth I turned to Yoshio and said, *Don't say a word. It will be all right. Do you understand? Everything's going to be all right.*

Apparently he picked up my message, because he responded by saying, *I know. It's impossible to take back something you've said, so I'm just going to stand here and be quiet.*

Our conversation was for real, even though our mouths hadn't moved. It wasn't telepathy, but we both understood because of something bright and warm that made its way between us.

A rather unusual morning, all the way around.

"I'll bring back souvenirs," my mother said, turning away from the door. Then she looked back and said, "Imagine those being my last words to you all!" She laughed aloud as she squeezed into the car.

~

"Paris is magnificent!" My mother's voice came clearly over the telephone, sending a flood of relief to my heart.

She had made the trip without incident. When I hung up the receiver, I couldn't help but feel a little stupid. I didn't feel bad that I'd believed in my brother's prediction; my thoughts came more from the fact that I'd been foolish enough to allow my own emotions to fluctuate so much, a trait so different from my mother. Looking behind me, I noticed that my brother wasn't feeling well.

Mikiko had already left for school, and Junko had gone off shopping for dinner that night, saying something about not wanting to be around when the phone call came from, or about, my mother. I told her I'd stay home as I plopped on the sofa and opened a book. That's where I was when the call came.

"So you made it," I responded, hanging up the phone. I didn't say a word to my brother.

He was quiet, which made things feel weird, like there was something out of place. There's no other way of describing the atmosphere in the room that moment. Since everything was so quiet, I turned on the TV.

The news was on, and they were showing a picture of an airplane on the screen. My heart skipped a beat.

The plane had split in two and large puffs of white smoke billowed out from inside. Hundreds of people were dashing about, stretchers were being brought in one after another, and the reporter ran to and fro, trying to describe the scene.

I turned to my brother and asked what happened. .

"A plane heading for Australia exploded as it was taking off from Narita," he replied.

"Did you know about it?" I asked.

He nodded. "Just a minute ago I found out that one of the planes was an hour late for takeoff. Mom was already gone."

"Why the extra hour?" I said.

"All I know is that Mom's plane left an hour before the plane for Australia blew up."

On the television the announcer was reporting the names of all the Japanese people who had either died or received injuries in the accident. Once he was finished, the names came up in graphics on the screen, printed in bold *katakana*.

"I wasn't wrong," Yoshio said with a tender look on his face. "Mom's trip and this other airplane just got mixed up, that's all."

"Of course you were right," I said. "You knew it all the time. And it wasn't your fault, either, so don't let an idea like that even cross your mind. It was just something that came to you naturally."

Again I had the impression I should do something for my brother. I didn't know what I would do, but whatever it was, it would have to be done quickly.

Chapter 7

Dear Diary:

I'm sitting in bed writing with my brother sleeping next to me. I can hear him breathing deeply.

With only a small light next to my bed illuminating these pages, the room is rather dark. Outside the trees blow violently in the darkness along with the heavy crash of the waves. I feel like I'm out under the stars.

Whoosh. Swish. Bang. The sounds are so gigantic they threaten me.

Everything is quiet in the room. My brother's face is shining faintly in the darkness. He's beautiful when he sleeps. The bridge of his nose stands out prominently from his face, and his lips are shaded in red.

Lately I've been thinking a lot about life.

I just finished a book that seemed perfect for living on a beach, my current situation. It was called *A Gift from the Sea,* and I think this diary has picked up the same style of writing. How foolish I am sometimes.

I haven't kept a diary since summer vacations during elementary school, but for some reason I've been writing this one for an entire month now.

Aren't I capricious? I mean, I only jot down what I did on a certain day, or I write whatever pops into my head, kind of like I'm doing now. I must be pretty tired.

Actually, somewhere in my subconscious I've had the desire to record the things that have been happening to my kid brother, and I believe that's why I've been brought to pick up the pen. But now I'm sounding like a stage mother. What a horrible feeling. I would rather think of myself differently.

Somewhere between the things that I say and the things that I sense there is a deep gorge which is impossible to fill. I figure there must be the same amount of distance between myself and my written words. But just like so many other people in this world, when I sit down to record my thoughts and feelings in a diary I turn into a coward, and I feel woozy, like I'm putting on airs, pretending to be something I am not. It really feels unpleasant.

Take, for instance, a man who holds a precious job in society, something that helps preserve mankind as we know it. Without warning one morning he gets a hard-on while standing at a street corner staring at this incredibly sexy woman from behind, and sometime during the same day he gets angry with his two-year-old daughter. When he talks with his wife, he is touched by the strength of compassion, but since we all get into a good story we start to wonder if we, ourselves, are really good or bad, regardless of the fact that there's so much confusion in life. I bet that man feels the same way, too.

Isn't that weird?

Putting the above example aside, I think I know why I'm going on in my diary like this. I have nothing better to do. Then again, I heard a nice story about a diary the other day that also might have had more of an effect on me than I realize.

When one of my girlfriends turned twenty-one, she moved into a new apartment. Up until that time she had been living alone with her mother. Her father had passed away years before. Since her mother was about to be remarried, they decided to vacate their old place. She was packing things away to start a life out on her own, her mother lending a hand.

As the two of them rummaged through articles her father had left behind after a battle with cancer, a brown leather satchel turned up. My friend's mother told her that before her father died, he'd given strict orders to throw the bag away. For some odd reason the mother was unable to go through with the command. The bag remained closed for years.

They opened it together, uncovering dozens of diaries. As they glanced through the pages, they discovered that the entries started with her father in high school and continued throughout his early life as a businessman. They even contained the description of a certain day when he met a young woman on a street corner and instantly fell in love. All his youthful days were represented.

"When I pick up my father's journals and flip through them before going to bed at night, it feels like I'm reading a fabulous novel," my friend said.

One man, unwilling to show his true self until he had passed on to a different world, only doing those things on this earth that fulfilled his responsibility as a husband and a father, later seeped through the pages of a diary to support his daughter, now out on her own.

One of the things I've tried so desperately not to think about lately has forced its way into my mind. Maybe it had to do with the impression that came from seeing a flying saucer.

What am I talking about? The transformation that took place when I fell down the stairs. My memory scattered, and friends tell me I've changed. I've just laughed it off, but clearly something profound really did happen inside—inside my head, inside the brain cells, inside the neurons and endorphins and all the other spinning and turning somethings within my head. Maybe at some point in time, on a certain date at a certain time, my memory will be lost forever, because I'll be dead, or just crazy.

I'm not exaggerating. It happened to that guy in *The Dead Zone.* He received a fatal injury to the brain. What would stop it from happening to me?

Whatever happens, happens, I don't really care. Even if I die.

My life has been fun; I have no regrets. Actually, I have nothing, not a single thing to show for my days and months and years on this planet—no children, nothing, zilch. If I died right now I'd just disappear from one side of me to the other.

I suppose dying is the same for everyone, because even those people who have some way of leaving something on earth still pass away so abruptly. Nonetheless, death holds a certain sense of loneliness. Up until the time Yoshio started acting strangely, my mother had been peaceful knowing her children were well. If I had died back then there would have been no regrets. Now things are different, because if I left now my mother would get stuck holding the bag. Actually, I'm the one feeling responsible for us now.

Okay, I admit it. I wrote about the journal my friend found simply because I was jealous. It's hard to say why. Every now and then I have the feeling I want to tell someone about how nervous I feel, exposing that small, helpless part of me. I want to show someone a childlike spirit frightened of tomorrow, the same spirit that shrinks itself away in the corner of my heart.

On a beach anyone can be a poet.

I've heard that when you stand on a beach and look out over the ocean, it's really 20 percent larger than you expected. When I looked at the ocean with an average idea in mind, it was true—20 percent larger than I expected. Even if you went to the ocean with a larger idea of its size in mind, it would still go beyond your imagination—20 percent, that is, even if you're only moved by the sight of a single wave, or picture a smaller beach. Everything increases by 20 percent.

I suppose this is what they mean by "limitless."

From a UFO to the loss of memory, from my brother to Ryūichirō, not forgetting Eiko, my diary, Paris, and everything else that came together over the past few months to form a portion of my life without boundaries, I sit and look out over it now. It occurs to me that everything was actually 20 percent larger than anticipated.

I've reached the point where I don't understand what I'm writing anymore, so I guess I'll go to sleep.

Tomorrow I'm taking Yoshio fishing.
Although I've never even been myself.
It should be fun.

∾

My head ached as I read over what I had written in my diary. I'd scribbled out the entry the night before and I was stone drunk when I did it.

Oh, did I fail to mention I was in Kochi with my brother at the time?

A few nights after my mother left for Paris, I was talking with my boss at work, telling him about how unhappy my brother was and about everything else that was happening in our lives. He suggested I take a break from the bar and go on a trip with Yoshio. I was impressed by his generosity, the ex-hippie.

That seemed to be the answer—a small vacation with my brother. The next problem was where. It didn't take long for me to find a solution.

Eiko had mentioned that the guy she was seeing owned a small apartment near the beach in Kōchi, on the Pacific side of Shikoku. Apparently he had grown up there, and he had the place ready in order to return home on weekends to see his family. Since he was so busy that he hardly ever managed to get home, the apartment felt more like a summer beach house.

I called Eiko, and she talked to her boyfriend. He cheerfully agreed to let us use the place, expressing thanks to have someone there to air the place out. I grabbed my brother, and we were gone before my mother returned from Paris.

∾

I'd made an appointment with Eiko so I could pick up the key to the apartment.

Once again her flashy appearance made her float amid the moonless night, even though her black suit seemed caught up in commotion. She approached me with a sense of urgency, but in a nonchalant way. Her life gave form to expression. In the simple way she carried herself, she never stopped the display.

"Eiko," I yelled. She saw me and smiled.

My heart dropped. A large white bandage covered half of her face. Seeing her in that way, with her downturned eyebrows and a majority of her face concealed behind the mask, I couldn't help but find it extraordinarily erotic.

"What's that?" I asked. "What happened? Come and let's talk about it over some tea."

Eiko smiled. "No, I've got to rush off to another appointment. Don't worry about this," she said, pointing at the mask. "It was just a run-in with his wife."

"How did she find out?" I said with surprise. "Please don't tell me it had something to do with us borrowing his apartment."

"No, no, it didn't have anything to do with that at all," she replied. "I guess she's been noticing things for quite some time, but out of the blue she just showed up at the house—you know, the condo that we're sharing in Nakameguro—and I was there all alone. God, was it scary!"

"You were frightened?" I asked.

"What else could I be?" Another smile came over her face.

She'd always been that way, it didn't matter what went on. Eiko was the type that never was defeated. Reality would go one way, her heart another. You could see it in her attitude and expression. Maintaining the word *refined,* she always allowed for extra space in her life, and from the look of it, things hadn't changed.

"I had to let her in. I mean, what else could I do?" Eiko said. "So I made some tea and took a seat beside her. We just stared at each other without saying anything for a few minutes, and that's when it happened. She blew up,

"crying,

"screaming,

"and getting all violent.

"I watched her transform into a writhing beast, right in front of my eyes. You know, women are remarkable creatures. It's probably not nice of me to say it, but I promised myself right there and then that I would never behave that way. It might be different for a first wife, but not me."

"You mean because she's married?"

"Well, we shouldn't rule out the possibility. Maybe I'd get that upset too, if I'd been married to a guy who cheated on me for five years. What do you suppose would happen to him if he picked up two or three other girlfriends on the side?"

The last part of her statement seemed almost sincere. Nebulous chaos in a person's life—a direct look at the foolishness we carry with us. At least her voice sounded innocent. As I watched Eiko talk about her incident with her boyfriend's wife, she appeared 20 percent larger than the Eiko I'd expected.

I just shook my head in reply.

"We'll talk about it more later," she said, placing a key and a piece of paper with a sketched-out map in my hand. I watched as her thin shoulders disappeared into the night.

∾

I felt unusual waking up to the sound of the waves, and Yoshio was always with me. It was the first time that my brother and I had spent so much time together.

For some reason waves hitting the shore bring uneasiness to some, especially when they look out over a scene that grows

20 percent larger than expected. But when it came down to it, I seemed to be in the middle of the road.

I connected with that miraculous line which brought the sky together with the ocean, a sensation of being a part of an endless horizon. Everything silent, everything real.

That's the reason I tried to cope with the truth about my own existence. In the meantime my brother showed signs of improvement, but it was different from the way Spenser grew up over the course of one summer in Robert Parker's *Early Autumn.* I think Yoshio was experiencing a tremendous amount of freedom.

Maybe it had something to do with the fact that I was a woman. For example, if we were walking along a path in the middle of the night he would go first and tell me if there were any large rocks. If we had two shopping bags he would carry the heavier one—we based everything on that kind of standard. I felt like I'd been able to glance through clouds into his anxious heart and see all the separate parts—everything his original personality was based on, his rough spots, and his humble generosity as well.

More than anything, I had the impression that Yoshio was probably just learning to feel comfortable with himself while we were away.

~

The place turned out to be a regular apartment, fifth floor up, with a nice view of town and the water beyond. It was small—two bedrooms, a living room, kitchen, and small dining area—with limited furnishings. Certainly the term *summer beach home* was pushing it. It was more of your run-of-the-mill apartment.

In the morning we jogged on the beach, and splashed about the neighborhood swimming pool in the afternoon. To be honest, though, we didn't do much of anything except watch each day come and go. That's how I felt one afternoon when I asked Yoshio what he wanted for dinner. Since breakfast had been thrown-together leftovers, my stomach was already growling.

"What'll it be?" I asked my brother. "Dinner at home, or should we go out?"

Thinking for a minute, he said, "Let's go out."

Outside we were witnesses to a sunset so dazzling it was frightening. I'll never forget it as long as I live, since it reminded me of the night we saw the flying saucer. My heart pounded inside me, and I felt alive—just in those few minutes we spent staring at the sunset.

We were headed for the center of town, no real destination in mind. Everything was as clear as a southern land should be, the dry sun assuming an orange hue, dark city streets floating like silhouettes in the crimson sky. But that was only the prelude. I recalled that back in Tokyo we would look at sunsets and dream about wonderful things that had to be happening far away.

For the next few minutes everything was completely different, like something you'd see on TV, or a picture from a tourist brochure, and I wondered if I could reach out and touch it. Everything was surrounded by a force that squeezed its way through an invisible wall between the air and town, a gigantic energy that burned softly in its own clarity, a vividness so fresh I almost stopped breathing.

I've always thought that when it comes time for one day to end, the sun makes its exit from the stage by showing off the most ravishing item of the day—something of true beauty, something so friendly and large it terrifies me. My thoughts were confirmed on that day.

I felt myself sink into the city. The essence felt pure white, drawing close to me from the western sky like the soft, rosy cheeks of a beloved wife. Every street in town shone with the brightness, and every face radiated the glow—that intense sunset shimmering in its own redness.

Feeling my soul wake inside me, I felt something tug at my chest as the sunset finally disappeared over the horizon, giving me a sense of invigorating gratitude and a feeling of not wanting to part. I knew I would never see another day like that one—the perfect composition of the sky, the formation of the clouds, the colors, the warmth—they'd never come back.

Locals strolled peacefully through town. Windows full of light from dinner floated against the clear screen of nightfall. It seemed like I could reach out and scoop everything up like water in my hand—drops trickling from the small ridges in my fingers, falling with a plunk, painfully hitting the hard concrete below. They seemed to carry a fragrance of that thick night and the beautiful scent of the afternoon sun.

How could such a simple thing like a sunset contain so much power? I didn't know until I saw it firsthand. Over the course of our lives each one of us reads a million books, and sees as many films—we kiss our loved ones the same number of times. But I was aware I'd seen something that night that I'd never see again in my lifetime.

Nature is something so powerful that when you try to capture it, it overwhelms you with a split second of something spectacular, forcing you to understand, even when you're not looking for it. Since the mysteries aren't biased they can happen to us all.

"I don't know why, but I feel really calm right now," I said.

As the last drop of sunlight was squeezed from the horizon, every corner of the small town plunged into darkness and night descended upon us.

"Me, too," Yoshio said.

"How about some *oden* to celebrate what we just saw?" I asked.

"Can I drink sake tonight with my dinner?" he said.

"Just as long as you don't get drunk, because I'm the one who'll have to carry you home."

"Can I order from the adult menu?" he asked, once again looking gloomy.

"Sure. But why the sudden change? You don't seem very happy."

Yoshio thought for a minute and said, "When we were looking at the sunset, I started to feel a little embarrassed about how I've been acting lately. I think I'm ready to go back and start things up again—at least get back into school."

"Wonderful," I replied. "You know, there are quite a few people in the world who've said that once you've recognized your own limits you've raised yourself to a higher level of being, since you're closer to the real you. Let's see, Yūmi Matsutoya said it, Ayrton Senna said it, John C. Lilly said it . . . "

"I've heard about Yūmin, she's a singer. But who are the rest of the people you are talking about?" my brother inquired.

"That's something you'll have to learn later," I said, knowing full well that a popular singer, a Brazilian grand prix winner, and an American neurologist had nothing to do with one another. I figured they'd give more persuasion to my argument, so I tried to fool my brother by dropping their names.

Because I've always thought the best catch in the world is one that passes right underneath you.

Chapter 8

"Let's go home," my brother said.

Yoshio and I sat eating dinner together on our seventh night in Kochi. I'd just put out my chopsticks to grab a piece of octopus sashimi, when I stopped and looked up at him, staring at him for a moment, since his comment had taken me completely by surprise. It must have looked like a scene straight out of a television drama.

The reason for my reaction was clear. That morning the very same thing had popped into my head, and I had considered mentioning it to my brother. He looked fine with the idea of returning home, and I suppose I wouldn't have been too out of line if I had suggested it. But I had been afraid of the opposite reaction. I could just see Yoshio throwing himself half-crazed on the floor and crying out loud like a baby. I suppose I wouldn't have been surprised by either response.

I wasn't reading my brother as well as he was reading me.

Within a few days of watching the sun rise and set over the ocean, Yoshio had made a complete turnaround, turning from the timid little pip-squeak with the pale look on his face into a kid actually fun to be around.

I'd made it a point not to bring up school with him—not during our walks along the beach, not during the times we burst out laughing as we hit it big playing *pachinko* at the beachside amusement center, not during the times we would stay up late at night watching TV, and not during the silent times we would lie in bed reading.

Ever since coming to Kochi we hadn't talked about why we were there, and with no idea of the extent of Yoshio's pain, I couldn't estimate how long we would have to stay in order for him to snap back to normal. Hence my silence. The two of us simply took a long-needed break. Without thinking about anything in particular, we allowed only the impression of how nice it would be to stay there to flow endlessly through our minds. Still, the time had come for us to leave. I hadn't been able predict when it would come, but in due time it fell upon us.

~

That afternoon we'd gone fishing.

We rented some poles and bought bait from the little shop at the beach, and strolled down to the ocean to try our hand at some amateur fishing. It was actually the second time we had been, and since on our first try we were able to bring in such a surprisingly large catch, the taste for fishing was still in our mouths. Now we were back for more.

We found a spot on a dike facing the ocean, but after casting our lines it was obvious that neither of us would hook a thing. The wind was strong, the smell of salt bitter in our noses, and the cement underneath us was cold. With all the forces against us, I had to frown, and my brother did the same. We just sat together, both lines drooping in the water. The sky was overcast, making me feel like I was looking through a white veil at the faint blue behind the clouds. The waves beat against the dike underneath us, sending up sprays of water that fell back to the ocean as foamy bubbles like cream. I thought the waves would stop abruptly once they hit the dike, but they continued endlessly fluttering against the shore.

As that happened, the word "tide" came to my mind. Perhaps it was telling me that it was time to go. I'd actually grown tired of the beauty. Below my dangling legs, the echoes of the waves seemed to be saying,

It's time for you to go home,
You've seen all there is to see,
and so on.

It was that kind of feeling. At the time I had no idea how my brother would feel about going home, and when I glanced over to see him I saw the frown on his face and his fishing pole drooping between his legs. What was going through his mind? Maybe he was contemplating school, or the universe; or maybe he was wondering about life, or just listening to the sound of the waves. In all honesty he was probably thinking about what a waste our time was, sitting out on the beach not catching a single thing.

When the idea of returning to Tokyo entered my mind, the faces of all of those people also came to me—my mother, Mikiko, Junko, Eiko, all the people at the bar, and even though we weren't that far away, they seemed distant somehow. It didn't take long for the most important face of all to force itself into my mind—Ryūichirō.

As I pondered over what he was doing in the world, I felt the need to see him. The thin, western sun shone hazily across a concrete tetrapod out in the sea, and the desire to meet Ryūichirō came to me so strongly I couldn't stand it anymore, even though I knew there was no way to see him. That desire, mixed with the reality of not being able to see him, brought a lonely feeling to my heart.

At that point a small fishing boat came in from the sea. There was a small pier not far from where we were sitting, and the boat moved its way through the waves and landed next to the dock. We watched two men get out from inside the boat—an old fisherman and a younger guy who I assumed was the older man's apprentice. Before long they had both gathered various nets and other fishing equipment in their arms, and they strolled in our direction.

"Are they biting today?" the older man yelled.

"Not a bit," I replied.

Laughing at my response, the younger man rushed over to the dike and threw us a small octopus. Overjoyed, we thanked them for their kindness. Then we gave up fishing for the day. More than anything, the octopus had proven to be our reason to stop our absurdity. After returning to the apartment, we cut off the legs and turned them into sashimi. The head became a nice stock for our miso soup that night.

It was over dinner that night when my brother revealed to me how much of my mind he was reading, giving me such a shock.

Before I responded to his statement, however, I breathed the smell of salt water from my miso soup, and then I took a sip. Finally I opened my mouth and said, "Why? Why the sudden decision to go home?"

"Something told me it was time to go home while we were fishing today," he said. "And chances are if we don't go home now, we might not ever get back."

Continuing to be impressed by his maturity, I could see that Yoshio was picking up on signs within himself. He wasn't afraid to face the things that frightened him, even though he really didn't need to go that far.

"Don't stress yourself about going home. If you're worried about me, don't be, because I could stay forever. And if you're tired of being here, we can always go someplace else."

My brother thought for a while and said, "No, I think we should go home. But before we go I have a favor to ask, if it's all right."

"What?" I said. "Anything."

"If I go back to acting weird, will you take me away again? And could you ask Mom if it's all right to be away—with this trip as well?" His face was serious as he spoke.

"Of course," I said. "I promise to take you away whenever you need it, at least until you're old enough to do it on your own." I paused for a moment. "You know, these seven days have been really fun. Let's do it again. I think I've gotten just as much out of this trip as you have."

∾

It happened that night.

Yoshio and I were watching a terrifying television show in the living room.

I said goodnight to my brother as he crawled off to bed. Thinking that I would have a nightcap before I turned in, I went into the kitchen and poured myself a glass of the whiskey that I had discovered sometime before. It was stale—obviously the bottle had been there for years. Then I trotted back to the living room where I'd left the TV on.

The station was showing a special edition of the Japanese *Tales from the Dark Side.* A number of prominent actors were being interviewed about frightening experiences in their lives. I found myself getting into the show, despite the fact it was scaring me to death. Before long I went into my brother's room and shook him from his sleep. I just couldn't stand to be in the living room all by myself.

Yoshio grumbled as I pulled him from his room, but before long he was caught up in the episode with me. Together we huddled in front of the television like two fools who can't get enough of a bad thing. We watched one segment after another, saying that we would turn the TV off after the next one was over.

"Sakumi," Yoshio asked, "have you ever seen a ghost?"

"No, never," I replied.

"Neither have I. So why do all these actors have so many stories to tell about seeing them?"

"Good point," I said.

"I wonder if Mom's ever seen one."

"I don't think she has," I replied. "Then again, there was the incident on the day that Mayu died—do you remember?"

"What?"

"When Mom got home from the hospital, the wooden doll that Mayu played with while she was growing up had fallen from the shelf with the other dolls. It was broken."

"Stop it!" my brother screamed. "You're frightening me!"

"Not a pleasant story, is it?" I said.

"But when I think about Mayu, I don't think about scary things," Yoshio said.

"Haven't you heard ghosts always stay in the family?"

We were sitting in the dark, only the flicking light from the television illuminating the room that night. As we sat telling ghost stories, I felt my chest tighten and every muscle in my body stiffen. Perhaps the worst part was that I was well aware of the fact that ghosts often assemble around people who talk about them, just me and Yoshio that night. That part was, by far, the most unsettling.

Around one o'clock the star performer came on to narrate his segment. It was Junji Inagawa, not a surprise considering how well known he is for his scary stories. We were pushed to the outer limits of our excitement, and just at the moment we were practically nailed to the floor in horror over what we were seeing on TV, the doorbell rang.

Ding dong.

I screamed. Yoshio jumped up, his eyes twitching like a cat. I was amazed by how well he managed to spring to his feet in that split second—people can really jump when they want to. I threw myself around my brother's legs, and continued to cry pathetically. "What was that? Is there someone at the door, right here, right now?"

"That's what I thought," Yoshio said in a voice too cool for expression. "I don't suppose . . ."

"You don't suppose . . . what?" I asked.

"No, that's impossible. There's no way he'd be here."

"Don't talk like that," I stammered. "Because I'm really scared down here."

Then it happened again.

Ding dong.

Okay. Thinking quickly to myself, I knew that it was either: (1), a person who just happened to be at the wrong door; (2), a drunken burglar; (3), a ghost.

None were appealing.

There wasn't a thing I could do but go to the door and check things out for myself. The apartment had a security camera at the front door of the lobby, and I walked over to the monitor to see who was there.

(Now as I look back over the incident I see my fear had changed to curiosity, and I was actually feeling warm at that moment. It wasn't a sad feeling, but I didn't realize that until later. As I think about it now, I feel hurt somehow by the sweet premonition I had during those few moments. It brings a swelling to my heart.)

Timid, I glanced into the monitor. A young woman was there. Since the image was in black and white, I really couldn't pick up any details, but I knew she was a stranger. I assumed her dress was red, her figure was small and defined. She had an attractive face. She appeared to be in a good mood—perhaps she was high or drunk. There was something familiar about her face, something that gave me the impression I knew her, even though I was sure I'd never met her before. Just at the moment I'd given up seeing her clearly, the image grew intensely bright. It felt strange.

She pointed to the monitor and laughed suggestively. Then, without saying anything, she opened her mouth and slowly began to move her mouth, forming words.

"What?" I said to the monitor. "Once more. I can't hear you!" I must have looked foolish, since there was no way this woman could have heard me. She repeated herself, trying desperately to tell me something with her lips. I pushed my face closer to the screen, irritated by the fact that I couldn't understand what she was trying to say. Suddenly she walked away from the camera, disappearing from sight.

I stood for a moment, not knowing what to do. My brother crawled over and stood beside me. Just as I was about to tell him about the woman, he pointed to the monitor. Again the doorbell rang.

"Look! It's Ryu-chan!" Yoshio exclaimed.

He was right. When I looked at the screen I could see Ryūichirō standing in front of the camera. Two questions came to my mind. First, why was he here? Second, what the hell did he think he was doing bringing a woman with him? I was in shock.

At times like this my mind works like that of a genius. Fresh recognition seems to swell up around me, and I see things without gaps or contradictions. It's happened to me more since I fell down and banged my head.

Whatever happened to the child in me? The one who sat with a grudge the day her mother broke her promise to take her shopping because of a hangover that day, the one who felt so hurt after the night she'd spent with Ryūichirō. After saying good-bye, she'd cried as she walked down the hallway of the hotel, the tears giving her a headache.

So pitiful.

I suppose she hadn't been lost forever. She was probably in a world where the atmosphere was congested with the anguish of people who lived there. I'm sure she's there now. Actually, I'm sure all of them are there now—all the young women who had spent time being me.

I grabbed the receiver and said, "Ryūichirō?"

"Yeah," he replied, his voice fuzzy from the intercom. Pushing the button, I heard the buzz, and the door on the first floor open. Before long we heard the sound of footsteps outside our apartment, and when I looked through the peephole Ryūichirō was standing there.

"Kombanwa!" He waved his hand. I slid the chain from its holder and propped the door open. Ryūichirō looked like a newborn—his face was all red.

"You've been drinking," I said, not bothering to ask the dozens of other questions that were rumbling through my mind.

"I stopped and had a drink before I came here," he said. "My god, Yoshio, you've sure grown up!"

"You're right," my brother said, smiling.

What a remarkable feeling. Only a few hours earlier I'd desired to meet Ryūichirō, now he was standing in front of me. The situation was almost harder to believe than the ghost stories we'd seen on TV.

"Where's the woman you brought?" I asked.

"Eh? What do you mean? It's just me."

"Liar!" I said. "Just now—in the monitor. There was a woman in a red dress. I'm sure of it."

"I have no idea who you're talking about. You mean you saw her before you saw me?"

"RIGHT EXACTLY BEFORE YOU!" I screamed.

My brother started jumping up and down. "Stop it! You're scaring me, Saku-chan!"

"There was no one in the monitor before me," Ryūichirō said calmly.

"Stop saying that!"

"Well then, it was a ghost."

"STOP IT!"

"It really is frightening."

"What could it have been?"

"I'm scared!"

It didn't take us long to calm down, and we knew that it would be impossible for us to explain the unusual appearance of the woman in the monitor. Together we had some coffee.

Reality seemed to be lost because of the frightening stories on TV; in fact, we could still hear the noise of the TV left playing in the background. I remembered something I had read by Yōko Ono not too long ago: You can think of television as your very best friend, but really it's no different than a blank wall. The reason is simple. If a robber was to enter the house and kill you, the TV would just go on playing. Something to that effect.

Up until our guest arrived the television had been the source of tremendous anxiety, in control of every one of our actions. Now it was nothing more than a box that provided background noise.

"We're thinking about going home tomorrow," I said.

"Serious?" Ryūichirō replied. "I thought you'd stick around longer. When I got into the airport in Osaka I called your house and talked to your mother. She said you were on a 'wandering exile' or something like that, so I assumed it would be a long trip. I knew I couldn't see you in Tokyo, so I decided to come down here instead."

"One more coincidence . . . ," I replied.

"I jumped on the first flight out. When we landed in Shikoku I stopped by a friend's restaurant before coming here. We started to drink, one thing led to another, and now it's this late. Sorry to bother you," Ryūichirō said.

"No bother. In fact, your timing was perfect," I replied. Yoshio nodded his head.

Then I remembered the woman at the door. Who could she have been? That familiar presence, and the faraway trace of someone I'd seen before.

I don't recall having ever seen a ghost, but I wouldn't be surprised if my mind had created an optical illusion separated by the large gap between memory and reality . . . or so the thought crossed my mind.

But her recollection was gone. That person was someone who I should have known and remembered, and . . .

Just thinking about it gave me a headache, so I decided to stop. She was not there, and there was nothing I could do about it. Despite her absence, there was someone else in the room who I hadn't seen for a while, and I was glad to have him around. I felt like we were celebrating a new year.

"Well, in that case, maybe I'll go back to Tokyo tomorrow, too," Ryūichirō said. "I've already spent time with my friend, and there's really no other reason for me to hang around here. Why don't we just go home together? How does the afternoon flight sound?"

"That would be fine," I said. "But we're in no hurry." It was nice to know my brother and I wouldn't be going home alone. I was a bit muffled, however, by the idea of Ryūichirō having friends all over the world. He even knew someone in Kochi. When I realized I was only one among thousands, I felt a sharp pain inside my stomach, because for him I was just one card in the deck, one of several landscapes he saw every day, something yearned for and remembered, but only from a distance. Maybe I was a summer beach he thought of during winter.

As those thoughts crossed my mind, a lonely sensation came over me.

Yoshio looked up at Ryūichirō and asked where he'd been all this time.

"I've spent the last few months in Hawaii," he replied. "Hawaii, then Saipan. I have a friend who owns a scuba diving company, and he let me work for him for a while. I even got my diving license."

"How nice, being down among the tropics," I said.

"Yeah, but the food was horrible. I eventually got used to it, but before coming over here I stopped and had some seared bonito. I just about died over how wonderful it tasted."

"You sure do a lot of different things, don't you?" my brother asked.

"Of course, why not? You should try some of them sometime," Ryūichirō responded. "I bet you'd like them."

"I haven't been feeling very good lately," Yoshio said. "I don't know what I want to do anymore. I knew you were coming, though. Today as we were fishing I saw your face in my mind several times, but I wasn't sure if something was trying to tell me I wanted to see you, or if I should just stay silent because you were on your way here. Everything's all mixed up inside me."

"You remembered Ryūichirō's face?" I said to my brother. "Are you sure you didn't get it mixed up with the octopus?"

Yoshio didn't find humor in my joke. Perhaps he was only playing with me, not being truthful about everything. Perhaps not. I remember when the door bell rang he'd commented, "I don't suppose . . ."

My brother himself put it best. His mind was completely confused. That, I imagine, was a better way of expressing it.

I looked over to Ryūichirō to see how he was reacting. His expression displayed casual recognition, genuine curiosity, a feeling of true belief, and a minute trace of doubt. Everything came through clearly. But like always, there was the reassuring confidence that he seemed to carry with him nowadays, a bright sensation that seemed to say, "Don't worry, I understand." It was a particular essence that hovered around Ryūichirō.

I enjoyed checking to see that he hadn't changed. It made me relax. I couldn't help but think how wonderful it would be to always have him around, and to always have that assurance. It seemed Ryūichirō stood alone in a category of people who were able to bring me such a strong sense of security. If Yoshio could grow up into a man like Ryūichirō, I would have nothing to worry about.

"Why worry about it?" Ryūichirō said. "Who cares if you saw my face today or not? Listen, Yoshio, people who use their minds in strange ways, those with highly developed brainpower, you know, people like you and me, eventually end up not listening to what their bodies are trying to say. It's as if their bodies and minds have separated. Believe me, it's not a pretty sight. Know what I mean?"

"Yeah. I know what you mean," my brother said.

"I work in a field where I constantly have to use my head, and that's why it's difficult for me to adjust my thinking properly. It wouldn't be right to let those thoughts take over. Instead I just listen to something meaningless, or go out for a swim, or go jogging, trying to focus on something else for the moment. If I don't do that my brain will just fry and burn out. Then it's gone, right? Something tells me you're just starting to face whatever cruel things await in this world, but don't worry. You'll be fine, as long as you learn the ropes. See, with every new thing you try, you'll hear people making different suggestions, and it's wrong to believe in what they say, unless it's coming from inside. Most of the critical people in this world are those who haven't had to put up with the bad, so all they do is just sit back on the side and point their fingers at what you do wrong. You've got to develop a sense that tells you who you are, and who to take advice from. If you don't find that sense it may be the difference between life and death. Just use the part of your brain most people waste on playing."

"I can't do that," Yoshio said. "I don't have any confidence."

"Then get some." Ryūichirō laughed. "Look at me! I mean, if a guy like me can be confident . . ."

My brother looked troubled. I had a feeling he was doubting some of the things Ryūichirō had said. Perhaps somewhere inside him he was saying to himself, "This guy hasn't had to face half of the trials that I have." But maybe that was a good thing, because it showed me Yoshio was making comparisons between himself and others, poking fun at the things that didn't stack up, disregarding what other people said. For me that was a sign Yoshio was envisioning his own image shining brightly in the light.

Ryūichirō had an expression on his face that seemed to read, "I understand, but think about what I've said for a while." When it came to forecasting the future, however, or making a rendezvous with a flying saucer, Yoshio was out of his league. I think my brother understood that. He just couldn't decide where to draw a line between confidence and behavior, because the one strong place inside him was the most confused.

Listening to the two of them speak, I stood off to the side thinking that if life were Tetris, Yoshio would certainly come out the winner, and if he could only pull together some of the skills it would take to not be defeated, then things would be much smoother. Another thought crossed my mind—perhaps Yoshio needed a father. But it wasn't my place to suggest it.

I could only stand by and listen.

Chapter 9

It had been a while since I'd been to a department store with my mother.

She always has a clear goal in mind whenever she goes shopping—in other words, she shops like a man, never getting lost along the way. Once she sees what she likes, *bang,* she grabs it. If something doesn't fall into my mother's hands with a bang, most likely it never will.

My mother decides exactly what she wants long before she ever breaks down to buy it. She must have a limit on her vision, blinkers of sorts, because apparently she can't see anything but what's right in front of her. Nevertheless, watching my mother makes me feel good. When something is suddenly missing from our lives, for example, my mother looks beyond it, and the rest of us know it will be okay. It's like—well, I really can't explain. Perhaps it's like a small quivering in your voice, something that you just can't stop. It's like irretrievable, meaningless things that were shouted out during a fight one bitter night, or ill temperament regarding love, or a heart hurt by jealousy, or a spirit that reaches out to save you, right at the moment when things are about to collapse. That type of thing.

No, my mother's different. Whatever it is she has inside of her clearly comes in excess. How does she handle it? I really don't know, but I have a feeling that a part of me knows what's going on. My mother is never distracted by simple things like shopping, or by unreasonable outpourings of emotion from people around her.

So what could it be?

I suppose what I'm trying to get at here is my mother's uncanny ability to "make things run smoothly." Even when things are crumbling down around us, my mother holds her head high, and keeps her eyes wide open to the world. When she allows a mood of "all is well" to penetrate every corner of our home, things slowly start to go that way. Maybe she's had to force it on occasion, but it's something she's done time and again. That strong will is her special talent.

I couldn't mimic her if I tried.

When I'm in a store browsing over this and that, I decide I want everything in sight. If I'm not in the mood to shop, then I just slide through the store gazing over the beautifully decorated displays. It's one way or the other.

Since my mother asked me to go out with her that day, I think I must have been in the mood for the second scenario, considering there wasn't a thing I wanted to buy. But my mother told me if I carried the bags she would buy me a new jacket, so I gladly went along. I loved going with her because she never tried to get me to buy the things that she liked, and she wasn't too cheap to purchase anything nice. That's when I discovered there wasn't another mom in the world as comfortable as mine.

~

After a couple of hours' shopping, we decided to sit down for some tea. Out of the blue my mother asked, right after taking a sip, "So how was Kochi?"

"Fine, I guess. We really didn't do much. It was just a nice rest, that's all."

"Well, Yoshio's back in school, and for the life of me I can't figure out what brought on the change." She smiled with her large eyes with an expression that seemed almost too normal. I knew that if she saw through me I'd have a hard time closing my heart to her straightforwardness. It didn't matter how much my mother grumbled, or how awfully painful things became—the one thing that never changed was the clarity of her eyes.

I think of Mayu whenever I see my mother's eyes, and wonder if she had possessed the same—just one more reason to doubt the things in my head. Still, whenever I let the opaque image of my younger sister run through my brain, I see the same crystal eyes, and I know she's smiling.

I also suppose that every once in a while I, too, looked upon other people in the same provocative way that my mother was looking at me. Maybe I did it to set that person free, or to ellicit truth from them. Another guess would be that I was trying to invoke a strange sense of nostalgia, a feeling of love and bewilderment.

If I was successful then they'd feel like I did at that moment.

"You know, Yoshio really needs a father," I said.

"Why?" my mother asked.

Late afternoon, a department store on a weekday. We could hear the rattle down on the street outside from the upper level of the small cafe where we were sitting. I had a cup of hot chai, my mother a tall espresso. Everything in sight was filled with the brightness of a new summer, and I felt glad. The short-sleeved shirts on the people around us, the green of the trees swaying in the breeze; sunlight that reflected from the tip of the leaves, the smell of the sky, everything—I couldn't get enough of it.

"Yoshio's absolutely enthralled with Ryūichirō. He listens to whatever Ryu-chan says. Yoshio's back in school because Ryūichirō convinced him to be there. It's hard, you know, for the four of us women to encourage him like that, since all of his life we've treated him like a baby doll."

"You're wrong," my mother said boldly. "Yoshio listens to what Ryūichirō has to say because he's an outsider in our home; it has nothing to do with the fact he's a man. People on the outside can wear a thousand different smiles. They never have to be around to scold or spoil the child, so it's only natural for them to have more influence. That's how it is for Ryu-chan. He isn't actually responsible for Yoshio, and I think the distance they have between them is just the way it should be. If we forced them apart, Yoshio would shift all his support to Ryūichirō, turning him into some kind of hero. If they came closer then the opposite would occur. You know, it won't matter what kind of man I bring home to father that child, Yoshio's bound to find fault with him. He'll compare him to Ryūichirō, making fun of him to no end. That's just the way Yoshio's been acting lately."

"Maybe," I said.

"Don't you think so?" my mother replied, lighting up a cigarette and puffing away. She laughed.

"I suppose it isn't a problem," I said. "At any rate, we had a good time together at the beach. The scenery was gorgeous."

"Seems to me the two of you have really bonded, and that's fine. In fact, it's a very good thing," my mother said.

"You mean me and Yoshio?"

"Of course I mean you and Yoshio." My mother laughed again.

"Are you telling me I'm par with a kid in elementary school?"

"No, no," she said, shaking her head. "I mean that both of you have something inside which seems to be working harder than the rest of us. Mayu had a little bit of it too, but she managed to keep it at a normal speed until she met Ryu-chan. I don't think she would have died if she'd been with someone else, but since she was with Ryūichirō she just lost control of whatever was happening to her head, and she just couldn't keep up with him. Don't get me wrong, I don't hate Ryūichirō. I just think things would have been different for Mayu if she'd been with someone else. Ryūichirō is more for you, Sakumi. You and he are the same. There's something anxious about both of you."

"I think I know what you mean," I responded.

My mother continued, "Right now Yoshio needs two things: strength and love."

"Love?" I said, recalling the conversation I'd had with Junko only a few days before.

"You analyze things too much, Sakumi, think about things far more than you should. In the end you wind up running around in circles, losing your timing, and so forth. Why don't you just stop and allow your own beautiful light to shine? When I say Yoshio needs love, I'm not talking about something sweet, or ideal. I'm talking about something that comes naturally."

"So it's wrong for me to be independent? A feminist would probably be offended by what you're saying." Every so often my mother had a hard time explaining herself; she always used the wrong words. As I listened to her talk I noticed how random her thoughts were.

"NO!" she yelled. "You haven't been listening to a word I've said! I'm talking about something a person can do for themselves. That's what I mean by love. Do you understand? It's a matter of how much you believe in it. But actually achieving something is much more difficult than just sitting around, talking about it. And no one knows how much effort it really takes."

"Let me see if I understand," I said. "What you're trying to say is that love symbolizes a certain condition."

"My, you're clever with words, aren't you?" My mother laughed. For the first time since the start of our conversation I felt as if we were really getting through to each other. I was finally seeing her purpose.

She went on. "When I look at my children, I think they lack the ability to concentrate. I've often watched you just stop dead in your tracks. Personally I feel it would be a lot better for all of us if we took one day at a time, living on the edge every once in a while."

"Why don't you tell Yoshio that?" I asked.

"You don't think he'd find my advice silly, like I have some kind of trick up my sleeve?" my mother replied.

"No, of course not. Yoshio wants to know that you care about him. It's always nice to know that there is someone in the world thinking about you like a mother," I said.

"Believe it or not, there are times when I do think about my children as a mother." In the back of her mind I could tell she was really saying to herself, So what do you think goes on in my head every day? Once again she threw back her head and laughed proudly.

~

It didn't take long for my mother to go to work.

As we sat around the dinner table that night we heard the front door fly open, and my brother stomped into the room. "I'm home," he said. My mother, Junko, and I had already started dinner. Seeing my brother enter the kitchen with his black backpack and cutoff shorts, I couldn't help but notice how much he looked just like a real kid in elementary school. He looked almost cheerful. There was so much happiness in him, in fact, that I felt it spreading all the way to my heart.

Yoshio grabbed a plate piled high with fried prawns and munched on them greedily in front of the TV. It appeared as if nothing unusual had ever happened to him, and I could see he'd developed a good way of stopping things that would try to get inside. At that point my mother leaned down and started to ask him questions.

"How's your food, Yoshio?" my mother inquired. "Does it taste good? Are your taste buds working properly?"

My brother swallowed and said, "Yeah, tastes great. Did Aunt Junko fry these prawns?"

"No," I said. "We bought them in the basement of the department store today."

Junko spoke up. "You know, frying is about the only type of cooking that I can't do. It's so frightening, throwing those creatures into that boiling pot of oil, practically still alive. Cleaning it up is a pain as well."

Her excuses were inconsistent, but there in the kitchen I was overwhelmed with the impression that we'd formed a family circle. The moment reminded me of the scent of an olive flowing through autumn wind, a faint scent, yet with a presence clearly noticeable. It had been a long time since I had smelled it.

"Okay," my mother said, moving in. "More questions. Do you look forward to waking up in the morning? Are you happy all day? Do you feel good when you go to bed at night?"

My brother paused. "I'm not so sure about that. I'm always so tired when I go to bed. . . ." He answered the questions promptly, as though he were under some kind of psychological evaluation.

"Now. You are standing on the street and you see a friend coming. Are you happy? Or is it a bother? Look around and notice the scenery. Does the beauty of nature strike at your heart? What about music? How does it sound? Think about a trip overseas. Is that something you'd be interested in? Do you get excited when you think about it? Or is it just another pain in your life?"

My mother stopped. Her voice had resonated like that of a skillful actress in a play, the words floating from her mouth as a soft voice would from a tape used for meditation. I was taken aback by her impromptu performance and the situation made me feel awkward. Something told me that if I'd closed my eyes while she was speaking, I would have actually seen a friend of mine approaching, and imagined what it's like to be overseas. Her voice was that clear, that deep.

We sat in silence for a while, each of us earnestly pondering over how we'd have answered the questions.

My mother started up again. "Do you look forward to tomorrow? How about the day after next? What comes to mind when I say 'future'? Does it excite you? Depress you? How do you feel right now? Are things going well? Do you look in the mirror and like what you see?"

My brother turned to my mother and said, "Yeah, I think I'm okay."

Personally, I wasn't so sure.

"I'm not sure," Junko said, taking the words right out of my mouth. "Yukiko, where on earth did you get those questions? Did you find them in a book?"

My mother started to grin. "These questions," she said, looking deep into my brother's eyes, "are the secret formula for living that was taught to me by my grandfather when I was about your age, Yoshio. He called them his 'checkpoints for life.'"

"He really used that phrase? He really used the word 'checkpoint'?" I asked, surprised by the modern terminology.

"Well, no," my mother said. "He might have put it differently, but the principle's the same. It actually comes from your great-grandfather. You know who I'm talking about, don't you? My grandpa who ran the traditional Japanese candy shop back in the country? Every day he went into the shop to work, and his sweets were so good that people would line up outside the shop for miles. A group even came all the way down from the north once just to buy some. Grandpa made candy every day of his life until he turned ninety. He was in perfect health, gentle to his wife, children, and grandchildren, and so bright and friendly all the neighbors loved him. After retiring, he lived another five years before he passed away peacefully. Such a wonderful man. Once when I was a child he gathered us all together, and he asked us these questions, starting with 'Are your taste buds working properly?' There was also a warning."

"What was that?" my brother said, completely taken in by my mother's story.

"He made us gaze deep into his eyes as he spoke, and he told us to remember them. Then he made us look around the room and remember the atmosphere that we'd created there. 'If you ever tell another soul my secret formula for life,' he said, 'you have to create the same kind of feeling in the room, and have the same look in your eye with the same deep resonance in your throat, otherwise you shouldn't say it, because when you tell the secret to life you aren't just asking questions, you're opening up your soul. Once you've established the right situation, you can tell the secret to someone else.' I remember staring around the room for a long time, making sure I knew exactly what he was talking about. My grandfather and grandmother, mother and father, and my younger sister and brothers—all of us were there. The room was filled with a special power, bright and warm. Every night after finishing dinner we sat in the living room together. Grandfather told us stories with his deep voice and his sparkling eyes. I knew that regardless of what would happen, as long as he was around, everything would be all right. I knew right then I would always remember him, each and every little thing. I wasn't worried so much about how he phrased his questions, I just made sure I wouldn't forget that night by thinking about it too much. I packed it all away in my heart, tried hard not to get too nervous, and I've savored the freshness until now.

"I remembered my grandfather today, and thought now would be a good time to review the secret formula for life. I'm not sure if I did it correctly, but I think you got the gist." My mother stopped.

"Can we ask ourselves the questions if we need to?" I asked.

"Of course, as long as your answers aren't lies. Just respond with an honest 'yes' or 'no.' Ask yourself every night before you go to sleep if you want to. Just close your eyes and question away. Don't worry if you've had a bad day, because we all have them sometimes. But I can tell you this much, if you ask yourself the questions every night you really can gain courage to move on. This might sound like I'm preaching, but everyone needs something in their lives to make it worth living. Another thing to watch out for is how you react to your answers. It's important to feel good about your responses, picking up on even the small doubts. It doesn't help just thinking everything's going to be okay. As I mentioned before, it's wrong to lie. But once you have a clear understanding of your own perception of the world, somehow you'll find courage to move on. Take me, for example, and my brother and sisters. There isn't one of us who hasn't gone through a divorce or bankruptcy. But thanks to what my grandfather taught us that night, none of us feel like we've led difficult lives."

"Isn't that a lovely story." Junko beamed.

I considered what my mother had said. Most likely the formula had come to my great-grandfather from his father, and he'd passed it along to his children and grandchildren. I'd learned the secret from my mother, and most likely I'd give it to my daughter as well. A neverending story, told from one generation to the next, like an ancient tale retold among American Indians. Never in my wildest dreams would I have guessed something like that was alive in my family. My mother had waited a while before disclosing the secret, but I'd seen her will and power to survive for many years now and I knew that rather than telling us about it, she had actually been showing it to us all along.

"Mayu never had a chance to hear the secret formula," I said, recalling that she hadn't been around enough to see it in my mother's actions either.

My mother looked sad. "You're right. But like I said, the thought didn't occur to me until we were drinking tea today. It's been years since I've thought about it."

"On top of that," I said, looking around the room, "Mikiko wasn't here to listen to the story, either."

"An outsider!" Yoshio said with a laugh. "She's probably out getting drunk with her friends."

"Well, she missed a nice story," my mother said. "It will be a hundred years before anyone brings it up again."

"What a fool."

Everyone laughed, it was so much fun. I sincerely loved my family.

~

On a day with a rich blue sky filled with the warmth of summer, the entire world seemed to be shining brightly. This weather had continued for some time now, so it was really starting to feel like summer—my favorite time of year.

Ryūichirō and I went to see the sunfish that day.

"Did you know they brought a sunfish to the aquarium while you were away?" I boasted. Ryūichirō seemed muffled by my comment. Since it was obvious he wanted to see it, we decided to go together, even though I'd been dozens of times already.

It was a weekday, and we were practically the only ones there. The sunfish floated gently in her huge outdoor tank. From the observation point I could see up into the sky and out into the city beyond. The view filled me with tranquillity.

I had been to this place many times. Really.

After hitting my head, they finally let me out of the hospital. Meanwhile Ryūichirō had once again been off traveling. Everyday life had returned to the same old routine, and winter had settled in. There were so many different things I had trouble remembering, even though I was back to a run-of-the-mill lifestyle. For example, there was a time last year—my mother's friends still laugh about it today—when I went searching for a particular bottle opener. I remembered exactly what it looked like, but when I couldn't find it I described it to my mother, and she laughed and grabbed a different one. "Don't you remember buying this new opener at the store the other day?" she said. With no recollection of having done so, I pretended to remember anyway, and I laughed along with the others.

I felt lonely, pushed outside the group.

The sunfish was wonderful then.

Her strange shape, the unusual way she moved around. Without thinking, she'd just bang herself against the glass wall.

Just like me, I thought.

I wasn't in a hurry to go through life either, but occasionally I found myself bumping into walls.

I visited the sunfish alone, spending hours next to the tank, staring into the water. When I entered the aquarium, I'd quickly go around and see the other animals, the seals and so on. And in the end I'd find myself with the sunfish, overjoyed. After countless hours it was a shock to discover the aquarium closing.

That's why everything was so familiar when I returned to see the sunfish with Ryūichirō. The thought of standing there with him under the warmth of the summer sun had never crossed my mind back then.

The sunfish was white, and she glided peacefully in the water. Nothing about her had changed, not even the way she quietly moved back and forth. She didn't seem as carefree as before—at least she certainly had appeared to be more relaxed. Back then even her eyes seemed to be having more fun.

I was the one who'd changed.

That was a time I viewed things through isolation and fear. Now things had changed. It was no longer winter.

"What a silly creature," Ryūichirō said. "I'd never get tired of watching it."

"I agree," I said, explaining how I had come to visit the sunfish during the days after my operation.

"It was your secret way of getting back into life, right?" Ryūichirō said.

Time felt like the movement of the sunfish, passing by us slowly as we stood with the sun shining on our shoulders. I felt serene when Ryūichirō was around. He was different than others. He wasn't in an unrecognizable dimension; I knew where he was coming from. Even if he wound up killing someone, and even if that person was someone I knew, something tells me I'd just forgive him in the end. My feelings weren't logical, they simply reflected the air around me.

How would Mayu respond to that?

One thing was certain. My sister had always existed in a time and place where she stood alone; not a person in the world could have reached her. Even Ryūichirō was helpless when it came to Mayu.

Now I was with him, and together we stared at the sunfish. A warm sensation spread over me like a bottle of ink tipped over—an indication that something was happening between us.

"I've been thinking about a few things," Ryūichirō said, "and I've decided I really like you."

Since nobody else was around, only the sunfish and I could have heard his confession. I stood silent for a while. Suddenly everything zoomed in on me like the close-up of a camera—the buildings around the tank, the touch of his hand, the touch of my own hand as well—a sensory indication of love.

"When Mayu left I decided that I needed to get out, too. So I took off to see what was out there, but things got pretty boring on my own. I thought about what it'd be like if you were there with me, always. When I was away people stole my stuff or were just incredibly rude. I'd sit there alone, staring at some strange television program in some foreign language, and the only thing that saved me from going out of my mind was the thought of you. That's what it finally came down to—you were my own secret formula for living. In the end I knew I'd return to Japan and see you. Once that thought entered my mind I could look forward to the next day. My attraction to you was really strong. Back when we slept together, when everything was so wild, I was really happy to be with you. I figure it must be love."

"Have you only liked me since I hit my head?" I asked.

"You must have always been in my heart, even before your accident. But back then Mayu was around, and I knew things would never go smoothly between us. Then something changed. Who knows? Maybe it was me—maybe I was tempered on my journeys. I don't know if anything really happened to you when you fell and cracked your head, but when we were together last time I saw how dynamic you really are, and I couldn't help but think that even if you were the same as before, now there's a whole new something about you. I think it has something to do with your spirit, an attitude that was with you even before you hit your head. It just took some time to surface. That's when I realized there might be something between us. It was a strange feeling, not really romantic, just a confirmation, something to fall back on the rest of our lives. When I went away and you fell down the stairs, something was stirred up, something that now excites me. Do you know what I mean?"

Troubled, I sat staring at the sunfish. I could feel myself turning red because I knew that inside they were both mocking me. "I think I'm only too aware of what you mean," I replied. "And something tells me you're sincere, and not just trying to trick me."

"I stand corrected," Ryūichirō said. "Even though I'm not sure if I asked for it." He smiled.

"In that case," I said, "let's do it. Let's go on a journey somewhere together. I don't care if it's only in Japan, just as long as we're together. We'll just see how we are, you and me, out in the world. Because I refuse to be some woman who just waits around for you to come home. I'd rather die first. And you can show me what you're like when you're out there. Let's see if these trips are as fun as you've led me to believe."

"Where do you want to go?" he asked. "Next month I'm headed back to Saipan to visit some friends, so why don't you come along? Is that too soon?"

I laughed. "Sounds wonderful."

"It'll be great."

The sun dipped down into the city around us. A faint tinge of orange expanded, and clouds in the west burned with color.

My hand reached out and took his. He squeezed my fingers tightly. A familiar feeling—the dry warmth of his hand. There really was something between us, I could see it clearly. I looked down at the white sunfish, and felt an urge to reach out and touch her as well.

I wanted to reach out and touch everything at that moment, just to make sure it was really there. That's how I was feeling.

Chapter 10

As I gazed over the ocean of clouds shining brightly in the afternoon sun outside the airplane window, I was overcome by an uncanny feeling. If someone had told me it was all just a dream, I would have believed them—one more indication that everything to this point in my life had only been an illusion, far away and simple.

Now, before I knew it, I found myself on board a plane headed for Saipan. We rushed to the airport and grabbed the first two tickets available, ending up in business class. I was shocked to discover how much space I could now call my own. After pulling myself out of bed earlier that morning, I lazily floated in my thoughts as the plane rolled down the runway. I was trying to keep my eyes open by reading and listening to rap music turned up full blast on my Walkman. It would have been pointless to fall asleep on the short plane ride and miss landing on the beautiful island, so I was trying to stay alert. My book was a biographical sketch of a saint who seemingly had no trouble collecting Rolls-Royces and cuff links like a kid with new toys, a sad story that thoroughly captured my interest.

Everything around me seemed to fit perfectly into my idea of "now," but even if I was to enumerate those things here, I'm not sure I could explain the sense of liberation I felt on the plane, as though the beer they served us over lunch had made me intoxicated.

Next to me Ryūichirō was sleeping, having reclined in his seat as far back as it would go. It hadn't taken long for him to drift off.

I noticed that his eyebrows looked like my brother's. Don't people have such warm looks on their faces when they're sleeping, something that seems far away and lonely? Ryūichirō was wandering about a world where I was not invited, my little sleeping beauty.

Behind me was a new friend, Kozumi. He was taking us to his home in Saipan.

~

Kozumi was out of this world. Never in my life had I encountered anyone like him, even amid the characters in the books I'd read or people I'd seen on TV. Two weeks ago Ryūichirō had called Berries, the bar where I worked, and given me the rundown on his friend who'd moved away and was now living in Saipan. He said he wanted us to meet since we would be staying with him once we got to the island. That night he wanted to bring him by the bar.

I told Ryūichirō that would be fine, but then it occurred to me how cumbersome the trip was going to be. Just a few weeks before I'd taken time off work to go away with my brother. Now this. Obviously my manager would not be pleased. In addition to leaving work, I'd already formed a bad image of Kozumi, because when I was told that in Saipan he ran a little shop that rented out diving equipment in the front and served sandwiches in the back, I thought, What kind of life could that be? I could just see his body—tan, and totally obsessed with diving. I was sure he was into drinking and women as well.

So I really didn't feel like going.

Then again, imagining myself diving in the warm waters, I realized I'd never been to a tropical place like Saipan. On top of that, I could spend time with Ryūichirō. It wasn't long before my attitude changed and I looked forward to going. I told myself not to think about what others would say and what would happen to me if I took more time off work. Before long, I was anxious to go.

~

"I've been invited to Saipan for a while," I said to my mother. "Will everything be okay around here if I go?"

"Of course." My mother smiled. "But who are you going with?"

"Ryūichirō," I replied.

"Well then, just be sure not to kill yourself." She laughed.

I also informed my brother.

"I'm going to Saipan with Ryūichirō. Do you want to come along?"

"Well," my brother said, "it sounds like a lot of fun, but . . ." He paused. "I think I'd better stick around here a bit longer."

"If you change your mind and decide to come, just give me a call."

"I don't know how to call overseas," he said.

"I'll show you how," I said. "It's really simple, and you can do it all in Japanese." I proceeded to write down the steps for dialing another country.

After I was finished Yoshio took the paper from my hands and said, "Saku-chan, do you really like Ryūichirō, or is this just a fling?"

Again, he knew exactly what to say.

"Why do you ask?"

"Whenever Mom falls in love she always leaves the house, and it seems like you're always here," Yoshio said.

"You're right," I responded. "I suppose that means I can't really be in love."

"So what is it then, fate?" he asked.

"I wouldn't go as far as to say my feelings about Ryūichirō are in the hands of fate, but I do know I'm sort of caught up in it right now, and maybe in the end that's what will bring us together."

"Yeah, that's what I was trying to say," Yoshio said loudly. "Caught up in fate."

I looked down and noticed he was happy. I couldn't tell if my brother was jealous, or if he was just saying those things to me as a kid with the ability to see what was coming. Certainly my love was something shiny, like a UFO, and I knew that in order for us to change the future we'd have to bend the rules so we could be together. Regardless of what was destined to happen, if the two of us didn't take each other by the hand and jump into the unknown, we'd just get lost, losing each other somewhere along the way.

It's like a useless automatic door opener you see in contests for new inventions. A bowling ball is sent down a funnel that ends in a bucket full of water. The ball tips the bucket over and water flows out. The water turns a mill operating a switch which triggers another switch, pulling a flap attached to the door. Finally, after all that, the cord tugs and the door opens.

The wind blows and the inventor becomes a millionaire.

Well, at least it feels like it happens that way.

By that point the person's powerless, or so it seems. But really she's in a position to do anything. With the help of some sort of power, and while playing some sort of game, all she can do is jump. Even though there's no need to worry—no one will die if they miss the mark—something inside of her starts to sparkle and say,

"No!"

"Now!"

"Not there!"

She reaches a point where she loses control, but she steps off the platform anyway,

and jumps. . . .

~

Ryūichirō brought Kozumi by the bar that night, and I realized for the first time how naive my first impressions had been. My image of a dark man lazily hanging out at the beaches in Saipan was anything but correct, because he was completely different than I expected. Instead of a golden tan, he was white, pure white, as if there was no pigment in his skin. His eyes were a clear brown, right along with his hair.

Kozumi was an albino.

Oh my, I thought to myself as Ryūichirō introduced us.

"Kozumi, this is Sakumi."

"Nice to meet you," he said with a grin. His smile was huge. It didn't matter how white his skin was, the warmth in his face at that moment made me feel as if I'd already taken a trip to the South Pacific.

With the exception of Ryūichirō and Kozumi, we didn't have a single customer at the bar that night. My boss was so startled to see Ryūichirō, he began a conversation with him immediately. Kozumi and I were left standing alone. He looked like a sculpture in the dim light of the bar.

"I have a wife in Saipan," Kozumi stated firmly. I was taken aback by his abrupt comment.

What kind of girl do I look like? I thought to myself. Does this guy think I look like some tramp who'd cheat on her boyfriend? The nerve of some people.

"Is that so?" I replied.

Kozumi started to laugh, almost like he had understood what I was thinking. As if to clarify his intentions, he looked back at me and said, "I'm sure the two of you will get along splendidly."

"Is she from Saipan?"

"No, she's Japanese. Her name is Saseko."

My mouth dropped open. I didn't want to be rude to Kozumi, considering this was the first time we'd met, but I couldn't help myself. I knew that *sasego* was a word generally used to describe a woman as a public toilet—you know, in the sense that anybody could use her for free. I couldn't imagine anyone having such a name.

"Saseko?" I said.

He nodded his head.

"Wow," I said, trying to imagine a mother who could be so cruel.

"Don't worry. Everyone's shocked when they hear it," Kozumi replied. "Her parents really had something against her." Again he sounded like he was responding to my thoughts, not just to what I had said.

Kozumi continued, "I'll tell you about her background—Saseko's mother was an alcoholic, and when Saseko was three her mother rolled over and died. By that time the man who was married to her mother had discovered that Saseko was not his child. Apparently the baby was the result of a casual fling outside the marriage, if you know what I mean. The father who'd been cheated on was angry, for obvious reasons, and to get even with his wife he went down to the city office building and had Saseko's name changed to 'free public toilet.' Her mother never found out."

"Is that so?" I said.

"But it doesn't stop there. Her father was a Yakuza and there was absolutely no way he could raise a young daughter on his own, so he took her to an orphanage where she stayed until she was sixteen. Then she went to Saipan with a man she'd met, and for the first time in her life she lived without people laughing at her name, since no one in Saipan thinks twice when they hear the word *sasego*."

"Is that so?" I said. I couldn't understand how Kozumi was able to go on with such a story without ever wiping that funny grin off his face. Actually, he almost sounded bored, like it was something he had rehearsed many times. His scratchy voice was also peculiar.

"Since I've been with Saseko, she has found her calling in life. You see, Saseko has special powers."

"And those would be . . ."

"Well, Saseko's always realized, even from the time she was in her mother's belly, that she was hated and unwanted. But she came into this world anyway, knowing throughout the entire nine months that the world didn't want her. She couldn't go anywhere, because she was attached to the umbilical cord. So she had to listen and feel all the things she didn't want to. The pain grew so bad that the voices inside her heart crying for her to get out was actually what allowed Saseko to start a new form of communication between herself and others."

"Others?" I asked.

"Ghosts," he replied.

Oh no, I thought to myself. How was I going to get out of this one?

"So now my wife has stopped selling herself to men, because she has a whole new reason for living. Using different sorts of chants and songs, she performs memorial services for the dead."

"She sings?" I asked.

"Does she ever!" Kozumi replied proudly. "By all means, we'll have to get her to sing for you."

"Aren't there a lot of apparitions in Saipan?" I asked.

"Countless!" he said, throwing up both his arms. "Now if you'll excuse me, I must use the toilet." He trotted off to the rest room.

Ryūichirō turned and saw that our conversation was over.

"Where in the world did you dig him up?" I said. "He's completely out of his mind."

"Give the guy a break," Ryūichirō said. "He's such an honest guy. He'd never tell you a lie—not even one."

After such a strong personal reference from Ryūichirō, I assumed it must be true, even if I couldn't help but be suspicious. Still, what would become of us in Saipan?

On the way out of the bar I turned to Kozumi and said, "Please give my regards to your wife. But are you sure I could get along with someone like her, I mean, someone with all those special powers?"

"Don't worry," he exclaimed, "I guarantee it."

The road sparkled under the moon, and Kozumi's brown eyes were crystal in the light. Seeing Kozumi like that made me think he wasn't so strange. It had nothing to do with his eyes, skin color, or even the things he said, it had more to do with the mood he conveyed—a sharp smell of a cemetery in the afternoon, or a moonlit beach in summer. Light and death were brought together in his small frame—illuminating chaos.

He was that sort of person. The kind I'd never encountered before in my life.

∾

The plane engine hummed in the background as my eyes flowed gracefully over the words on the pages, rap music echoing distantly in my head. I was feeling anxious. Then it happened.

Eiko was suddenly there.

Her smell, her presence, her touch—everything about her came rushing inside me, and I felt embarrassed and confused. My head was dizzy. I couldn't run away. A few seconds later I'd returned to feeling normal, but my heart was still pounding and I couldn't get it to stop, no matter how I tried.

Those eyes and hair, voice and profile, the way she looked from behind—everything had sprung up in my mind in a split fraction of a second. Next the memories of being with her came to mind, one after another. Everything was vivid and painfully sharp. I couldn't just sit there and let it all happen, so I got out of my chair and headed for the bathroom, even though I really didn't need to.

Inside the gray interior I took several deep breaths.

Wasn't there a scene just like it in *The Shining*? A boy was in trouble and he used mind signals to cry out for help. Was he able to get through and attract anybody's attention? I wondered if Eiko had done something similar, just moments before.

With the initial shock finally over, I opened the door and returned to my seat. I decided to wait until we'd landed and then I'd give Eiko a call. I'd been so shaken a minute ago that I couldn't even come up with such a simple plan as that.

By the time I was back in my seat, Ryūichirō had opened his eyes.

"We're almost there," he said with a smile. The seat belt light was on, and the usual drone of the stewardess's voice filtered through the compartment. Looking out the window, I saw a number of small islands in the water. Their brilliant green shone brightly against the blue of the water, reminding me of a postcard. The ocean was filled with gradations of blue, and the waves were topped with white bubbles appearing like crest patterns from the window.

"Wow!" I said. "It's beautiful, really beautiful."

"It is nice, isn't it?" Even Ryūichirō, the seasoned traveler, allowed his eyes to sparkle. So this is what it takes to impress him, I thought. He's like bread dough you fill with yeast and then set out to rise—once he's swollen up enough his true feelings finally show through.

"Hey!" Kozumi leaned over from behind our seats.

I turned to him and said, "Saipan is so beautiful. Do you ever get tired of seeing it?"

"Of course not," he said. "It always excites me. But there's something more urgent right now. Did you get the message from that woman just now? She was calling out, trying to reach you."

"Who are you talking about?" I asked.

"Umm . . ." Kozumi closed his eyes. "I can't really make her out very clearly, but she seems to be a rather attractive young lady, slender, with a high-pitched voice."

"Yes," I said. "She reached me." At that point it was clear that the place where we were about to go was far from normal reality. Perhaps this place would give me access to all my lost information.

"You'd better call her when we get in," Kozumi replied. Far different from the undulations I had just received, Kozumi warned me in a voice that sounded natural and calm, like the warning of a mother on a cold day.

Be sure to wear your jacket!

I looked up at Kozumi and said, "I understand."

~

Once off the plane everything became sticky in the sweltering heat as if the island were diluted somehow. Maybe it came from the sky, which was too blue, or from the sweet greenery in the air.

I told the others to hold on, searching for a public phone. I rushed over to the money exchange machine and threw in a couple of bills, then I quickly found a phone that would accept overseas calls and dialed Eiko's number. I strained to listen as the phone started to ring, but the commotion inside the airport prevented me from hearing well. The phone rang several times, which I thought was odd since Eiko's mother always seemed to be at home, and if she wasn't around then the maid was always there. As I debated whether or not I should hang up, someone quickly picked up the other end of the line.

"Moshi, moshi." It was the voice of Eiko's maid.

I was relieved.

"Is Eiko there?" I asked.

"Actually there's no one here. I just ran an errand, and when I got back everyone was out. It's rather strange because Eiko's mother didn't mention she'd be going anywhere."

My relief returned to panic. I relayed as much information as I could, including the number of our hotel, and told her that I desperately needed to talk to Eiko. There wasn't anything else I could do.

I collected myself, and joined the line for customs. Ryūichirō and Kozumi were in another line way ahead of me, and I could see they were just being processed. After leaving the counter, I saw both of them standing by the wall, talking to a small Asian woman. It had to be Kozumi's wife. She had long black hair and she was wearing a pink suit. Ryūichirō glanced in my direction, and waved me over with his hand. The woman turned around and looked at me too. I froze. I'd seen her somewhere before. Her face had appeared in the monitor during our stay in Kochi.

Her eyes were narrow, her nose round. And she was smiling. There seemed to be an indescribable force about her—something sweet, as if she were seeing me from a distance. It wasn't like I saw through to her rebellious years, despite the thick makeup and the heavily painted nails. But thoughts of people like Mayu, drunk and heavy with drugs, also crossed my mind. Still, there was something incredibly gentle about her.

I returned the grin.

She put out her right hand and said, "Pleased to meet you." Her voice was soft, and somewhere there was a deep resonance. It was all so unwieldy.

"Konnichiwa," I replied. "Thanks for having us." I shook her hand.

At that point she stepped back and said, "Oh, my."

"What's wrong?" Kozumi asked.

"It's been a long time since I've seen someone like you," she said. "A very long time, indeed." Then she said to Kozumi, "So you're not the only one."

"What do you mean?" I asked, my curiosity only natural.

Turning to me, she said, "You're half dead."

I stopped, unsure how to react to such a statement. A broad grin came across Ryūichirō's face, and it was obvious he was enjoying the conversation immensely.

Kozumi leaned into his wife and said, "Don't be so rude!"

She smiled. "Please don't take that wrong. It really is a wonderful thing."

Really? I thought to myself. Being "half dead" is such a wonderful thing?

She tried her hardest to explain. "When a person is about to die and they suddenly come back to life, they bring with them the resources to tap all the powers they have inside. They've actually been reborn. Some people try to accomplish the same thing with yoga, but that takes an entire lifetime. You should be happy you have access to something so rare."

~

We piled into Kozumi's car and headed toward the hotel. Kozumi kept offering to let us stay at his home, but we turned him down, saying the hotel where we'd made a reservation would be fine. It was just a block away from their house, we could stay as long as we wanted, and it was right in the middle of all the large resorts on the island—just north of Garapan in a little place called Susupe.

The sun shone brightly in the west, and the trees swayed softly in the wind as though they were coming from the jungle. There was nothing on the road, just dense jungle growing up on both sides. Staring lazily out at the scenery, I noticed something strange had happened to my heart, a feeling only described with a word like *becoming.*

My chest ached. The air that surrounded me was so heavy it felt like it was winding itself around my heart. The trees and plants and flowers of the jungle twisted to form weird shapes, and the ground and the sky began to shake as if I were seeing them on the other side of a great kettle of boiling steam.

Maybe I was just getting carsick. I took a deep breath, but nothing changed. I had a feeling that the fine line which separated my body and my soul had somehow lost its shape, and the feeling of oppression that accompanied it was dark and heavy.

As I thought about how strange things had been, the car pulled into Susupe. Instantly those strange feelings were gone, and I forgot about them immediately. But that wouldn't last for long. Eventually they would catch up to me.

The buildings in the town were so sparse it reminded me of a tiny movie set. The huge amount of foliage covering the area made up for what was missing. Large white puffs of dust trailed behind cars as they drove through the jungle, completing the illusion.

We passed the hotel where we would be staying, but instead of stopping to check in right away, we went to Kozumi's house first, just a minute away by car. The front of their house faced the road, an average home with an orange facade. From the car the house looked like it would be huge inside.

"Let's go around to the store in the back," Kozumi said. We got out of the car and followed.

"Right this way," Saseko said, motioning to us with her hand. She walked along a small path that was next to the side of the house.

"They really have a nice place," Ryūichirō whispered to me as we walked along the path. Not a second after we came out of the thick jungle onto the beach, the ocean spread out in front of us for miles.

My mind made a quick mental note: store in front, facing the water, house in back.

The blue ocean water was clear and peaceful, the white sand smooth.

"We're back," Saseko said to a Japanese man working behind the cash register.

The man nodded his head and said gently, "Welcome home. Nice to have you here." I smiled when I saw his dark skin and thick beard, because he was the type that should be here, I thought to myself. He was obviously into water sports, and I'm sure he was fond of beer.

"Come over and have something to drink," Saseko said, waving us over to one of the tables that were lined up outside the shop, each facing the beach. They were covered with large parasols and blue tablecloths. The southern sun made the definition between light and shadow clear on the tops of all the tables.

Sitting down at the table nearest the ocean, I noticed that aside from Ryūichirō and I there was only one other group of customers, an American couple dressed in colorful swimming suits. They appeared relaxed as they munched on huge sandwiches. The young man inside the shop who'd greeted us so kindly was putting some very sweet-looking drinks on a tray behind the black counter as Kozumi, who had just come back from parking the car, went up to him to say something. Under the tropical sun Kozumi looked like he was melting, but those arms and legs also appeared as if they were firmly planted in the soil of Saipan. This must be where he belongs, I thought.

Little by little our bare arms were exposed to the sun, and a breeze blew over us, cooling our shiny foreheads. Small beads of sweat trickled down our glasses as we carried on a casual conversation.

By then I'd grown accustomed to the scenery around me, and I already had a feeling like I could live that way every day. In fact, I felt like I'd been there for years.

"I'm going to the storehouse for a while," Kozumi said. "I'll be back in a little while, so you guys just take your time and rest up until tonight, then we'll go out for some drinks. I'll give you a call."

We waved and said good-bye, and then it was just the three of us again.

Saseko turned to me and said, "Do you see that building over there?" She pointed down the beach, and I nodded my head. "That's the beach bar next to your hotel." I could see a row of white tables that looked similar to the ones in front of Kozumi's store, and the wind carried soft music which seemed to be coming from the bar. "See, you're that close."

"So we wouldn't be lying if we said we have a beach house," Ryūichirō replied.

"Exactly," Saseko said. "There are dozens of them along the beach. And you're just a few steps away from cold drinks, beer, and light snacks."

"But the sandwiches at your place are particularly nice," Ryūichirō said.

"We get so busy during lunchtime."

"Well, don't forget to leave a table for us," I said. "We'll definitely stop by for a sandwich sometime." At that point I felt like

I did in the car, the inexpressible sensation of being thrown in a pressure cooker—that warped air, painful breathing.

Blue sky. Fresh air. Wonderful sandwiches. Faraway places.

Things looked forward to on vacations. Feelings of release.

It was only the sharp pain in my breast that wouldn't go away. It completely took over me, like a bad cold, hay fever, or mountain sickness. I couldn't get a hold of what was happening.

But why?

Did it have something to do with Eiko?

I became depressed. Without breathing I searched inside myself, gaining the confidence that my feelings had nothing to do with her.

Then I saw Eiko's lovely hair fluttering in the mind. It was wet, as if she had just stepped out of the shower. Flinging it back and forth, she shook off small drops of water. I closed my eyes to savor the image. Even after opening my eyes the image of her remained, almost in slow motion, the curved strands bending like small leather whips, thousands and thousands of them cutting into my heart.

Strange, my chest was suddenly relieved.

Once the feeling was gone, it was like it had never been there, along with all indications of why it would have been there in the first place. Maybe Saseko had had something to do with it, maybe not. Without a clue, I turned and looked at her.

"What's the matter?" Ryūichirō asked.

"I know, your head just hurts a little, right?" Saseko paused for a moment, and then she smiled and said, "That sort of thing happens all the time around here."

I nodded.

A whisper came into my head, forming a word that sounded like *ghosts*.

Millions of voices started singing in my heart, voices of each Japanese who'd died on this island long ago. Their spirits were still hovering across the beaches and oceans, through the branches and leaves of the trees in the jungle. There were millions of them on the island, literally millions.

I thought for a moment. There hadn't been that many ghosts in Japan, and if they were there I certainly hadn't felt them. Now that I was in a place where their numbers were so overwhelming I had a clear understanding of their existence. On top of that, I think I had learned a lot about this kind of thing from my brother as well, because the more time I spent with Yoshio the more keen my senses became. The amount of spirits I felt in my heart was increasing by the day.

Was that the source of my pain? Or did it have something to do with the young woman sitting next to me, the one with the talent to sing to the ghosts?

Was it because I was half dead? Or just getting closer to dying?

That last premonition made me grieve. With each passing second every one of us grows closer to death. Still, new cells are constantly being created inside each of us, one right after another. Maybe I've slipped out of this neverending cycle, in that strange continuum where everything is constantly changing as it glows with a radiant light.

I wasn't hoping to be young forever. My feelings had more to do with the cells being born inside me every moment, those little creatures with the power to see everything so clearly.

On the other side of the beach the sun was beginning to set, and even the sound of the waves seemed to fade away into the distance. The palm trees surrounding the store turned a pale ocher as they swayed gently, ever so gently, in the wind.

"What a beautiful sunset," Saseko said calmly. She started to hum the song we heard coming from the bar next door. Listening to her sweet voice, I felt like I was listening to a faraway radio playing songs from the memories of my childhood, each familiar, soft, and comforting. I realized for the first time that my eyes were awakening to who I was and where I belonged.

The sky hung over us like an enormous dome, the wide ocean spread out before us. Gazing into the western sky with the two lovers sitting together beside us, I felt like a happy puppy wagging a tail at her master.

We'd been blessed.

But only for a short while.

Staring out across the sea, we watched the sun fade away. Saseko continued to hum, not necessarily singing a specific tune. Still, I could practically see what she was singing because it fit so perfectly into our surroundings. Her harmony rose into the air like the world's greatest fragrance. She had a beautiful singing voice, sweet and precise, and it concealed any sort of vibrato.

It was my first chance to hear her sing.

Chapter 11

Lights shimmering over the night sky in Saipan looked like diamonds. The buildings were small, their illumination big. The air had cleared and everything was filled with damp humidity from the sea.

As we walked through the streets we heard people singing karaoke inside the bars. We glanced into the dark windows of odd souvenir shops, and read signs written in strange Japanese. The neon lights swirled powerfully in the night. After a dinner of Chamorro cuisine we strolled in our short sleeves down wide streets that looked like they'd been made for a set of an old Hollywood movie, and I savored the sensation of independence. It was as if a whole new life had begun for me.

I often feel this way when I'm away, particularly when I have gone to a place where time goes by slowly. Maybe it was okay that my memories were scattered. Perhaps the order of events in my life wasn't so important anymore, or so the thought crossed my mind. Surely there had never even been a sequence to it all. Right now I was in Saipan with the scent of the salty air seeping through my mind, something that I hadn't breathed as a child, or even with Yoshio on our recent trip to Kochi. Nor was it the smell of liquid moving through my nose while I was still inside my mother. At the same time, however, it was all different smells put together.

Certainly I was exposed to the ocean's scent now, in that time and in that place. It rushed in through me, covering every inch of my being, and I decided to file it away in my mind as one pure recollection.

Rather than confuse myself with the progression of events, it was just nice to savor the sensation of something far more magnificent. In order to let the feeling sink into my entire body, I relaxed and opened my senses. Within the atmosphere of Saipan it seemed to be rather easy to do.

I was reminded of an article I saw once in a weekly magazine that depicted the Ginza during the early part of the Showa era. When I looked out over the people, there was a certain nobility in the air. The same thing crossed my mind now—I couldn't help but wonder what it would be like to walk down the street in such a wonderful fashion: the sky opening up all around you, the faces of the passing people so clear and refined, like something you see in panorama.

Back in Tokyo I was frustrated with my unclear perception of life. But all that was far from me in Saipan, including those bad feelings of emotional distress that bordered on nervous disease.

~

"I was born with this mop," Kozumi said as he stuck out his finger and pointed to his silvery hair. "And I was also blessed with a family."

The four of us had gone for a drink at a bar next to the beach. We'd just finished eating. All of us had several cocktails, but no one had reached their limit yet. Saseko had said she wasn't drinking, and she managed to go all night without putting a drop in her body. That night she'd been the designated driver.

I could see that the beach bar was doing well. It was packed with locals, and tourists from practically every country in the world, everyone pleasantly sipping mixed drinks and beer. Candles flickered brightly on each of the tables and a live band was playing music in the back, but they weren't very good. In fact they were downright awful. At any rate, the bar was booming.

Right in front of my eyes the sea had subsided, and the moon cast a narrow strip of light across the ocean waters. The white sand nestled close to the sea as it curved around the small bay where we were sitting. Amid that landscape Kozumi continued his unusual confession, so different from his typical shy appearance.

I thought about his wife sitting next to him. Surely she'd heard her husband talk about these things a hundred times or more, and I wondered what her expression would be.

Would her face be saying, "Do I have to listen to this again?"

Or would it be a look of respect?

It was neither. Saseko was merely resting her hand on her chin, her face an image of indescribable beauty. Her figure was soft and white like the goddess of mercy, Kannon. It was so sweet I felt I was melting.

At the same time her eyes appeared to glow as they reflected light from the candles on our table; I'd never seen anything like it. No, I take that back. I had seen it once before. It was the same expression I saw in my cat's eyes after she'd given birth to her litter, her countenance of natural instinct, fresh and alive. After only three days of caring for her children that look disappeared from her eyes—that look of pride and blood smeared all over her children, a visage of motherly love.

"Now that you mention it," Ryūichirō said to Kozumi, "I don't think I've ever heard you talk about your family. Where did you come from? I don't know why, but I've always assumed that you were just born here."

"I grew up in a small fishing village in Shizuoka," Kozumi said with a smile. "My parents were cousins, or something like that. At least they shared the same blood."

Fortunately the rest of his speech wasn't quite so revealing.

"All my brothers and sisters were born with regular skin. I was the only one without color."

The band took a break and before long the stir of people around us mixed in with the sound of waves. Everyone was in good spirits and we all talked rather loudly. The ocean was beautiful—so smooth it looked like it could vanish into the white sand.

"My parents were just two happy people who bumped into each other on the street—completely average in every respect. My father was bronze and buffed from fishing, Mother a plump woman from the country. There was nothing more to them than that, except that they were wonderful. Everyone in our village loved them.

"There were five children in our family. My older brother and sister—I came third—and then came my two younger brothers. Since we didn't have any dividers between the rooms in our house, we all slept cuddled up on the floor, the five of us together. We would tickle one another and laugh, never going to sleep. Our mother would have to scold us. Every day brought something new. It was fun. Really fun.

"When the whole family ate at night, everyone would be in an uproar. Plates would fly and we'd all laugh and soon I'd forget where I was and what I was doing. Since my brother and sister were a lot older than the three of us younger brothers, they were the ones who really took care of us. We were happy—I don't know how else to describe it. It never occurred to me once when I was a child that my skin was different from everybody else's.

"But I knew I was unlike my siblings. Sometimes I had premonitions of the future. Even now I don't know why. I could guess the weather, see accidents before they happened, and I knew my score on tests in school before I'd even take them. There was always one thing, though, that terrified me most. Something I couldn't bring up with anybody. I'd hold off until night so I could pounce on my brothers and sister in my pajamas, and then jump into my futon at the sound of my mother's footsteps. We only had one small lamp so everything was always dark. Mother would throw the door open with a bang and yell, 'GO TO SLEEP!' We'd wiggle with laughter, somebody whispering under the sheets. Before long the others were asleep, and I would fade off, too. One good day was over and we looked forward to the next.

"Every so often, though, maybe once a year, my eyes would pop open in the middle of the dark night.

"It would happen so quickly I'd think someone had flipped on a light switch. It was that way every time. Then a thick smell of sulfur would surround my body, and I would wonder where on earth it was coming from. At first I thought one of my brothers had farted, but the smell was never that fresh. It had to be coming from somewhere inside my own dizzy head. Regardless of what I tried, I couldn't get rid of the smell. I glanced around at my sleeping brothers and sister, their small frames glimmering under the light, blissfully snoring away. They looked dead, all spread out on the floor, arms and legs twisted together. Our house was so small I felt relieved by the closeness that we shared. My sister's prominent face; my brother's thick eyelashes; my little brother's nose squinted between his eyes. I'd stare at them for hours. They appeared so different from when I'd look at them in the daytime. Something about them was sad, weak, and defenseless. I knew when morning rolled around everything would change. The first one awake would jump on the others, and the party would begin. We'd beat one another to the toilet, flip channels on the TV, tear into one another's faces, and in the end treat one another nicely. But that only happened in the morning, only after we'd gotten up. That's when things would change. The deadly silence of the night would be gone, and I'd no longer be alone. Once I woke up and felt that relief, I'd want to go back to sleep. Still, the smell crept back to me, night after night. A soft voice would sneak into my head saying, 'You'd better get used to it now, because you'll be the only one left in the end. The only one.' I heard it clearly each time, but I didn't know what it was trying to tell me, and I really didn't want to understand. I could see my brothers and sisters around me. I didn't want them to go away. I enjoyed their beauty and their brightness, and I thought if I recognized what was being said then my brothers and sisters would all disappear. Eventually I couldn't help it, though, I knew I would end up alone. The thought frightened me. I'd get so scared

I'd roll over to my sister and wake her. 'I'm scared,' I'd say, tightly gripping her warm hand. She'd squeeze my hand tight while she dreamed. In the morning, after checking to see that my siblings were still alive, I'd feel so happy tears would roll from my eyes. But that one thing remained—a dark shadow that fell on my parents first, and then my older sister. It was dark and foreboding. I didn't want to see it, but I did.

"In the dim light I could see my sister's face, and before I knew it I was drifting off to sleep. When I opened my eyes the next morning, the first thing I'd notice was the sulfur smell was gone. The room was filled with the usual lively atmosphere and morning sunlight. My sister would say something like, 'You must have had a nightmare because you came and slept with me last night.' By then I'd forgotten all about the terrible feelings of the night before, with only the words and an image remaining—that deep voice saying, 'Only you will be left.' But everyone would be in such high spirits, getting ready for the day—my father out in the ocean already, my mother working away in the kitchen, and everything else in wild confusion.

"I never forgot that smell. It took some time, but in the end I understood the meaning of my premonition. Sulfur is the scent of death. It started long after I left the house, long after all my brothers and sisters had grown up and moved away. My father died first in an accident out at sea. One of my little brothers was next, dying in a bike accident. My sister moved too close to some wires while working at her factory, and received an electric shock. A few years later my older brother got sick and was gone. Then two years ago, my second younger brother left Japan to study and died of AIDS. Now only my mother and I are left, and she's never been out of Japan. Right now she's living in a mental institution. I haven't informed her about me and Saseko, since she doesn't understand much of anything anymore. Whenever I think about my family and Saseko, I get her mixed up with my older sister. It must have something to do with the fact that I'm the only one around. But even now I won't go to hot springs, or any other place with the smell of sulfur, unless it's near the ocean like the hot springs in Izu. I know if I breathe that scent someone will die.

"The voice has stopped coming to me at night, but I still have strange dreams, often of my childhood. I see my brothers and sister sleeping, their arms and legs intertwined. I hear them snore in their sleep, deep breathing and teeth grinding. They're sound asleep, their faces at peace like children should be. I know they are dead, despite the fact they're right next to me. And everything's okay because they're surrounding me, although I know I'm really alone.

"When I open my eyes the next morning I feel tears on my cheeks. It wasn't a bed I'd shared with my siblings, it was a coffin. In my dreams they're healthy and asleep, but in reality they're gone. In the end I lost it. With a tortured heart I locked my mother in a hospital, and quickly ran away to Saipan."

Just as I was about to respond with "Is that so?" Ryūichirō piped in.

"I'd hardly say you locked her up," he said. "Sounds to me like she needed to be there. You shouldn't feel like you've done anything wrong."

I wanted to voice the same thing, but then I realized it wouldn't have been effective if I'd said it. I was reminded, once again, that Ryūichirō is a writer, and he had the power of telling truth when he wanted to. His skill was clearly visible, sending out an echo of truth along with a tremendous amount of energy—something wrapped in sympathy for whoever sat next to him.

"I wish I could see it like that," Kozumi responded.

"Think of it this way," Ryūichirō said. "You're a winner, the final survivor. You've escaped the weak gene, or the bad luck of an early death. Don't worry, you'll bounce back."

Saseko nodded.

"You're right. Things are going well for me," Kozumi said. "But now I'm petrified over the thought of Saseko dying. Sometimes

I can't even sleep at night, thinking about what might happen to her."

"Do you smell sulfur?" Saseko said, taking a large lock of her hair and waving it like a fan in front of Kozumi's nose.

"No, just shampoo and some salt water." Kozumi laughed at his own joke. I felt relieved. The conversation was getting unbearable. Kozumi's confession seemed to dance in the darkness of the beach that night like a terribly sad dream, cutting through me like a long knife.

Kozumi leaned over to me. "Right now my younger brother's with us, and he's telling me that you have a little sister who's dead, right?"

I nodded, not surprised. There was a chance Ryūichirō had mentioned Mayu to Kozumi before we came to Saipan. But whether he'd told Kozumi or not, I couldn't be surprised to hear he knew about Mayu passing away, not someone who'd lost so many brothers and a sister himself. To him, it was nothing new. When I thought about how many people have died in the past, I realized there were probably even more people in situations worse than what we'd been through. A long time ago in small villages and towns in Japan, people had seen entire families depart right in front of them.

"She looks a lot like your friend who sent that message to you while we were on the plane," Kozumi said.

Ryūichirō asked me about it, and I told him. He agreed by saying, "Now that you mention it, they do have the same eyes."

For the first time since I'd been with Ryūichirō, I was overcome by jealousy which reminded me that Mayu had been with him before me. But it didn't take long before the feeling went away.

"That woman on the plane . . . what was her name? Aiko? Ieko? She was stabbed by another woman."

"Are you serious?" I said, my eyes popping open. I was horrified. Kozumi looked off into the distance as if he were staring at someone who wasn't really there. His head bobbed up and down like he was responding to what was being said.

"What does she mean by 'his wife'? She keeps repeating, I was stabbed by his wife. Oh, wait a minute. She was having an affair." Kozumi got a bit excited. "I get it. She was stabbed by her lover's wife!"

"Is she dead?" I asked in a hurry. There wasn't anything else to say.

"No, she's alive."

I don't think I've ever been so relieved in my life. Kozumi had given me vigor, like we were watching a movie on television and he'd pressed the pause button to explain what was going on for me.

"She's in the hospital. The wound doesn't look serious—she's just in shock right now. They've got her sedated with heavy pills. Don't worry, her chart says her condition isn't bad. But she's not to get out of bed for a while."

"That's so nice to hear," I said, placing my trust in what he had said. Most likely everything he'd said was correct, because somewhere deep inside me I knew it too.

"My younger brother tells me everything," Kozumi said with a smile.

"Are you sure it was your brother?" Saseko asked with a cold look in her eyes.

"What do you mean?" Kozumi said, getting angry.

"I can sense when a spirit's around," she said. "And I know what they're saying. But I haven't received one impression that your brother's here, even though I've always felt him in the past."

"So you're calling me a liar? Or are you just blabbing away like you always do?" Kozumi looked as though he was trying to remain calm as he questioned his wife, but he couldn't hide his rage.

Saseko responded callously, "You don't know what you're talking about. You're the one coming up with this stuff about a woman in a hospital, not your brother, because everyone knows ghosts don't impart that kind of information so easily. They do their own thing, completely independent of human beings. They're never that compassionate. In fact they hate people who are alive. You think someone who died as a baby is going to suddenly change into a spirit with such a gentle personality? Of course there are guardian spirits out there, but they don't just turn into saints."

"You're saying my brother isn't here with us now?" Kozumi said with a dejected look on his face.

I glanced at Ryūichirō. We were both thinking the same thing—It doesn't matter if your brother's here or not. Just stop your fighting.

"No," Saseko said, "your brother is out there, somewhere. But you know, the reason he doesn't tell you things is because you have your own spirit inside you that's doing all the watching for you. I know how it must feel to want to get information from your brother, but it's wrong to think you can depend on him for everything. One of these days some weird ghost pretending to be him is just going to pop up and surprise you." Saseko smiled.

"I've had to be strong," Kozumi said through his drunken speech, "because they left me here all alone. That's why he's here protecting me."

I could see that Kozumi was upset with his wife, but the alcohol was starting to take control and he was becoming overly emotional. He'd already denied a number of things he believed right there in front of us that night. But since he spoke so kindly, and since his wife appeared so soft and pure under the moonlit night, I just sat watching them in silence. Ryūichirō was with me.

The clamor of the people around us, the quivering light of our candle, and the sound of waves on the coast all came back to my mind. At that point the band began to return to the stage to warm up. I was sure their performance was not about to improve, but once the music started a group of women sitting close to the stage, who appeared like they lived in town, turned to our table and simultaneously started to chant, "SA-SE-KO! SA-SE-KO!"

"I was just waiting for this to happen," Kozumi said. "Whenever we come they make Saseko sing at least one song. She's a star on this island."

Saseko stood up and announced that she would "be back in a jiffy." Then she moved toward the stage, everyone cheering and clapping. Saseko returned their gracious welcome with a smile.

Until that moment Saseko had been the same woman I'd met at the airport, perfectly fitting the description Kozumi had given me back at the bar in Tokyo. Nothing about her seemed any different. As I watched her getting ready to sing I couldn't help but think how wonderful it would be to attract so much attention from your neighbors by having such a wonderful talent to sing. The band came to a halt and everything was silent for a moment. Then, to my surprise, they began to play "Love Me Tender." Saseko held the hand mike. When I turned back to see what Ryūichirō was thinking, I was startled to see how earnestly he was concentrating. His eyes were glued to Saseko. Maybe this would be the start of something incredible . . .

. . . or so I thought as I turned back to look at the stage. Then her song began. Even though her song had been immortalized by Elvis Presley, it wasn't like the rock version, and it didn't remind me of Nicolas Cage, either. The words lifted from her mouth in a way I'd never heard words come from a human mouth before. Even though she was belting her voice into the mike, the quality of sound was something you'd expect from a faraway bell, something from a dream. The world began to spin around me, and her song began to represent what kind of person she was for me. If I was to describe the voice here I would say it was a strange mix of nobility and flattery. Something sweet, sad, and so full of energy that even though I knew it would never come back, I wanted to hold on to it forever.

Everyone was hushed as they listened. A few couples swayed together next to the stage. She was able to send something out across the bar that night, something like ripples in water, silent and gentle as they flowed. And just as those thoughts were going through my mind it happened. A gust of hot steam came rolling in from the sea and lingered around the bar as she sang. Without thinking I grabbed Ryūichirō by the arm. He gave me a firm nod of his head. Kozumi sat silently next to us, apparently unaffected by the strange phenomenon.

That rush of air had come over us so unexpectedly it seemed to create a small lining between us and the world. That's why it appeared as if Saseko were standing on the other side of a beautiful fountain and we were looking at her through sprays of water. Everything trembled softly, melting in my vision. Her voice became even more ghostly as it took in the humidity surrounding it.

By the time my limited perception had picked up on that much of what was going on around, her song was over. I grieved because it seemed so short. I wished I could just go on listening, but the steam from the ocean was quickly dissipating. It happened so quickly I wondered for a minute if something or someone had brought the mist with them.

I turned to Ryūichirō and inquired, "What happened just now? Was that natural, or did it have to do with the power of her voice while she was singing?"

"I'm not sure," he said. "But I think it was spirits coming in from the ocean to listen to her song."

"Are you sure?"

"No, but you have to admit things got distorted for a while," he replied.

I nodded. But if that was the case, why hadn't I felt sick to my stomach like I did earlier that day in the jungle?

Ryūichirō turned to me so that Kozumi couldn't hear what he was saying, and whispered softly in my ear. "Personally I think there's a different way to explain it, but I have a feeling that Kozumi and his wife would like us to think of it that way."

The music turned to a song a bit more upbeat. Saseko danced her way off the stage, and an older man who also looked like he was from town grabbed her as she strolled by and kissed her on the lips. She put her arms around his shoulders and returned the favor. Then she sauntered her way over to our table.

"So? How was it?" She grinned.

"I'm really not sure what to think, but it was really wonderful," I said. "I'd give anything to hear more." That's all I could say for the moment, since I was having trouble finding the right words for my impressions. I was sensing a primeval desire, something I wished would be with me forever.

"Yeah, I'd like to hear more, too," Ryūichirō said.

"Let's walk around a bit," Saseko said.

Without saying a word, Kozumi stood up. He was quiet, and his face appeared even paler than usual. I figured he wasn't feeling well. As Saseko stood up and walked out of the bar, she received another round of applause. She stepped inside to pay the bill, and the manager at the counter gave us our first round of drinks free of charge.

Rather than go all the way through the building, we slipped around the side of the bar and found a shortcut to the street. When we had walked a few steps in the direction of our hotel and turned around to say good-bye, we saw that Kozumi and his wife had stopped a few yards back and now they were in a heated discussion on the street. I'd just turned to Ryūichirō, telling him how nice it would be to walk home together, and I'd failed to notice they hadn't come along.

By the time we went back Kozumi was yelling at Saseko.

"You whore! Why did you let that old fucker kiss you?"

Oh boy, I thought. Here we go.

"You're drunk!" Saseko screamed. "Why do you have to make everything a fight? I can't change the way I am. I was brought up this way."

Glancing over at Ryūichirō, I saw he was trying to examine the situation, even though his efforts were pointless. He whispered to me, "I think Kozumi's just in a bad mood. He's been trying to pick a fight for a while now. It doesn't matter if there's a true reason or not."

"He's really drunk, isn't he?" I said.

The two of them were screaming: I'm so embarrassed to be seen with you! You're so thick-headed! Why don't you open up your heart? You never say anything when you're sober! You always get your own way!

Their fight continued as Ryūichirō and I looked on.

"Do you think we should stop them?" I asked.

"No," he replied. "They'll work it out."

I shook my head, and we turned and walked away. "They really occupy themselves, don't they? One minute they're in the height of spirituality, the next minute just like two newlyweds." As we walked around the street corner I glanced back for the last time. The fight was still going on.

"That's what makes them so interesting," Ryūichirō said.

"Have you ever heard Saseko sing before?"

"Only when we went to Garapan and I heard her sing karaoke. But tonight was amazing, wasn't it? I mean, that audience coming in from the ocean to hear her song. That was really a first."

"You mean the fog, right? What was that?"

"Don't ask me," Ryūichirō replied. "But apparently that happens quite often—she turns to the ocean and sings to a crowd without human form. When Kozumi told me about it, he said the phenomenon is impossible to describe."

"He really loves his wife, doesn't he?" I said.

"Yeah, he does. But it was your first time to hear her song too."

I had heard it, that much was true. But I hadn't heard a song. No, it was something entirely different. It was closer to those things my brother saw and heard in his mind, translated in the form of a song. Various smells, tears, the touch of a person's hand, regret that never reaches you, light from the gods, heat from hell. Everything brought together to create something so impressive that even that old man knew how to respond. Something so amazing that it would cause a couple to burst out fighting.

We grabbed our key from the desk and went up to our room. It was a large suite with a kitchen and a small balcony, and we could see the street outside. As I stepped out to look across the road, I thought once again that the facade looked like a set in a movie, small and unstable. I went back in and took a seat on a fluffy red couch in the living area. Ryūichirō grabbed a beer from the refrigerator and we drank it. It felt like I'd been there a lifetime.

I tried calling Eiko while Ryūichirō was in the shower, but no one was home. After he finished I took a shower myself, and then I found myself dozing. I rolled into bed with Ryūichirō, and like an elderly couple who've shared their nights for decades, I gave him a soft peck on the cheek and told him I was tired. Then I snuggled up next to him. His body felt warm.

Please don't let his warmth disappear during the night. Please let him stay until I awaken tomorrow. Death awaits both of us at some point; I just hope I don't know about it beforehand.

Oh, and please don't let him just get up and leave.

. . . or so a small prayer whispered in my heart on that sultry summer evening.

Chapter 12

When I opened my eyes, I detected a sharp pain in my head and my temples felt hot, as if I had a fever. It would have been a real bummer if I'd caught a cold on a tropical island.

Ryūichirō asked me several times if I wanted to go diving with him and Kozumi, but I told him I'd already made plans to spend the day on the beach. Listening to him say, "Come on, just come with us," and seeing the sad look in his eyes as he got ready to go diving, I wondered how a man like this was able to spend so much time traveling alone in the world, exposed to so much danger. Then I realized one simple fact. Ryūichirō was the type who had to go off on his own, otherwise he'd just be spoiled with someone else around. My heart went out to him as I watched him roll up his wetsuit on top of the musty hotel carpet. I went into the kitchen and made him some coffee.

"Thanks," he said, taking the mug and putting it to his mouth. I glanced over his shoulder and saw the patio behind him sparkling in the morning sun. Bunches of large red flowers swayed outside, soaking up the morning light.

Where would he be off to this time?

Perhaps I'm exaggerating just a bit, but take, for example, a monk who leaves his home and journeys out into the world. Does he carry with him the thoughts and memories of the mother and sisters left behind?

I glanced outside and saw Kozumi drive up to the front of our hotel. I waved to Ryūichirō from the window as he left the front door and squeezed into Kozumi's car.

The shadow of loneliness accompanied by the smell of death, momentarily entering into the heart of the person who is sending someone off . . .

Is it the same for the person being sent off?

~

Once he was gone I felt lazy. I returned to the room and sprawled on the bed. The bedroom was separate from the living room and a huge window ran from one end of the wall to the next. I pulled back the blind and beheld the beach. It was luxurious. A dry breeze blew through the open window and made the cheap white lace curtains you see in so many hotels flutter about wildly. The skylight in the wide hallway filled the entire room with sunshine.

Lying there all alone on the bed, staring up at the sun's rays shining from every corner of the ceiling, I thought back to a time when I rested on a bed in the school health center after feigning some kind of illness. When I closed my eyes, the feeling was even stronger. I could almost hear the sound of the bell and the confusion out in the hall as students jostled about, moving on to their next class. It was a peculiar image that brought peacefulness to my heart.

I think my spirit was restored to me completely when I had dreams of my past like that one. I could return to my childhood in my sleep—a suspicious slumber that made me feel marvelous.

As I dozed off I watched the white curtains continue to sway in front of my eyes. They reminded me of flying pigeons or a crisp, waving flag. Once I'd fallen into a clean, deep sleep, I saw past the curtain into a white brightness beyond. Cool, sweet, and soft, it visually reminded me of a firefly. In my mouth I could taste the sweetness of pear-flavored sherbet—it was that kind of light. I could sense it drawing near to me. I watched it move from the front of the hotel up the stairs and over the landing covered on one side with flowers. I'm sure the light was approaching my room. I felt like radar picking up subtle undulations of the light as it moved closer and closer to me.

Then it stopped.

My eyes popped open and I heard a sound. Someone was knocking on my door. Rising out of bed, I saw Saseko through the peephole in the door. Of course it was Saseko—I knew it all along. I really didn't have any strange powers inside me, but for some reason I could always feel when she was around.

When I opened the door it occurred to me how odd it was to have such premonitions.

"How are you?" she asked as she let herself into the room. She was wearing a beautiful sundress of yellows, reds, and blues, and it felt as though she'd brought the morning sun into the room with her. When she passed I breathed in sunshine emanating from her.

"I think I've come down with a cold," I said.

"You might perceive it as that, but you're wrong," Saseko replied. "You're such a nice person, the ghosts are swarming around you, that's all. Once you get used to life in Saipan—you know, once you know your way around—they'll leave you alone, I'm sure of it."

"Get used to life in Saipan? Know my way around?" I looked at her doubtfully. "No, it's really just a cold."

"Okay." Saseko smiled. "Let's try singing your sickness away."

"Singing?" I asked.

"Yes, but we have to do it together. Now let's see, what's something we both know. How about an old folk song from Japan? Let's sing 'Hana.'"

"Wait a minute!" I gasped. "Sing with you, a real-life singer?"

"Sure," she exclaimed, grasping me by the arm. "Let's start. One, two, three . . . go!"

"Haru no, urara no . . ."

Saseko started singing and I joined in. As we sang the first verse I listened to her beautiful soprano voice, and all at once I started feeling better. It had been so long since I had sung with anyone I'd almost forgotten what it felt like to experience something so loud and clear. I could almost see the sound rising up from the bottom of my chest into my throat and vocal cords. It was a magnificent sound. Standing across from Saseko I looked her straight in the eyes. We harmonized together. When I smiled she followed suit, and soon the song itself seemed to be smiling. I'm sure if we'd been thinking about sad things during that moment the song would have reflected our sad feelings as well. It might seem such a natural sort of thing, but thinking about it makes me realize how complex singing really is. Experiencing it with Saseko brought that realization to mind.

The weather outside was gorgeous and the ocean was spread out before us. Time went by slowly. It was warm. The echo of our song reverberated around the room as the cool breeze came flowing in from the window.

Once the song was over Saseko asked if I felt better.

"Now that you mention it," I said, "I really do . . ."

. . . feel better. I did feel better. I felt like leaving the hotel room to go swimming. Saseko had done it for me.

"When you live on this island you just have to let it out every once in a while. If you're ever caught off guard, or just lounging around, the spirits will creep up from behind and get you. They'll never let you win."

I started to laugh. "Sounds like you've made a study of it."

I knew so many things existed, even though I couldn't see them all—like those things running through my brother's head and the intimacy I felt when Saseko was around. Those things and many more. I'm sure you could define them in a variety of different ways, but whatever they were, the thing Saseko had done for me then was one such phenomenon. Rather than give her actions a name, I just wanted to recognize how they'd truly served their purpose. She'd showed me a wonderful way to improve my condition, which was far better than any label I could have slapped on it.

"How about a sandwich?" Saseko said, reaching into her bag. "They're from the shop." She strolled over to the kitchen table and motioned for me to sit down.

"I'd love some."

Once she had finished placing the wrapped sandwiches on the table, Saseko stood up and asked if I'd like coffee or tea, boiling some water on the stove.

"Ummm . . . coffee, I suppose," I replied, as I moved over to the sofa and sat down, turning on the TV. I could have cared less that Saseko, practically a stranger, had just come into my room and willfully started making coffee and feeding me. In fact, I kind of liked it. I didn't feel she was being patronizing at all. Instead I felt more like a dog or a cat—like something that could just lie back and have everything brought to her. On top of everything else, the sandwiches were incredibly delicious.

"Don't compliment me on the bread. We don't bake it ourselves, we have it delivered," Saseko said with a giggle. Still, it was clear she took pride in the sandwiches.

A small fever in my head. Hot coffee and wonderful sandwiches. The sun and the old furniture in my room. Flowers swaying on the balcony. I felt like it had been years, literally years, since I'd first come to Saipan. The air wrapped itself around me as though I were a native, causing me to feel utterly relaxed and calm.

The colors of the flower petals were different than they were in Japan, and the way the sun shone down upon the water. I know I was thinking differently as well—the strength and brightness of it all. All of it came together to form a sensation I hadn't enjoyed in years.

~

When I mentioned to Saseko that it would be nice to go shopping, she said she'd be happy to take me, and we drove to the largest supermarket in town. As we left my hotel I noticed how strong the sun was beating down upon the island. The pure white road we took seemed sterile. As we went north along the parched road running parallel to the beach, white clouds of dust barreled from behind our car as we moved forward.

The supermarket was right in front of a huge hotel, and even though it appeared run-down from the outside, I couldn't help but be amazed at how spacious it was inside. I felt idiotic pushing a cart down the seemingly endless rows and aisles, and I surprised myself when I didn't get lost in the end. Unhealthy food lined the shelves in huge containers with brightly colored labels, so I picked out a few fruits and vegetables we could eat in the small kitchen back at the hotel.

When I met Saseko at the registers, I asked how she survived on such horrible food. She laughed and said, "Mostly on sandwiches from the shop. But we cook Japanese a lot at the house, too—miso soup, fish, meat marinated in soy sauce, all sorts of different things."

"Come to think of it, did you ever make up with Kozumi after last night?" I said, recalling the encounter they'd had on the street the night before.

"No, but that sort of thing happens all the time. It's nothing to worry about." She made it sound so simple.

"I see," I said, satisfied by her remark. I suppose I get preoccupied when I spend time with other couples.

∾

We stopped on the way home for some tea at the Philippine Cafe. (I just named it that because the woman who owned the place was Filipino.) We also had some Filipino dessert with our tea. For some reason they had turned half of the cafe into a barbershop, and as we talked over tea, the sound of clipping metal scissors seemed to never end. I couldn't tell if it was an amazingly clean way to run a business, or just the opposite. Sun filtered in from the front window and covered the table where we were seated.

Weak coffee and sweet cake. Beer straight from the tap. Intense sunlight. Incomprehensible Tagalog flying over our heads.

Such a unique place; I couldn't form a single impression. Everything brought such uncanny feelings. The people on the island appeared blurred, as if I saw them in a photograph, and the landscape was warped as if it were heat rising off a road in the desert.

"What a strange place, what a strange time," I said. "It must be weird living on an island like this."

"It's better than being back in Japan. To me, nothing's worse than home. You can get by without concerning yourself here."

"You're right," I said. "I do find myself less troubled."

Gazing out over the view; eating three meals a day; swimming in the ocean; watching TV—those were the only skills needed to survive. It was an enlarged version of the life I had experienced in Kochi. Everything became unsharp and loose—at least those things that frightened me, or the things in Japan I had always longed for.

"I ran away from my own country like I was being chased," Saseko said with a smile.

"But I saw you in Japan," I exclaimed. "In fact, you came to me while I was in Kochi."

"I remember meeting you too," Saseko replied. "Just once. I had a dream that I walked up to your door to pay you a visit when you were living in an apartment with a young guy." Saseko acted like it was no big deal.

"You're right," I said.

"It happens every so often. I see someone I'm destined to be friends with long before we ever actually meet. Kozumi was the same way. I had a dream one night that I went to the airport to meet him, and the next day I actually did go. I'd never seen him before and I knew nothing about him, but when he laid eyes on me he said he'd talked to me in a dream. Even though he was there with some friends, he told them to go off on their own and we had our first date. Next time he came by himself, and it's been that way ever since."

"Well," I said, "the two of you sure seemed to click fast. You're amazing."

"It's nothing really," Saseko said. "I mean, I've always wanted to get away from Japan, or to get away from my own body. Always. I've felt this way ever since I was inside my mother's womb. But when you compare how intense my thoughts and feelings are to what actually goes on, they're nothing, really. Believe me, there were times in my life when I hated myself so much I'd develop hives or break out in a rash. There were even times when I lost so much control over my mind that they had to put me in a hospital. That was really hard. But then I went through puberty and found that I could release a lot of my built-up energy on the men who liked me. When I thought about my body, and when I realized I was attractive and wanted by many, I was overjoyed. In the end I slept around with hundreds of different people. My name wound up fitting me perfectly. Guys would ask me what my name was, I would tell them, and it would all be downhill from there." At that point Saseko laughed so hard it was difficult for me to keep myself from giggling along with her.

"Yes," I said, "I suppose you're right."

"Don't you think so?" she replied. "See, when I was little I had a vibrator as a toy. For the longest time I actually called it 'Mother.'"

"Vibrator?" I asked. "Do you mean *that* kind of vibrator?"

"Exactly. Well, at least it was something shaped like one." Again she laughed aloud. "You see, once my father was out of the house, the woman who took care of me threw out everything that reminded me of my mother. By the time I was old enough to know what was going on, there wasn't a trace of her left. Then I found it, the one thing I could remember her by. Obviously I didn't know how to use it. I mean, how was I supposed to know what it was?

I was still so young. It was just something I'd come across tucked away in a small cupboard somewhere. I started calling it 'Mother,' and in the end I couldn't go to sleep without it; it was my only memento. When I went to the orphanage they took it away from me, angry that a child would be carrying such a toy. I was crushed. I've never been so sad. . . .

"But it didn't take long to find it again, right between men's legs. I loved it. When I was with it I could see my mother, and father, and friends. . . . It began to represent everyone for me." Saseko became excited. "Can't you see?" she said. "We were together again! Suddenly I could be with my mother anytime I wanted, but it came with a new sensation I hadn't felt before. Now my mother meant even more than before. I admit, in the end I became sort of a tramp, a sex maniac perhaps—which gives you a better feel for where I'm coming from. Over the course of the years I've seen it all. So compared to the story of how I was reunited with my mother, you can see why meeting people in dreams hasn't been a big deal."

Saseko sat still for a while with a smile across her face.

After hearing a story like that, I had the feeling that this woman sitting next to me was even more sublime than I'd previously imagined.

I must have been looking rather dazed, because Saseko turned to me and said, "But I'm happy now, so stop looking at me like that." She smiled and continued, "I was born for only one reason, and that's why I keep going. I'm here just to be happy."

"I know what you mean," I said.

"Sometimes I get really jealous of Kozumi. Sure, he appears to be unhappy, but he still has all those wonderful memories of being with his family. He has a mother who he remembers well. He was brought up in a world where there was no reason to be frightened or worried. He has memories of . . . of . . ." Saseko paused for a moment and then stated in English, ". . . being fed."

It was an English expression I recognized. Throughout Kozumi's life he had been *fed*.

"Now if something was to come between us and ruin the happiness we've found, perhaps I'd go back to being unhappy. But it's funny, because I think once I sense something it stays with me to a certain extent, even after the first sign of that feeling has been lost. Still, it frightens me to think I might lose it someday. I suppose that's the way it is with happiness.

"Does happiness come from knowing the value of everything in life? I don't know what the sad darkness of losing someone special feels like. Maybe Kozumi's the great one, having survived after losing so much. If he ever does leave me, I'm really going to be troubled. I've never lost someone I really love." Saseko smiled.

It seemed pointless to make comparisons, but since she was looking at her life and Kozumi's, I couldn't help but think where my life would be if it was stacked up next to hers. When I looked into the past and saw my occasional (?) run-ins with dying—the deaths of my father and sister, my concussion, the jumbled mess of past and present that I refer to as my memory, not to mention all that was happening with my brother—I still felt my own experiences paled in comparison to hers. When I looked at how stable and sober my own life had become, I couldn't help but feel a little ashamed.

"Well, you should be happy," I responded. The melody by which I replied to her statement made its way into her heart; after all, she was a singer.

Once again a broad smile slid across her lips, and she said, "Let's get out of here and find a nice spot on the beach and go swimming."

~

The ocean water was clear, wide, and shallow. It seemed to stretch out that way forever. Everything was peaceful and calm, but when

I planted my bare foot in the white sand I felt an icky, squishy feeling. The sand was covered with slimy sea cucumbers.

As I walked boldly into the water, each footstep brought more unpleasant contact with the sluggish creatures. However, once I was away from the lagoon I stopped stepping on the things. At first I was disgusted, taken aback by their ugly appearance. Before long I realized how harmless they were and I got used to just bending down and tossing them aside.

Diving deep into the water, I looked up to see the sparkle of the sun hitting the surface. Below me the white sand covered the ocean floor. I watched rays of light filter through the water to cast shaky, brightly shining polka dots across the floor of the ocean spread into eternity.

There were thousands—no, millions—of the sluggish black creatures. The sea cucumbers littered the bottom of the sea. Some lay nestled together, others lay contorted and twisted. But all of them appeared like strange vegetables breathing calmly under the water.

Being underwater was an unusual sensation. It was such a peculiar scene. A strange silence filtered its way into my body, so far that it seeped into the furthest reaches of my heart and into the darkest depths of my brain—a silent, overwhelming new world.

∾

I came up out of the water and made my way through the sand to the place where Saseko was waiting.

"I can't believe how many sea cucumbers there are!" I said, shaking water from my hair.

Saseko had on a blue bathing suit and had a cold bottle of beer in one hand. She opened her mouth and said clearly, "The sea cucumbers are the spirits of those who died in the war. They sleep on the ocean floor."

"Don't say that!" I screamed as I pulled my beach towel out and laid it next to hers.

"Why not? It's true. They're asleep down in the sand. Every morning a group of people come out here to throw them back in the ocean so the tourists won't be afraid, and every afternoon they've made their way back to the shoal."

"They're disgusting," I said.

"But don't you think their numbers reflect the same amount of people who died here during the war?" she asked.

"Yes," I said, thinking about it for a while. "I suppose you're right." During the war Saipan had become a grave for tens of thousands of Japanese soldiers who had lost their lives in battle. It was a fact I'd picked up in history class, but that still didn't explain the strange feeling I had on the island. Something told me that it has little to do with the anguish of war, because I could go to any cemetery, for example, and feel the same thing—thousands of sleeping dead people. They lie here and there—various people, various ways of dying.

But this place was different somehow.

Everyone died together in an instant, by the same harsh method of extermination. That is what seemed so strange. The greenery and blue sky. The silent beach. The absence of noise. Natural whispers of thousands of spirits rising ever so silently over the waters—silent voices without sound.

The sea cucumbers inspired that feeling.

"Sea cucumbers!" I said.

Saseko was laughing. "So now you won't go swimming?"

"No, I think I'll go back in."

"Exactly," Saseko said, firmly nodding her head.

~

I fell asleep sitting on a beach chair as I sipped a beer I'd taken from the cooler. Determined to get a tan, I'd smothered myself in oil. Saseko was well known on the beach, and people close enough to notice her shouted out a friendly "Hi!"

Folks from the shop, the karaoke bar, the neighborhood—there were many, and Saseko was a popular item. She sat next to me waving cheerfully as people strolled by.

A few young men also tried to pick her up. I'm sure it had nothing to do with how I was lying next to her in the sand showing my butt to the world, because they all turned their attention to Saseko, sliding up to her gently. I couldn't understand their English very well, but I know a pickup line when I hear one.

"Hey! So what you girls into?"

"How about washing those swimsuits off with some beer?"

"Looking for a dinner partner?"

"Come on, let's go for a ride. I've got something to show you."

As I listened to the conversation I realized why Kozumi was so worried about his wife. Saseko was also adroit at saying no. I had the feeling she'd heard every line in the book, and she was quite used to these conversations by now.

"So what's you name, cute thing?"

"Saseko."

"What does that mean?"

"LOVE. It means 'love,'" Saseko responded in perfect English.

I could see how she was able to get away with a lot more here than in Japan. I could also feel myself baking away little by little under the heat of the sun. I dozed off again. At some point a dream crept up on me from some dark place in my mind. It must have happened between that brief period when the song coming from the beach bar ended, and the sound of the waves filtered into my ears.

Summer.

The cry of cicadas. I'm back at home and I'm still a child, curled in a fetal position on top of the tatami mats. My father's naked feet cross in front of my eyes. Dark feet and stubby toenails.

My sister is watching TV on the other side of the room. The bamboo blind; green trees and bushes outside my window.

I watch my sister's back. I see her two pigtails. I hear my father's voice say, Mother, Sakumi's asleep. So why don't you put something over her? she replies. I'm making tempura right now and I can't hear a word you're saying! The sound of dripping batter falling into the splattering grease. The wafting stench of cooking prawns. Squinting into the kitchen, I see my mother standing in an apron behind the large wok, long chopsticks in her hands. My father brings a quilt over to where I'm sleeping and places it gently over my shoulders. My sister looks back. She's awake! she exclaims. It's been a long time since I've seen her double tooth.

Feeding someone.

Being *fed*.

That's what Saseko was talking about. I had the recollection. Even though my thoughts had been washed away, my memory trickled back to me like that. Aren't we all the same? Don't we all have memories of a father and a mother engraved in our minds? I supposed most of these thoughts wouldn't come back to me until I became a mother myself, but now my memory was alive. It would be like this forever, or at least until I died. Even after my father left, even after my mother went away, or I lost my entire family. Even when I grow so very old . . .

~

"Roll over or you're going to get burned!" Saseko said, shaking me out of my sleep. My eyes snapped open. I was lying on my stomach in the sand, and I felt hot tears on my cheeks.

Turning onto my side, I looked up at her and said, "Huh?"

"The sun's getting stronger. It's late afternoon, you know." Saseko grinned a painful kind of smile.

I realized she'd been planning on spending the entire day with me, since sitting at home all alone would have been boring. She'd been so nonchalant about staying with me it had taken me a while to catch on. It probably would have been okay not to notice, since my life on the island was moving by so slowly anyway.

Saipan was that sort of place, and Saseko was that kind of person.

"The men are home," she said, turning her body around and waving in the direction of the shop. Looking over, I saw Kozumi's car driving into the garage next to the sandwich shop. Ryūichirō stepped out of the car, carrying a lot of equipment. He looked almost black, and I knew he'd spent the entire day under the sun. He also seemed to be having a good time.

The sun was fading in the west, and the world turned into the same crimson as before. The ocean seemed to settle in for the long night ahead. Buzzing, the neon signs and other lights flickered on around the store.

The two were laughing as they approached. My thoughts turned to Saseko, and for a moment I thought about how pleased I was she'd found such a comfortable lifestyle. I stood up. We talked about the things we had done that day, and then we went back to the hotel to clean up and have dinner.

That was the life I was so pleased Saseko had discovered.

Chapter 13

There wasn't a breeze that night, and with the humidity we'd taken off all our clothes and sprawled ourselves naked on top of the bed. Sometime during the middle of the night the phone rang, and since we knew only one couple on the island, I knew the call must be from them. Ryūichirō probably thought the same thing. He was closest, so he grabbed the phone and said, *"Moshi, moshi."*

Without warning I had a sensation that someone else was on the line, and I watched through the darkness as Ryūichirō said, "Hang on, I'll get her." I knew it. The call was from Eiko.

Taking the phone, I put my mouth to the receiver. "Hello?"

"It's terrible." Eiko's voice came over the distant line. Ever since we'd come to the island, I had been sick with worry. After wondering whether or not she was okay for so long, it was a tremendous relief to hear her voice—a sign she was still alive.

"What are you talking about? I've been freaking out over you!" I screamed. "I was afraid if I called your house your mother would try and get some dirt out of me. What on earth happened? Was their another blowup between you and his wife?"

I heard Eiko chuckle on the other end of the line. Finally her soft voice filtered over the ocean. "I see our maid filled you in," she said. "She probably informed you that I got stabbed. I'm still in the hospital, calling you from a public phone out in the hallway. I'm really getting tired of this place. It's been awful."

"It sounds awful," I replied. "How's your boyfriend? Okay? Was he there when it happened?"

"You know about our condo, right?" Eiko said.

"Yes."

"Well, he'd gone off to work and I was in the kitchen eating breakfast. All of a sudden his wife shows up at the front door, holding a butcher knife. She rang the doorbell, and without thinking I went over and opened the door, even managing to say 'Hi' before she attacked me. I was more shocked than hurt. But the ambulance came and took me away in my bathrobe. Can you imagine? I was so embarrassed. It probably looked like a scene out of a movie—you know, me, all sexy, smeared with blood. Actually, once his wife caught sight of the gore she got nervous and started jumping around. I begged her to call an ambulance, so she did. Isn't that strange? If she cared enough to save me by making the call, wouldn't it have been easier not to stab me in the first place?"

Again I heard Eiko's laughter.

"Well, at least you're alive," I said.

"Luckily it wasn't deep. The thick cloth of my bathrobe saved me. Still, I seem to be having a run of bad luck lately."

"You sure sound calm about it."

"Sakumi, I was scared, really scared," she said. My thoughts returned to high school. Her voice had echoed to the humble voice with which I was familiar.

She continued, "I mean, think about it. Earrings, bracelets, rings—they're all made of metal, right?"

Taken aback by the unexpected question, I wondered if maybe her mother had come up behind her in the hospital. Was that the reason she'd jumped into such a different conversation? Maybe she was trying to fool someone standing next to her in the hallway.

"It's completely natural to have jewelry touching your skin, all through the day. A lot of times you don't even bother taking it off. I normally just leave it on, so I wouldn't be lying if I said my skin's used to touching metal. But when I looked down and saw that butcher knife sticking out of my bathrobe, I realized the true feeling of metal connected to skin. It hit me that bodies and metal are made up of two totally different substances. That's what went through my mind as blood gushed from my side. The knife felt like a strange, foreign object."

After hearing the intensity in her voice I was at a loss for words. Without knowing what to say, I ended up blurting out something moronic like, "It is foreign, isn't it."

"But you're the one who's been in for brain surgery!" she replied.

"Yeah, but I was passed out from the narcotics. They gave me anesthesia for weeks. But speaking of brain sickness—how are you holding out mentally? Everything okay upstairs? Have you recovered from the shock?" I asked.

"I was a bit excited and confused the day it happened, but since then it hasn't been a problem. Then again, I suppose you never know. Right now all I can think about is getting out of this place and going to Shinjuku. I have this huge craving to eat curry rice at Nakamuraya, or maybe a steak at Wadamon. Just thinking about it makes me high. I can't wait to leave. I want to relax in a long Borghese bubble bath back at home, or throw on one of my Dolce & Gabbana dresses. My mind's just filled with things I want to do. Ever since I've been here I've realized how wonderful everyday life is. Outside I feel so happy. But once I get there, I don't know what I'm going to do. The thought of going back to that same condo really terrifies me, even though I heard he's vacating the place. Then again, what will I do if I'm living in a different apartment and someone rings the doorbell when I'm home all alone? I get scared just thinking about it. Maybe it's just in my mind. I won't know what things will really be like until I'm finally out of this place."

"So have you seen him since it happened? Have you talked to him at all?"

"Only once," she replied. "On the telephone."

"How are your parents? Are they mad?"

"Are they ever! It's a blend of anger and tears. My father refuses to come to the hospital. He's what frightens me the most about leaving this place. I've no idea what's going to happen. That's why I try and look depressed when my mother comes to see me during the day. Ha, ha. I've pulled the wool over her eyes. The police have also been here. But my boyfriend won't show his face, and you're not around to come and see me, either. I'm going nuts with boredom. Hospitals are the worst!"

Thinking about how the place had practically saved her life, I started to laugh. Then I stopped and asked another question. "So what about his wife? What happened to her?"

"Sounds like she's in a hospital, too," Eiko said. "But I think it won't be long before they let her out again. What's going to happen between us? Right now I just don't care. I think I'm probably more concerned with late-night reruns of *Tokyo Love Story*."

"Just consider your time there a short vacation. Once you're finished I'm sure you're going to have to face the music, so just relax while you can," I said.

"Sounds like homework over summer vacation," Eiko replied. Then she paused for a moment and said, "Sakumi, I do want to tell you something. While I was waiting for the ambulance to arrive, all I could think about was you and my boyfriend. For some reason your face popped into my head and stayed there." I heard her chuckling again. "Shows you how many friends I've got in this world!"

I chose not to say anything about how she'd come into my mind on the airplane as well, or about how I, half dead, probably sent my image to her that day. That was all.

"When you get back to Japan I'm sure I'll be out of the hospital," Eiko said. "Give me a call. Most likely I'll just be rotting away at home." She hung up.

I passed the phone to Ryūichirō.

"Sounds like she's okay," he said. "That's nice." There was nothing more to his comment and nothing less . . . or so I felt as I listened to his bland remark. I looked down at the wrinkles in the sheet, which had picked up the trace of his shoulder and the warmth of his body, his chest rising and falling as he breathed. . . .

. . . everything seemed in contradiction.

How should I take such a comment?

He was so healthy and alive, along with everyone else who took their lives for granted.

Feeling the air in the room, my mind started to sail with the smell of salt, and the sea that spread widely over the base of our window. I thought of the sea cucumbers out on the beach getting washed by the tide coming in and going out under the dim light of the moon. Cold slime and thick blackness.

Stars burned brightly against the dark sky. The palm trees swayed gently, surrounded by fresh oxygen. I strained my ears so I could hear night unfold. I wanted to savor the gentleness.

People draw closer together, reaching out to touch another body made of their own genetic material, snuggling next to a universe of the same chemical compounds.

Heavy breathing, snoring, teeth grinding, and talk going on in our sleep. Eyebrows and fingernails growing; tears and mucus bubbling up from within. Boils and blisters forming on our noses and legs, popping and fading away. We take in liquids and expel them; the process everlasting. It continues on, flowing through our bodies, never stopping, never coming to an end.

One thing was for certain—that flowing was a part of me now.

I could feel my heart pumping. The pounding, the pulsating. It created a perfect rhythm in the darkness—my own heart audible in my own ears.

I turned to Ryūichirō and said, "Tell me something. How can Kozumi look out at the ocean and see danger in somebody's life, even though he's never seen her, or been introduced before?"

"I don't know," Ryūichirō replied. "But haven't you ever heard that if you have a desire to know something, you can, as long as you want to badly enough?"

His comment sounded like something from a bad poetry recitation.

"What do you mean?" I asked.

"Let's suppose there are people with special powers—famous or not," Ryūichirō replied. "Apparently we'd be surprised if we could see how many there are. It's like they just pop up naturally. When I think back to the time when I was in India and Tibet, I can certainly recall people who'd attest to that. There were some amazing individuals who could predict almost anything. But aren't there amazing people in all walks of life—people who go out for adventure, those who sit home behind a desk? They seem to be wanted by everybody, the rest of us never come to mind. When you think about humanity, in all its various forms, you can't help but be impressed. But most inspiring are those who've found a way to balance everyday life along with their amazing talents. I really have to wonder about people like that, eating and sleeping every day, just like you and me."

"Of course they're just like you and me," I said. "After all, they're only human."

"Still gives me the creeps."

"Are you writing another novel?" I asked.

"Don't be rude. You know I'm gathering stuff to put in my next book."

"But what's stopping you? Why don't you take what material you have and get going? I'm sure your readers are out there waiting."

"The best reason not to write," he said.

"So who do you like? Name your favorite author."

"Every time I go off on another trip I ask myself the same question. It sort of turns into a problem. I mean, I can't take my entire library with me each time I leave. In the end I always grab Truman Capote's *Music for Chameleons*, so I suppose that means I like him. The book's not even in paperback yet. I take this damn hardback novel with me wherever I go and leave it next to my pillow when I get there. Even though I must have read it a dozen times, I still find myself flipping through the pages."

"Do you mind if I take a look?" I asked.

"No. I've even got it with me now," Ryūichirō responded. He reached under his pillow and took out a thick hardcover book and handed it to me. In the darkness I could see the spotted cover and yellow pages. I knew in an instant this book was still very much alive.

"Writers are such happy people, aren't they?" I said.

"Wouldn't it be nice to be living proof of that," Ryūichirō said. "One thing's for certain. I bet the author of that book never imagined his work would support an unknown Japanese man on his journeys."

"I'm sure you're right about that."

"Do you like my novel?" Ryūichirō asked.

"Yes," I said. "I do like your novel, although it's really dark."

"Really?" He paused for a moment. "Anything else?"

"No, that's it," I said laughing. I figure my reaction told him a lot more than my words ever could. He laughed along with me. The atmosphere in the room that night was perfect for the wonderful mood of our conversation. We were both there, but I felt more freedom than I would have felt if I'd been alone. My heart felt full of energy. Aside from our words, everything seemed fresh and rounded like a new fragrance. We were sleeping under a dome of silence and forgiveness. I felt engulfed by the cool air.

Still conscious for a few minutes after I heard Ryūichirō fall off to sleep, I turned into a puppy whose master has placed a wristwatch around her collar so she can sleep well that night. The sound of Ryūichirō's breathing created a rhythm in the room, a soft lullaby. It was not long before his song surrounded me and I drifted quickly off to sleep.

∾

Life easily falls into routine.

Regardless of where I am in the world, as long as I sleep and eat in one place, I consider it home, and that's the fundamental rule. Even though I'd been taken from my familiar surroundings to a place where I saw and heard only English, even though the beach seemed so lonely at night, even though every piece of clothing they sold in the stores seemed so coarse and unrefined, there wasn't an easier place to live than the island, regardless of the stifled sensation on the beach from those left behind during the war. I felt them in a sharp pain that entered my head for a split second every morning, making me see crookedly. I sensed them in the middle of the night when every so often nightmares rumbled through my mind. I could hear them the loudest when I closed my eyes on that barren beach shining brightly in the sun. The voices of millions crying out to me.

Yes, even their cries were a part of the routine.

Despite the energy piled up in my heart from all the deaths I'd seen, I still craved to cuddle up like the sea cucumbers and fall fast asleep in the midmorning sun, but maybe it was that same energy that often got in my way. Even though I was a native Japanese, and those were my ancestors calling, there was nothing I could do for them.

~

"You can't do anything for the dead, unless you're like Saseko and make a living holding memorial services," Kozumi said. "It's cruel to listen to them and then not do anything about it. That's why it's best to stop listening."

I nodded, and he smiled and continued, "Apparently it was hard for Ryūichirō when he first came here, too. He's such a nice person, just wanting to listen. But then it made him sick. Now it seems he's caught on. It's perfectly up to you to decide if you believe in spirits or not, or to take any interest in them at all. Still, there are places on earth where there is so much power radiating from the living dead that only professionals, people skilled at controlling such energy, can survive. That's the only thing I'm certain of. You've felt it too, haven't you, Sakumi?"

"Yes," I said. "Ever since that first trip through the jungle I've had a funny feeling in my chest."

Saseko had her songs. Kozumi could summon his brother. They paid respect to the spirits by holding memorial services. This might be offensive to the ghosts, but I couldn't help but compare them to two people collecting empty soda cans at a resort spot after the season has ended. The task was endless, the location barren. Occasionally when I'd see Kozumi and his wife, I'd bring a retired couple to mind, their efforts seemed that devoid of life. They'd left their country to spend their lives gazing out over the sea. Even though they were still young, their youthful vitality was gone.

What an unusual existence.

The next day I resolved to sit in front of Kozumi's shop facing the beach and read the book Ryūichirō had loaned me. I also did my fair share of sleeping. In the afternoon when the sun was hottest, I read under the shade of a parasol. But once again I was troubled. The sunlight danced from one spot to the next and I watched the reflection of the sun's rays change with the color of the ocean.

The shop was full of people. When I asked the Japanese man who I thought looked so right for the island if he had time to go diving, he grumbled and said no, sliding me a lukewarm beer from behind the counter. The commotion of bustling people and blaring music from the shop restored life to a spot on the beach that seemed dark somehow, even though everything was so bright.

Wouldn't it be nice to stay on the island always—in a rhythm so easily melted into . . .

. . . or so the thought crossed my mind.

I couldn't write novels or call ghosts in from the sea. It was just me; I was the only one living that way. Nature on the island seemed to share my burden with me. I just kept telling myself it was helping me because I was there, doing what I was doing.

Eventually Ryūichirō returned from diving and collecting information for his book. I didn't always stay at the hotel, I'd go out with him once every three times he'd go. Had I prolonged my stay I would have thought about getting a license to dive. Whenever I felt like not going, Ryūichirō grabbed Kozumi or some locals.

The sun was so low in the west and everything was getting dark so quickly that I couldn't read my book anymore. Ryūichirō came walking up from the beach, burnt by the sun. I noticed he'd already taken a shower and changed clothes. He looked at me and smiled.

An image of my lover against a golden ocean and a western sun.

I stood up, shaking sand from my body, asking him about dinner that night. I could never have experienced such a simple thing back in my native Japan.

For an instant I wondered if my brother was watching over me and feeling my thoughts—my brother, so excited to go fishing back in Kochi, going to bed so early and getting up so early, his childlike arms and legs.

"Saseko said she's having us over to their place for supper tonight," Ryūichirō said.

∾

Kozumi and his wife lived in a spacious one-bedroom apartment on the second floor of their sandwich shop. The interior was decorated in lively oranges, perfect for a house in the southern islands. Even though everything was nicely organized, the decorations were simple, and in the center of the room was a humongous TV.

Dinner was delicious, but right after we'd cleared the table I started to feel a sharp pain through my forehead as if a fever was coming on. I walked over to the sofa and collapsed.

"It has nothing to do with dinner," I quickly said as I wrapped my arms around my head. "Everything was absolutely wonderful."

As I toppled over Ryūichirō's face grew pale, and Kozumi rushed into the kitchen to prepare an ice pack for my head. Saseko came over to the couch and held my head on her soft breast, singing a soft lullaby, but it didn't work this time. My head just continued to pound.

"This happens every now and then. Before you know it, it comes on really strong," Saseko said as she gave me some medicine. "Here, take this and go lie down on our bed."

"No," I said, objecting. "I think I'd rather go home. We're just down the street. . . ." Even though I tried to convince them I should leave, Kozumi and his wife wouldn't hear of it. They took me to their bed saying I could stay there as long as I needed, because the shop was closed the next day. I collapsed on their Western-style double bed. It didn't take long for the foreign aspirin Saseko had given me to completely knock me out. I remembered glancing over at the clock, despite my dizziness, to see that it was eight o'clock. That much I remembered.

I was taken aback when my eyes popped open, like someone had just flipped on the light. Looking over at the clock, I saw it was almost eleven. I'd been asleep for almost three hours. I turned my head to one side, trying to get the kinks out of my neck. Even though I'd only slept that short while, my headache was gone, along with the fever.

Saipan was bizarre.

The bedroom door had been cracked open, and I heard laughter and sounds from the TV. I looked out the window and saw a line of white chairs in front of the closed shop below facing the dark ocean.

Listening to the others laugh in the other room brought a peacefulness to me, rather than making me feel alienated from them. I didn't feel alone. It reminded me of catching a cold when I was little. Even then the sound of laughter gave me a reason to be happy.

I loved Saseko's kindness. It seemed so natural.

I don't know if she was able to be that considerate of others because she'd received so much unkindness in her life, or the other way around. Perhaps she'd been treated so poorly all she could do was be kindhearted. Regardless of where it came from, it was a selfless love, free to all.

After pulling myself out of the bed, I stumbled to the door.

Saseko saw me first.

"Oh, look. Sakumi's up," she said.

"How about some coffee?" Kozumi asked as he stood and walked into the kitchen.

"Are you all right?" Ryūichirō asked.

They were all sitting comfortably in their chairs, smiling as if they'd been having a good time. As I wondered if I had died and gone to heaven, I jokingly answered, "Maybe I should hang out with ghosts more often, if this is the way I get pampered."

Was the pain in my heart an endemic disease, something that would leave me once I was away from the island?

I took a bit of some cake Saseko had baked, letting it slide into my mouth. The aspirin was still in effect, so everything seemed cloudy. I recalled a lingering melody that had apparently come from the hard-rock MTV that the others had been watching in the living room.

"Is this a special version of MTV?" I asked.

Kozumi got excited. "Yes! That's exactly what it is. There isn't anything like it back in Japan. There's only hard rock on this channel—all day long. It's great!" He was so enthusiastic all I could do was comment on how much he seemed to like the music. "I just flip out over it!" he replied.

What a shock. I wouldn't have guessed someone as gentle as Kozumi could be so into that sort of music.

Saseko turned to me and said, "I didn't care for hard rock either. But ever since I moved in with Kozumi I've gotten to know a lot more about it."

"Where else would he get his energy?" Ryūichirō asked.

"You mean you've known about this hard-rock thing, too?" I asked, surprised to see I was the only one who didn't know. "I mean, when you look at his clothes and the way he acts, he looks so quiet and reserved."

"Of course I knew," Ryūichirō replied. "Every time we go out he has hard rock blaring from his car stereo, and he sleeps in a black Metallica T-shirt. I've labeled him 'The Hard Rock Closet Junky.'"

"You never know about a person, do you," I said. So that was it, the one thing that brought happiness to a man who'd lost his family and run away to Saipan, the support of Kozumi's soul as he operated a busy store in this land full of spirits.

I'm not exaggerating. I'd never seen Kozumi so happy. After asking him only one simple question, he went off on a crusade to convince me of the intricacies of the music. He discussed things with so much vitality he reminded me of a mother bragging about her daughter. Harsh vocals poured from the TV set as blond guitarists went crazy on the stage, screaming out muddled lyrics. Thinking of her husband, Saseko turned up the volume, and soon the room felt like a convention of hard-rock zealots. Kozumi talked on about how one player had actually been in a different band, but this and that happened, and now he was with the other, so that's why the lyrics say this and that—and so on. He looked delighted as he drank, watched, and listened to the music.

Basically I'd been brought up with the music that we played back at Berries, a sort of sixties reggae, so I couldn't say I was familiar with this genre. For some reason, however, I wasn't opposed to hearing the hard rock that night, nor was I upset over Kozumi's explanations. I suppose my forgiveness came from the fact that I could see Kozumi honestly loved what we were listening to.

"I remember when this song was popular. We'd just heard it, and we liked it so much we hopped on a plane and went to the mainland for the concert, didn't we?" Saseko joined Kozumi's conversation.

"Yeah, and you taped over the video we took there—just one more reason we got into a fight."

"They've come out with three songs since then."

A history of a couple depicted through song.

When I look at a man and a women I'd much rather see them lined up together looking out into the world than see them staring romantically into each other's eyes. It doesn't matter if they're watching their children, or a movie, or the view outside a window, as long as both of them are calm and happy. I love to see their support.

Great White. Thin Lizzy. Tesla. Iron Maiden. Quiet Riot. AC/DC. Motley Crüe. The names passed me by like the words I'd heard in chants or spells, but I knew they had quietly saved the two sitting near me, just as Capote's novel rescued Ryūichirō on nights he couldn't sleep. They brought support to the lives of people who never clued in to what they were there for. Such trifling little things, but so needed.

You would never think of them as "presents," but maybe they were.

"It must be nice to have something you can really sink your teeth into," I said.

"I really get into it," Kozumi said with a smile. His humility must also have been a guiding force in his life.

More and more thoughts just came into my head.

At that moment Saseko suddenly got a stiff expression on her face, and Ryūichirō said, "What the . . ." Both of them glanced at the doorway in front of the stairs. Startled by their sudden reactions, Kozumi and I followed suit.

It was my kid brother.

My brother—Yoshio—was standing in the room.

He wore blue pajamas and his eyes looked distant, although there was something warm about his face, and he carried with him a tranquil mood from beyond this world. When I saw the stare in my brother's eyes, I recalled how my sister Mayu looked in her coffin.

He gazed slowly about the room and then moved in our direction.

I opened my mouth. "Yoshio?" But he acted as if he couldn't hear me. He continued walking past us as he moved closer to the balcony. At the precise moment he was surrounded by palm trees and buildings and the starry night sky coming in the window, he faded away.

I realized then that it couldn't have been Yoshio in the flesh.

"A living spirit," Saseko said. "And so vivid. Who was that?"

Turning to me, Kozumi muttered, "It was your brother, wasn't it?"

I slowly nodded my head.

"Why don't you give him a call?" Ryūichirō suggested, the color drained from his face.

"I will." I hurried over to the phone and dialed.

My mother picked up the phone. "Oh, Sakumi, how nice to hear from you. How are things in Saipan?"

"Just fine, Mother," I said quickly. "Where's Yoshio?"

"He's upstairs," she replied. "Do you want me to get him?"

"Please."

"Hold on."

I heard her press the pause button as she set the phone down. The background music that filtered over the line only increased my anxiety. After a few seconds I heard the rustle of someone picking up the phone, and I heard my mother's voice again.

"I'm sorry, but he's fast asleep. He doesn't want to get up."

"Are you sure he's asleep, and not dead?" I asked.

"Not unless his corpse has found some way to snore. But to look at that child sleeping you'd think he is dead." My mother laughed and I let out a sigh of relief.

"Well, tell him I'll call back later. By the way, how are things at home?"

"Nothing has changed, dear. Mikiko caught a cold and was laid up in bed for a week, but other than that nothing's new. A boy from school came over to see her while she was sick and we all got a good look at him."

The scent of my house came over the phone as I talked to my mother that night. It was a strong fragrance, something that would surely disappear once my mother was gone, a smell unique to our home alone, something so natural that none of us ever picked up on it during our everyday lives.

Mother continued, "He was very attractive, the young man who came to see Mikiko."

"I wish I could have seen him," I said.

"Well, it looks like they're an item."

After a few more minutes of idle gossip, I said good-bye and hung up the phone.

"He's fine," I said. The other three had listened intently to the conversation. "Mom says he's asleep in bed. I wonder if he had a dream about Saipan. My brother's a little strange that way."

It felt awkward talking about my supernatural sibling in a room full of experts.

"Wonderful! He has special powers, doesn't he?" Kozumi said. "You've been followed around by ghosts since you got here. Chances are you've been sending him messages with your mind, so he showed up to see how you are."

"He came all this way just for me?" I said in a loud voice. "That's so sweet."

Everything was so exciting. I felt like I was in the middle of a psychic horror novel.

Kozumi continued, "That's why he won't wake up. He's exhausted from the journey. It really takes a lot out of you to appear in spirit form as strongly as he did."

Still stunned, Ryūichirō shook his head. "I've never seen anything like that."

I was delighted. I mean, I'd seen my brother and I hadn't been drunk or stoned, nor had I been alone when it happened. For that single moment we'd witnessed him, we'd all come together. It wasn't a curse or spell, not even a song. It was simply knowing my brother cared about me, and he'd come from Japan to let me know, his intentions shining through his clear and rigid expression.

"But it must be tough for a kid his age to have so much power. Almost too tough, I imagine. How old is he, anyway?" Kozumi asked.

"Eleven, I think."

"When someone's able to realize that kind of power as a child—unlike so many other stories you hear about people developing it later—that means he's somehow managed to sharpen his senses and establish a remarkable balance. Wouldn't it be wonderful if his initial power wasn't necessary for him to progress, but that's not often the case. I have a feeling he's still too young to control it, at least not right now anyway," Kozumi said.

"Well, I think your brother's adorable," Saseko said. "He's going to be so handsome when he grows up."

Everyone was so calm, acting as though we were cooing over a picture of Yoshio. I felt saved. Ordinarily if something like that happened most people would be hysterical. I suppose I was in the right place at the right time to experience such an amazing thing. Then it occurred to me how comfortable my brother would be here, with no need to shrivel up like he always did back home. I think Ryūichirō could see what I was thinking.

"Why don't you get him to come down?" he said. "Even if you have to force him onto the plane."

I nodded enthusiastically. "That would be nice, and it would only have to be for three or four days."

It would be a difficult thing to do, but not impossible.

Kozumi and Saseko lent me their full support. "We'd love to meet him," they said.

~

Another phone call came that night.

Ryūichirō and I were back in our hotel room, but due to my nap a few hours before, I couldn't go back to sleep. Instead I was sitting in a lounge chair reading under a single light. Ryūichirō was in bed, and I could hear him snoring.

It didn't take long for me to pick up the receiver.

"Moshi, moshi." It was my brother.

"Yoshio? You're awake? How are you? Do you feel okay?"

"Okay, I guess. But it's sort of boring around here without you." It sounded like he was whispering.

"Is everyone asleep?"

"Yeah," he said. "It was a good thing you showed me how to call Saipan. Actually, I had to call you because I had a crazy dream and you were in it. You were surrounded by a bunch of men in soldier uniforms. I tried to reach out and pull you away from them, but then this loud, blaring music came from the walls, and I saw you in a different room sitting with three other people. Ryūichirō was there with a woman and a strange-looking white guy. Am I right?"

"You came to Saipan," I replied. "We saw you walking across the carpet in your pajamas."

"Travel with me and you don't need money for a plane ticket!" My brother started laughing. "But I really couldn't make out what was in the room." He must have been able to see only certain things.

"Why don't you come down here?" I asked, totally serious about having him come.

"No way," he said. "I can't do it."

"Let's talk to Mom about it. It would be so much fun."

My brother was silent for a moment. He was calm, but he didn't sound like he was pleased. I don't think his disposition had anything to do with the activity he'd experienced in his dream. The vitality he'd gained on our trip to Kochi had all but vanished, or at least I figured out that much over the phone.

"Think about it," I said. "You want to come, don't you? Please be honest."

"I'm worried that Mom will . . ."

"Don't worry about her," I stated.

"Umm . . . Okay. I'll think about it," Yoshio said.

"I bet you'd enjoy Saipan a lot more once you get on a plane and come to see it in person. It's always best to smell the ocean with your own nose."

"I really want to leave."

For a split second I thought he said, "I really want to live." There was a sincere echo in his voice.

"So don't worry about Mother. I'll take care of everything. Why don't you try staying in bed for a couple of days. Just tell Mom you're not feeling well. I think that will help us convince her to let you come."

"Gotcha," my brother said. Now I could hear excitement in his voice.

After hanging up the phone I knew I shouldn't have been so concerned with romance. It would have been best to have just brought him with us from the beginning. I would be lying, though, if I said I hadn't longed for a chance to be with Ryūichirō alone, without my brother.

There was one thing about my brother that I knew the others weren't aware of.

When my brother was a baby he had a habit of walking purposefully through the living room as we sat around in a group watching TV. He did it whenever he needed help or he wanted to attract our attention. After passing us, he'd walk out onto the balcony.

That night I knew exactly what his spirit was trying to tell me.

Chapter 14

Lately I'd found myself thinking a lot about cycles.

While traveling with Ryūichirō in the car on the way to pick up Yoshio at the airport, I let the warm air from the open window fly through my hair. The thick foliage covering every inch of the island murmured softly in the wind and the sky above me was so blue it was frightening. As I sensed all these things with my ears and my eyes, the same thoughts kept running through my head.

We stopped the car along the wide road next to the airport, just like Saseko had done for us at some point in the past. When I got out of the car I felt my skirt moved by the wind and I gazed up into the blazing sky. Suddenly my thoughts formed a beautiful conviction that rang in my mind like the melody from a music box.

I believe in cycles. People associated with religion would probably label them karma, but I choose not to call them anything but what they are—simple and ordinary. Nothing more.

Take, for example, me and my brother. We flew off to Kochi and had a glorious time. Our trip was a seed planted in my heart, something that eventually grew into my trip to Saipan. Now the seed was bearing fruit, and my brother was on his way to partake of it with me. The only thing that had changed was the scenery, and it had grown much larger. I was sure my brother was on the plane looking forward to the same happiness we realized on Shikoku.

Basically everything is the same, everything follows a pattern. A seed is planted and a bud starts to grow. Eventually a fruit is

born. There are reasons and results. It doesn't matter how trifling they might be. Something is invited, and something is achieved.

But I was beginning to understand that this cycle had brought a different change in me, as if a distinct seed had found its way into my heart. At some point in time I'd been pushed so far away that I would never go back, never return to the reality that existed before hitting my head, despite my longing for a chance to make a reconciliation with the "me" that existed so long ago. I'd love to meet her and shake her hand. I would give anything to go back in time and understand the life that she led.

But then would I be lying?

Ever since coming to the island I realized that something inside me was, without question, out of place. Over the course of a few weeks that confirmation grew stronger by the day as I took in air almost too painful to breathe and recalled sights so nostalgic my chest started to ache. I knew returning would be impossible.

By now I'd been pushed too far into my own revolutions, and I would not be allowed to go back and do things over again. Cells containing my expectations for what lay ahead in my unknown future rotted away in my heart like some evil form of cancer.

I would never return.

My newfound knowledge didn't excite me, nor did it make me depressed. I was satisfied being alive, here and now, melting into my own existence and the scenery that came with it.

I found myself dancing through life as if it was the most natural thing in the world. Nothing more.

"I think his plane's here," Ryūichirō said.

Leaving him with the car, I went inside the airport and made my way to the immigration counter. My brother came out of the gate, and I couldn't help but smile when I saw his small frame carrying such an enormous suitcase. A wide grin spread across his face and I knew he was delighted. He was also pale—paler than most people I'd seen living on the island.

So overjoyed I could hardly contain myself, I waved my hand frantically in his direction.

~

The task of bringing Yoshio to the island had been both easy and difficult.

When I suggested the idea to my mother over the phone she told me to wait and she would think about it. Then, after pausing for a minute, she said, "Fine." I was startled to see her give in so easily. Next there was the school issue—convincing his teachers to let him out of class. A further challenge was getting Yoshio to ride on the plane by himself. But in the end, Junko was the biggest obstacle of all, even though I tried to convince her that someone would practically be with him every step of the way. We'd leave the island together, I'd get him home as soon as possible, and so on. Still, Junko never relented. I ended up making numerous phone calls home and there was quite a bit of heated discussion over the issue.

Ultimately, the deciding factor was Yoshio himself, pretending like he didn't want to stir up a lot of commotion. Like an obedient little sheep he calmly shed a few tears, and showed his enthusiasm by telling everyone through his sniffles, "I'd really like to go."

~

Yoshio's first words to his older sister were simple: "Saku-chan, you're so black you look like you're from a different country!" As we left the airport he made several comments about how hot it was on the island, and once we got outside he planted his feet in the ground and took a deep breath of air, as if he were smelling a flower.

Ryūichirō was leaning against the side of the car, where he'd been waiting. When he saw Yoshio, he smiled and waved.

"Ryu-chan, it's been a long time!" my brother yelled, flinging himself at Ryūichirō. Within moments his luggage was in the trunk. It was already fun having him with us on the island.

As we traveled down the highway my brother leaned over to me and said, "The air seems stuffy here, like there's a whole bunch of people around. Wait a minute. Are they ghosts? Are spirits living on this island?" Yoshio shuffled in his seat. I noted that it was exactly in the same spot of the jungle where I'd first felt a tightening in my throat when we drove in.

"Don't worry," I said, comforting Yoshio. "It only takes a little while to get used to them."

Next Ryūichirō looked back and said, "You're not here to work, so leave the spirits and ghosts up to the professionals. While you're here your only assignment is to act like an ordinary kid on vacation."

A huge grin came over his face and he yelled, "You've got it, Ryu-chan!"

~

Precisely at that moment the thought of returning to Japan came over me, and it brought with it heartrending anguish. I couldn't stand to think about leaving all the things that mirrored my eyes on the island—our room at the hotel, the wetsuits hanging like dry squid on the balcony, the loud sound of the radio coming from Kozumi's shop, white chairs aligned on the beach, the ocean and palm trees, people scorched by the sun, the neighborhood dog, blasting wind from the air conditioner, and the small red baskets we shopped with at the market.

Everything.

Even though Ryūichirō and I'd been on the island only for a short while, I felt as though I'd been there for years.

I woke up every morning and went to the beach for a swim. Then I had a sandwich, threw in a load of laundry, and headed off to town. At night the same crimson sun cast golden shadows all around and I would lay my tired head on my pillow amid the somber breeze blowing in from the window.

Glancing quickly out over the ocean, everything seemed to be washed over in orange. I'd hold up my nightly glass of beer and pay respect to its beauty. Then I'd head off for a shower.

Occasionally Ryūichirō and I would go out for dinner, strolling along the paths on the beach on our way home. Once we got back we'd watch some TV and fall fast asleep.

Daily life was filled with dozens of special things. It felt like a faraway dream.

So simple it felt foolish.

So cursed it was beautiful.

~

Not long before we returned to Japan, Ryūichirō said he'd like to take me for a drive. Kozumi and Saseko had fallen head over heels for my brother, and they had invited him on a date to the city, souvenir shopping. In other words, they were kind enough to babysit for a while.

With Yoshio out of the picture, Ryūichirō and I found ourselves free to go off on our own.

"Let's go somewhere," he said.

"How about the botanical gardens?" I suggested. "We could eat lunch there." The gardens covered a large portion of the upper north end of the island. I'd been there once with Saseko, and we'd each washed down a tall cup of freshly squeezed juice at the small stand near the park.

"Sounds good," Ryūichirō said, putting his foot on the accelerator. We took off.

The wide road shimmered in its own whiteness. There were hardly any other cars on the small highway, and the dense trees that covered both sides of the road quickly passed us by. Every so often I'd get a glance through the forest at the sparkling ocean beside us. The chaos caused by the faraway light seemed to go on forever amid the waters.

I left the window open and my cheeks and hair were blown by the wind. It was almost difficult to breathe . . .

. . . the salty fragrance of the water, dust stirred up from the road, pure white buildings. Colorful patterns on clothing and the peaceful tempo of the people coming and going on the road. Cars speeding by—whizzing by us in just a fraction of a second.

I felt like turning to Ryūichirō and saying, "Stop driving so fast, you're going to get us killed," but I knew my words would only get chopped by the wind, so I gave up the idea completely.

He took his driving seriously, and as we moved forward he wouldn't take his eyes off the road. The landscape around us seemed distant anyway—almost as if it was reflected in its own freshness.

Then the idea came back strongly in my mind. It happened amid the scenery, as though I were the center of the world and all was revolving around me. A feeling so sharp that it caused me to ache.

Oh, yes. At some point in time Ryūichirō and I will have to leave this earth.

Cycles never change. One day our bodies turn to bones which eventually turn back into dust. Then we melt in the air, and become vapors covering the earth in an atmospheric dome. All are connected—Japan, along with China. Italy would be there too. Everything and everyone together in the air. A time will come when I become a part of the wind blowing around in endless circles. The arms and legs that I see below me will one day dissolve into thin air.

It will happen to all of us eventually, each and every one.

Like my father.

And Mayu.

Every living creature on this earth.

What will happen to us then? What great things await us?

How wonderful it will be, leaving this body so limited in comprehension and moving into a permanence of complete perception. The impression of that image was so strong it left tears in my eyes.

Speed never forgives injury. In the air, however, wounds will dry up, and at some point dissipate into the running continuum of time.

Tears will dry up, too.

~

After hiking through the low-lying hibiscus flowers that grew along both sides of the path, we came out on the top of a tall hill overlooking the whole area. Eventually we plopped down on the grassy lawn, deciding that was where we'd have our picnic. We had brought the sandwiches and juice along. Now everything was picture-perfect.

The trees and bushes flourishing before us were so thick I couldn't imagine what disaster would befall anyone who would try to explore their inner depths. Nature went on forever—so green the sky looked like it was melting into it. From where we sat on the hill we could practically see the entire island around us, a view clear enough to see the wind blowing in the distant city, and the jungle which continued endlessly in between.

Ryūichirō started speaking. "I'm glad you brought Yoshio here. He seems to be having a good time."

"I think it's wonderful that he's having a chance to see so many different places at such a young age," I said. "He got to ride on the airplane by himself, and when he goes into the city he gets a chance to talk to people in another language. I think it's particularly good for children like Yoshio who have a lot going on in their minds. He'll probably gain a lot of confidence through it all."

"You're right," Ryūichirō replied. "I mean, look at me. I didn't start doing things like that until after I was grown. It makes me seem wretched, like some kind of worthless slug. It's good to try things out, but don't get me wrong, I'm not talking about things that inflict pain. I just think it's good to have your luggage stolen every once in a while. What would you do if your passport was inside? Say you don't have lodging for a night. You're renting an apartment and you don't have hot water so you have to go and talk to your landlord, but the guy doesn't speak Japanese. Those experiences build character. When faced with the challenge, you're struck with the feeling of conquering the world. You feel like you can do anything, like a new seed has sprung up inside you. You aren't afraid of things you can't do, like speaking a different language. Your little comfort zone breaks down, and you begin to think before you act so you won't wind up doing something foolish. You stop panicking as much. It's a good thing. And think, it's happening to Yoshio at his age."

"Yes, I know," I said.

Delicious sandwiches made by a friend, the sweet, natural juice; a sky so blue it looked like it would come down and meet me, even though it was so close and pure I felt like I could reach out and touch it as it quietly covered our heads, extending out into neverending distances; sweet clouds, flowing and fading away.

From where we sat I caught a small trace of the ocean.

As I looked down I saw the landscape spread out before my eyes like piles of beans, endlessly changing from foliage to town, controlling spirits, people, forests, and oceans, exposing without regret everything that created balance on the island. The brilliant blue of the sky seemed to mesh with it all, adding a bright touch of sweetness.

"The sky's amazing, isn't it?" I said, straining my neck so far back it hurt.

"Wow. You're right," Ryūichirō said. "I could stare off into it for hours."

The two of us grew silent.

Then I remembered Mayu, and I bet Ryūichirō did the same. I'm not sure why, but talking about my brother and looking into a sky like that brought back a flood of memories about Mayu, my sister, who had actually been between me and Ryūichirō. Something about her was identical to the landscape in front of me. I'm surprised I hadn't made the connection earlier.

White teeth like pearls. Those small hands she was born with.

The way her shoulders hunched over as she sunk her teeth into a slice of dripping watermelon.

Curled-up toes. The pedicure on the foot she took out of its shoe.

The brown color of her hair piled high on her head.

Everything.

She loved sunny days. In her small apartment she was always concerned with where the light was shining. Her smile, that never-ending soft, sweet smile, and her voice which rang through the air like a bell, the highest and most refined of its kind.

All the images of my little sister came into my mind with such force that I was frightened. I longed to be with her, to be back with her. My response was so strong that it tormented me to the point where I could hardly contain myself.

I felt strange. I'd longed for my sister before, but this was the first time those emotions had come over me so profoundly, under a foreign sky. Something else must have provoked my vexation over my sister, the one who'd felt privileged enough to just go off and die of her own free will.

Somewhere in my heart I felt hated.

Somewhere in my heart I had been betrayed.

~

The next day while the men were out diving, I watched Marilyn Monroe's final film on video with Saseko. It was a comedy the actress never finished, and it reminded me a lot of shows with bloopers you see on TV.

The actress was beautiful, soft, and brilliant. It felt curious watching her laughing, so full of life in front of the camera, and knowing that it would be only days before she'd no longer be alive. I think anyone watching the cheerful film would have thought the same thing. She wrapped her arms around her dripping wet children coming up from the pool. Without thinking, she grinned at a dog who couldn't perform her tricks well. She swam naked in the pool. And she released such a natural glow that no one looking at her would have guessed how tipsy she really was, smothered in her drugs and alcohol.

But there was some kind of divergence. She seemed to melt, bathed in the white light, an enigmatic ray of light that looked as though it would vanish. She was too beautiful, and even though she could attract the attention of all who saw her, she emanated that thin, pale light.

After we finished watching the movie I felt as if I'd been taken by it somehow, and I pondered my reaction for a while.

Only after I'd gone to sleep that night did I receive a clear understanding of my feelings. She was Mayu. The same thing had happened to my sister. She acted just like Marilyn in the final few years of her life—looking as though she'd melt into clear sky, bright air, and fading sunsets. With no life or energy to her existence, she managed to radiate a Marilyn kind of glow. People saw her only as a person who had skillfully absorbed her surroundings.

So that's what plagued my mind as I viewed the film with Saseko. Had they done the same drugs, or was it due to the fact that they both faced death when it happened?

Who knows? Maybe it was a combination of both.

~

Mayu.

Was it true, was she really not around? Couldn't there be a place out there, somewhere in the world, where she would be?

Even with the sky so blue and the shadows so dark, even though it was so clear that everything in the world was amazing and frightening, was it true? Was she really gone?

The one who'd lost her talent to feel.

Mayu.

~

"Welcome home!"

Yoshio came rushing up to us from the beach like a little puppy. Then he whispered, "So did you get a chance to talk?"

"No, not really," I replied. "But we had a nice conversation about things that go wrong on trips."

"But did it feel like you were on a date?" my brother asked.

"What are you talking about? Is this jealousy that I see? Are you mad that I'm spending time with him, or are you really concerned about how we're getting along?"

"You know I'm concerned about you," my brother replied.

We sat together outside the sandwich shop. Droplets of water dripped off my brother's hair. He'd just come from swimming in the ocean spread out in front of us. In the back Saseko was piling slices of watermelon onto a large plate. I watched her approach with the platter in her hands.

How is it she always managed to smile so much during times like that?

Perhaps it made the watermelon she had in one arm look tastier. I felt happier, like I'd just seen an old movie filmed in the South Pacific.

I really loved Saseko. I admired her and her talents, so much that it hurt. My feelings tugged at my heart.

"Here's some watermelon, on the house," she said. "I've still got a bunch of things to do in the back, so the two of you just relax and sit here." Leaving the plate, she went back into the store.

"Where's Ryu-chan?" Yoshio asked.

"He went to put gas in the car," I replied. "He'll be back in a minute. Stop worrying about him so much, you sound like a fool."

"But if I wasn't here you wouldn't want to leave, right?"

Again my brother managed to say the one thing that went straight to my heart.

"You don't have to worry about me, little brother. I'll worry about myself," I said with a smile. "Just tell me what you're feeling. Do you want to go home?"

"No," my brother said. "What's wrong with me staying here forever? I could just live here and work at Kozumi's shop."

Such an earnest desire; I couldn't help but be touched.

"You know that's impossible, don't you? You understand that, right?"

"Yes, I do," he said with a firm nod.

"It's the same for me as for you," I said. "I mean, I would love to stay here. But when I think about all the places we haven't visited and all the things in the world still left to see, not to mention all the people we haven't met yet—I know it's wrong to just get up and run away. I mean, think about it, Saipan's so close we could just come back anytime."

Yoshio thought for a moment and then said, "Yeah, I guess you're right. The things going on in my head don't really matter at all, even if I have seen them. I'm still a kid, and maybe it would be best to push them aside and get on with life. From here on out, lots of things are bound to happen. Pretty soon Mom'll be married and our house will change, too. We won't be able to go on living like we always have." Yoshio spoke so seriously about his life that I began to confuse him with an eighty-year-old man.

"Don't worry, Yoshio. You're going to make a terrific young guy. Every girl in Tokyo is going to want to date you."

Once that happened my dream from the start would be realized. I could see myself tucking my hand in his arm and walking together with Yoshio, attractive, and half my age, through the streets of downtown Tokyo.

My brother looked off into the distance. "There are so many different people in the world, aren't there? Take Kozumi and Saseko for instance. I don't think I've ever met people like that before." I glanced over at his sunburned profile and saw his childlike nose, still small for his face, his skinny arms and legs.

He turned to me and I looked in his eyes, too dark for the eyes of a child. The brown color was nebulous, concealing a power that made me think of something rolling about in inexhaustible supply like the millions of sea cucumbers on the bottom of the ocean. There were so many different paths in those eyes—so many that if I tried to list them all here I would be the one acting foolish. Endless possibilities of an endless future.

~

"Yoshio and I are on our way home," I said to Ryūichirō. "How about you? Are you going to stay here?"

When Saseko had heard I was taking my brother back to Japan, she instantly scheduled a small recital in our honor. It would be at the beach bar that night.

We really hadn't discussed plans for going home, but I felt safer leaving Ryūichirō this time than I had in the past when we'd been forced to go our separate ways. I felt comfortable asking him about it now. Yoshio was taking a shower, and I was changing clothes in the bedroom with Ryūichirō.

I figured I should be dressed in white for my last night on the island. I stood in front of the mirror as I slid my white sundress over my shoulders. I was almost afraid to look at myself after realizing how dark I'd turned on the trip. The white dress looked good against my brown skin.

"Well . . . ," Ryūichirō stammered, and then he took a deep breath.

"Well what?" I said.

"I was just wondering what I would do if you just took off without saying good-bye." He chuckled.

"Just how would I go about leaving and not saying anything to you?" I laughed along with him. "You're really weird sometimes, you know that? Explain to me why men are so strangely delicate."

"It's obvious," Ryūichirō replied. "When it really comes down to it, we aren't friends. Not even close. We're strangers. We see each other off at the airport, but that doesn't mean another day won't come when we'll be forced to say good-bye. Chances are we'll never see each other again." Ryūichirō was sober as he talked. Thinking about it for a moment, I realized he was right. We were strangers. The sensation was almost too sad. I couldn't find myself feeling comfortable with the idea. Not even close.

"So what are you going to do? It's too late to buy a ticket. Will you ever come home?" I asked.

"I'll head back to Japan in a week or two. After that I plan to live there for a while."

"Where?"

"Someplace near you. I'll get an apartment or something."

"Are you sure?" I said. "That would make me so happy."

Finally, things wouldn't be boring when I got home. What a relief. For the first time since we'd arrived I looked forward to life after Saipan. Clearly everything would be okay. There was no need to rush into anything. I'd only have to wait for time.

"Hmm . . ." Ryūichirō paused for a second. "I think once I get back to Japan I'll write another book. Then I'll think about what the next step will be."

"So you'll be around for a couple of years at least," I said with a smile.

"Yeah, and we can take trips around Japan together."

I stopped and considered his statement. Either he was completely dependent on others—the type who can't live a day without being with someone else—or it meant he really liked me and wanted me around. To this day I don't know what he was trying to say, but perhaps the meaning would eventually become clear to us—together, the two of us as one.

Ryūichirō stood in front of the mirror and buttoned his shirt. "Yoshio will hear Saseko for the first time tonight."

"Yeah," I said. "He's in for a shock."

I looked beyond the window at the pale dusk of Saipan. Our trip had been fun. Really, truly fun. That impression struck me that night as I looked out over the air, which seemed to be singing its own song. Silently the scent of darkness came floating in from the window. Outside I could hear the leaves of trees rustling together.

Fun. We'd had fun. Really.

~

Since the night was still young, only a few people were scattered about the bar.

The sound of the waves reminded me of music you hear softly floating about a concert hall before the concert begins. It made me even more excited.

By now the smell of the salty ocean had stained fast inside my hair and in every pore on my body, a strong fragrance that filled every inch of the island.

The moon shone brightly in midair with an intensity to stir a person's heart.

Kozumi had volunteered to accompany Saseko on his guitar. I'd never heard him play before, but he was on the stage tuning his instrument as we sat and waited for things to begin. Oh, please don't let him start into some heavy Def Leppard . . .

. . . or so I thought for a moment.

Then she appeared.

She wore a colorful dress designed completely in the colors of Saipan. I could see how much of her Japanese identity she'd lost as she strolled gently onto the stage.

Yoshio stirred in his seat. "Wow," he said. "I'm starting to feel funny inside. Saku-chan, is this going to be strange? I mean, is there something weird about Saseko's performance? My heart's pounding."

"Wait and see," Ryūichirō said, patting my brother on the shoulder.

Then it happened. Saseko began to sing.

Chapter 15

When we arrived home everything was winter and the city was rapidly getting colder. I had the impression that Tokyo was a place full of people with too much time on their hands, but even then there wasn't a mountain or an ocean in sight. No wonder their eyes were never at ease. This was the only thing rolling around in my empty head, because I had nothing else to think about.

You won't believe it, but I'd lost my job. After returning from Saipan, I discovered my manager had closed down the bar. Apparently he caught the vacationing bug and ran off to Jamaica. After making numerous phone calls for three days I decided to go and see if I could talk to him in person. As I approached I read a sign posted on the door:

The bar will be closed for a while. We apologize for any inconvenience—Berries

I smiled and shook my head. Exactly how long is "a while"? The fact of the matter was my master was more of a playgirl than I was, but that had completely slipped my mind. I suppose I'd known all along this day would actually come, but I was shocked to discover it had happened so fast. At least I knew one thing—if I had stayed and worked at the bar then my boss wouldn't have flown the coop. My presence alone would have kept him from leaving.

I stood in front of the door for a short time with my head blank. The sky above me was a pale blue. Trees, thrusting their dead branches out, lined the road. People muffled by their enormous sweaters passed by.

Feeling sorry for myself, I decided it was time to leave the bar behind. That night I called a friend who knew my boss at Berries.

"Get this," he said, "your boss went to some friend's house for a party where he met a traveling fortune teller from Tibet. The fortune teller told him that 'it would be wise to go to Jamaica,' so he did! He grabbed his wife and kids, and they were gone, just like that. I figure he'll be back in a year or so. He told me to say 'hi' if I ever got the chance to see you again. I think he'll send you a letter as well."

I told him thanks, but as I hung up the phone I tried to figure out how Jamaica and Tibet got into the same story. It must have had something to do with his appearance. My boss looked like he came right out of a reggae band. The fortune teller probably took one look at him and came up with that cockeyed prediction. What a quack.

Once again I was reminded that people get separated, and it always happens without notice. The idea made me sad. I had known my boss for years, feeling close to him ever since I'd been a customer at the bar. Every night as the doors opened for the evening all the elements would come together so nicely—the way the water squirted from the faucet over the sink in the kitchen, the arrangement of odd glasses and plates, and the atmosphere coming from the music in the background. Despite the fact that everything still seemed to be soaked in my skin as though it had been only yesterday, now there was no reason to return.

On the night before we left Saipan, when Ryūichirō turned to me and said we were strangers because as far as we could tell that would be the end of our relationship as we knew it, I thought his comments were just the foolish remarks of a lover. But I also remembered the earnest expression in his eyes. Now with the bar closed I understood what he was talking about. The speed at which things change, the feeling of losing something special. It could happen to any of us, at any point in time.

Ryūichirō had known that throughout our stay on the island.
I hadn't clued in yet.
Now I was fully aware of it—only too painfully.

~

On account of the bar closing down I now found myself with plenty of reason to think of what my next job would be in Japan.

I hated offices. I'd go crazy if I had to work in another one. It was a choice between a part-time job at a restaurant or bar that took my fancy, or I'd find work as a receptionist. Those were about the only things I could do. Even in the world of hotels and restaurants I knew I didn't have much of a chance, my skills were so limited.

I figured I would tell all my friends that I was out of work, and head back to the pool each day. Mikiko was so into her new boyfriend that she didn't have time to come with me, and Yoshio had gone diligently back to school as soon as we returned to the country. Without anyone else to come along, I went off to the pool alone.

Each night on my way home I'd look into the western sky and remember Kozumi, Saseko, and Ryūichirō. I'd get so homesick I could hardly stand to be around myself.

That sky over the people who truly understood what I was going through, that ocean lit up with the dim light of dusk. I wanted so badly to be back with those who could understand. I wanted to be with someone who knew I was alive—the one who could explain to me why such a strange thing had been forgiven.

Dear Sakumi:
How are you? I'm happy and my life is going well. I just have one small favor to ask, hope you don't mind. Would it be possible to get some of Mom's pickled plums? Ryūichirō

can't stand them and I haven't had one since I moved in. Can you believe it? I'm sure you remember I practically lived on them each summer. So I suppose that's what you call marriage—giving up things in life you crave. But I've just got to get my hands on at least one *umeboshi*. Do you think you could bring some by the day after tomorrow?

I know I could have called and asked for them, but for some reason I felt like sitting down and writing a letter. I don't know how else to pass the extra time on my hands. Remember two years ago when I was back in show business, only sleeping a couple hours a night? I was never on my own. My manager was always there with me.

I didn't know how she felt about me. I'm not trying to say she had a thing for me, nothing like that ever happened. (Not that she hated me either, because she didn't. I wouldn't talk back much.) I suppose it was her job. I know because now we never see each other. She probably doesn't even want to see me anymore. I'm sure the thought doesn't even cross her mind. It makes me feel kind of sad. Even though we were together every day, sleeping in the same room, eating the same food, traveling in the same cars, she never really wanted to be with me, even though we got along so well as women.

I watch my movies a lot on television. I suppose that makes me sort of a narcissist, but when I see myself I realize what a terrible actor I was. It was horrible. Ryu-chan's kind enough to say otherwise. He says I carry a special, unique mood about me. Still, it's obvious my acting was really bad. I suppose there's little that can be done about that now. Retiring was the right thing to do.

You know, seeing yourself in a movie is really strange. It's like having a dream. I see myself laughing, or asleep with my eyes closed. I discover what my own face looks like when I'm wrapped in someone's arms.

It's a pleasant feeling. I feel like I've met a new friend.

Funny, that new person is me. She looks so pitiful I want to walk up and throw my arms around her, and tell her that I want to see her.

Well, I'm blabbing on. I'll see you the day after tomorrow. I'm sure I won't be this moody the next time we meet.

I'm really looking forward to it.

Mayu

As I was cleaning out my bookshelf the letter came tumbling down from between some books. Without warning a huge lump formed in my throat.

I couldn't even remember getting such a letter. Surely my memory block had something to do with falling down and hitting my head. My sister must have sent it at a time when things were starting to get dangerous—that time when she had shut herself off to the world and refused to listen to what others had to tell her.

She was so tired that every word in her letter released the same emotions.

I'm here, don't forget me.

It was Mayu. Mayu was out there.

The letter, her way of speaking—everything became a swelling mass of bittersweet memories that seemed to fill the entire room. For a moment I wondered if I should let my mother read the letter, but then I gave up the idea. If I showed it to her she would have gone off on how we could have prevented Mayu from dying. The old pain and remorse would be revisited.

Rather than place that burden on others, I allowed only myself to go through with the experience.

The smell of death. The image of defeat, exhausted and dried up. Personal demands. The spot in a person's mind that expands what is lost to a size hundreds of times bigger than that which is obtained. I could have said it about anything, but couldn't I have stopped it from going on? It went forward on its own without me.

~

Bored out of my mind, I decided to pay a visit on Eiko.

Thinking that surely things in her home would be in an uproar after Eiko came home from the hospital, I opted to wait for a while before I visited her. It didn't take long, though, before she called me.

Apparently I hadn't been to Eiko's house since we were in high school together. I say "apparently" because I had no recollection of ever having been there.

Eiko pointed it out to me over the phone.

"You haven't been over since we graduated," she said.

Again I realized how many memories I'd lost in the fall, since I really had no thoughts of being there. But once I stood in front of the gate to her house I felt a tremendous burst of energy coming from within me. Everything gushed in all at once.

I recalled the fringe of my skirt. My penny loafers. I remember walking through her far-too-spacious garden and stepping on the stones leading up to her entrance. That huge wooden door, and the gorgeous chime next to it.

See? I told myself. You've been here before. You've seen this garden, and you've walked on top of this dirt.

It was thrilling to remember.

It was as though I'd jumped in a time machine and gone to meet my own self back in high school. It was a Western-style building I'd seen in a vision. A building so lovely it was dreamlike.

I cheerfully rang the doorbell. Eiko's mother came with the maid to the doorway. Both had aged slightly from the cloudy way I remembered them. Somewhere in my blank mind I felt like Rip Van Winkle.

"Thank you so much for coming to see Eiko," her mother said with a smile. "It's really difficult to be a mother during times like this. She just shuts herself up in her room and never comes out."

Eiko's family was beautiful—perfect and sympathetic, free from any kind of imperfection. That's why it was so hard to see something like this happen to them. I just nodded my head and moved past them into the doorway, moving straight up to Eiko's room.

"I'm so happy to see you!" Eiko cried as she playfully threw both arms around me. Dark rings rested under both eyes and she looked like she'd lost weight. I knew she hadn't been doing well, but I was relieved to see she was still as strong-willed as ever. Even though we both possessed the same disposition, there was something different about us. As I pondered our differences, the word *upbringing* came to mind. It was lonely.

The maid came in behind me rolling a cart with a perfect English tea service. Silver sugar pot. Wedgwood tea set. Biscuits and bite-size cucumber sandwiches. Smiling, Eiko sent the maid away with a thank-you. Something about the way she said it reminded me faintly of the sensation I had around her mother.

"So you aren't allowed to go out?" I asked, taking more than my fair share of sandwiches.

"Well, they say I'm not a child anymore, so they haven't gone as far as to place any restrictions like that on me." She giggled. "But when I do go out they ask me who I was with, and I'm not allowed to spend the night anywhere."

"Of course!" I laughed. "That would be awful."

"Really?" she asked with a grin. "But seriously. I think my mother is taking me to Hawaii with my grandmother. We'll probably be there for half a year or so, or at least until the storm blows over, if you know what I mean."

"How would it be to have as much money as you!" I screamed. I was beginning to remember how wealthy Eiko's family was and how difficult that made it for her, coming from a home otherwise very comfortable.

Outside the thin winter sun shone on the window. Lace curtains. The perfectly manicured garden that lay beyond. Carp swimming in the small pond outside in her garden, seemingly too red. The entire scene quivered in wintry misery.

This was the nest where she'd been born and raised, the place where she'd been loved and kept all of her life. Even now they refused to let her leave. Perhaps Eiko's only problem was being cooped up in the house.

"Don't say that," Eiko said. "It's not like I want to go to Hawaii. Of course, I'm not opposed to the idea either."

"I think you'll change your mind once you get there," I said. "It's only six months. Time will go by like that." I snapped my fingers. "I'm sure it will be a nice break for you—physically and mentally. Even after a month in Saipan I felt like I'd been reborn. And it's always nice to see a different landscape. That's really the only thing that will change."

"Are you sure?" she asked. "Well then, maybe that's how I'll think about it from now on. Yes, that would be nice. I won't work, or even allow the thought to cross my mind. I'll just spend time shopping and swimming, and I'll call it filial piety." For the first time that day Eiko threw her head back and really started to laugh.

It was a sure sign she was tired. I thought about how scary the whole experience must have been. She wore a white cashmere sweater, not a trace of makeup on her face. Her hair was pulled back in a French braid. She looked like a child—sweet and unprotected. That's why I hadn't brought up her boyfriend right away. We talked further about my trip and movies we had seen.

At that point it occurred to me how slowly time went by inside that box garden of a room. Even if she went to Hawaii it would never go away—that sad feeling of remorse.

Once those feelings had passed, I turned to Eiko and said, "So have you seen him since the accident?"

"No," she said with a smile. That was her only reply. She didn't provoke any more questions. "I don't want my parents to go and apologize, and then pretend like nothing ever happened between us. The very thought makes me feel like a teenager all over again.

First I want to meet him face-to-face and talk things over. But it's not as easy as it sounds."

"Why?"

"After an incident like that you can't expect me to show up at his office. I've talked to him a bit over the phone, but I just can't summon enough courage to ask him out on a date. I'm trying to do my best. But I also need a better understanding of what I want out of our relationship. The thoughts have been rolling around in my mind for weeks now."

Perhaps the thing that concerned me most was the sincerity of her desires. Eiko coming out and saying "I want to see him" meant that she would go crazy if she didn't get the chance.

"Okay," I said. "It might not be much, but if you want, I'll give you a hand."

"What do you mean?" she asked.

"For the next two hours I'm taking you for a walk. Isn't his company over in Ginza? It'll take us forty minutes to get there and back. You meet him and talk to him in person. If we both come home together then your mother won't think twice about it, I'm sure. Nothing will look suspicious. I'll put my name in at the reception desk in his office. You won't have time for sex, but if things work out I'm sure you'll have time for at least a cup of tea."

"You really don't have to go to such trouble." Eiko's eyes began to sparkle. "But you'd really do that for me?"

"Just this once," I replied with a smile.

∾

"Can Sakumi eat dinner with us tonight?" Eiko asked cheerfully as she told her mother we were going out for some tea and shopping, but that we'd be back promptly before dinner. Her mother nodded, and she and the maid led us to the door, smiling as they waved us away.

We hailed a taxi and jumped inside. Once in the car Eiko fell silent. I figured as much. Getting stabbed is not drama, and murder isn't a simple thing, either. Then there are those who simply want to kill themselves. It all creates pressure.

After a while Eiko said, "It's been a long time since I've been anywhere outside my own neighborhood. The city looks pretty."

She was right. The winter sun was falling and it cast long rays of light on the shops and display windows we were passing, so beautiful it reminded me of a fairy tale. Eiko, buried next to me in the dark backseat of the taxi with her pale face glimmering in the light, also appeared a part of that story. I knew how strongly she wanted to meet her boyfriend, considering this was the type of girl who piled on makeup and wore a designer suit or dress whenever she went into the city. Now she was in a simple sweater and a house skirt, even though she was off to meet her man.

I walked into the main floor of the office building where Eiko's boyfriend worked and placed my name on the register with the woman at the reception counter. I'd never met him before. While I waited for a reply, I could feel myself getting nervous. Before long a good-looking, older gentleman stepped out of the elevator. At once I could see he was a somewhat tired, run-of-the-mill businessman with a lot of money. He also looked as though he'd had a good upbringing.

I was impressed by the fact he wasn't bothered by the glare he received from the woman at the counter. He fearlessly left the office with me. I remembered Eiko's father—he seemed to be just like him.

"Eiko's waiting for you at the coffee shop over there," I said, pointing my finger to a quiet place on the other side of the street. After thanking me, he quickly crossed the street.

We'd planned to meet thirty minutes later at the Tiffany's section of Mitsukoshi department store. I started cursing her name after she was ten minutes late. But five minutes later I saw her approaching, and the look in her eyes was enough to make me forgive her. She looked like she had undergone cosmetic surgery or at least had a new makeover.

The reason was simple: she was glowing. Life had been restored to her eyes. The light that emanated from each pupil was something different than I'd seen before. Her clean face and white sweater shone like a half-moon floating softly in an afternoon sky. Her cheeks were rosy even though she hadn't put anything on them, and her feet were so weightless she appeared to be dancing.

"Sorry I'm late," she said.

"How was it?" I asked.

"As soon as I'm back from Hawaii he wants us to consider marriage," Eiko said.

"You're kidding!" I screamed.

"No," she said. "I'm not." She blushed.

So that was it—she really did want to get married. I hadn't been informed of this, although it really wouldn't have changed my opinion of her in any way. I had really been in the dark about Eiko and her boyfriend. I also wasn't aware of the unusual earnestness that seemed to surround her parents and upbringing.

Aren't people simple creatures?

. . . or so I thought.

But at the same time I figured it was that simplicity which made them great.

Winter dusk settling over Tokyo, the flash of the neon lights on the street. Caught inside the confusion of the people leaving their offices and heading home, Eiko, with her tiny little frame, turned to me and said, "Shall we go, Sakumi?"

I nodded.

She paused for a moment before saying, "Thank you."

I felt myself turning red at her remark, which seemed almost too childlike for words. I was impressed, however, by her beauty. It made me feel like a small boy who falls in love with his gorgeous second-grade teacher, turning red when she smiles and thanks him for the huge bouquet of flowers he put on her desk the last day of school.

~

Late that night while I was sitting at home watching a video by myself in the dayroom, my brother came bounding down the stairs.

"Sakumi, whatcha up to?" he asked.

"Just watching a video," I said.

"Oh." He went into the kitchen and poured himself some warm wheat tea from a pot on top of the stove. After I asked him to pour a cup for me, he was kind enough to bring my mug over to the sofa.

"Maybe I should be the one asking you what you're doing," I said. "Were you asleep?"

"I went to bed at nine, but then I woke up and I've been wide awake ever since. What time is it now anyway? Three?"

"Yeah," I said. "It's three."

"Wow. Sakumi, you stay up late," Yoshio responded with a bright smile. He looked like a healthy superchild.

"I guess you're right," I said.

On the screen there was a scene at a nightclub, and a singer was on the stage.

"I wonder how Saseko's doing," my brother said.

"When I talked to Ryūichirō on the phone yesterday he said everyone's fine," I replied.

"I miss Saipan a lot," he said.

"So do I."

Yoshio paused for a moment and said, "That was really great, wasn't it? That night we heard Saseko sing."

"Uh-huh," I said with a nod. "But wasn't it a shock?"

We went through such an amazing experience that it wasn't something we felt comfortable talking about. That was the first time my brother had mentioned it since coming home.

~

That night was our last in Saipan.

Bits and pieces of the evening floated up in my mind, one right after the other.

I was dressed in my white sundress. The salty smell of the ocean hovered in the air around me, along with Ryūichirō's dark arm resting on top of the table. Next there was the moon and the sliver of white light it cast across the ocean. My brother was wearing short pants, and each of us sipped on cheap, sweet cocktails. The people at the bar were laughing and talking, while the sand on the beach remained bright and still.

Saseko began her performance, accompanied by Kozumi's horrible guitar. I suppose I should be fair, however, and say that Kozumi's music had flavor. They went through a number of older songs, starting with a not-so-famous number by Billie Holiday. I was completely absorbed in the music, feeling like I would sink into it at any time. At the same moment I felt a nervousness in the back of my heart. A dam seemed to stop something from going around and around, something familiar, something that made tears fall from my eyes when I realized I couldn't flow with it. If I were to float off now, I know my heart would tighten under the pressure of having felt too many beautiful things. Taken away by Saseko's soft but powerful voice, I felt myself moving with the clear night of Saipan.

I wanted to be there forever.

Parents, siblings, lovers.

I didn't need any of them, because they all seemed to be right there.

I wanted to go swimming just once inside the freshness of the air around me.

I'm sure anyone would have felt the same way—if they'd heard with what talent Saseko could sing. Her voice was pure, composed of hundreds of minuscule particles. Sweet, and shining brightly, blowing like a despondent wind made from that tiny matter.

My brother was also taken aback. He just sat with his eyes wide open.

The applause and cheers from the people around us seemed loud enough to surround Saseko like she'd just performed in a large concert hall. Every person in the bar was full of joy at having witnessed what had gone on that night.

"Please forgive my selection of music," she said as she came over to where we were sitting. "I have to plan my concerts around what Kozumi can play on his guitar and what the regulars in this bar go for."

"Saseko-san," my brother said. "You were wonderful."

Saseko leaned over and kissed him on the cheek. Kozumi laughed. Apparently he was okay with his wife kissing children.

Ryūichirō smiled and said to Kozumi, "You're not so bad on the guitar, either."

Everything seemed in balance, all was in harmony with the world. Within seconds the sound of the waves came floating back over the bar, now rather subdued. Our server brought out one free cocktail after another. Saseko was loved by the people around her.

Each of us, including my brother, had more than enough to drink.

Before long it was two o'clock, and the bar was closed for the evening. The lights were turned off, and the beach was plunged in darkness. A number of people filed by and thanked Saseko once again before they left, and then headed off in various directions in the dark.

Saseko was the one who suggested we take a walk along the beach.

All the adults were tipsy, and my brother was just plain drunk. We had to struggle to get him to walk straight. We danced and sang as we romped around the beach, moving our party to a small inlet not far from the hotel and the sandwich shop, where we found ourselves alone facing the dark ocean. Saseko took off her shoes and began to wade in the water. Then suddenly she dived into the ocean and began to swim with her clothes on.

"Oh my god!" she cried as she sat down in a shallow spot in the lagoon, which shimmered in the gloomy darkness. "This feels wonderful!"

"It's not going to be a pretty sight if a shark shows up." Kozumi stuttered the rather irrelevant remark as he took off his shoes and went splashing out to pull Saseko from the water. "Don't even think about swimming out into the bay!"

"They make such a cute couple!" The rest of us laughed from where we stood on the beach.

Finally Saseko came out of the ocean looking like a mermaid straight out of water. Her clothes and hair stuck thickly to her body. After pulling herself through the sand until she was standing directly under the light of the moon, she began to sing.

It was an elegant sound that mixed with the mood of the night, but rather than call it a song, I think it was more of a heightened hum. Without thinking I looked down at my wristwatch and confirmed the time. Through my drunken eyes I saw that the hands of my watch were reading ninety degrees.

It was 3 A.M.

Just as that clicked into my brain, someone somewhere turned up the volume on Saseko's singing. It was scary. Goose bumps rose over every inch of my body. For the first time in my life I wanted to leave the spot where I was standing. I would have given anything to have been able to run away.

Saseko was frightening.

She was no longer human. She had turned into something else, something resembling pure beauty, but I'm not referring to the beauty of her song. I don't want to say she looked like a god, or even a spirit for that matter. It was something different still.

She turned into a feeling that directly reached out to the source of why people are people.

That's why she was so astonishing. It had been something I'd tried to grasp all my life, and never had been able to reach. I was looking at an abyss so dark and deep I couldn't see to the bottom, or staring straight into the sun at high noon without wearing any sort of eye protection.

Her song felt as though it would continue on forever; then again it felt like only a split second in time.

I looked down at Yoshio, who had gripped my hand in fear. Even though both of us were hiding our faces from the terrific sight, I recalled looking up and seeing Ryūichirō standing beside us, a look of conviction in his eyes. He was ready to experience it all, and remember everything for us.

I don't know what happened to Kozumi.

However, when I glanced out over the ocean I saw it coming. As I turned back I saw it coming from inside the jungle as well, a heavy dark cloud tumbling in from every direction in the sky. I felt as if I would be swallowed by it. That was the only way to perceive what was happening. What was my brother, or any other person with his type of power, seeing in that cloud?

"SAKU-CHAN!" Yoshio screamed as he threw himself around me. He was practically sobbing.

At that point it happened. The entire world flashed before us. I'm not lying.

The light was so bright my eyes became dizzy. I couldn't stand to be there anymore.

Saseko's song was over.

With locks of hair clinging to her neck and her clothes still stuck to her body, she stepped back and bowed deeply. The rest of us were dazed, but we started to clap anyway.

Silence was restored to the beach. It was a dreadful silence, something that evolved not only from the world around me, which was no longer blessed with Saseko's singing, but from somewhere inside my heart as well. Everything was so silent it felt empty.

~

"So what do you think that big flash was?" I asked Yoshio.

"Promise me you won't laugh," he replied.

"Yeah," I said. "I promise."

"When Saseko was singing a bunch of spirits came together. There were so many of them I don't think anyone could have counted them all." My brother's eyes grew wide. "And when the whole world burst into light, I saw it."

"Saw what?" I asked.

"Saw *it,*" he said. "Eternity."

"Oh," I quietly responded.

Chapter 16

A letter arrived two weeks later on a cold morning in winter. It was from my boss.

Dear Sakumi:
Sorry for closing the bar so abruptly. I've included a check with this letter that covers the income I still owe you along with a small bonus to help out while you find a new job. Please don't worry about me or the bar, your hard work was greatly appreciated.

I am having a wonderful time in Jamaica. My wife and I have made going to the dance hall a part of our nightly routine. We've also made a lot of new friends. Time goes by slowly here. I feel like I'm in paradise.

We plan to stay a while. Feel free to visit anytime.

—Manager of Berries

I was familiar with the delicate penmanship. The letter looked as if it was written by one of those men you see dressed so wonderfully in women's clothes. But after reading the letter I knew it was over. My chances of finding work back at the bar had been completely demolished. They faded away with the old records and the sound system we played them on. So my boss had finally grown tired of trying to lead a life of the seventies in modern-day Japan.

With no other choice, I went on a diligent search for new employment. Much to my surprise, a job fell right into my lap. I would work for a bakery located in a high-class suburb of Tokyo, six days a week, 11 A.M. until 8 P.M.

The owner of the shop was a lively Frenchman who spoke only a few phrases of broken Japanese. He was the second son of a man who owned a famous bakery established in Paris decades before, and apparently the shop had quite a reputation. With an earnest zeal to open a similar shop in Japan, my new boss had stuck it out and realized his dream rather quickly.

Ironically, my new boss had the same personality as the bartender back at Berries. For some reason that type of man always took a fancy to me. Even though dozens of other applicants had interviewed for the job, I was hired after he talked to me once. My boss worked in the kitchen with two older ladies preparing and cooking the bread, and I sat alone behind the counter in the front of the shop working the till. It was a really small setup, and my job was the most relaxing. On top of it being easy, I picked up tips on how to make wonderful French bread and learned French conversation as well.

We specialized in baguettes, and they were cooked only three times a day. I'd punch in for work thirty minutes before the first batch of bread was scheduled to go out on the shelves. When I came through the back door into the kitchen I saw row after row of neatly formed bread, just waiting to be bought and sold. We'd always wait a few minutes before putting out the bread—just enough for the steam to vanish along with the acrid smell of the yeast.

Afternoons were always my favorite.

As I stood behind the counter I watched one person after another come into the shop, followed by yet another. Students and housewives, old men dressed in nice sweaters and ties. They would come into the store and form a small line. Since there wasn't another bread shop for miles, I'm sure the bright light that poured from our little store window glowed like a lighthouse amid the skyline of the dark suburban streets. People never came from very far away, nor did we ever have so many customers that we ran out of bread, so I never felt hurried by the lines. In fact, I never encountered a customer who seemed to be in a rush. Everyone seemed to be silently overjoyed by the thought of having wonderful toasted French bread for breakfast.

I wasn't sure why, but the fragrance of cooking bread that permeated the air was somehow familiar, but in a dreadful sort of way. It invited a nostalgia that made me feel homesick, as if I longed to return to a place with sparkling sunrises. Even if I were, for example, to devour one hundred slices of the bread hot from the oven, it still wouldn't be the same as reaching the images that invaded my heart with the smell.

Within that air I stood and watched the line of customers grow longer and the night slowly unfold before me. Soft lights from the windows of neighborhood houses, the spirit of a late-afternoon meal, shadows of homes rumbling like mountains. Eventually the bread would be brought out from the kitchen, and I'd start to quickly pound the register and collect the cash. Sliding the bread into the bags and passing them back over the counter with a smile gave me a lofty feeling, as if I had aspired to being a goddess—a quick reason to fall in love with my new job.

Just like I loved Ryūichirō, my brother, and Saipan.

I was sure life would be fine, as long as I continued doing the same things over and over.

∾

It was one of my few days off work.

The afternoon was drawing to a close, and I'd made the decision to go to the bookstore. Wondering if my little brother would like to go along, I peeked into his bedroom. Just as I saw him sitting in front of a small TV fervently pushing the buttons on his Nintendo joystick, he quickly glanced over to see who was there, his speed just slightly faster than my own. Even though there was nothing unusual about his reaction, I was startled.

"So you're going out?" my brother asked.

"Yeah," I said. "To the bookstore. Want to come along?"

"Umm . . . no," Yoshio said with his eyes glued to the screen. "I've got to see if I can beat this game. You go on without me."

"Okay," I replied. "I'll see you when I get back."

I shut his door. There was nothing wrong with our encounter. My brother was happy, and we were acting like a real brother and sister. Everything seemed so normal. The atmosphere in his room felt natural and so did the tired expression he had in his eyes.

However, I wasn't sure if his fatigue was just one more aspect of being a boy growing up or if it had something to do with his brain overworking. I suppose I couldn't help it if his mental powers were affecting the status of his mind. What I could see was that my brother wasn't acting like he did back in Saipan, where a life force had bubbled over inside him. I'd figured out at least that much. And there was something else. I knew his heart wasn't opening up to me as much as it had back then.

The city was cold, and the people I passed on the street were buried in their coats. I picked up a scent of early spring in the soft rays of the afternoon sun. It reminded me of something new, something sweet. Only a small bit came through with the light. This was something I'd experienced only in Japan. The people who lived in Tokyo were well aware of the change of the seasons, and the conditions that were brought by spring. It was like it was a part of our skin.

There was a huge bookstore inside the shopping mall built over the neighborhood train station. When I was released from the hospital I found myself with so much time on my hands—so much that I didn't know what to do with it—I went to the aquarium to visit the sunfish. Then, on the way back, I stopped by the bookstore and bought up stacks of books. Under the dim lights at Berries I read for hours before finally going home. It seemed like every day was the same pattern for me then. My friendly boss at Berries was sympathetic to my peculiar situation and he told me, "Any person who takes a tumble down a flight of stone steps shouldn't be allowed to work for a while." But it didn't take long before he put me back on the schedule.

It was winter . . .

. . . when the new me took the first step in my new life by going back to work at Berries.

. . . when I gazed silently out at the maze of dead branches outside my window, desperately trying to untangle them in my mind.

Why was I so emotional? Because I had so much extra time. While allowing my thoughts to relax, my mind became a dead spirit, floating lifelessly throughout time and space. It was a pleasant feeling, but I got tired of it fast. Seriously wanting to get over it, I would force my consciousness to dive back into the intense beam of light that blared in my eyes, but only for a second or two. Soon I'd snap into place. Even when that was happening to me, I knew Berries was the one place I could go to feel relaxed in this world.

~

The bookstore was packed full of people—a confused mass of students and office ladies just off work. Pushing my way through the crowds, I found a number of books that I liked. There was an interesting book of simple French conversation, a guide for making bread, a couple of magazines . . . and so on.

Then I passed the shelf with new publications.

Before going up to the counter, I saw a huge stack of books that were lying flat on their sides, one thick book in particular catching my eye. *A Secret Room of Philosophers,* written by Kiyoshi Kasai. I'd never seen it before. It was a detective story, something

I rarely read, and on top of that it was hundreds of pages long. Pulling it from the pile, I could feel how much the book weighed. I don't know what made me do it, I mean, I didn't even have enough money to buy it with all the other books in my arms, so in the end I gave up my bread-making guidebook.

I suppose one could call it fate. I simply had to have it.

I don't know what it was, or how far away it came from, but clearly something was close enough to reach out and touch my heart, a strong appeal that seemed to be saying, "Buy it! Buy it! Buy it!"

When I returned home my brother was gone.

"From the sound of it he's made some friends," Junko said.

I thought that was strange, but I realized Yoshio was at a perfectly normal age to go out and make friends on his own. I returned to my room and, opening my new book to the first page, I slowly began to read.

The story was set in Paris; the main character was an intelligent Parisienne named Nadja. Next came her Japanese lover, Kakeru, a young man who was quite enigmatic.

. . . Nadja was a woman with the perfect ability to love, almost to the extent that she was prideful over it. Curious to know the woman, Kakeru existed in a realm of uncontrollable darkness as he viewed the scheme of the world from an entirely different perspective.

Air flowed through my teeth, and I continued to scan the pages.

Halfway through the book something happened. A strange feeling suddenly overcame me and I couldn't stand to read it any longer. I just couldn't take it. For some reason the characters in the novel were familiar to me. I felt tenderly toward them, as though they were long-lost friends I hadn't seen since I was a child. The feeling was almost irritating.

It was similar to the déjà vu I had experienced as I walked to the front door of Eiko's house—that unstoppable feeling of having been somewhere before.

Why?

I thought about it for a while. Did it have to do with the fact that the character of Kakeru was dark, even though he was still a nice person, just like Ryūichirō? Did it have something to do with the strange similarities between myself and Nadja? Or had I just found a way to sympathize with the radiant spirit of the characters?

No, that couldn't be it. There had to be something more. I don't know how, where, or why, but I'd met these people before. I'd never synchronized so closely with characters in any other novel.

Why?

I suppose the way I allowed myself to be overwhelmed by the book would have appeared suspicious from the outside. I wrapped both arms around my head as I searched deeply, ever so deeply, in an attempt to discover even the slightest clue that could tell me where my feelings were coming from. Even now I find it hard to believe that such a small thing could have been the springboard for something so drastic, because I hadn't seen it coming. But the knot holding everything together until now had slipped and loosened. At that point the answers were clear, coming to me like the flash of a brilliant light. It was like dusk settling quickly into night. The pace was exactly the same, and the result was clear.

I'd read this book before.

The author, the whole series—they were my favorites as a teenager. I'd read them with passion—*Bye, Bye Angel*; *Woman of the Rose*. And there was at least one more, I was sure of it. Oh, yes, *Apocalypse Murder*. I'd bought each of them the day they came out in the bookstores. The story continues with Kakeru going off to study in Tibet. His guru commands him to go out into the world and fight against all evil. There was no air-conditioning during the summer, and he couldn't even open a window. Nadja lost her mother and went to live with her father. Her father was a policeman, perhaps the superintendent of police.

I remembered what had happened when I read it for the first time. I'd stayed up most of the night to finish the entire book, too excited to stop. After sunrise I lay down for a short nap, then I heard a knock on my door. My mother and Mayu came to my room, inviting me to go flower-watching with them. With a break in her film schedule, Mayu had come home for a while, sporting a new short hairstyle. All of us went to a park lined with green, lush trees to eat fried noodles under the branches of the cherry blossoms. I remembered I had yellow curtains at that time. They glowed in the afternoon sun.

I suppose I was barely four feet high by then. My kid brother was still a baby, running around in his rompers and bumping into things. Before long he graduated to short pants, and then he went off to preschool. I remembered him coming home in tears because the other kids had made him eat dirt from the sandbox. My mother was already separated from her second husband, so it must have all happened during the fall of that year. I remember her drinking and crying. She was so upset that even Junko didn't know what to do. It was about that time when Junko came to live with us.

One memory after another, a deluge rushing in. I was doing more than just articulating what had happened; the things I remembered couldn't be described with mere words. The flood of memories was more like perceived, sensual experiences. It was as though a soft spirit had crept into my soul and, with a miraculous touch of her hand, opened the database that was blocked in my head. Now information just surged through my mind.

I trembled. Why did something like that happen after only reading a novel? The memories continued to spin about in various directions and patterns until slowly they pieced themselves together to form a continuous, unbreakable story. As proof of that fact I was only able to sit back and watch it all happen. I could tell it was the beginning of something spectacular.

I was seeing my own story, something called *Me,* but rather than kicking back and watching the events flash before my eyes, I saw them in a higher, more perfected form. Each scene was completely finished, completed rounded, and each episode was so densely connected there wasn't even a slight gap through which my emotions could show. I was sucked into a huge, swirling whirlpool of people, places, and events—all of them looking like helpless bubbles in the sea. There was only one world, stained in my color. In other words, I imagined a flowing helix that had formed a thick silhouette bringing all the rest together.

It was the faraway form of Andromeda, that beautiful form I was so familiar with.

Pulling my eyes up from the book, I saw myself exist inside that history. The whole world looked different. Had my memory returned? I asked myself the question out loud, because by that point I had trouble remembering what it felt like to be confused.

Within seconds the objects around me, which I knew really hadn't changed, seemed different. It was as though separate databases had formed in my mind, each containing information about a different item, and I suddenly had access to them all.

They came to me in chronological order, one right after the other:

My bookshelf—Mom had bought it for me when I was ready to go to elementary school.

That corner of my room—I sat staring at it the night my father passed away.

The scar above my eye—it came from Mikiko when she was still in high school. She tried to stand on the window ledge to reach something high, but she tumbled over, bringing the bookcase with her. I happened to be standing by her side. We'd picked up the case at Seibu department store. At that time Ikebukuro was the only place you could find Seibu. My mother found her china cabinet downstairs on the same day. I remember a fight between my mother and my stepfather not long after they married. He yelled, "You can't forget your dead husband!" and was so angry he beat his fist against the cabinet, putting a crack in one of the panes of glass—just like in a TV drama. My brother started to cry.

All those simple, minute things were popping back into my brain. I felt like my mind was the Internet, and I'd just gone on a random surf under the heading, http://www.bookcase-in-the-corner. My head was filled with so much information, both of quality and of quantity, that I couldn't keep it all straight. Everything was the same:

http://www.scissors-in-my-desk;
http://www.hallway-near-my-room;
http://www.door-to-the-bedroom;
http://www.pencil-in-my-hand.

~

Excited about my new information, I decided to go downstairs. My mother was there sitting at the walnut-colored table we had bought the year before last. We'd gone shopping at Isetan and my mother had ordered it from their catalog. She fell in love with the table instantly, ordering it right away. The delivery man who showed up at our door reminded me of Robert De Niro. When my kid brother crawled on top of the table my mother got really upset.

The memories wouldn't stop coming.

Somewhat frightened, I looked at my mother. Her memory contained her childhood, and all the time she'd spent in the womb, things only felt and not seen. After all, she was only human. But they still created a mass of disorder, dancing together with only a minute fragment of true recollection.

"What in the world happened to you, Sakumi? You look so strange," she said.

"What do you mean?" I asked.

"Your face looks relaxed, like when you were a child."

"I just woke up," I said, walking into the kitchen. The database continued throwing out memories of the past, one incident after another. Amid the confusion of everything bouncing together, I began to make some coffee.

After looking closely at what was happening to me, I realized that the memories I'd gathered since falling and hitting my head were slowly being painted over like butter spread lightly on a piece of thick bread. They continued to spread naturally, one on top of the other, rich in information. It was a strange sensation. Everything seemed too harsh and bright, like I was understanding too much of what I now had access to view. When I compared this life to how I'd felt a few minutes before—that time when I'd existed only for "now," living on the edge with the mere touch of my hand and an inner sixth sense for survival—my new life felt heavier, as though I'd suddenly become a walking encyclopedia of events and information, dozens of volumes bulky and difficult to manage. From here on out I'd have to live in this unusual, new world. It frightened me to think about it. Perhaps it was perfectly natural, something that had never been a problem all along.

Once I had placed a mug of hot coffee in front of my mother, I turned and went back upstairs to my bedroom. I had to show thanks to the two people in my life who had made all of this possible—Kakeru and Nadja—and I figured the best way to express gratitude would be to continue to read their book. I bounded up the stairs, but just as I came to the top of the landing my brother appeared. I could sense a certain amount of fear in him.

Before I could say anything, he looked into my eyes and asked in a distant voice, "Sakumi, your memory came back to you?"

I was shocked. "How do you know?" I asked, quickly pulling up a new search.

http://www.kid-brother.

The file from the day he was born to the time we were together in Saipan came rushing through my mind. I was forced to concentrate so my mind would not become overloaded—the amount of memory was that intense. It was getting difficult to manage.

"By the feeling in the house," Yoshio replied. "Just a few minutes ago I saw the two of you, Sakumi, the old one and the new one, separate. Then there was a strange feeling in the air."

At first I was offended. I wanted to tell him to stop classifying people as old or new, or even seeing any kind of alliance between them like you see in the science fiction cartoons where a person gets in and out of a robot's body, but I didn't. I figured he was picking up on all my thoughts anyway. It was clear he understood what was going through my mind.

I suppose an experience like this would just make some people toss about with the energy of their own memory fervently unfolding images before them, like reflecting mirrors bouncing back and forth forever, driving someone mad. I was different, however, because I enjoyed seeing both sides of myself. If possible, I wanted to hold on to this feeling forever.

Then it occurred to me that a person's mind is a computer without the capacity to discern between things unnecessary or inconvenient. It's not a comparison, or anything else for that matter, but various expressions on a person's face change to correspond with what she's feeling. Computers, on the other hand, tend to be foolishly honest and thoroughly precise. If you input something negative that's what you're bound to get back, because a computer doesn't contemplate whether or not it should reshape something like a dark past, or change anything at all about the original makeup of the data you put in. The only thing that comes out is what was there from the start.

However, I wanted it to be distinct, simply because I was alive and I'd come all this way. I hoped to do a bunch of different things to bring me both pleasure and fear. Someday I even wanted to be so jealous that I could just kill someone . . .

. . . or at least that's the new impression I'd formed of the world. It was like I'd gone back to preschool and my teacher had asked me, "Sakumi, what do you want to do when you grow up?"

"You might be out of it for a while," Yoshio said. "But don't worry. I'm sure your memory will straighten itself out pretty quickly."

"Well, I appreciate it, but what's with all the gloom?" I asked. His face reminded me of a chicken about to be slaughtered.

"I feel kind of lonely, but I don't know why," he replied. "I think the Saku-chan who lost her memory understood more of my pain."

"Oh, stop it!" I yelled. "You sound like an idiot." Then it occurred to me that up until that morning I probably would have agreed. Looking down at my brother, I said, "It's nice you can talk about how painful things are right now, but nothing will ever come out of thinking that way. I mean, nothing's worse than two people who've come together because the only thing they have in common is pain. You remember what it was like back in Saipan, that wonderful weather and the gorgeous sun. You saw it yourself. We all had a great time together, didn't we? All we did was laugh all day."

My brother nodded.

"See, you're acting foolish. I mean, think about it—we're from the same past. We've grown up together, eaten the same food, and our mother's always been the same. So our fathers might be different, but there's really no change. You really are just a kid, aren't you?"

I don't know why, but Yoshio felt tender to me at that moment. I looked down at him for some time. I had the faint feeling I could feel his future inside a bright light, but I couldn't really see it.

He sniffled. "Yeah, you're right. I'm sorry," he said in a small voice.

I smiled and returned to my room.

∾

Thrilled to have my memory back, I gave Saseko a call.

"It's so weird. Everything just came back to me, one memory after another. And it just won't stop," I said.

"Is that so?" she replied. "My goodness, Sakumi, you do have a lot of different things happen to you." She laughed. Then I heard her pull away and yell to Kozumi in the next room, telling him that my memory had returned and that nothing was the matter with me anymore. I loved the way I could announce such a thing to Saseko and Kozumi and they acted like nothing was unusual.

Saseko put her mouth back over the receiver. "Kozumi says that when a person's memory comes back they're confused for a while, but that goes away quickly and the person feels calm. At least that's what his brother said."

Yoshio's comment exactly.

"Tell him thanks," I replied.

"Does Ryūichirō know?" Saseko asked.

"Not yet. I'm thinking about writing him a letter since this isn't something that happens very often."

"Okay," she said. "We'll be sure to keep it a secret."

"I'll call again sometime," I said.

"Well, you know us. We never change. Things are always the same in Saipan and you're always welcome back," Saseko replied.

It was the first time my new self had spoken with her, but there appeared to be no problem. My mind was no longer confused. Rather, I felt relaxed by our conversation.

So when I really felt calm—the way Kozumi had mentioned over the phone—what would become of me?

Dear Ryūichirō:

While killing time with loneliness, I have decided to write you a letter. Don't you find this white ink attractive? I think the blue stationery it rests upon is rather unsettling.

Wasn't there a song with those lyrics?

Ryūichirō, how are you? I really miss Saipan. There have been a few subtle changes in my life here in Japan. As I mentioned to you on the phone, Berries shut down. Now I am working as a clerk in a French bakery. I have an enjoyable time at work, but the thought of how much more wonderful it would be if I could be doing it facing the mountains or the oceans of the island crosses my mind. I really miss the sandwich shop.

I feel bad when I think that people gave up mountains, the scent of the ocean, and the commotion in the trees just to build an upper-class suburban neighborhood.

Luckily I still have the feeling of comfort inside me. Instead of feeling the rays of the sun on my shoulders now I stand under the splendor of a light you can turn on and off with the flick of a switch, and instead of looking out over oceans and mountains I now look out over a skyline of the roofs of houses. Even though I can no longer find that space which existed before men created their magnificent edifices on this earth, it was there in Saipan, wasn't it? So much of it that some was even left over. A girl might even have grown tired of it. The ocean, mountains, and jungle.

When I compare the things we've created to the power of nature, I can't help but realize how the work of men pales in comparison, and I feel misled in some way.

Still, box gardens are beautiful, and I suppose they're rarely affected by typhoons and cold waves.

I must say that the earnest and refined desires of the people who live here in the rich areas of Tokyo to understand and appreciate the aesthetic sense of nature is rather an unusual phenomenon. You could probably write a book about it.

You know my house. It was built years ago, alongside the garden, the cherry blossoms, and even the caterpillars. Compared to the suburbs where I'm working, I feel it's one place that still has yet to be affected, or so I find myself thinking as I pass away idle hours.

Please come home soon.

A majority of my memory has come back and right now everything from the past seems rather coherent. I suppose you're wondering what made it return. Let me tell you.

It was a novel.

That resplendent space created by a piece of fiction can really expand the width of time. I'm so thrilled you are a writer. It's such an important job, such a refined art. I find that now more than ever I hold a deep respect for you.

Unless something extremely awful happens, I think the majority of us just read a book for pleasure. Seldom do we remember the people and places that formed in our minds as we read it. Clearly there is a spot somewhere inside our heads that records the feelings we had when we read the book, and it stays with us forever.

It's like a group of people living in separate parts of town. They think things, feel things, have distinct personalities. It's possible to pick up the book and see those people all over again, just like meeting an old friend from high school. When the intense memories of my past caused my heart to start dancing again, I realized that I had been reunited with a cast of characters I'd been introduced to in a novel. I hope you can understand what I'm saying.

Regardless of whether I liked them or not, I've come to know Heathcliffe and Cathy, and that disgusting character Joel who seems to show up in the Capote novel you like so well. Despite his repugnant nature you still understand him. Did you even find yourself liking him?

Novels are alive.

They live on the other side of our lives, influencing us like good friends. I learned this from my own body. It might be for only a couple of hours, maybe an entire night, but we still have a chance to go across to their side of reality. I'm telling the truth.

The book I'm referring to is Kiyoshi Kasai's *A Secret Room of Philosophers,* the first book in a series that I read avidly in high school. Even though the memory of having read such a book completely left my mind, I bought it again at the bookstore thinking it looked interesting, unconcerned with anything else. But when I read the book I couldn't get over the sensation that I knew these people from someplace else. That's when it happened—my memory came crashing back into my mind. I was almost disappointed by how simply all my forgotten thoughts chose to make their reappearance.

It all started with seeing you for the first time, being with my brother, and going to Saipan. A number of different things made me recall small memories a bit at a time, like meeting Eiko again, or getting close to you, or just everyday life in general. Over the course of those months I managed to read miscellaneous books, and see dozens of different movies. I was even able to recall a few I'd seen before my fall. But none of them forced my whole memory to come back to me like that one novel. Was it just a hallucination? Perhaps there're still things I don't remember, but I really do feel as if all of my memory has returned. Did I think I was the only person who'd gone through such a thing? It's impossible for me to compare myself with others, because I'm all alone.

Ultimately the connection wasn't made with an old friend, or by looking through the family album. It came from a fictitious reality, a made-up world. Funny, don't you think?

It's like the conviction of knowing certain things are out there, even though you can't see or touch them.

Maybe I got you and me mixed up with the couple in the book as I was thinking about how much I long to see you. Things are so boring here without you. All those things came together and changed from being pointless to intense, something disordered but alive. And I'm sure when the thought crossed my mind that you, yourself, are a writer, the feeling just got stronger. It was similar to when people with supernatural powers claim to see and hear ghosts. I felt the same way about you.

Putting it more clearly, I would say that when you write a book you actually create a special universe that continues to function forever. You have the power to kill or take away people's lives. What a frightening line of work! No wonder you appear to have so little freedom, since you always seem to be putting together something new. It's almost as though you're held down by a force stronger than gravity.

How amusing.

It's really strange. The main character in the book I read, a Parisienne named Nadja, reaches a final conclusion that seems very similar to my current situation. It goes like this: "I hold in my heart an earnest desire for comfort and happiness—all things indescribable. I know I have to go on living the life I see in front of me, and in turn the love that comes along with it."

Her words gave me a strong impression. Maybe that's because I'm like Nadja—I've been raised knowing little hardship. Or maybe that's because I'm a woman. Then again, maybe it's both.

Even though all my memories are from a distant past, I feel as if they happened yesterday.

I wonder how much information the things in my room are hiding, or what is concealed between the cracks in the narrow sidewalks in my neighborhood. Living is a process of forgetting. I really believe that. Since everything came back to me all at once, my mind was probably more confused with all the information than it was without. I felt like a computer gone haywire.

How would I look if you could see me today? I'm sure a drastic change has come over me once again.

Even though I was able to return to the past just like in the novel, I haven't forgotten anything that's happened since then. So there's no need to worry. I'll never forget what happened in Saipan, those nights we sat together on the veranda watching people walking down on the street below. I won't forget the stars we saw or how wonderful it all made me feel.

Right now it seems as though I've become a convenient encyclopedia for family and friends, since I can suddenly remember the name of a distant relative's son or the place where somebody hid something years ago.

My mother says I've made a habit of losing my mind.

It's an interesting life.

Oh, and one more thing. A long time ago, not long after Mayu passed away, someone said we were the "sisters greedy for happiness," didn't they?

Now I fully understand.

It was something passed down through our genes. My mother, our father—everyone was up front about how much they wanted happiness and comfort. Maybe you could have called us Italians.

But the difference between me and Mayu, despite being subtle, was really quite big. It was clear when we'd go on trips to places where the scenery was absolutely gorgeous—Nara, for example.

Once our family looked out over the sunset from that observation deck on top of Mt. Miwa. The landscape resonated with the spirit of Yamato, old Japan. The feeling was clear and distinct, but it was growing somewhat hazy.

Everything was tranquil and mellow. The buildings below us shone softly in the western sun—an ancient golden city lying serene, looking like it was about to emerge from obscurity.

The four of us stood there, my mother and father, young Mayu and I, taking in the delicious air of the mountains. When I turned around I saw the dark green of the huge mountain soaring even more brightly in the western sky.

If someone would have announced to us then that my father would soon pass away, my mother would remarry and divorce, not to mention giving birth in between, my sister would go on to become an actress, quitting her job, living with a man as if they were married, dying by her own hand, and finally, on top of it all, me, destined to hit my head and fall for the man my sister had lived with . . .

. . . we would have gone crazy.

But none of us knew what would happen. We just stood with large smiles on our faces as we looked at the setting sun, talking about how we were looking forward to the delicious dinner waiting for us back at the hotel. My mother and father were getting along well. It had been a while since they had taken a trip together, and they acted like newlyweds. I'm sure none of us would have believed what would eventually come to pass.

Then fate took over and everything really happened.

It hurts me to realize they were there.

Anyway, at that point Mayu became frightened by the beautiful landscape spread out before us, and she started screaming that she wanted to leave. "Let's go home!" she cried. I'm sure her reaction came from more than just being tired or bored.

But I was different. I knew there were even nicer places to view the scenery, so I started crying because I wanted to go higher up the mountain. How could the two of us turn out so differently?

It seems like we had a spirit before we were born, something that we brought with us when we first came into the world. I suppose that's what defined our differences. But why? Why do people's paths go in such opposite directions? We both had the same parents. Yet one of us lived and the other one died. . . .

I want to go on living, understanding more. I want to see the world around me. I'm overjoyed by my differences. I don't know if this thing that resembles hope is the source of all of my desires.

When I wander the streets of the city where I was born, attacked by the flood of old, frightening memories, I get an urge to turn to the fading sunset over the skyline of Tokyo and yell aloud, "Papa!" It's all so familiar. I recognize the scent of my own childhood—the smell of the wool on my father's sweater, the smell of water straight from the well at the side of the road. I feel it all.

Unlike the powerful sunsets in Saipan, the scenery of Japan is more elegant, more sentimental, more subtle and refined. If you don't open yourself up to all your senses then it's impossible to see it all.

The fact is I was born and raised here, and for a while I could recall only bits and pieces of my life until now. Somewhere inside all of that, I had the opportunity to meet and start a wonderful new relationship with you. I think of you as a pleasant dream that I will have when I doze off during a midday nap. A cool pillow of water for my deathbed.

The dream is far away, lovely, and sweet.

It's like the peculiar melody of Saseko's voice when she sings, like the white sand on the beach in Saipan where millions of people are living.

At some point in time it will happen. The day will arrive when everything is brought to an end, and all will be forgiven. I will simply disappear.

Then will I be able to meet my father and Mayu again?

For now I suppose I'll just stay right here. Outside my foggy window rain comes pelting down. Inside my lonely heart . . .

. . . I can't write what I feel.

No, I should probably be honest with you. There's not a cloud in the sky today. We've had wonderful weather all morning. Even the clear air of a Japanese winter is hard to brush aside.

Please come home soon.

Let's have a dinner of hot pot.

I want to see you, and tell you many things.

I don't want us to grow distant. I want to keep telling you the things I know no one else can comprehend. I want to continue to force you to understand them.

What on earth am I writing?

The past we've formed together is beautiful.

It's like a fable in an ordinary, everyday sort of way. But as the novels and movies around the world tell us, our story is altogether unique.

In order to feel such a simple thing, apparently it's good for one to fall down and knock the memory from her head, then struggle to retrieve it.

Everything feels wonderful. I feel good . . .

. . . like the sound, smell, and color of the dried leaves in autumn.

Perhaps this sounds like a line from the classics, but I leave it with you as my parting word anyway:

Now I understand why everything is here.

Lately this has brought me a tremendous amount of pleasure.

With love,
Sakumi

Looking back over the letter, one thing became perfectly clear. I really wanted to see Ryūichirō. I knew there was something I wanted to tell him, the one person who I knew could understand me. I wanted to etch the swelling and immaturity indelibly in my heart as a memory of my feelings from a painfully bitter night.

With the memory firmly in place, I decided to go on living. It would stand in my mind as a single moment—the color of my skin, which seemed to melt into the stationery, my hand, which glimmered under the light of my overhead lamp. I would remember the memory of the heat from the stove, my flushed cheeks, the voices of my mother and Junko talking together downstairs in the kitchen, and the lingering smell of the curry rice we had had for dinner that night.

I found myself falling asleep as I thought about so many different things.

Then I had a dream about my boss from Berries.

∾

I'm hanging over the edge of the bar at work, wishing for time to move faster so I can go home. Twilight begins to settle inside the soft brown interior of our little business.

For some reason it's summer. The smell of fresh grass comes in through the window. I can see the bright green amid the settling dusk outside.

My boss is behind the bar frying thin slices of meat. The entire bar's full of the wonderful sound and smell.

There aren't any customers. My boss hands me a small plate with the meat and tells me to eat it discreetly. I see the ring he always wore on his finger. It's embedded with a large turquoise rock.

The meat's soft and delicious. I mention how wonderful it would taste with a beer. Before I know it he hands me a large glass, telling me it will be fine to drink it since customers haven't yet arrived. But we know Z and his friends will be coming that night, so things will eventually be busy. It would be best to recharge our spirits now.

My boss laughs, and I think to myself what a wonderful man he is. I like him a lot. He tells me what a nice place we have. The staff's wonderful, and it's a comfortable environment. Everything is always calm. He says he never would have thought he could have created such a nice place back when he was in his twenties.

Outside I hear the shrill of cicadas. I also hear voices of mothers with their daughters as they travel past in the late-afternoon sun.

I flatter my boss, telling him his meat and beer bring a soft, warm atmosphere filled with love to the bar, a feeling so good it's painful. Then I tell him not to talk about how he never imagined he could make a place as wonderful as this, because once he starts to say things like that then everything will come to an end. I mean, I also love all the people who work here. I don't want to lose this place.

My master just laughs. He says not to worry, because the bar will stay open forever.

~

Opening my eyes, I found I was back in the cold morning of winter, thrust from the warmth of my dream. It tormented me almost to tears.

Why do people act so foolishly? I thought quietly to myself. Why is it so hard to go on living? And why is it so painful to watch the number of people and places so dear steadily increase as the days go by? We just keep throwing ourselves into the same pattern of evil cycles like we are slicing ourselves with daggers.

Why on earth would anyone keep doing such a thing? Why?

The thoughts ran through my mind as though I'd been assaulted by the tremendous energy of my dreams.

Chapter 17

"I don't know what it is," Ryūichirō said, "but there's something really different about you. Really." His reaction came at the precise moment he opened the door and saw my face.

I have a confession to make. I really don't like meeting people at the airport, it doesn't matter who the person is. And I dislike it even more when they've just come from overseas. To me, picking someone up at Narita is just about the worst thing in the world. Perhaps it has something to do with how I feel when I come home from a trip. I stumble off the plane looking disheveled, my skin pale. Can you blame me for not wanting to be seen?

On the way back to Tokyo from the airport I fell asleep, and a century of love was awakened inside me. I think it was only natural for me to want to jump into the shower and fall quickly off to sleep.

That's why I opted not to go to the airport to pick up Ryūichirō. Just knowing that he and I were again living the same mornings and evenings, caught up in the same flow of time, was enough to make the sunset appear much sweeter every day. Now when I call him on the phone, we can talk forever.

The nights felt long and silent.

Feelings that had made me numb trying so hard not to miss him seemed to thrust out, one right after another, the way flower petals extend themselves to receive the sun of the season, quietly and with certainty.

* * *

I went to see him at his hotel the day after he arrived in Tokyo.

In the past I used to love it when my father returned home from foreign business trips. Anyone who arrives from a different country is somewhat strained, but at the same time they seem to bring with them a special kind of fragrance, almost as if they've come back to life. A renewed sensation.

Having slept peacefully for the first time in a long time, Ryūichirō looked refreshed, although I could tell his heart was still wandering along the beaches of Saipan. I looked out over the large windows in the hotel room. The weather was fine and the view across the skyscrapers was spectacular. I could practically see the new spring breeze blowing through the city below us.

Ryūichirō poured us some tea.

"Do you want to go out and get something to eat?" I asked.

"Yeah," he replied. "I'm starving. I haven't had a thing since breakfast." Then he was silent.

"What?" I asked.

Ryūichirō looked over at me and smiled. "I've been trying to come up with the right word to describe how you've changed. I think I just discovered it."

"And what would that be?"

"Happy," he said. "Yeah, that's it. You look like you're enjoying life."

He was right. I was happy.

My feelings, however, came from a natural high, not from being stoned or drunk, because my condition was different from that of people who find themselves tripping out on drugs and alcohol. Without fail, an unfair price must be paid for the latter. On a night when you least expect it, a caller comes to collect on the unpaid portion of the bill.

Rather than "happy," I'd say my situation was closer to "content."

Somehow I felt relaxed. I suppose I was stressed out most of the time after falling and hitting my head, simply because I was forced to use ambiguous energy to take charge of everyday life, which became my top priority. There was more than enough opportunity to think about how much I'd retained and how much I'd forgotten, an uncommon way to survive. I was always questioning how much I remembered, when really I only wanted to know what I was missing. It wasn't natural.

I tried not to allow myself to be bothered by it, but angst always found a way of sneaking up behind me. Once the threat of that was gone, I found myself enjoying daily life. I felt like I'd been relieved of the nervous feeling that had previously wrapped itself around me whenever I would meet and talk with other people.

When I opened my window in the morning, I discovered the fresh scent of spring mixed with the smell of sun and grass. Small buds forming on the cherry trees, later turning into huge blossoms of faint pink. Looking out over this miracle, I gazed out on the past twelve months, living that way. Everything seemed mysterious, something so puzzling that I had to question how it was so strange. I felt an essence floating up inside me from the very bottom of my soul. I labeled that fragrance "me," and realized that with it I could see things far better than before.

You read a lot about druggies who love themselves, and the word that's generally used to describe them is "blissful." But the same books also question how close their feelings are to happiness. I admit I was scared when it was my turn to see things that way, to understand true happiness, because I fathomed for the first time how wonderful the perception can be. Once you get to a certain point, nothing in the world can stop you.

My boss at Berries recommended a book to me that depicted these thoughts. So I allowed myself to read it, but at first I was turned off because the author seemed to be using her own happiness just to prove a point, on purpose. I look at her differently now, because ever since receiving my own joy I've felt like I should be the one sharing it with others. Surely the same thing would happen if I went through a painful experience as well. Maybe that's just one more reason for our hearts: that future inner self trying to teach a lesson to the "I" who existed in the past.

Now that I've gone through it, I really understand. Happiness, unparalleled.

A feeling as strong as depression or complete neurosis.

~

Once he told me I looked happy, Ryūichirō wrapped his arms around my waist and squeezed tightly. Then he continued to speak. "I've realized something else as I've watched you go through so many different changes these past few months. Human beings are nothing but empty containers. Yes, I really think so. It doesn't matter what you choose to fill your container with, even if it's someone else, because you still won't be any different from another woman off the street. There's no doubt about it, Sakumi, you've really changed lately. But I'm also sure that deep down inside there's always been 'Sakumi.' I don't know, maybe I'm talking about your spirit, but whatever it is, it's the one thing about you that never changes. Chances are it never will. It's been with you from the beginning, absorbing everything going on around you, trying to be happy. When I think that spirit will always be around, I feel lonely and sad. I can hardly stand to be around you."

I burst out laughing. "You really know how to flatter a woman, don't you?"

Ryūichirō laughed along with me.

There was something I'd learned about life from him as well, something that reminded me of the sparkling warm rays of the sun filling the room where we stood. Its tone seemed to go on forever.

I know how two people with strong personalities like ours were able to maintain balance and not find ourselves drowning even though tossed by that terrifying thing called love. It had something to do with the remarkable way Ryūichirō was able to maintain distance. You see, when one person hooks up with someone else, they have only each other in the world. The space they make between them is theirs alone, unique, the only one of its kind, anywhere. Once they realize they have created that area, then they both unconsciously try to break free from it in order to see each other more clearly.

But he was a writer, and as such he was able to hold his own ground. Between the two of us there was some other vessel, bright and warm, something that couldn't have existed with only one of us alone; there was a strange atmosphere that gave rise to a medley of different things.

The most interesting thing about Ryūichirō was his clear list of priorities. Something tells me that was Mayu's greatest worry when she was with him.

∾

Once in the middle of the night I awoke extremely thirsty. Moonlight reflected off the ceiling, and for a moment it was so quiet that I thought time had stood still. None of those things that preoccupied my life were there. When I checked the time, I saw it was three o'clock in the morning.

I stayed awake for a while, just lying in bed with my eyes open.

Then I realized it was happening.

It had been quite some time since I'd felt that way before. In fact, I couldn't recall when the sensation had come over me last. After falling down the stairs and going into the hospital, I would often wake up like this in the middle of the night. It was just a feeling; I didn't know when it would come. And it was impossible to put into words.

It was nothing. Just that, nothing. Everything around me was gone. I found myself floating in empty space. Simple logic let me understand what was happening and I could easily familiarize myself with my surroundings: I knew who I was, I'd been asleep, and I recalled the things I'd done that day.

But distance separated me now. I'd lost all emotion. The only thing I could truly feel was my own body resting vacantly. I didn't know if I was three years old or thirty; there was no distinction between today and yesterday. Everything was just a dream and in that dream if a voice had told me, "You're a premature baby waiting to be born," I would have thought to myself, I see, because now I would understand. Everything was so silent, so bare. A blank page of white paper.

Was I going crazy?

The same question crossed my mind every time it happened.

But as I lay on my bed the flow of memories slowly came back to me, just in the nick of time, to save my life like a ship that lands on a familiar shore. . . .

. . . I recalled my mother's face saying goodnight to me before bed

. . . those people I loved in life

. . . the friends I could no longer see. And the wonderful, brief moments I'd spent with them.

Fireworks on summer nights. Phosphorescent animalcules sparkling on a beach. Stormy nights with snow. Listening to the radio playing my favorite song under the light of a small lamp while leaning over the window ledge with my sister Mayu as we viewed white crystals dancing in the darkness, harmonizing our voices to the music.

Strangely, those were the thoughts that came back to my mind. Reality returned to me slowly, one small piece of it after another, saving me in the nick of time.

The brilliant crimson sun of Saipan, so gorgeous you'd never think it a part of this world; the spot where it dipped in the sea. Saseko, and her red cheeks softly glowing in the twilight. Her hair, so dark and so brown.

It was no different from peering down into a blooming tulip—a combination of scent with visual appeal. My crying baby brother as he stumbled around looking for our mom—making me laugh. Ryūichirō, and all the other people in my life with whom I'd slept—our naked feet touching in bed. A matinee in a darkened movie theater—stepping out into the harsh rays of the sun. The touch of dirt as you transplant seedlings—the cold sensation of earth.

Various perceptions were flowing into my mind, stirring up my desire to be connected. I wanted to remember them forever. I simply wanted to live.

And I wanted to be a part of it all.

It was like a prayer: Please let my children, my family, livestock, and fields go without harm over the upcoming year. Please let our crop be a good one. Please let me feel the peace and happiness that come with a good season.

Or so I cry out to a place where the generations of people had gathered since the beginning of time, from the deep past to the present.

Fate is unexpected. One can't control what will happen tomorrow. Hitting my head and living to tell about it was exactly the same as falling down, cracking the skull, and dying right there on the spot. Everything was the same. I couldn't foresee the future, but I was there just the same. The thought of it was frightening.

Coming to an understanding of innumerable things, I came to, and pulled myself out of bed.

My throat still dry, I went downstairs to the kitchen to get something to drink. After filling a mug full of coffee, I walked over to the table and sat down. In front of me there was a large white envelope. When I picked it up and read the address, I was taken aback with surprise. It was an application for a private school that specialized in treating autistic children, or other kids who were unable to cope with regular school. I had a hunch why the pamphlet was there, but it was a shock to discover no one had informed me. In fact, I recalled Yoshio going off to school only yesterday, just like usual.

I thought, what in the world has happened? Yoshio and I were so close back in Saipan, huddled together like teammates. Now he seemed distant, even though we were both living under the same roof, eating the same food.

At least I was sure of that much.

~

The next morning when I asked Junko about it, she said, "He was the one who wanted to go. Yoshio brought the application to us. Yukiko's off at this moment checking out the place with your brother."

"But what's he going to do about regular school?" I asked. "Couldn't he wait before running off to a place like that?"

"Actually," Junko replied, "Yoshio hasn't been to school once since the two of you returned from Saipan. We just found out last week."

"You're kidding!" I said, my mouth dropping open.

"I'm not."

"But he left the house with his schoolbag every day."

"True. But apparently a man called the school claiming to be Yoshio's friend. Once the school found out he was home, just not showing up to classes, they called your mother. That's why it took us so long to find out."

"I had no idea," I said shaking my head, still shocked by the news.

"Which is odd, because at first your mother and I assumed it was you who'd called the school to report on him, so we didn't take it all that seriously. But when we talked to the ladies in the office they said the caller was an older gentleman. We were both a bit surprised."

"Didn't he mention some new friends? What are those people like?" I asked.

"I have absolutely no idea," Junko replied. "He won't say a word about who he's been running around with. All he said was he hated his public elementary school and wouldn't go back, he would only go to the children's center. Whatever do you think could have happened?"

"I'm sorry you have to deal with this," I said. "Every kid in this family has something wrong with them at some point in their lives."

Junko began to laugh. She wasn't concerned with our family because she was trying to stick her nose into other people's business, she was just a part of our home. Families never stop getting larger. The more someone steps out of the place where she lives and journeys out into the world, the bigger her family becomes. The process is neverending.

I'm not sure if Junko, who looked like a typical housewife off the street, considered that good or bad. But the strength of her personality came shining through the minute things started happening with Yoshio, a talent that neither I nor my mother possessed. I suppose I'd call it the powerful strength of a mother—well, something like that. I found myself loving Junko dearly during those moments, and even if she were to leave our home she would always be a welcome member of our family.

What a peculiar thing.

As we talked in the kitchen, my mother came in the door followed by my brother, who looked as though he'd been crying. His eyes were swollen and red. Yoshio turned and went straight up the stairs. My mother looked at me and said, "Do you think you could take him somewhere for a while? I'll explain what happened later. Right now he's just got to get rid of some steam. Unless someone takes him out he'll sit up in his room until he rots. We can't leave him up there crying all alone."

When I looked into my mother's eyes I could clearly see what she was trying to imply: *You're responsible for this, so do something about it.*

"That's fine," I said, moving around my mother and heading up the stairway. "Leave everything to me."

Something pulled at my heart when I saw the sad look in Yoshio's eyes, but it wasn't the same kind of pain I'd feel, for example, for an innocent stray kitten. The feeling came more from looking at complete helplessness, and of knowing too much about the boy who was wrapped in that torment. My newfound happiness, however, was not affected by his sullen expression.

"Yoshio," I said, "let's go get something to eat."

"I don't want to," he replied. "Just being around you when you're so happy tires me out."

Once again he managed to say the one thing he knew would affect me the most. Why did this small boy possess such a power to see through me? And where did that power come from? At his age he'd mastered a delicate technique few adults ever aspire to. But what was the purpose? What good was it in his life?

"If you stay around here you'll get hungry, because they aren't making anything for dinner downstairs, they're too busy gossiping about you. So you've got to go out. It's just what the doctor ordered. Don't worry, nobody's going to ask where we're going. But tell me something, so I know if the rumors are true. Do you really want to leave school?"

Yoshio nodded his head.

"I've also heard that you've been skipping classes lately, and I want you to know I'm impressed. You fooled all of us this time."

My brother's face brightened just a bit, and he lifted his head with pride. "It wasn't easy! I told myself I'd do it on my own this time, without causing any trouble for you, Saku-chan."

"So where were you?" I asked. Apparently my curiosity was getting through, because now he was starting to talk.

"I'd ride the trains mostly, hanging out at a bunch of different places, like at the park or along the banks of the Tamagawa. I even made some friends—older friends, mostly. I hooked up with some because they're clairvoyant, and with others just because I like them. They taught me all sorts of different things, and they even took me out to eat. Once I met a homeless kid off the street and we shoplifted some candy from a store. That only happened once, but he was a great guy. I haven't seen him since running into him at the game center when he bought me some shaved ice."

"Listening to you speak, I realize how much of a sucker you are for anyone who'll buy you something," I said. But I also figured out something else. Yoshio needed to be involved in many things. It would have been cruel to put a child like that in regular school, because he was obviously beyond what other children could do. He was well on his way to becoming an adult.

"What do you expect? It's not like I have any money," Yoshio replied.

"You're right," I said, thinking for a moment. He'd come in contact with various people, New Age and delinquent, and although I could never say that was a wonderful thing, it did show me that Yoshio was trying to make it on his own. I also saw he was dying to show off how successful he'd been—to me or to anyone else.

Knowing there was something inside my brother that brought him even the slightest happiness brought a peacefulness over me. Up until now I'd seen Yoshio only as a kid who was picked on, or things even more sad.

"Friends are good things," I said to my brother. "But when you do it out on the street you'd better be careful. There's a whole bunch of bad people out there just waiting to kidnap a cute guy like you. They'd just love to get their hands on someone your age. You'd better make sure that they don't."

"Don't worry," Yoshio replied. "When I look at a person I can see if they're good or evil. When I go into the city, I'm always surprised to see how few and far between bad people are. You hardly ever see them around. On the outside, a few might look like they're just hanging around, but oftentimes their hearts are so busy they practically have a storm going on inside. It's the same for people in the park and on the banks of the river." My brother paused. "Whenever a weird person approaches me, I get a strange tingling inside. So I make it a point to become friends only with those people with good intentions."

"I see," I said. "But how about finishing your story in a restaurant somewhere? Let's go get something to eat."

"Can I ask you a favor?" my brother blurted out. "Because there's something I've been wanting to do and I haven't got the money to do it."

"What?" I asked. "Don't tell me you want to go out for steak."

"No," he said. "I want to go see my father, but not for sympathy or because I want to rat on somebody. I just have something to ask."

My mother had made it plain to us that she didn't want to see her second husband after the divorce, even though none of us knew why they'd split up. My mother wasn't against Yoshio getting together with his father, but she wasn't pleased with the idea either. As such, my brother had naturally been kept away. I suppose we assumed that he'd go if he wished when he was old enough to do so. I'm sure it was still uncomfortable for Yoshio to bring up the subject with my mother. His father lived in Yokohama at the time.

"That's fine. I'll go with you. That way we can eat in Chinatown."

"Are you sure?"

"Of course I'm sure," I said. "Mom's bound to find out about it sooner or later. But who cares?"

"Okay." My brother nodded.

Without a quick way to get there, I suggested we call Ryūichirō and have him drive us. Yoshio was completely against the idea.

"What's wrong?" I asked. "It seems like you've really had it in for Ryūichirō lately." Thinking back, I realized that Yoshio hadn't been with him once since he'd returned from Saipan. Maybe it was jealousy.

"Okay," I said. "I understand. We'll go together by train."

Yoshio looked as if he had something to say.

"What is it?" I asked.

He sat still for a moment. "Do you know about Ryūichirō?" he asked. "Saku-chan, he's been fooling you all this time."

"What do you mean? Does he have a wife hidden away in a closet or something?" I started to laugh.

"No," my brother replied. "Something else."

"Now I'm worried. Tell me."

"I bet you didn't know that Mayu had an abortion—twice. Both times it was Ryūichirō's baby."

"You're right," I said. "I didn't know." I was shocked, but not by what he'd said. I was more taken aback by the word he'd used, and in the correct context. "Keep using that kind of language," I said, "and pretty soon you'll be getting a girl pregnant." Perhaps Yoshio's time out on the street with hooligans hadn't been all that good for him.

Without a doubt my brother had a special talent that gave him access to things regular people couldn't see. In addition, he knew how to benefit from the information. On top of everything, he made people tremble as easily as he made friends. I didn't want to pardon him for those things simply because he was a child, but now things were different. Something told me he was only trying to be compassionate, and I felt sorry for him.

"When did you find that out? Did Ryūichirō tell you?" I asked.

"I'm sorry," Yoshio said. "I suppose I gave you a shock."

"No, not a shock, but let me think about it for a while." Thinking about it for a while, I began to speak. "Even if something like that did happen, it was a long time ago. And I suppose it was Mayu's decision all along. She must have said that she didn't want them. Except for you, Yoshi-chan, Mayu never got along with children, since she was still a kid herself. It would have been nice, though, if she had mentioned the babies to me.

Keeping something like that a secret until you go off and kill yourself . . .

"If anything surprises me, I suppose it would just be that Mayu and Ryūichirō were having sex. To just dive into something like that, at such a young age—I think it's rather tasteless." At that point I allowed my true feelings to show through me, but just for a short moment. My brother had been there for it all.

"So you aren't upset?" he asked.

"You always did like Mayu, didn't you?" I asked.

It was true. More than my mother, the goddess Shiva, more than me, the tough big sister, there was something about the graceful Mayu that Yoshio had loved even as a baby. He was foolish, and I was sure he'd end up in a lot of trouble with women as soon as he got older.

Even though I seemed to be getting along fine, there was a similar quality inside me. People like Mayu tend to lead men into their lives, burying them in their swamps, never letting them leave. They go through life playing by their own rules, and the minute you've gone out with them once, you find yourself caught in a web that makes you lose the ability to find happiness in another reality, regardless of how worn out you are. On top of not having a conscience, there was a place in Mayu so dark it was frightening. Each time I was exposed to her seduction I thanked heaven I was not a man.

Her charm seemed unrelated to personal happiness, but due to that skill she had no female friends. Only men could stand to be with her. According to her, she was the only person on earth who felt pain, and when she was hurt she unconsciously coiled up in her own little universe where she dominated as queen.

But I was still me, going out with a man who'd been struck by her power. Mayu was passionate; Ryūichirō was smart enough to know how painful Mayu's life had been. I'm sure he found some way to love her because of it.

"You still haven't told me how you know," I said to Yoshio.

"I had another dream," he replied. "But I really can't call it a dream. Do you believe me?"

"You don't have to keep asking me that," I said. "Of course I believe you."

"Well then, I'll tell you. I saw a vision of Mayu."

~

Yoshio said that when his vision opened he found himself standing in a place he'd never been to before. There was a long hallway full of different wreaths and vases. Doors lining the hallway seemed to lead into small rooms or closets; and curtains of various colors had been draped in front of each door. There were posters on the walls, and my brother had the impression he was "behind" something.

I knew exactly what he was talking about. It was behind the stage at the theater nearby. At the time Mayu started living with Ryūichirō, she'd been cast in a play. It was by far the most acclaimed of her stage performances. I knew my brother was referring to the backstage dressing rooms.

Apparently Yoshio was thrust down the long hallway as people bustled in and out of the rooms. Everything was in commotion. He looked and saw Mayu's name printed on one of the doors, so he pulled back the curtain and looked in.

The room was in disarray, but he noticed Mayu right away. She was sitting on a small, round chair in the middle of the clutter. Her hair was pulled back, her face painted pure white with makeup. In front of her was a mirror surrounded with lights. Yoshio said she wore a costume with lots of gold patterns, yes, he said, he was sure of it. I knew the robe he was referring to. She'd been cast in the role of Kannon, the Buddhist goddess of mercy, and a famous costumer had been brought in to design the show. The outfit was spectacular.

My brother was so happy to see Mayu he wanted to reach out and touch her, but he didn't. Her face appeared ghostlike, it was so white, which frightened him. In his dream he was well aware that Mayu had died long ago.

"Yoshio?" Mayu asked. "Come over here and sit down."

Yoshio did as he was told. He tried to keep his eyes fixed on our sister, but when he looked at her directly they became clouded. Her image was that vivid.

"I have two children who were never born," Mayu said.

Yoshio didn't understand what she was talking about.

"I'm only tormented by one thing in my life, and that was giving up my two children. Please tell Sakumi that I'm only troubled by that." Mayu paused for a moment. "And tell her thanks for remembering me when she was with you in the jungles in Saipan. Oh, and tell her that her name doesn't mean 'crescent moon' like she's always telling people. I guess Mother forgot the real reason a long time ago, and that's made our father sad. Just remember those things, and take them back to Sakumi. Can you do that for me?"

Yoshio nodded.

"You're a wonderful brother. I'm sure you'll be a handsome young man someday." Mayu sat back and smiled.

"I'm going to be happy when I get older, there's no question about it!" My brother said with tears in his eyes. He knew how hard it was for Mayu to appear in spirit form like that.

"Do you know what a 'grand finale' is?" Mayu questioned.

My brother shook his head.

She began to speak faster. "Well, once I get to perform something like that, everything will be fine. You see, I think I'm going to have a chance to go back and live my life over again. But I plan to do things differently. I'm going to take things much more slowly. In my previous life I jumped into everything too quickly, and I didn't slow down until it was too late. No one was to blame.

"But I've noticed you, Yoshio, and I can see you're quite eager for your age. Please take care of yourself. Don't hurry through life like I did. Take time to savor the dinners that Mom makes, and look closely at the sweaters she buys you. Remember the faces of the boys and girls in your school class, and take time to stop and watch that old house they're tearing down in your neighborhood. Sometimes when you're alive you fail to realize it, but when you're waiting in the dressing room for your next chance to go out on stage, then everything becomes so clear.

"Yoshio, the sky's really blue. You have five fingers on each hand. Both your mother and father are alive. Strangers greet you when they pass you on the street. All those things are just like gulping down delicious water. Let that water flow inside you. We all have to drink the water every day of our lives, otherwise we will cease to go on living. Everything's exactly the same. If you don't reach out and drink it, even though it's just sitting there waiting for you to, then your throat dries up and you die. I've never been good with words, so I have a hard time expressing myself, but please understand what I'm saying.

"Tell Sakumi that I don't have any regrets. Tell everyone, for that matter. But don't rush out and do so. I remember back in school when we had an assignment to keep a journal over summer vacation. I'd write an entire month's worth of entries in less than a week, and then feel jealous of my friends who stayed up late at night a few days before school started to finish their own. They seemed so involved, but not me. I was afraid if I didn't do mine quickly, it would never get done. Next time I have a chance to write a diary I'm going to write it like it should be written, one day at a time. I'll describe the warmth of the sun, and my thoughts and feelings of that day. You see, Yoshio," Mayu said, "I hurried through life, that's all."

My brother nodded.

Mayu stood up and went over to a small stand and placed her hand on a teapot. Just as she was pouring water into two cups, Yoshio opened his eyes.

He was back in his bedroom, alone on his bed.

Mayu was no longer around.

And that was the extent of my brother's vision.

~

On the train bound for Yokohama I sat silently trying to figure out what my sister had had to say. Outside the window city lights sparkled in the distance. We traveled from one train station to the next, watching various lives of various people as they were silently shaken by the train, heading off in various directions.

I felt sad. As I thought of Mayu, I was overwhelmed with melancholy, but that's all I could feel at the time. Were those the only feelings I would ever have of my sister, until I died and went on to a different place?

I longed to see her, to make things return to the way they were.

I loved her. I hated her. I wanted to reach out and touch her. The same cycle, rolling around and around, my emotions right in the middle. Endless revolutions, never to be broken.

We called Yoshio's father from the train station once we arrived in Yokohama. He was surprised by the call, but quickly agreed to meet us at a small cafe in Chinatown.

It had been years since I'd seen him, so I began to feel slightly nervous. I recalled with a certain amount of nostalgia the days when I lived together with that stranger I called "Father," even bothering to do his laundry. That was an unusual time in my life.

Yoshio and I were happy as we drank several different cups of Chinese tea and munched on sweet sesame cakes. Before long "Father" walked in. He wore a casual sweater and some Levi's, looking younger than before. As he approached us, however, I noticed the lines in his forehead had increased since we'd lived together, and his overall frame had grown smaller.

"So the two of you ran away from home." "Father" smiled. Next he squinted at Yoshio, and leaned back with a relaxed look on his face. I could see he was pleased. Surely the pleasant look on "Father's" face had cured my brother's anxiety. Yoshio himself was probably pleased, his father looking at him like that. Even though their feelings weren't expressed in words, it was easy to tell that he loved his son and had longed to be with him for some time.

"You've gotten so big!" "Father" said.

Yoshio looked like he would cry.

"And Sakumi," he said, turning to me. "You're a completely different person, practically an adult. When was the last time we saw each other?"

"It must have been Mayu's funeral," I replied.

"Oh, yes," "Father" said, looking glum. "That was so unfortunate, wasn't it? She was so young. But has it really been that long since we got together?"

"Yes, sir," I said. "But 'Father,' you haven't changed a bit." It occurred to me how strange I must have sounded speaking so politely to a man who had been married to my mother. But how else should I have treated him—like any other man off the street? When you think about it, "reasons" are always important.

Our pretend family left the cafe and began walking down the main street of Chinatown. Everything was full of commotion. The bright faces of the people around me reminded me of a festival in some foreign country. Vendors lined both sides of the street selling hot Chinese cakes still sending forth clouds of steam. Rows of exotic vegetables and ingredients for various dishes lined the shopfronts.

I loved Chinatown. The first time I ever went as a child I got so excited from all the running around that my nose started to bleed. My mother told me later she was really embarrassed by the commotion I caused.

All the excitement awoke a part of me that had been asleep. Layer after layer of signs flashing with cheap neon lights, the looks on the faces of those who had come here to eat, the inexpressible way they seemed to float in the air. Crammed shops and stores lining every alley and street, regardless of how narrow. People just kept coming.

Chinatown created its own country with its own civilization. It had its own system of preserving order. Everything was rare and wonderful. It inspired those kinds of feelings.

Yoshio was walking with "Father." They were holding hands. Both faces were shining: "Father's" face as he explained what was going on in this shop or the other, and Yoshio's face as he earnestly tried to listen.

How splendid, I thought. It's like an illusion. Strolling carelessly through the streets. The faces of people I love, the faces of people all about. I feel equally for each of them. The poverty, the smell of cooking dinners, an image of a pot of hot tea eventually placed on the table. The grandfathers, grandmothers, weddings, and funerals. Summer celebrations. Foreign countries visited, souvenirs brought home. The scent of sweat, and a familiar feeling in the look of it all.

The smell of a place where people lived and worked. Each had their own father and mother; each changing diapers, fighting with their spouse. More and more of the same people. Everyone increasing in number. Regardless of how rich or poor, each crawling into bed and into their dreams.

Once again it dawned on me that even though I was walking on this road, at some point I would die. It was a strange and lonely sense of knowing that this road would continue on in its own lively animation, even after I was gone. My body felt like a part of the atmosphere.

Sauntering down the street, I figured I was only a passing apparition.

"Are you still teaching at the university?" I asked. By this point I was rather relaxed. We'd finished a huge Chinese dinner and were working on our tapioca dessert when the topic of conversation suddenly changed.

"Yes," he said. "They haven't found a reason to fire me yet."

He taught Asian literature, and could speak many different languages.

"Maybe I'll go to your college sometime," Yoshio replied.

"I'd better be through with my job by the time you make it to college, son. Or at least stop being a lecturer. I'm tired of standing in front of bored students."

"Sounds like things are going well with your new wife," I said. "We heard you have a new baby."

"Would that make her my sister?" Yoshio sat with a puzzled look on his face.

"You heard right," "Father" replied. "I have a little daughter. She just turned one. Her name is Shoko, and you spell it with the Chinese character for *villa*. I think the name makes her sound kind of cheap. It was foolish to have given it to her."

"Sounds to me like she's really going to make something of herself," I said. In the back of my mind I completely agreed with him.

"Even though her name has a Chinese origin just like yours, it's not quite as pure as *Sakumi*." "Father" smiled.

Huh? I thought to myself. I suppose my brother was taken aback as well. We glanced across at each other.

"The *saku* in Sakumi, doesn't that mean 'crescent moon'?" I asked. "That's what I've always heard from my mother."

"Well, I wasn't the one who named you, so I'm only speaking from hearsay, but the story I heard was quite different. I'm sure your mother either forgot the true meaning or she just remembered it wrongly from the beginning."

"So what does it mean?" I asked.

"I'm not sure about the details, but if you remember, your father used to read a lot of economics reports and books about success, right?"

I nodded.

"Apparently *Sakumi* came from one of those. The reference goes back to a story in ancient China. I remember reading about it myself in my studies."

"What story?" I asked.

"A long time ago in Han, or old China, there lived an eccentric man named Tōhōsaku who curried favor with the emperor. He received gifts from the palace, but he treated them as though they were worthless. If they gave him a piece of silk cloth, for example, he carelessly flung it over his shoulder. If it was raw meat, he would stuff it into his pants, right into the pocket of his kimono, sticky and wet. Then he squandered all his money on women—that sort of thing."

"What's so good about that story?" I asked.

"Just wait, it gets better," "Father" replied. "You see, all the people around Saku told him he was strange and eccentric, so he fought back, saying, 'No, in the old days people used to go deep into the mountains to hide from their enemies, but those like me who are smart enough know that if you want to hide somewhere the best place to do it is in the palace of the Imperial Court.' And that's the story."

"I still have a hard time finding the good in a story like that." I'd caught the gist of what he was trying to say, but that was all. What I couldn't understand was what Mayu had tried to tell me in her dream.

"Actually, I like the story about her name coming from the moon. It's more ladylike," Yoshio said. "It sounds more romantic."

"Perhaps. But I think Sakumi really takes after her namesake," "Father" replied.

Yoshio agreed. "Yeah, I guess I can see that."

"I know what you're trying to say, but . . . ," I said. I really did. There was just one point that didn't seem to fit—Mayu's kindness. Something was odd about her compassion.

"Maybe that's all you need to know," "Father" said.

I recalled how bitter and jealous he could be at times. When we lived together I never got away from it, but now he seemed calm, almost overflowing in confidence. I don't want to think he made a mistake by getting together with my mother, but I couldn't help noticing how he'd changed. Now he seemed pleasant.

~

As we climbed into a taxi, "Father" told us over and over again how he would come to visit sometime, telling the driver to take us over the Yokohama Bay Bridge. When we drove off Yoshio and I looked back to see him waving his hand in the air until we'd gone so far we couldn't see him anymore.

In the end Yoshio never asked any important questions of him in particular, but something told me the thing Yoshio wanted to confirm more than anything was, "Am I still your son?" I'm sure "Father" provided Yoshio with an answer the split second he put his eyes on him and smiled so broadly. The way he waved his hand as we left was also a clear indication that Yoshio was loved by his father. I was impressed. It felt like we were headed on something like a trip around the world. Everything felt that far away.

Me and my brother. So endless, so distant.

My feelings swelled up even more as we turned onto the freeway and began to cross the bridge. Amid the carefree silhouette of the H-shape, the glowing lights came together to form a solid body in the middle of the sparkling bay. Across the water a number of boats were sleeping peacefully, and they cast reflections over the face of the sea—red, orange, and white lights. Some far, some near.

The beautiful, curving edge of the road went on in a perfect line. Driving through the line was like going through the light. Everything appeared glorious and spectacular for a split second, then we glided away from it.

"Looks like the Milky Way!" Yoshio exclaimed. Then he asked me if I'd ever driven across the bridge before.

"Yeah," I said. "I have." Dozens of times. But out of all of my trips across the bridge, that night was the most spectacular, more beautiful than I'd ever seen it in the past, many times more beautiful.

"It's like we're coming home from a trip," my brother said.

By now we were quite far from the curving line of light, and our taxi was back on the highway. So that's what a "trip" really is—an intense concentration of time that goes by in a few simple seconds, and when you look back you feel sorry that it's over.

My new definition of the word.

After we got home I called Ryūichirō and gave him the rundown on what had happened. I didn't feel ready to bring up Mayu, though, so I didn't. I figured I'd tell him about it in person. I just told him about the origin of my name, and he burst out laughing. When I told him to calm down because it really wasn't that funny, he only laughed harder.

Now whenever I hear the laughter of someone I love that much, I'm reminded of the things that were said by my sister, and the wish of my dead father. It was as though the laughter was showing me how much they cared. To this day it gives me a feeling that is not altogether a bad one.

In fact, it feels rather good.

Chapter 18

A letter arrived from Eiko. A love letter from Hawaii.

Dear Sakumi:
How are you?

I'm here. It feels like Hawaii. Every day feels the same.

I am so thankful for having you there the other day—really, really thankful.

Now all my meals taste delicious. Swimming in the ocean is fun. All because of what you did.

I'm pleasing my parents, and having a wonderful time shopping. I really appreciate having a friend like you.

I love you so much. So very, very much.

Eiko

The words were just scribbled across the page as if a small child had written them. But as I read the letter I honestly felt as if I could see Eiko in Hawaii. The smile on her sunburned face, and her thin arms and legs sticking out of her fashionable sports wear.

The letter had also shared with me Eiko's thoughts as she remembered me so many miles away. As I considered the things she told me, I could feel myself getting better. I felt purer in a way, almost as if I'd become a better person.

My brother left the house on a warm morning in May.

The branches on the trees were swaying wildly in the wind, and the clothes on the people walking back and forth on the street were fluttering about them. The gust was so strong the entire landscape seemed more dynamic somehow.

I pulled myself out of bed rather early and walked over to Yoshio's room. Peeking in through the doorway, I watched him pack his suitcase surrounded in morning light. He was desperately trying to get a number of important items into a rather small bag. He really looked as though he were traveling someplace far away.

"What's wrong with the school you're going to now?" I asked. As I stood in the doorway looking into the room where my brother was packing, I realized how abrupt my question must have sounded.

"Because I've tried everything and nothing seems to work," he replied. "I just can't get along with the other kids."

"Couldn't you just commute to the children's center from here? Then you wouldn't have to live in the dormitory. Aren't there students who do that in your school?" I asked.

"No, there aren't," he replied. "Besides, I've already made up my mind. I'm going."

"I'm going to miss you," I said. "Things are going to be pretty boring around here without you."

As I stood in the doorway pouting, Yoshio reassured me that it wouldn't be long before they would let him out on weekends.

My mother pranced out of her room dressed in a suit that made her look like the perfect "provider" for our family. She took my brother and went out the door. As I watched them disappear out of sight I looked out over the garden shining in the morning light. It appeared so empty.

Junko and I turned around and went into the kitchen. My mother's mug was sitting on the table still half full of tea, next to the cup my brother had been drinking from.

All at once I couldn't stand to be there any longer.

He had just been in the house, muddling about like he always did, like some noisy dog or cat. Now he was gone. From the day he was born until the minute I saw him leave, the thought of us ever living under separate roofs had never crossed my mind. Even though it was obvious that such a day would eventually arrive, I never figured it would happen so soon and in such an awful way. It completely blew my mind. Had my little brother been forced to grow up sooner than expected because of the way we had treated him?

"Won't it be wonderful if things work out for Yoshio?" Junko paused for a moment before continuing. "I've been thinking about a lot of things since he made the decision to leave, and I realized that perhaps I can't stay here forever, either."

"You mean you're going too?" I asked, hearing the miserable tone in my voice.

"I'm not going right away, so stop looking at me like a child," Junko replied with a smile.

Once something becomes an everyday matter, even something uncommon, you stop thinking of it as strange. A housewife, a cousin, my mother, my brother, and me, all living together in the same home. We took our meals together. We each had claim to our own rights, but we functioned together anyway. Perhaps that imbalance finally showed itself within my brother. There really wasn't an answer. I can't say it had something to do with losing my memory, but then I can't say that it didn't. I also can't say it had something to do with Berries closing down, or with me dating Ryūichirō. I'm sure everything had some impact on his departure, and now this was the shape it had taken.

The world around us often goes through changes. It doesn't mean it gets better or worse. It simply continues to change, endlessly moving on.

~

I helped Ryūichirō find an apartment. We went around to several places, actually going into over twenty of them. Ryūichirō was so fickle about finding a place to live. Regardless of what I or anyone else had to say, he refused to make a compromise.

It felt peculiar going into so many strangers' apartments. Each time we opened a new door, for a split second the air would seem to indicate the thoughts and feelings of the person who'd been living there. If it was a new place, the only thing floating in the air was the smell of fresh paint. Each time we went to a different room Ryūichirō would speculate on how it would be like to live there. Looking down from the window and seeing a small road or alleyway, he would imagine both of us coming home from shopping at the store. In this way dozens of different futures were born in a short space of time, and at the same time many others died.

No one can stop a person from daydreaming.

I was amused at Ryūichirō's criterion for finding an apartment. "If you can't see the morning sun, then it isn't a place to live. It doesn't matter how far away the closest train station is. I've just got to have windows facing east." It was one of the few times I'd ever seen him so passionate about something. It was refreshing to see him so determined.

Ironically, the day we found the perfect place for Ryūichirō was the day my brother left the house. Whenever something unfortunate happens in my life, something fortunate always seems to follow.

To make matters even more strange, the room that we found for Ryūichirō was across the street from the staircase I fell on and hit my head. It was an older apartment building, and when you looked down from the window you could see the cold cement flight of stairs. I'm sure you could see me walking up the stairs as well.

I turned to Ryūichirō. "I can just see it now—me on those stairs, looking up when you're standing here in the window. I'll get excited and start waving my hand, and the next thing I know I'll be back on the cement, everything forgotten. What would I ever do then?"

We had left the realtor waiting for us outside the building. The room had been vacant for some time and it smelled strongly of dust and bright sunlight, the floor just slightly chilly. Our voices echoed as we spoke.

"Don't worry, your memory won't leave you now," Ryūichirō replied.

"Oh, look!" I said. "Down there."

"What?"

"My bloodstains."

"You liar!" Ryūichirō squinted out the window. "Stop saying things like that. It's gross." He really sounded disgusted.

Windows lined the east and south walls. White curtains that had been left by the former tenant fluttered in the breeze, reminding me of the aurora borealis. If I were to set their movement to music, I would choose a melody played by a pipe organ.

"I think I'll take it," he said.

"Are you sure you have the money?"

"Of course I do," Ryūichirō said, offended by my comment. "You always ask me that, but believe it or not I'm still getting a lot of revenue from my book because it keeps selling. You should try asking yourself such a question."

"So you have savings?" I asked.

"Uh-huh." He nodded.

"Are you sure?" I grinned.

The room was nice. It was filled with warm light and decorated with nice wallpaper, reminding me a lot of our hotel room back in Saipan. Ryūichirō agreed by saying, "I thought when I opened the window that I'd have a view of the ocean."

For a split second he looked familiar.

. . . or so I thought.

Even though we had been separated, living in different areas of the world and experiencing different things, I no longer felt distant. Things had been this way between us ever since the beginning.

It must have had something to do with our location, a vacant room that stood empty like ruins, that made me understand my feeling so clearly. Maybe it was the sound of both our voices that caused me to realize so much. I didn't pick up on any living ghosts in the room. It was always different in the city, so that must have been why I hadn't thought about it before.

Everything was a blank sheet of white paper, so the feeling intensified—that feeling of something rich in color, formed by two individuals.

~

Life without my brother was like a silent movie—there was something missing with him not around. A lump formed in my throat every time I passed the door to his room, the same lump that was there whenever I saw pictures of my father and Mayu, even if Yoshio was far from being dead. Somewhere a shadow had fallen.

Regardless of what I was doing, I thought about my brother. Mikiko had picked up an extra cake on her way home and I helped her eat it in silence.

After a while she started to speak. "I suppose this is our first taste of what it's going to be like when Yoshio gets big and goes off to college, or finds a girlfriend and spends all his time with her. But don't you think it's happened too quickly?" Mikiko sounded so innocent, as though she was living in self-denial.

Funny, if Yoshio had just stayed here I wouldn't have noticed him. But now that he was no longer with us I was completely aware of his absence. I felt remorse from having let him go, as if I had misplaced something important.

~

She approached me in a cafe. I was there for a quiet cup of tea after work, and I'd just opened my book and started to read. Moreover, I'd sat down at a huge wooden table and right in front of me was a large flower arrangement filled with pure white Casablanca lilies, lace flowers, and a bunch of twigs and branches. It was so big that I couldn't very well see around me, so I wasn't aware she had watched me for as long as she had.

"Excuse me . . . " A soft voice filtered through the lilies in front of me. Glancing up, I noticed she was standing on the other side of the table peering down at me, and I saw her white face among the branches and flowers. She looked blurred in the foliage. It was beautiful.

"I'm sorry to interrupt you like this, but I have this impression that you know a dear friend of mine." The tone of her voice was distant.

Her thick brown hair was wrapped in curls down her back. She appeared elegant and refined. With her eyes slightly upturned, her eyelashes grew thick and long. There was a dark brown look in her eyes that seemed to go on forever. Her lips were thin, her skin perfectly clear. She was wearing a regular white sweater with a long black skirt tight around her waist, and she reminded me of English royalty, but I don't say that from personal knowledge. That was simply the image she conveyed.

"Eh?" I couldn't believe I'd just run into another mysterious being. With so many unusual characters in my life I was thinking I should open a business. I would be lying, however, if I said I didn't need those people. With my curiosity aroused, I smiled and continued the conversation.

"Perhaps," I said. "But who exactly do you mean?"

"Actually, he's a boy still in elementary school," she said.

"Then maybe you're referring to my brother," I said. "Why don't you come over and sit down?"

She smiled for the first time that night, and I noticed the small wrinkles that formed on the end of her nose. I also got a glance at the perfect row of ivory teeth inside her mouth. Her smile was mystifying, something that would attract just about anyone. She brought over a cup and saucer of Royal Milk Tea and took the seat next to me. I couldn't help but smile at how appropriately her tea seemed to fit her, even though we'd only just met.

"Where did you meet my brother?" I asked. "His name, by the way, is Yoshio. I'm Sakumi."

"Oh, please forgive me for not introducing myself," she said. "I'm a student at the university. Everyone calls me 'Noodles.' It's a nickname I was given because I eat *kishimen,* you know, the thin, flat noodles, every day for lunch." She giggled to herself for a moment.

Now it was obvious, this woman really was odd. I started to wonder if something inside my head was sending out signals like a television show that specialized in discussions with telepathic people or otherwise strange individuals.

"I met Yoshio at a park one day during lunch," Noodles continued. "He looked bored, like he was playing hooky from school and he didn't have anything to do. I'd just come from the college, where lectures had been canceled for the day. I approached him before he even saw me. Once we started talking, we realized we had a lot in common, and our conversation just took off from there. It didn't take long for us to become the best of friends. We would meet regularly in the park, but it's been days since I saw Yoshio on our bench. I couldn't contact him since I forgot to get his address or phone number, so I've been wondering if something happened. He's my little friend."

"How did you know I was related to him?" I asked. "We were born years apart, and we don't even look alike."

"Actually," she said, "there's something inside me that tells me things like that. Aren't you aware that your brother has the same talents as well? For example, I was just sitting over there enjoying my tea when you walked into this cafe and sat right down in front of me. Even though there was nothing unusual about either of us, all at once I got this tingling feeling inside me, and after staring at you long enough an image floated up in my mind. I remembered Yoshio telling me about an older sister who had lost her memory, so I just had to come over here and talk to you to see if my hunch was correct."

"Is that so." I understood what she was saying. After spending so much time with my brother and the people back in Saipan, I was more than ready to accept this kind of story. I'd grown immune, so to speak.

"Yoshio dropped out of regular school and checked into a center for special children. It's kind of like a boarding house, since they all live together. Apparently they keep the students busy from morning until night, so I suppose he has little time to get out and go to the park."

"Oh, really?" she said. "I had no idea. Well, as long as he's healthy and happy, then nothing else matters. Still, I wasn't sure if he'd gone back to school, moved, gotten sick, or whatever. With no information I was beginning to worry." She started to laugh. "Tell you what. I'll write down my name, address, and telephone number and the next time you see your brother you can pass the information along and tell him to keep in touch."

Noodles grabbed a paper napkin and scribbled on it. I glanced down at the name she'd written: Kaname Suzuki. Her real name, of course.

"I'll make sure he gets this," I said, taking the napkin.

~

"I should never have put him in that center!" my mother hollered a few days later after walking in from an interview at Yoshio's school. "It's run like an army barracks. He'd be better off sitting at home all day long than live in a place like that." She was hysterical. Since Yoshio had been in the school only a week or two, he wasn't able to come home on weekends.

"What makes it so bad?" I asked. "Don't the students have freedom? Or are the people there just not friendly?"

"No, no," my mother replied. "It's not that at all. Everyone's really nice. But listen to this. They made me talk about the divorce. Can you believe it? The nerve of some people! I was so mad. I blocked that out years ago."

"What about Yoshio? How does he feel?" I asked.

"Oh, Yoshio seems to be doing fine. He says that it's better than going to regular school, and it looks like he's made some friends."

"Well, then, what's wrong with that?"

"I'm the one who doesn't like it there!" my mother screamed. "Why should I have to go in for counseling?"

"I can't really say I agree," I said. "Considering you're his mother." In her own strange way my mother was full of generosity, but at the same time she could really be selfish.

Mikiko was sitting in the living room watching television. She turned to me and said, "I understand what Aunt Yukiko's trying to say. I mean, there's nothing wrong with Yoshio. He's not autistic and he's never been kicked out of school. All he did was play hooky for a couple of days. Everyone seems to think there's something wrong with him mentally, but that's not the case. I think the kids who live at that center are special in other ways."

"Exactly!" my mother said. "But what was I supposed to do? Yoshio said he wanted to leave the house and stop going to regular school, so sending him to the center was the only thing to do, right? There has to be something better. Yoshio just doesn't know that yet."

"I think you're right," I said. "You could always send him to a private boarding school, or even to a school overseas."

"No, we don't have money to do anything like that," she said.

"Well, then, we could at least let him transfer to another school," I replied.

"Yes, that went through my mind too."

"But why did Yoshio want to go to that center so badly? I just don't understand," I said.

"I have no idea."

"Maybe I should go and see him, just to sort of check things out. Is it all right for sisters to go in for counseling as well?"

"I'm sure it would be fine. If it's not, all they can say is 'no,'" my mother said.

Ever since I'd gone with Yoshio on our trip, I had the feeling that I'd been put in charge of his welfare. Placing my hand over my pocket to make sure Noodles's address was with me, I said, "So that's what I'll do. I'll go to the children's center and check things out for myself."

~

Counseling was held on Saturday afternoons.

For some reason I imagined myself seated behind a wire screen with my brother on the other side, but when I got to the building it was far different from the prison I'd conjured up in my mind. The school was just a regular building, no different than its surroundings. It was bright and well maintained, and as I walked through the doors I had the impression that it wouldn't be so unpleasant to live there. The walls were covered with colorful posters that would easily appeal to children, and toys littered the corners of the rooms. There was absolutely nothing lonely or dark about my brother's new home.

As I approached the front desk, I looked into the room behind. There were a number of children coming in and out of the room. Everything was in commotion, but all the children looked like they were having fun. From what I could see, none of the children showed signs of being "special" either.

I turned to the receptionist behind the desk and said, "I'm Yoshio's older sister. Would it be all right to take him out for a bite to eat?"

She smiled and said, "That would be fine. Just as long as he's back before seven-thirty."

I was relieved to find things so friendly.

Then it occurred to me—perhaps some of these children had come to the center just to find rest away from their homes, and something told me that my brother wasn't an exception. His life hadn't been easier than that of any of the other kids. No one but Yoshio knew exactly what was going on inside his head. For all I could gather, the psychic things that were a part of him had confused him so much he couldn't fall asleep at night. Moreover, it was impossible for him to tell our mother or anyone else at home and expect them to understand. That must have been what was in his mind when he made the decision to come to the children's center.

A pleasant-looking old man brought Yoshio down the hall. My brother smiled and waved to the woman at the desk, saying, "I'll be right back!" Then he walked right up to me and said, "Hey! Haven't seen you for a while."

"Let's grab something to eat," I replied. "What do you feel like having?"

"Cake," he said. "I've been craving cake."

I lowered my voice. "How's the food around here, anyway?"

"It's okay, I guess," my brother replied.

"Oh yeah?" I said, starting for the door. I didn't like whispering.

"Air feels so good on the outside," Yoshio said as we walked down the sidewalk. He laughed at himself. The sun was setting and everything was bathed in a warm light. I could see that Yoshio was calmer, but perhaps he was just less nervous about the little things in life that apparently had bothered him before. Now he was living in an atmosphere free from care, as though he'd found protection.

"So you like your new school?" I asked. "The people there are nice?"

"Yup!" My brother nodded his head. "I've made lots of new friends. Some of the kids are autistic, but when I spend time with them I feel like we really connect. Sometimes they act up, or just start to cry. One of my friends won't speak to the teachers, but she'll talk to everyone else, and another kid seems fine until his parents come to visit. He'll blab along with the rest of us until his mom or dad shows up."

"That must be tough for everyone," I said.

"Yeah," my brother said. "At night before we go to bed we all talk about how awful life is at home."

"How have they diagnosed you?" I asked. "What do they think is wrong? Have you been in for counseling?"

"They just tell me I'm too sharp for my age and that I respond to things too quickly."

"I think they're right," I said.

"So far I've just been telling them about Mom and Dad breaking up, and how rough it was for me. That's about all I've said."

"Well, I'm sure that's enough," I replied.

"Maybe Mom gets in hot water when she goes into parent counseling."

I smiled. "There might be some good in that as well."

"But I don't think I'll be at the center much longer," Yoshio replied.

"Oh, really?" I asked.

"Yeah. At least that's my intention."

We walked through the station and jumped on a train headed in the direction of our home. There was a small shopping mall with a dozen or so different places not far from where we lived, and I thought we might go there. But first I asked Yoshio if he wanted to stop by the house.

"No," he said. "I don't want to."

I was a bit taken aback by his response, since he really was only a child. There was no reason for him not to go home.

The view outside our window was soft, as if it was clouded over with mist. Trees full of cherry blossoms were growing here and there in the city, making the streets look as though they had been inlaid with diamonds. Since it was Saturday afternoon only a few people were riding on the train with us. Our car was filled with the light from the setting sun.

Yoshio turned to me. "Why do you suppose I get along so well with the other kids at the center? I feel like we understand one another, like we can read one another's minds. I get along with all of them, even though some of them are crazy or do weird things, or get frightened because they don't know what to say."

"You're more precocious than other children your age," I said. "You have a bunch of weird things running through your head and you're smarter than most folks. I suspect that shows up in the aura that floats around you. The other kids at school have normal thoughts running through their heads, but every now and then they get a sudden burst of energy and they see things like you do. That has to be the reason why you get along so well."

My explanation would have to remain at that for the time being. If I honestly compared the things Yoshio saw and felt to what other children normally experience in life, I knew my statement hadn't been very convincing. Still, my brother nodded his head as if he agreed. Then he turned to me and said, "I'm sure if I look hard enough there are kids in a normal school I could get along with as well. I just didn't have the energy to go out and find them."

Just as the words "Don't worry about it" were about to slip off my tongue, I stopped to think whether it would be appropriate to say something like that to a kid who'd been through so much. Eventually I gave up on the idea completely.

Because there was nothing I could say.

~

I took him to my regular cafe, and after passing through the front door I took him to the large table I was so fond of sitting at. Even after we sat down it still had not occurred to me to mention to Yoshio that I had met his friend. Then, as my brother rattled off his order of four slices of different kinds of cake, I tried to remember what I'd eaten there the last time I was in. Out of nowhere the image of Noodles came floating up in my mind. I turned to my brother and said, "I met someone here the other day who wanted me to give you their address and phone number."

"Who was it?" Yoshio asked, his face turning stiff with fright. His expression was so taut it would be impossible to put into words. "Was it a man?"

I was surprised he would have such a strange reaction. I sensed he was really scared. "No," I said. "A woman." Then I reached into my pocket and took out the paper napkin.

Yoshio scanned the characters for a moment before saying, "Is this that lady who calls herself 'Noodles'?" I suppose he was a bit unsure since she'd only written her real name.

"Yes," I replied.

Then my brother smiled, looking genuinely pleased. The soft inflection in his voice seemed to be hiding some kind of secret.

"Do you know her?" I asked.

"Yeah," Yoshio replied. "I met her in the park and we became good friends. She's a really nice person. We got to be really close, but then this old boyfriend of hers started to hang out with us, and I hated him. He scared me to death. I don't know what happened to him because Mom checked me into the center and I haven't seen or heard from either of them since. I was wondering if Noodles was okay."

"What do you mean he scared you to death? What made you so nervous?"

"I don't really know how to explain it," Yoshio said. "But it seemed as if he really liked me."

"Was he gay?" I asked.

"No, but I don't think that had anything to do with it."

"So what made him so weird?"

"He found a way to get inside my dreams. He came to me every night. Then he would send me messages, you know, through his mind."

I thought for a moment and said, "You know, you're starting to sound like a model case study. Tell me something. Do you ever feel like you're being watched? Do you think there's someone in this cafe spying on you right now?" I figured my brother had finally gone over the limit. He must have been schizophrenic.

Yoshio looked at me with an angry glare in his eye and said, "What are you talking about? I just got frightened, that's all. I got so scared I couldn't go to school anymore. I thought about running away to my dad's house. That's why we went to talk to him, to see if I could move in for a while. Really."

I had no idea those things had been happening to Yoshio. Hearing him talk to me like that brought a sharp pain to my heart.

"Oh, really?" I said softly.

"But Dad has a new baby now, and I figured if I asked him he would just say no anyway, so I gave up on the idea."

"You're really amazing," I replied. "Taking matters into your own hands like that."

"Uh-huh," Yoshio said, nodding his head.

His cakes arrived and he began to devour them greedily. I'd ordered only coffee and as I took my first sip I noticed that the flower arrangement had changed since I had stopped in last. The new arrangement was decorated with a bundle of brightly colored orange gladioli with dark brown twigs. I recalled the white lilies and the lace flowers that had adorned the arrangement before.

. . . then she came into my mind.

"I really like Noodles," my brother said with his mouth full of chocolate cake. "Doesn't she seem kind of strange?"

"I know exactly what you mean," I replied. "Last time I was here she came up to me and just started talking. I could see her face inside the petals of the flowers and, and . . . How should I put it?" The image of Noodles became clearer in my mind as I talked to my brother. It was like a faraway memory from my childhood, carrying with it a beautiful fragrance. There was no difference between how I thought of Noodles and how someone falls in love, madly. The image of her face was that vivid. It was painful.

"Maybe I should give her a call," my brother said.

"Now that's thinking positively," I replied.

"Why not? She's a friend."

I watched Yoshio get up from his chair and go to a pay phone in the corner of the cafe. After a few seconds he returned. Apparently she wasn't at home, or so Yoshio said as he sat back down in his seat and began to finish the rest of his cake.

I managed to swallow the last of my coffee. Then, without thinking, I glanced over to the window, lined with various ceramics. All the plates and cups at the cafe were stoneware made in Japan; and usually the coffee was roasted and ground in the back, right before you drank it. Each piece of furniture was made out of wood. The interior was spacious, but I still felt at home. As the servers walked over the wooden floor, it made a soft creak. They never brought out huge slices of cake piled high with whipped cream. The style was more refined and elegant, almost European. I really liked the little shop. I'd made it my nightly routine to stop in for a cup of tea after work. It was the one small piece of joy I'd found in my life in the city.

Even though I went in several times a week, it occurred to me I hadn't taken time to look at the other people in the cafe until after Noodles spotted me.

. . . or so I thought as she came through the door.

A small bell rang and the front door flew open. A group of noisy girls in their school uniforms came rushing into the store, giggling as they pointed at the display case full of desserts. Our waitress turned and bid them the traditional in-store greeting, *"Irasshaimase."* Somehow our friend had managed to slip in just a few seconds before, nothing more than a shadow. Her presence was as soft as a light breeze in the air, but my brother picked up on her instantly.

"NOODLES!" he cried.

She turned to us and smiled warmly.

I could see in her eyes she was saying to herself, "So we meet again. I knew if I came you'd be here."

Chapter 19

As we talked to Noodles, I became fully aware of my feelings for her despite the fact that they were far too complicated for me to understand at the time. Even though I was able to reach back in my memory to find the words to adequately describe those emotions, I couldn't bring myself to express them. The feelings in my heart were that complex. I'd never felt this way with anyone before, not even Ryūichirō. For a brief moment I wondered if I was actually falling in love.

It went beyond arbitrary things like enjoying her personality and taking a fancy to her face. I'd always known I was attracted to other women, but there was a big difference between thinking Eiko and Saseko were beautiful and my newly formed, acute feelings for Noodles which went far beyond what was normally required. I'd never felt this strongly about anyone.

Everything was fine now that she was around—that was the sensation. I also felt a certain sense of peace knowing that there'd never been a reason a person like this should not be in my life.

Take, for example, a grand cathedral in the middle of an ancient village in Europe. It's something you've seen many times brightly shining in postcards and on TV. You picture it in your mind under a perfectly blue sky, surrounded by crystal-clear air. Then you get on a plane and fly thousands of miles to see it in person, and there it is, just like you imagined it. For me, Noodles was my cathedral. I always knew she was there, but now I was actually seeing her in person. I felt a great respect for such a presence.

She inspired nostalgia, a sweet sense of homesickness. Like a soft lullaby I listened to as a child, I could hear that soft melody around her. She appeared misty and far away, like a beautiful light in the distance.

What was with me? Why was I having such feelings?

Confusion. Whenever someone is confronted with the unknown, she only runs into confusion.

~

"I'm sorry," Noodles said, looking over at my brother. "I'm sorry he was such a pain."

"Don't worry," Yoshio replied. "It didn't have anything to do with you. I just told Sakumi the same thing. Right when I thought he was driving me crazy, he just disappeared."

"The man you were so afraid of?" I said.

"Exactly," Noodles replied, turning to me. "My old boyfriend. He's kind of freaky, and it looked like he took a real fancy to Yoshio."

"What do you mean, 'freaky'?" I asked.

"You would have to meet him to see," my brother and Noodles said simultaneously. Perhaps I should say they "whispered" simultaneously, because both said it under their breath. Now I was even more curious to find out who this guy was.

"He's the kind of person who can capture people's minds, and bring them into his own," Noodles tried hard to explain.

"Is he evil?" I asked.

"Well," she said, thinking for a moment, "I'm really not in a position to say."

"Yes," I said. "I suppose that's always the way it is with people you've dated."

"I do know one thing," Noodles replied. "He was very serious about starting a new religion with Yoshio."

I'd just taken a sip of my coffee when Noodles made her abrupt announcement, and before I knew it I'd spewed coffee all over the table. Apologetic, I turned back to her and said, "Please forgive me. I suppose when a person's surprised they really do spew coffee. I've always thought that only happens on television." I glanced over at my brother. A sharp line had formed between his eyebrows. He was obviously thinking hard about something.

"But it seems to be true," Noodles said. "He was so persistent about asking me to join him that I finally had to leave. That's when we finally broke up."

Since I was such a newcomer to this conversation I couldn't follow all she was saying. It seemed like every time she said something a flood of new thoughts entered my mind—important things, and things I hadn't remembered. Even though things like that aren't often associated with love, I couldn't help but find them romantic.

"He still tried to get me to join him, even after I stopped hanging around him too," Yoshio stated.

"Well," I replied, "if I was to use what little brains I have to come up with a reason for what you are feeling, I'd have to say that somewhere inside you there is a large dish that attracts things that are frightening. I mean, I'm sure if I met him I wouldn't be scared. Isn't there also something inside you that hopes people recognize your special powers? That has to be it."

"Well, maybe," my brother said.

"I know what you're saying," Noodles said. "I felt the same way, you know, that feeling that he was strong. I also knew he was the only person on earth who understood me. That's why it took so long for me to break things off, and it had something to do with Yoshio, too. Now I feel like I'm back to finally being me. Thank you, Yoshio." She turned to my brother and smiled.

"So do you have special powers as well?" I asked.

"No, not really," she replied. "Every now and then I'm able to heal people's wounds and see what's inside an unopened box, that's about it."

That's it? I thought to myself. If that was "all" she could do, then I really couldn't do anything.

Noodles had her hair pulled back in two braids that ran down the length of her shoulders. She wore a black sweater with a green skirt. Even though she appeared so casual, there was something solid about her appearance. In fact she carried herself like she was participating in some kind of formal ceremony. No one had the power to break down the atmosphere that she carried with her, her presence was that strong. It was as though she'd been alive for centuries. Somehow the sensation was thin like a shadow, and somewhere it just plainly hurt me to see it. Even if she was not necessarily laughing or talking so much, I received the impression that she loved me.

"I have this feeling, Ms. Sakumi, that I, I . . . ," Noodles stammered.

"Please," I said interrupting, "just call me Sakumi."

She smiled. "Okay, Sakumi. I have a feeling I know you from somewhere. Isn't that odd?" she asked.

Something told me I couldn't answer her question. Now I just knew we were both thinking the same thing. If the two of us were mutually aware of our own feelings, what would come next? Sex?

Maybe not.

Perhaps we'd just be friends. Certainly that was the answer.

It had been a while since something so simple had entered my head. I remembered back to the first day of kindergarten, when I walked into a classroom full of strangers and was forced to search among them to find at least one who I could be friends with. Then I left it up to fate to decide whether or not it would happen. It was all so restrained. Although I was now an adult, and my freedom had expanded to allow me to go all over the city to find friends, that habit I was sure I'd packed away in a box after elementary school continued to show its face.

Maybe my brother, who was trying to get along by making new companions on his own, was going about it more healthily than I was.

Turning to Noodles, I boldly asked, "Why don't we get to know each other better?"

"No," Yoshio replied. "That's not good. I only have a few more hours before I have to be back. I want to have fun before I'm gone."

He had a good point.

"So why don't both of you come over to my house?" Noodles replied.

"What have you got there to eat?" my brother asked.

As I was about to kick Yoshio under the table, telling him how embarrassed I was to hear him say such a thing, Noodles said, "Why don't we just order pizza?" Then she started laughing. The air seemed to quiver with her smile. Dimples returned to her nose like she was trying to hide some kind of secret.

∾

I dreaded nightfall as a child because it always made me feel lonely. On several occasions my friends and I ran out of our houses so we could continue to play together into the night. But when things grew dark I'd be overwhelmed with fear, and I'd go home for my scolding. When night fell, the color of the green trees that rustled in the wind appeared deeper. Darkness draped a cold blanket over the future, and the light peeking over the horizon the next day seemed unbelievably far away. That's why my friends and I would try and make the best of the few minutes we had together. My favorite friends were the ones who lived next door.

I want to be with you more. We've got to play together, forever.

The thoughts ran through my mind.

Did I know back then that it would be impossible for two little girls at play to remain together until adulthood? Did I realize how much things would change, like the way I would think about life, or the path on which I was walking?

I think things were different back then, because children have a natural way of knowing that "now" is the only chance they'll ever have. I was sensitive enough to know on my own that "nows" were flying away as quickly as my legs and arms snapped and popped as they grew on my journey to becoming a woman.

But I had closed my eyes to that pain.

While the three of us were sitting around the table, something told me I was becoming aware of all of those feelings that I'd forgotten so long ago.

We returned to Noodles's studio apartment, and amid the perfectly white interior we munched on greasy slices of pizza. I began to notice the incongruity that comes from feeling like you've known a person all your life when really you don't know a thing about them.

Before long, six-thirty rolled around, even though we hadn't had time to talk about anything particularly important. Once again I was reminded how lonely it is to leave a friend. We'd just met, so there wasn't one urgent matter that needed to be brought up between us anyway, but my brother looked even more unhappy about going than I did. His face reminded me of Mayu when our cousin Mikiko would come over during summer vacations to spend the night with us. When she had to leave the next day Mayu looked so lonely, and I saw the same look in my brother's eyes. When she gazed at me with that expression, I felt as though I'd lost control of everything. All three of us seemed overwhelmed by the same melancholy.

"Michelle" was playing on the radio and I figured there must be some connection. When the Beatles were together it must have been just as hard for them to break up. John and Yoko probably experienced the same thing that fateful evening when they talked all through the night. From the beginning of time, the entire world has just moved around and around in circles.

After saying good-bye we took the elevator to the first floor. Stepping out of the building, I looked up to the fourth-floor window and saw Noodles's small hand waving down to us. The light in the room shone behind her, forming a silhouette over her body that prevented me from seeing her face. Somehow I knew she was smiling as she watched us go off in the night.

"People seem to be saying good-bye to us a lot lately," I said to my brother when we'd finally traveled so far that the light from the window floating in the darkness was nothing more than one of hundreds of tiny, twinkling lights. The night scene was cool and I could feel my loneliness leaving me. I actually felt refreshed.

Yoshio shook his head. "At first I was so terrified by Noodles's boyfriend that I had to keep running from him twenty-four hours a day. I got Mom to put me in the center so I could finally get away—that's half the reason I went there. But now things are different. At least I've got friends."

He really wasn't speaking to anyone in particular. His words were just full of whispers. I don't know why, but as I listened to what he was saying my mind suddenly became completely empty. Yoshio was no longer my brother, he was just a young kid off the street, and I was no longer his older sister. I really had lost understanding.

On a certain night, in some kind of weather, there were a woman and a young man walking together down a lonely street. When did it occur? How old were they? All of it seemed so pointless.

A fresh feeling hovering intensively in the darkness.

∾

Like always, I'd just finished work that day and returned home for the evening.

When I opened the door and kicked off my shoes in the entryway, I felt a peculiar silence inside the house. It was only a slight feeling, but something completely different from what

I was used to. I suppose I could say the air smelled of death. I immediately sensed that something was finished, an impression clear and intense. I became frightened, and I realized that because of all I'd been through in life, I really was returning to the past, and my outlook on life was rapidly returning to the feelings I'd had as a child.

Actually, the only real difference was that the light in the entryway hadn't been turned on. Still, I was entirely aware of the unusual atmosphere as I stepped up into the house and made my way through the dark into the kitchen. When I got there I glanced into the living room to see my mother sitting on the sofa in darkness. She was drinking red wine. An old monochrome movie was showing on TV and for some reason my mother hadn't bothered turning up the sound. She stared blankly at the screen. Her face flickered oddly in the light. The darkness of the room and the bloodstained color of the wine reflected off my mother's white cheekbones.

The image was so beautifully strange that for a moment I thought I was dreaming. Certain things that happen on a regular basis, despite their different meanings, really don't exist. For some reason I lost all fear as I stood and gazed at my mother in that light. Still in the dark, not knowing what was wrong, I asked my mother if something had happened.

Without moving, my mother responded by saying, "Oh, Sakumi, you're home." Then she turned her head until her large eyes met mine. I had a hard time reading the expression on her face. It was a mixture of humor and pain, as though she'd lost hope, or was just livid with anger.

"Junko's gone," she said. "She ran away from home."

I stood for a minute in silence. I was shocked. Speaking of Junko, I thought to myself, wasn't she just standing in the kitchen talking to me that very morning? Wasn't she the one who made the breakfast that Mikiko and I scarfed down as we sat around chatting about the tabloid news shows we'd seen on TV?

When I left the house she smiled and said, "See you when you get back." There was no secret in her statement, no depth to her emotions.

For breakfast she was kind enough to have thrown together a simple menu of omelets, miso soup, and marinated spinach salad. Junko's spinach salad was particularly sweet, and almost too soft. That was the trademark. I was sure the leftovers were still in the refrigerator. But after they were gone, would I ever eat her salad again? My feelings became clear as I pondered over what I was thinking. Her white hands. The bathrobe she walked around the house in—I'd just seen it the day before. The sound of her slippers on the floor. The soft echo of her voice as she and my mother stayed up all night gossiping in the kitchen.

"Why did she leave?" I asked.

My mother answered my question even though it was obvious she wasn't in the mood to do so. "I have no idea," she said. "I suppose we'll be getting a phone call or a letter before long, or she'll come back to pick up what's left of her things. I just can't believe she took all that money."

"What?" I cried. I couldn't believe what she had just said. Even though I had understood my mother perfectly, it was as though my ears had refused to listen. My heart wouldn't accept such a thing.

"What money? Where did she take it from?" I said rushing up to my mother. "Are you sure it's gone?"

"I'm sure. It was over there in that closet," my mother said, pointing across the room. "My secret savings. I had over eight hundred thousand yen."

"Why on earth did you leave that kind of money lying around the house?" I said, getting angry.

"Banks are so unreliable," she said. "I know you can't earn interest on cash in the house, but it was always there for us if we needed it, never a reason to fight the crowds at the bank. If I ever had the urge to take a trip or something, the money was right there for me."

Our conversation slowly moved away from the original topic. We didn't want to discuss the new absence, neither of us. Reality was hard enough.

"Junko didn't mention anything?" I asked.

"Now I think about it, she did say a few things lately, but I wasn't aware of anything specific." Mother paused for a moment. "If she had asked me for the money I would have loaned it to her."

"Of course you would have," I said. "That's really strange."

"Something really huge must have blown up in her face. It would have been nice for her to tell us about it."

"You just never know," I said shaking my head. "But what about the money? Are you sure she was the one who took it? Do you have any kind of proof?" It occurred to me that we were finally accepting the fact that it had happened and moving back into reality.

"She left it over there," my mother said, pointing to a small note scribbled on a piece of paper. It was on top of the table. As I walked over and picked up the letter I noticed the air had finally begun to circulate in the room. I recognized the penmanship right away. The letter really was from Junko.

I promise to pay you back.

"Wow," I said. "People are so unreliable. You never know what they're going to do next."

"That's right," my mother said, taking another sip of her wine.

That was our simple conclusion. We sat together in silence for a few minutes longer and then I got up and busied myself in the kitchen. My mother poured herself another glass of wine and drank it slowly. I nibbled on a few pieces of toast for dinner, but somehow that didn't seem to be enough. I remembered the leftover miso soup and salad, deciding to save them for later, for a special occasion perhaps. They seemed too precious. I was saddened when I realized there was no longer an endless supply, and tried to push the idea out of my mind. In the end I would relate the events to my brother and Mikiko, and eventually this strange occurrence would just melt into the neverending cycle of life all around us.

I imagine one could also point out that it was strange from the very beginning, having my mother's friend living with us.

Now there was only reality.

Junko no longer lived here. Chances are she'd never return.

Nothing more could be said about it.

I knew it would take time before I could remember what she looked like when she smiled. The sound of the shock resonated in my heart as I tried to come to grips with the whole idea of her leaving.

"Oh, I just can't stand it anymore!" my mother said, pulling herself from the sofa. "I've got to do something to get my mind off this. I'm calling my boyfriend and having him take me out for a drink." With that she left the room.

Once she was ready I saw her off at the door. As she made her way through our garden I called out to her from the porch, "Drink to your heart's content. There's no reason to be concerned with things at home tonight."

∾

When Mikiko got home I explained to her what had happened. She freaked in the typically gentle, Mikiko sort of way. Then she began to analyze the situation from every angle, exactly what I would have expected from a student at an all-girl college. Mikiko came up with every reason from lost love to her daughter prostituting herself to a member of the Yakuza. Perhaps her boyfriend needed the money to pay back a debt or . . . her reasons seemed endless. As I listened to her go on and on about all the different possibilities, I found myself distracted. It was almost as if this scandal had turned into something delightful.

We were so thrilled by it we were like two sisters forced to spend a night together during a typhoon or winter storm or something of that nature. Inside that peculiar environment, we managed to stay up the greater portion of the night sitting around the dining table gulping down beer and munching on chips and candy.

Eventually Mikiko went upstairs to go to sleep and I went into the bathroom and drew myself a hot bath. After I was finished I went back to the kitchen with my wet hair and made myself a pot of coffee.

In the dark I flipped on the TV and began to watch a midnight movie with the volume turned down. Two A.M. rolled around. Figuring my mother wouldn't be home until morning, I went to the entryway and pushed back the dead bolt on our door. I returned to the kitchen and painted my fingernails. Then I thought it was about time for me to go to bed, too. But all of a sudden I was overwhelmed by loneliness. It flooded my heart like a tsunami. I would never see her again. We would never have a chance to share a life under the same roof again.

Even though I had completely understood the conversations I'd had with my mother and Mikiko, why had it taken me so long to finally realize what had happened? When I asked myself that question alone and in the dark something else came to mind.

For the first time that night I realized our home was void of the feeling of a family. I remembered the nights when my father passed away, and when my mother finalized her divorce. The feeling was also there on the night that Mayu died . . .

. . . that cold chill of a storm

. . . uncertainty of absence

. . . absolute solitude of separation.

Amid my discouragement, I came to an understanding of what had happened inside the strange silence of that space. The air was stagnant and unsettled, a perfect setting for the tone of departure. We had all been asleep together in the same home only twenty-four hours earlier. Now I could never expect the same thing to happen again.

No words could adequately describe the overwhelming power of that loneliness. I felt like crying, as though someone had knocked me over. Perhaps it would have been better for me to cry, but I couldn't bring myself to do it. I just got a huge lump in my throat as I thought about the unusual distance between myself and all that had happened.

Junko's presence lingered.

The energy created by the memories would take time to dissipate from this space, just like it would take time for the impression of Junko to leave the home, too.

Loneliness surrounded my thoughts and filled the room, wrapping itself around the entire house where Mikiko and I were the only ones present. The days when the five of us crowded into the kitchen seemed like only yesterday. Now that was completely gone.

I should have been used to losing people by now. But the emptiness always visited me too quickly.

Pain that resolved all time.

I forced myself to crawl into the kitchen, even though I really didn't feel like moving. After draping an apron over my shoulders, I slowly washed the dishes. When I was finished I went over to the wall and flipped off the light, realizing how desperately I needed sleep. That's when I saw it.

There was a faint outline of a person in the kitchen window. My heart sank as I moved a little closer. A rapping sound came from the window, and I knew that whoever it was, they wanted in. I watched the small hand tap on the edge of the frosted glass windowpane.

It occurred to me that it might be my mother, having just forgotten her keys, or perhaps it was Junko coming home. I slowly opened the window and looked out.

"Who's there?" I asked.

"It's me," my brother said.

For a split second I thought I was in another world. Yoshio should have been asleep at the center. I looked closer to see if it was just another apparition of him like I'd seen in Saipan. But he was for real. His own voice had echoed in the darkness.

I flung the window open. My brother was standing straight up, almost on his tiptoes, trying to reach me.

"What in the world happened? Did you run away from the school?" I asked as if I were talking to someone in a dream. My own voice sounded like it was resonating in a different existence.

"No," Yoshio replied. "I was just worried, that's all. Did something happen to Junko?"

"We'll talk about it once you're inside," I said. "Go around to the front door and I'll let you in."

My brother looked so defenseless as I watched his shadow surrounded by the trees in the backyard. At the same time there was something timely about his coming.

Sliding back the bolt, I let Yoshio into the house. I took him to the kitchen and poured him a cup of hot chocolate.

"Haven't you ever heard of a doorbell?" I asked. "Did you want to scare me to death?"

"I figured you'd all be asleep, but when I saw the light on in the kitchen I decided to go around and check it out," he replied.

"So how did you get here?" I asked.

"It was simple. Everyone back in school was asleep. I saw my chance and came."

I glanced over to see that what he said was true. Under his overcoat he was still wearing his pajamas.

"This hot chocolate's great," he said with a smile. "Can I have another cup?"

I was still feeling uncomfortable with the strange feeling abiding in the room. It must have also had something to do with my brother, who came to visit in the middle of the night like he was coming to visit me in my dreams.

"How did you know about Junko?" I said. "Because there really was something."

"She's been sending me messages all day long. They're strong, like she's really in pain." Yoshio talked lightly, as if there was nothing unusual about his power.

"You really are telepathic, aren't you?" I said, once again taken aback by my brother's abilities. "I'll tell you what happened—she ran away from home. Junko's not living with us anymore."

For fear of complicating the issue I didn't bring up the money. I supposed my brother already understood the strange circumstances surrounding her disappearance.

"I get the impression that Junko's daughter took a lot of money from her father and then ran away from home. That's probably why Junko left. Seems like she's the only one who knew what was going on, and I think she blames herself."

His comment was similar to Mikiko's. It would take time before any of us could confirm what had happened; then again, there was a chance we'd never find out what went on. Regardless, Yoshio's and Mikiko's predictions must have come close to the truth.

"Junko was in so much pain she even went to the doctor's," Yoshio continued.

"What did they say when she got there?" I asked.

"I don't know. I can only see the image of her face at the doctor's office. But it's clear she won't come back to live with us again. I started missing her and wondering what would happen to the family. I've been so worried about it I couldn't sleep tonight. I had to find out if Junko had died or just left the house, and I assumed Mom would be pretty upset about it. I could almost see her crying."

"She's not crying," I said with a smile. "She's out getting stone drunk. I'm sure the tears will come later."

The person who looked like he would cry was my brother. When I glanced down at his eyes he casually looked at Junko's apron, which had been left hanging over the small cart we had in the corner of the kitchen.

"What should I do?" my brother asked. "Do you think I should go back tonight?"

"Do whatever you want," I said. " But there isn't a thing we can do about Junko right now. The next few months are bound to be difficult for her, no matter where she is or what she's doing."

"Do you think Mom will get remarried?" Yoshio asked.

"It's possible," I said, finally clueing in to Yoshio's greatest concern. Now that Junko was out of the house it would be much easier for my mother's boyfriend to move in on us.

"Saku-chan, if Mom gets married what'll you do?"

"At my age it would be uncomfortable living in the same house with such a young father," I replied. "So I guess I'll have to leave too."

"Are you going to live with Ryu-chan?"

"I don't know," I said. "But chances of that happening are slim."

"So what am I supposed to do?" he asked.

It was a good question, one that even made me feel funny when I heard him ask it. My brother reminded me of an unwanted pet tossed from one home to another.

"I don't think you should worry too much," I said. "Mom isn't that stupid. She ran off to Paris, but getting married will be an entirely different story. You've just got to make up your mind what you want to do and stick to it. It's still too early to think about anything else."

Yoshio nodded, looking calmer than before. After a few moments of silence he turned to me and said, "When one person does something big it's like a wave that sends out ripples. Everyone ends up feeling the effect."

He was staring off into space as he talked. When he spoke he sounded like he was talking to himself, his words were that sober. I couldn't help but be amused by the serious way my brother acted.

When I questioned whether he wasn't going back to the center, he shook his head no, saying it would be better for him to get back before anyone discovered he was gone. He told me he'd call if anything went wrong. But before returning the thing he wanted more than anything was street-stall ramen. The next thing I knew I was standing at the all-night, temporary ramen stand down the street. In my burned-out mind I figured we must have looked like a bar hostess and her child who had just gotten off work. That didn't stop us from ordering the largest bowls on the menu.

As we walked along the street headed for the school I turned to my brother and said, "You reek of garlic. Don't you think someone's going to find it strange that a kid who was supposed to be in bed at nine o'clock now smells like ramen? You're going to get caught."

"You're right. Maybe it wasn't such a great idea."

"Try fooling them with some gum," I said, reaching into my purse and taking out all my extra candy and gum. The rattling of tiny aluminum wrapping paper echoed in the darkness.

The road was completely empty and silent. It felt like the day had fallen fast asleep.

As I pondered the next day, the day that would come just as soon as this one was over, I suddenly brought to mind Junko's face. Once that happened the bitter, sharp pain returned to my heart. There was no reason for it. It just hurt. Everything before me turned black for just a moment.

"WOW!" my brother said, lifting his head to the sky. I followed suit and right before us, right in the middle of the sky, was a sudden streak of light. It was a shooting star, so bright and white it remained in the sky for a few seconds, shimmering like a fallen pearl. The trace had stayed there so long that any prayer would certainly have been answered if someone was into that sort of thing. I didn't wish for anything at all. I just continued to gaze at the millions of other stars that remained stable in the night sky.

"Sakumi!" Yoshio cried. "Was that a falling star? Or was it a UFO?"

"Why are you asking me?" I laughed. "You're the expert."

"It was so beautiful and long!" my brother exclaimed. Then he thought for a moment and said, "Oh, I see."

"See what?" I asked.

"When you're having a great time with someone you love and both of you look up at the sky, it doesn't matter if you see a star or a UFO, anything will appear so beautiful it will astound you."

Chapter 20

I peeked into the mailbox one afternoon and discovered a mysterious package. It was addressed to me. Opening it, I found a single cassette tape, nothing more. There was no letter—not even a return address. As I glanced at the outside of the envelope I could tell the characters had been written by a man; the strokes were bold and big.

I had an unpleasant feeling with the tape in my hand, but eventually curiosity got the best of me and I took it up to my room to play it on my stereo. Convinced that it would be a moaning voice like something off a 900 number, I was surprised when music drifted out of my speakers. A young woman's voice sang the lyrics with intense rock music in the background. It was a dark, but otherwise pleasant song to listen to.

And that was it—just that one song. The rest of the tape was blank.

My confusion mounted. But I continued to play the game, even though my instincts told me I should just stop right there. I grabbed a pen and some paper and played the song back over and over again, writing down as many of the English lyrics as I could understand. I knew a hidden riddle just had to be there. Eventually the words on my paper formed the following. There was nothing about the song that made me disapprove of it.

Close your eyes and imagine
You're so different from before
The thinnest girl I saw dancing at the strip joint

You knew just what to do to be the hippest girl around
Tell me stories from your crazy trips
Your unkempt stars and tongue-tied tricks

Close your eyes and imagine
That was different than before
A glass house atop a distant hill
You downed your drugs and ditched your classes
Yesterday Bruce Berry stopped in
A wild kid who I thought was pretty cool

Close your eyes and imagine
How it's all supposed to end
You're a Cinderella of the Night
You don't know your left from your right
So hungry you bite and snap
You've forgotten what forks and knives are for
Who could that be screaming outside the door?

I'm afraid, hold me tight

All the women scream when they see how smooth I am
But that was then and this is now
So things are different
I remember how tight I held those women
And that's okay, it was fun
I remember the darkness, 'cuz that's where I'm from
It's only a joke, if you believe me

I was lost, even after writing out the lyrics. What were they trying to tell me? After making a checklist in my mind of all the people who could have sent the package, the only person I came up with was Kozumi, since I remembered how much he liked rock music in Saipan. I even went as far as to call him to see if he'd sent the tape, but he wasn't the one. Later Saseko got on the phone and talked with me cheerfully for a while. For another tender moment I was reminded of the never-changing blue sky and salty smell of the ocean. But that was all.

Over and over I listened to the song, trying to pick up the words. In the end only the melody was firmly embedded in my mind. Still, there was something earnest coming from the music, a message of some kind. The same familiar echo kept ringing, as though someone was reaching out to connect with me.

That was the image the song inspired.

~

Just as I'd imagined, the days and weeks passed without any word from Junko. Her presence alone had formed a knot in our home, binding the rest of us together. When she left she was for me the perfect idea of "mother," even surpassing the image I had of my own.

Once Junko was gone, my mother made getting out of the house a habit, and she was gone as much as possible. Mikiko fooled around with her friends from college, only showing up at the house to sleep. In turn, I found myself spending more time with Ryūichirō than ever before. He'd never really bothered to decorate, so his place still lacked taste. But it was nice just to be in that free atmosphere. Ryūichirō let me do my own thing, that's why I found it so easy to be there.

I asked if he knew the song, playing the tape for him, and he said, yeah, he'd heard it, but it was a song from a pretty old band. He didn't know anything more. "And are you sure it's not a love letter from a old boyfriend?" he said with disdain.

"No," I said. "But for the life of me I don't have the slightest idea where it came from. Don't you think if it really was a love letter someone would choose a different kind of music? Nothing in this song indicates love."

"You've really thought about these lyrics, haven't you?" Ryūichirō replied.

"My, aren't we jealous," I said, amused by his reaction.

There wasn't a thing in his apartment, really. All his clothes were stacked in a big trunk as though he was ready for another trip overseas. Upon realizing that, another sensation of loneliness came over me; it was that odd. I'd just stopped in to say hi, but when I looked out from his window I saw the sun fading far into the west and the sky turning a faint crimson. Before long Venus glowed brightly. The color of the sky grew thicker.

I saw grandmothers coming home from shopping and heard sounds from the children playing below. Lights shone out of various windows here and there. My stomach was growling, and it hit me that time was ticking away inside me as well. It was such a strong emotion, so painfully bitter, almost too much to bear. I felt alone, but alive.

I bet those thoughts wouldn't have come to me then if Ryūichirō hadn't been with me. Two people in the same spot, watching time pass by—that alone provoked the images . . .

. . . a thick forest apparently continuing forever, so dense that even the sun can't penetrate its foliage; or

. . . a lake shining with morning light; or

. . . the color of tall mountains that seem to reflect like mirrors.

Those kinds of images.

I looked far into the Milky Way and saw a perfect triangle of stars: Altair, Vega, and Deneb forming a silence that hurt my neck when I looked up at them, but bringing to mind the image of an enormous swan as well.

That kind of sensation. A moment where you think time has actually come to a stop, knowing too painfully that somewhere, something is continuing to flow, unceasingly moving forward.

Somehow there was a way for the two of us to get away from it all. I saw us as two spirits, living forever in a world without ticking clocks. I felt we could find ourselves in a world so far, so very far away—a world so beautiful no one could grasp the meaning of its beauty. There would be no other human beings, just the mountains and the oceans to talk to. A place where our existence in bodily form would simply fade away . . .

But my stomach was still growling and I had to decide if I was going to call work to see what time they needed me to come in the next morning—the same mundane things. Can I read this magazine? I ask. Sure, he says, I've read it. That's all I had power over. My body and my voice. Places reachable and places too far out of reach. Limited and unlimited concepts driving my thoughts onward.

Power over simple things, everything encompassed in those very same things.

If something took those things away from me, I'd be left with nothing more than the end of a luxurious day.

~

"That song was talking about you. Did you listen closely to the lyrics?" asked the stranger who stopped me on a street corner a few weeks later. He was older than I was, with a keen desire to know how I felt when I listened to the words of that song.

I was shocked, and once again I felt like I had moved onto a different dimension, becoming an entirely different person.

With that in mind, I turned around to see a tall gentleman standing before me, in front of a clear red sky. I figured he must have been in his late thirties—maybe forties? He was almost too young to call a "sir," but far too old to have been one of my friends. He was simply a thin individual with a very lonely, limpid shadow and translucent brown eyes that reminded me of Kozumi.

"I'm sorry. Can I help you?" I said, thinking I'd thrown away the WEIRDOS WANTED sign that apparently was still written on my forehead.

"Unless I'm mistaken, I believe you received a tape in the mail a few weeks ago. I was the one who sent it." His voice was like a whisper, but he spoke with authority.

"Oh," I said. "You mean . . . yes, you mean the tape." I paused for a moment to gather my thoughts. "Please forgive me for asking, but do you mind telling me who you are?"

"Would you prefer my real name?" he asked.

"Actually, I'm simply wondering how it is you know me. I'm also wondering why you'd send me a tape out of nowhere, not to mention the message you were trying to get across with those lyrics. That's what I would like to know," I explained.

"People call me Mesmer," he said. "Mr. Mesmer. It's kind of a nickname, but I generally go by that."

One named "Noodles," another named "Mesmer," I silently thought.

"I heard most of what I know about you from your dear brother. The more I thought about your situation, the more I realized how perfect the song was for you. It occurred to me that if I aroused your curiosity by sending the tape first, you'd be more apt to listen to what I had to say. I will soon be departing on a rather long journey across the ocean, and I'm afraid a certain amount of confusion has evolved between myself and your younger sibling. I was hoping you'd know some way to resolve it."

"By any chance do you know a woman who calls herself 'Noodles'?" I asked.

"Yes, of course," he replied. "Kaname."

I nodded.

"She was my girlfriend until just recently," he said.

"I was somewhat informed about your relationship," I said. One question kept running through my head—how could my brother be frightened by this silent, gentle man? I'd imagined someone much younger, someone far more pushy. Now I was simply confused. I hadn't pictured in my mind a frail, mature gentleman, but when he caught my attention by sending me a tape (I'd never been subject to anything so naturally clever), I had a hard time keeping my reactions to myself.

"Would it be possible for us to go somewhere so we can talk for a while?" he asked.

I was on my way to Ryūichirō's apartment, but I wouldn't be missed anytime too soon, so I told him an hour or so was fine. Rather than going to my usual cafe, I suggested the outdoor beer garden in front of the train station. I feared running into Noodles.

Since it was still early afternoon it seemed like we had the entire place to ourselves. Nevertheless, there was a soft commotion from the few people who came into the bar and the servers dressed in their pressed uniforms running briskly about, serving beer in large mugs. A cluster of buildings surrounded us in the afternoon sun shining brightly against a relaxed blue sky—the whole scene reminding me of a puzzle with half its inner pieces missing.

Mr. Mesmer and I chose the table in a far corner of the restaurant. I didn't quite know what to say. I only knew his reputation was not good and Yoshio and Noodles didn't want to speak to him. As for me, I had no idea who he was.

He spoke first. "I'm sure you've only heard bad things about me."

"Well, everyone—by everyone I mean only Noodles and my brother—acts like they don't want to talk about you, so we don't. I don't know who you are, or what happened between you and the others."

"At one point I thought of taking your brother to California with me," he replied. "Perhaps that's when things got out of hand."

"Cal-California?" I stuttered, taken aback by his sudden announcement.

Our conversation came to a halt as our server arrived with a heavy tray of beer and a basket of dried beans. I'm sure he saw us as a couple of colleagues, maybe a subordinate and a superior, who were secretly having an affair. We took the beer and clinked cheers to our meeting and, for the first time that summer, I sipped draft beer from a mug that large.

Everything around me smelled of summer. It was different from the feeling I'd felt in Saipan; this was much more transitory, a summer with a deeper shade. Eventually my drink and the greenness of the trees came together and touched my naked arms, and before I realized it the sky had opened even wider with a tenderness that penetrated the entire city.

"Now that I think about it, Noodles mentioned you're forming a new religion," I said. "Was that part of the confusion?"

"That certainly wasn't my intention," Mr. Mesmer replied. "I would hardly call it a religion." He was shocked I'd even brought up the word. "I just knew your brother was having a difficult time here in Japan, so I thought about taking him to a place where it would be more comfortable for him to live."

"Why California?" I asked. "What's so special there?"

"An institute has been set up at a California university that specializes in your brother's abilities. They've brought a group of very talented people together for the purpose of studying the phenomenon. If you get accepted to the program they have a place for you to live, and it's all rather harmless, nothing like the stories you read about in science fiction novels, you know, where people get turned into lab rats or human weapons. There are no religious affiliations, either. It's simply a program where you can casually experiment with your own powers. I figured it would be perfect for your brother, since he wouldn't need to impose on any of you for support. I sincerely thought it would be good for him."

"Have you ever been there yourself, Mr. Mesmer?" I asked.

"Yes, I've been in and out ever since I was a teenager. Actually, I basically grew up in California, because of my father's job. That's also where I met Kaname, or Noodles, as you call her."

"I had no idea," I said, shocked by the news.

"I get the impression she's not pleased with her own clairvoyant capabilities," Mr. Mesmer explained. "To make matters worse, she went hysterical at the institution because of some complications in her treatment. I quit my own therapy to bring her back to Japan, and we've both been here ever since. Now she's insisting on leading a normal life, rather than go through something like that again. But she's always been refined that way."

"What do you mean?" I asked.

"Haven't you heard?" he replied.

"No, nothing."

"I'm sure it displeases her to even think about it now. There was a time when she was able to conjure up feelings from missing and dead people. The police even asked her to join in an investigation back in the States. After receiving thoughts from dead people, or even worse, thoughts from missing people on the edge of dying, she finally wore herself out. Apparently the sensation was stronger when she was a child, and the older she got the weaker the feelings became. Once she recovered from her neurosis, she claimed that she no longer had the power to receive thoughts from the dead or dying. I'm not sure it was the breakdown that did it, but whatever the reason it was clear she'd never go back to the institute with me. To this day she talks about how restricted she felt there. Her point is valid, since the people in the institute rarely talk about anything but New Age phenomena. Quite a change from a conversation with your average foreign student."

"I had absolutely no idea," I stated. Then it occurred to me why she was in college at her age. She'd "studied abroad" for a few years. Up until then I figured she'd just held off school for a while. "And what, Mr. Mesmer, would you say your special power is?" I asked.

"I have the power to hypnotize people. At least that was my specialty back in the institution. Are you familiar with the name Mesmer?" he asked.

"Wasn't he a famous doctor? I think he did some experiments with magnetism or something like that back in old Europe. Didn't he heal people that way?" I paused for a moment. "I guess I'm not really sure."

"No," Mr. Mesmer replied, "you're exactly right. That's where I picked up my nickname. I studied his work extensively back in the States, even writing a dissertation on him. In the late 1700s, using hypnotism and trance formation, he performed epoch-making experiments on people, eventually learning how to heal them. That's where we get the term 'mesmerism.'" He looked thrilled to be discussing such a thing.

I'm always amazed at how many different hobbies there are in this world. It seemed like everyone in life has something to keep their thoughts occupied. When I thought about the specialists coming together in a place across the ocean to talk about this sort of thing on a daily basis, it seemed nothing more than a strange dream. Until things started happening to my brother, topics of this sort were from another world.

"I see," I replied. "That's why you're nicknamed 'Mr. Mesmer.'"

"Exactly."

"And what do you intend to do when you get back to the States?" I asked.

"There is a psychological clinic where I will volunteer my services for a time, using what I know of hypnotism and over-the-counter counseling, and if I find I'm not needed there, then maybe I'll turn my sights to studying further as an official medical doctor. But right now I'm in the process of exploring the chance of becoming a true hypnotist, since I'm still only a beginner."

"Is that so?" I replied with a nod.

The bar was slowly filling up. People just off work thronged noisily into the tables around us and we could hear one group already shouting and laughing in the corner. The wind outside was strong, and the empty bean pods we'd left on the table looked as if they were about to blow away. Even with the harsh wind, the sky above us grew continually darker, overflowing once again with a blue too clear for expression.

While gazing up together at the sky with Mr. Mesmer, I suddenly felt a strange sensation, like I was in a different country. Perhaps I was just feeling lonely.

. . . Once, quite some time ago, I saw a homeless alley cat on the street. Rather than recognize its presence, I acted as if I didn't see it. But the sound of its pitiful meowing wouldn't leave my head that night.

. . . Once in elementary school my desk partner transferred to a different school, and I didn't know who I'd be sitting with the next day in class.

. . . Once I broke up with a boyfriend. I didn't cry, but as I was walking home, twilight on the street in front of me suddenly appeared pitch black. I knew if I called I could still see him, but there was little chance of us ever getting back together. As I yearned to hear his voice, the road in front of me got blacker and blacker. It was painful.

The images continued to float up in my mind.

I decided it would be best for me to be off to Ryūichirō's. I just needed to be in a place with nothing but warmth, just return to a place where someone was waiting. The light in his apartment never changed.

"I suppose it's up to the individual to decide whether or not he should go to a place like the institution in California," I said. "Still, after meeting and talking with you today, I can't understand why Yoshio would be so frightened."

Mr. Mesmer got a sad look on his face and said, "Your brother is extremely sensitive. He was able to understand far too much of me." He looked so dejected as he spoke that I thought he'd just vanish right in front of my eyes. Yoshio was the source of his pain. But I still wasn't sure why my brother felt the need to escape from this man. If anything, this Mr. Mesmer was just sad and hurt. I didn't know what to do for him.

"I have also confused Kaname more than I should have. She said I was trying to force your brother to go to California with me. That was never my intention. I simply sympathized with his situation and I just wanted to help him channel those feelings into a source of useful power. I wanted to be his friend. Having experienced the same thing myself as a child I know what he's going through, and I know there has to be some way to take his natural talents and turn them into productive energy."

"What do they feel like?" I asked. Mr. Mesmer looked closely at me. "Because I, myself, have never possessed such a thing, and even though Yoshio is my younger brother, I really have no idea what it is he's going through."

"You can never understand another person's powers," Mr. Mesmer replied. "It doesn't matter how closely related you are to that person, or even if you live with him." He began to chuckle to himself. His laughter was so humble it could have caused a small flower to bloom. "I lived next door to an old man who knew the power of hypnosis when I lived back in America. I often went to his house to spend time with him. I suppose that's where I first picked up the tools of my trade, and up until the time I became a teenager a lot of things happened to me. I could feel something strong about a person, and it would have a slight effect on them as well, there was no question about it. Those feelings just came naturally. The worst, though, was when I was in New York as a high school student. I have always been shy and I've never tried to stand out or be known. But apparently my power to influence the feelings of others was too strong. By the time I realized what was going on, five people had committed suicide around me, and dozens more had gone completely mad. I didn't know what to do. It was truly an awful time. Because of my age I couldn't control my own thoughts and how I felt around others."

"Really?" I asked.

"Yes, I wouldn't lie to you, and besides, it was something I saw happening before my eyes, so I feel I can express it with a certain amount of validity. You see, after contemplating killing myself and so on, I decided to go to the institution in California.

Other people were there like me who carried with them the same tragedies in their hearts. They informed me that this evil spirit I had living inside me was actually a talent that could be used for good. Growing up so close to hypnotism as a child, moving from one spot in America to the next as my mother got married and divorced time after time—gradually I became aware of how boldly my trauma had manifested itself in my life. After a few months of training at the institute, I learned I could use my powers to heal, mentally and physically, rather than causing pain. In the end I became comfortable with my situation."

"How old were you when all that happened?" I asked.

"About seventeen," Mr. Mesmer replied.

"And how exactly would you go about doing those things to people? Would you hypnotize them?"

"No, no, not at all. Hypnotism never hurts. Painful things only happened when the situation got out of control, when I had no intention of hurting anyone at all. There were many young women in my life who I grew fond of, but it never resulted in typical love, because I'd always end up bringing them pain. Whenever strong thoughts came to my mind about a certain person, I'd wind up in their dreams at night. I suppose I appealed too strongly to their consciousness."

Mr. Mesmer was completely serious as he talked, but I found myself doubting what he said. I mean, think about people in love. Is it possible for a person in love to ever say they're "normal"? And don't a lot of shady people just want to think they have power over others? If that was really the case, what was I supposed to think about my brother? I suppose that if those people really wanted to believe in that, the idea that sensitive people like Yoshio really do exist as primary targets for hypnotism, one could say the phenomenon was for real. I guess that would be similar to love. But since there's always a partner involved, there would have to be a mutual exchange before that special pattern could be woven. Perhaps the people who bring this sort of thing up are just thinking too much at once. Isn't there an easier way to go on living?

Mr. Mesmer continued to speak as if he were talking to himself. "I really can't explain myself well, but wouldn't it have been wonderful if all those awful things had been a dream."

I felt like crying. I could tell he really meant what he said by hearing the echo in his voice. I'm sure it pained him to talk about all the things that had happened in his life, all the little things that had turned into such catastrophes.

"Pardon me for asking," I said, "but how were things between you and Noo . . . I mean, Kaname-san? Were you able to fall in love without hurting her?" Out of all my questions that evening, I believe that was the one most impolite.

"Actually," Mr. Mesmer replied, "I did. Kaname was still quite young, and a very powerful woman at that. I'd never met anyone with her strength before." There was a longing in his voice. "She was the only one who didn't find me frightening, and she never received any of my bad influences, either. It didn't matter how much I felt for her, or how often she came to my thoughts, apparently none of it affected her. That's why I call her my first love. She brought me true happiness. She understood everything about me. How thrilling it was for me to fall in love with someone who didn't fear me. It gave me a tremendous amount of confidence."

"Is that so?" I said.

On the outside Noodles seemed rather unaffected by their split. From what I gathered she was just a special woman, never changing. She had no past, no expectations of the future, or at least that's what I read in her eyes. It seemed like she'd been alive for a very, very long time, perceiving all that was around her.

I looked up at Mr. Mesmer and said, "Apparently she's just enjoying life now as a young woman in college, nothing more."

"The very thing she desired," Mr. Mesmer said. "If she'd stayed with me she would have been stuck in the same lifestyle with the people she despised the most. We had no choice but to break up. The decision was mutual; we both agreed. Now there's just a bit of confusion regarding Yoshio."

"Well, I suppose," I said.

"Please give Kaname my regards. Let her know how I feel. Tell her that I forgive her, and tell her that breaking up in the midst of confusion was a difficult thing to do."

Once again Mr. Mesmer looked painfully sad.

I spoke up. "If possible, I think we all should get together and talk about it. I'll see what the others think. Noodles, I'm sure, is perfectly aware of what went on, and she's not the type who would hold a strong grudge."

Now I felt like staying with him longer. The degree of pain resonating from his sadness was as deep as human history is long, and the breeze that blew past him felt chilly, as if it were a breeze blowing over the tops of lonely tombstones. Since his grief resembled the essence of sadness that we all face at one point or another in life, I found it difficult to leave. Even though nothing could be done about it, the countless painful nights I spent trying to fool myself that loneliness didn't exist came bursting out of my heart at once. In order to avoid getting swept away, something told me, I had to stay with this man.

Had I been hypnotized by his power?

It was painful. The windows on the buildings. Laughter from people around me. The light shimmering from large lanterns. Sorrow and discouragement.

"Do you mind if I ask you one more thing before we go?" I said. He shook his head. "Why did the lyrics of that song remind you of me?"

He looked me straight in the eye. "I'm not sure if I can provide a clear answer to your question, but I've picked up a number of clues over the course of our conversation tonight. Please forgive me for asking, but would you mind if I tell you what I've discovered about you since we met?"

"Please," I said.

"In that song there's a line about a 'Cinderella of the Night,' and when your brother told me about you that single phrase came to mind. Perhaps that's what made my image of you stay for so long. After meeting with you today my suspicions have been confirmed. You're lonely. You're so starved for someone that there's nothing that any of us, including yourself, can do. Before you fell and hit your head you'd lost a number of people very close to you. I can only say you're next—it's something in your blood."

I thought about the phrase Saseko had used to describe me, "half dead."

"But somewhere inside you was a plan 'A,' and you were able to survive right up until the time that plan ran out. I'm not psychic and I can't see the future, nor do I turn to the stars for advice, so I can't guide you in that way. But I can tell you that the impressions I've received of you are strong. Your life after the concussion was a clean slate, a piece of white paper, a special gift from the sky. It was something unexpected by all, something that came with no scenario attached. However, I believe you know that too, somewhere deep inside. You've paid a tremendous amount of attention to yourself to avoid feeling lonely. But you are lonely. Your boyfriend's a well-liked guy, and he's close to your solitude, but compared to your confusion he brings little consolation. It's so easy to become hopeless. Everything inside you is trying desperately not to fall victim. You've already died once. Things from your former life have taken on new form."

Mr. Mesmer paused for a moment. "Maybe your mother possesses an inexplicable gene that she passed on to you and your brother. I'm sure there have been times in your life when you've woken up in the middle of the night only to ask yourself who you are. Well, the answer to that question is simple—you are you, the only one easily broken. People come and go in life, everything rolling right past you, and all you can do is stand by and watch. You've wandered through life because there was nothing else you could do, always. Chances are it will be the same way when you die. So much conflict and chaos is going on in your mind that it's kept you from understanding. You should try to give yourself a little bit more credit."

"Who? Me?" I asked.

"Lonely people are the same everywhere, because whoever thinks they're unique needs to be in front of an audience . . . " As he spoke an image of Mayu came into my mind. ". . . even though they don't want to lead such a life. Your support is not the power of your will, but something hidden in that thinking, something beautiful, like a baby crying for her first time, like people forced to pick up an enormous piece of luggage for a single second, or like the smell of bread when you're starving. It resembles those things. Your great-grandfather had it, and you've inherited it naturally in some way. Your sister didn't have it, but your brother does. What could it be?" Mr. Mesmer asked.

"A secret formula for living, perhaps." I smiled.

"You have a lovely smile. It expresses the essence of hope."

Loneliness. Sorrow. The "me" that this man was seeing. The same night. Fleeting stars in the sky. A breeze blowing softly over us. The buildings and the tables and the cold sensation of hard iron chairs. Even the servers who tediously hauled endless rounds of beer about the restaurant would have noticed something different had they looked at me in the same way as he did that night.

Realizing something can really be a dismal experience.

The things I tried to put inside my heart looked like faraway landscapes. (But not the kind of things that Mr. Mesmer was talking about, per se.) His crystal-clear eyes.

As one who never looks on others to pity, I'd fallen victim to the trap. I'm not sure when it happened—but it must have come sometime during the harsh half-life I'd been given.

Just like my brother.

And Noodles.

It was too agonizing. I could never be saved. My realization was that clear. Fate could not be avoided now.

* * *

Smiling, I parted with Mr. Mesmer, but feeling like I'd been knocked over, I found my way to Ryūichirō's apartment. When I got in the door he greeted me with a friendly "Welcome home."

He rushed up to me with a huge grin on his face, and I saw a snapshot in his hands.

"Since you were so late, I've been fooling around with my camera. Here, look at this," he said, holding out the picture. Ryūichirō was standing in my white sundress with a broad smile on his face. It looked nice on him, but I thought he looked funny wearing it without makeup.

"What is this? Why on earth would you do such a thing?" I asked.

"Well, I just came home and saw your dress hanging up in the closet. Thinking it would be a nice way to welcome you home, I put it on and waited for a while, but you never showed. After an hour or so I figured it was futile to stay in the dress, so I preserved the memory with a photo."

"I've been through a lot the past few hours," I said.

"So let's go get something to eat!" Ryūichirō said.

That day was one of the few times I'd been together with Ryūichirō when he was in such a good mood, but that was fine.

I think it's wrong to put into words a person's life or their position. It's also not good to reduce yourself to information so limited. Just leave things like that. Be secretive. Stand back and watch what happens. I knew he'd been aware of those things—there was no doubt about it.

But I wanted to say it, and I wanted it to be said. Because I knew I was sad, living in front of that backdrop of loneliness.

While Ryūichirō was in the bathroom I glanced down at the picture again. He was grinning so wildly wrinkles had formed near his eyes, looking like a picture I'd seen once of his mother. With the thought of him standing about his stark apartment wearing nothing but my white dress, I suddenly burst out laughing.

As I giggled my thoughts, my face, and my whole being seemed to melt into emptiness. We simply faded into laughter with the same speed with which a crowd surges down a long hallway. There was no salvation, no restitution. And there was no loneliness. The laughter called on more laughter, and in the end I took the shape of the very thing I'd imagined. The way my life had always been.

It only happened for a minute. A familiar sensation.

Even if something else came up, my feelings would remain clear.

Like a jewel in my possession.

Chapter 21

That night I had a scorching fever.

After all the time in the cold open air of the beer garden, I'd managed to catch a head cold. On top of that, there had been the shock of hearing what Mr. Mesmer had to say.

Usually I don't allow myself to worry about such things, and actually I didn't allow myself to be bothered by it then, either. Still, as my eyes closed my head spun in the darkness, and even though I was desperate to go to sleep, I couldn't. I suppose that with my enormous headache strong feelings had come rushing in one right after the other. I was overwhelmed with an odd sensation of wanting to cry, coupled with a strange feeling of not being able to breathe.

Precisely at the moment I thought how weird it was to feel that way, I found myself submerged in the sweltering world of fever. That's why I hadn't picked up on it so quickly. Once during the middle of the night I pulled myself out of bed and stumbled to the bathroom, barely walking straight. Thinking something was wrong, I went back to wake up Ryūichirō, and asked him if anything seemed out of place.

"Is there something funny about me?" I said.

"What do you mean?" He sounded shocked.

"My forehead's burning up, and my legs feel like water."

Reaching out and touching both, Ryūichirō quickly diagnosed the situation. "You're right," he said, going to the bathroom and returning with a thermometer.

"Here," he said, thrusting out the instrument. "See how hot you are."

I placed the thermometer under my tongue for a few minutes, then pulled it out and read the temperature: 103°.

"Oh my god!" Ryūichirō exclaimed. "You're amazing. You should be congratulated on a temperature that high." He strolled into the kitchen and filled a Ziploc bag full of ice. Then he brought it back to me.

"Everything looks so strange right now," I said.

Physically I felt restricted by the cold, but I was happy with the idea that everything seemed fresh, almost as though I were levitating.

"Are you going to be sick? Do you need something to drink?" Ryūichirō asked.

"Maybe some water . . . ," I said.

I drank a cupful, but then I felt like throwing up. My body just couldn't tolerate it. Within a few minutes, however, my stomach calmed down. Next my feet started burning. The ice bag was extremely cold. And my head felt hot enough to cook an egg on.

"The world looks really nice with everything spinning," I said.

"Your fever made you drunk," Ryūichirō replied.

Even in the flow of our conversation my head was seeing a number of dizzy things. I saw Mr. Mesmer and heard the things we talked about at the beer garden over and over in my mind, images just coming and going. Mr. Mesmer had truly shocked me. It wasn't like I was trying to be defeated, but I don't think I was as tossed aside as he made it seem. Everything confirmed that—my fever, my feet which were so cold they felt like something not of my body, the guy next to me in bed so healthy he had no way of comprehending how I felt. Everything.

Regardless of what Mr. Mesmer had said, I liked myself. It was amusing. It was a rare sensation that I didn't often understand.

"Looks like the only way we're going to get you to sleep is by giving you some medicine," Ryūichirō said as he brought a bottle of aspirin back from the medicine cabinet. After I swallowed a couple of the small white pills, they seemed to take immediate effect on those of my senses that had turned so keen all of a sudden.

At that point I was unable to recall my family. If someone had asked me to describe them, I wouldn't have been able to do it. I remembered the faces of strangers. Even then I was lonely.

So that's what it was. I'd sunk that far.

Don't children act the same? A person, or a place she lives in all her life, isn't limited to the household where she was born. You can't expect the only woman in your life who'd offer a suckling breast to be your mother. One things leads to another and you find yourself in the box of a stranger. My feelings were the same.

After seeing the way people liked me, I didn't think what Mr. Mesmer said was possible. And I didn't think they were bad, either. Aren't babies just the same? If they could speak I'm pretty sure they'd repeat similar things.

When I considered the loneliness Mr. Mesmer had talked about I couldn't believe it was something boiling up naturally from deep down inside my spirit. But I realized that only after we'd spoken, and I didn't feel like going back, because I remembered what I looked like without the support of my old memory. I could still see the outline of myself within faded colors. It was true loneliness.

It hurt. I don't know why. It resembled a kitten oblivious to the fact that she'd be taken to a different home the next day.

That was the only thing that registered. Nothing more.

With my mind continuing to run around in circles, I found myself drifting off to sleep.

~

When I woke up the next morning everything felt amusing.

My fever had dropped, and I felt fresh enough to be reborn. A note was lying on the pillow next to my head.

Called your house and told them what happened. Please stay in bed for the rest of the day. I'm leaving now, but I'll be back this afternoon. Food is in the refrigerator.

—Ryūichirō

Light streamed brightly through the window. Air around me tasted good. It felt easy to breathe, and the light dancing on the edge of the window and in the breeze was much more vivid than usual. Only my body felt languid, but at the same time, soft. I figured everything in the world had adjusted itself for me. Maybe sweat from my fever the night before had been good for me.

Turning over in my futon and looking up into the morning sky, I contemplated what I'd do that day. It had been a while since I'd been able to stop and conjure up limitless thoughts like that, endless thoughts of the world around me.

I figured I'd take a shower, grab something to eat, maybe drink some coffee, and then be out on my own. Just thinking about it made me happy.

Freedom, I felt as if I had tasted freedom. I had been liberated from a world boiling with heat. I knew my entire body was rejoicing because of it. "Fevers aren't so bad," I whispered to myself softly. I must have sounded foolish.

For the time being, I decided to drink a large glass of water and call my brother at the children's center. I had to tell him about my run-in with Mr. Mesmer.

My brother was extremely composed over the phone. The moment his voice came over the receiver he said, "You've caught a cold? I hear a fever in your voice."

"Yeah," I replied, and then I gave him the lowdown on what had happened with Mr. Mesmer. When Yoshio found out Mr. Mesmer would soon be leaving the country, he seemed to want to meet him. Maybe he was ready to make up as well.

"You actually talked to him?" Yoshio said. "Wasn't it hard? I mean, didn't he say a bunch of things that really made you think?

Because when I met him the first time he told me so many different things, I got this sick feeling inside. Now I don't feel anything at all. Actually, I think it was good for me. But he told me things most people wouldn't dare say. It must be really hard, being a person like him—you know, with that kind of personality and, well, talent. . . ."

"I know exactly what you're saying," I said. "At first I couldn't understand why you were frightened of a guy like that until after meeting and talking to him myself."

"I thought he might say mean stuff to you, too. That's why I didn't want you to see him. But it's probably a good thing that you did. Noodles also regrets how we broke things off with him and I think she'd like to see him before he goes."

"Well, then, it's settled," I said. "Let's all get together sometime. It would be awful to let him go back to California thinking the way he does. I'll call Noodles and see what she says."

"Gotcha," my brother said. "Don't worry about me. I'm perfectly fine with the idea. In fact, to be honest I think one of the main reasons I was scared was because half of me really wanted to go."

"To California?" I asked.

"Yeah."

"Well, if you want to go, why not?" I said.

"I'm sure I'll go sometime, but if I left now I'd only be running away, because I wouldn't be there of my own will, I'd be there because of someone else's desire. I'd be stuck to Mesmer like poop stuck on a goldfish, and I couldn't do anything on my own. Also, I don't think I could live with the people at the institute."

"Well, if you really feel that way," I said.

"You know," he said, "just as you were telling me about Mr. Mesmer and California I suddenly had this desire to go. Maybe I just feel things too easily, but a trip to the States sounds like happiness from a distant star, something really familiar. But I don't think the foreign country I imagine in my mind is the same as the real thing, at least not the same as the memories I have of Kochi and Saipan. And if I went together with Mr. Mesmer, then as long as he was around I'd see things through his eyes, right? Always there with him, perhaps I could look from behind and see the ocean or the sky or friends, whatever he was seeing. It would be like a pleasant dream, because I feel the same way when we're both in Tokyo. There's something about him that I can't get enough of. Maybe I could live anywhere if he was around. Would there be a reason to go if he wasn't there? Once something like this hits me I can't get it out of my mind, like that's the only place in the world for me. The thought of his powers taking over again kind of scares me, but maybe I'm just not sure. Do I really want to go there? I'm still not sure."

Listening to how helpless Yoshio's feelings were, I couldn't help but feel sorry for my brother. Then I said, "But Japan isn't a friendly place to be in if you're uncomfortable here. Regular school, at least, hasn't suited your needs. So why don't you go to California and see what it's like? If you really want to, that is."

"Yeah, well, that's why I want to see Mr. Mesmer once more before he goes. People's feelings can change. It won't be like the past when he made me so shook up in my dreams that I couldn't figure out what was going on. My life is different now."

∾

Getting the four of us together proved to be easier than I'd thought.

Noodles was the first to suggest we take her car. She figured if we were getting together we might as well make a fun trip of it. There were no ulterior motives; we seemed to know what was going on before any of us mentioned it.

All we had to do now was move forward.

So it was decided that on a hot, hot afternoon we'd go in Noodles's car.

We made plans to meet in front of Tokyo Station. I felt my heart pounding with excitement as I pulled my brother out of school, even though we were only going on a day trip with a man who was leaving the country. I had the impression we were in for something pleasant. When the burning summer day first began we had no idea that it would ever end. The sun beat down too strongly, trees seemed too green. It never occurred to us that at some point it would all be over.

Mr. Mesmer, under the sun shining like a silver bell, appeared a little bit more relaxed than he had during our previous meeting. When he exchanged a few words of greeting with Noodles I could tell that all the old negative feelings had been erased. It was clear Mr. Mesmer understood who he was, and recognized that the upcoming departure would finalize their decision to walk in separate paths.

As I looked out the open window into the blue sky, I thought that today, all day, would be a dream coupled with a song floating in the sky. All of us were on a natural high, laughing out loud. Since it was a weekday there was no traffic. We flew along the white highway under the midday sun.

Bits and pieces of my life over the past six months came rolling in. Days riding in a car along the highways in Saipan, the people I'd met, all the things that had happened. Those bits and pieces weren't like the fragments of remembrance popping into my mind after I'd lost my memory, they were more like a poem, each making a dance with brilliant flashes amid the greenery of Japan and over the horizon of the summer ocean.

"Please forgive me for what I said last time," Mr. Mesmer said. "Unless I'm mistaken, I expressed myself too frankly. I'm afraid I was impolite."

"I was so startled by what you said I had a horrible fever." I smiled.

"Really?"

"Really."

"I'm sorry."

"But it was a fabulous fever. It's so rare to get a really good fever once you're an adult," I said.

"Perhaps I was a bit hasty," Mr. Mesmer replied. "I wanted us to get to know as much of each other as possible in the little time that we had. Now I know I took things too quickly. Please forgive me for being so rude." He sounded humble as he spoke.

Noodles looked over to him and casually mentioned, "You know what happens when you say such harsh things to other people."

Her driving was excellent. Most people who obtain their driver's license overseas tend to have a peculiar, audacious style about how they manage a vehicle. But she seemed perfectly natural behind the wheel. We felt no anxiety.

~

"Mesmer, stop worrying about it so much. Can't you come up with dozens of reasons why a person might get a fever?" Noodles said. "I mean, it was just a coincidence. None of us here have power to control things like that, right?"

Mr. Mesmer wouldn't stop apologizing for being so frank during our first conversation, and for causing my fever. Noodles was trying to prove otherwise.

"She's right," I said. "I tend to be hypersensitive sometimes."

"Me, too," Yoshio replied. "Because we're brother and sister, I guess."

Hearing that didn't bring me any comfort. I knew he wasn't telling the truth.

Everyone else knew it, too.

But if I'd opened my mouth and said those things I'd have been like King Midas in the fairy tale, everything I touch turning to gold. All the dark things in my past were bleached by the summer light, and they disappeared along with the waves. It was that kind of feeling. I figured anything I said would actually come true. Eventually our conversation stopped having any kind of real meaning; we just laughed instead. My mind played tricks on me as I looked out of the car. It didn't take long for me to notice that Yoshio and I were once again back in our old familiar location—a place with ocean and sun.

During times like that, moments that felt like they were removed from the flow of time, I'd gaze out over an ocean. Then I'd glance over and see Yoshio right beside me. Regardless of whether we were near or far from home, every time I came to this kind of place under the hot, hot sky, so hot I could barely stand it, with my head just clear enough to make me feel good, all the elements would be there: the sound of waves, sand, a distant ocean, and clouds shining brightly over the meridian of light. As we stood on a beach where I felt I could simply melt into the bright sky, as we stood on the beach only gazing out over life, I supposed that the kid at my side was forever reading my thoughts, thinking right along with me.

In places like that things were simple. There was ocean, sky, and an intense premonition of departure. Our group wouldn't reassemble next week, or the week after. Each and every path of our lives poured gently from the clouds like brilliant rays of light, each sweet and straight, yet separate and distinct from one another.

Between our bouts of laughter and silence, I was sure each of us was impressed by the very same thing.

~

Sadly, night fell upon us. Every inch of our dark blue landscape was fringed with a golden border.

We had been walking for some time along the edge of the ocean. Silently the mood of night increased, a repose created by a soft silhouette filled with passing people and a small dog rushing home. When Mr. Mesmer saw the puppy he was reminded of a Great Dane he'd raised back in California. He told me the story. Apparently Noodles had been fond of the dog, or so Mr. Mesmer said. Whenever I broke into conversation with him Noodles became somewhat flirtatious, and I found it extremely charming.

Out of nowhere Yoshio announced that he wanted to have a barbecue, Japanese style. The rest of us glanced down at him with a puzzled look in our eyes.

Barbecue? How would we go about doing that?

"You know what I mean," my brother said, turning to me. "You and I had it with Mom when we went to Izu—that kind of barbecue where you cook all sorts of meat and clams on top of a skillet. You get to throw everything on by yourself and watch it sizzle!"

"I understand," I said. "You're talking about restaurants where you cook the meat right in front of you over an iron skillet, kind of like cabbage pancakes."

Yoshio anxiously nodded his head.

"Great!" Noodles exclaimed. "Now we know what we're having for dinner."

At that point, regardless of how much I wanted to hold on to the day, the orange and gold stripes across the ocean and the light reflecting in the windows of the hotels eventually faded away. Unconsciously someone let out a sigh.

"We would often say goodnight to another day as we stood on the beach in California, wouldn't we?" Noodles said. "It was like saying a prayer."

"Yes," Mr. Mesmer replied. "I remember." He nodded as he strolled lazily with Noodles by his side.

She looked back and continued, "But it really wasn't a sad feeling, was it? We'd just think about how long the upcoming night would be, and play until we couldn't go on any longer. We'd get so tired we wouldn't have energy to miss the precious daylight. That's when we'd crawl into bed until the light would visit us the next morning, flashing through the window to wake us. Maybe that's why we never forgot to bid farewell to a day like this, out on the beach, precisely at this time. But wasn't there a gap, like a quiet break, when everything felt so wasted?"

"Yes," Mr. Mesmer replied. "I remember."

~

There was a very fine, rather expensive restaurant with small rooms for group barbecues inside a hotel on the beach. Mr. Mesmer announced he was treating us to dinner to pay us back for spending the day with him before he left the country.

The four of us entered the room covered with sand, our shoes still sticky from walking on the beach. After throwing fat upon the grill we watched as it sizzled. Soon we were grilling all sorts of different things. Somebody squirted clam juice and we all burst out laughing. We played hockey with our chopsticks, trying to decide who would eat the burnt onion that stayed on the skillet for too long, and then we laughed even more. I'm sure people on the outside were thinking something strange, perhaps even dangerous, was happening in our room.

As we finished our meal Mr. Mesmer decided to show Yoshio how Robocop flew in the movies. "See," he said, "he jumped like this!" Once again we all broke out laughing, without a real reason. Noodles tipped over the soy sauce jar. It didn't matter. In fact, nothing mattered anymore. We had a marvelous time.

~

We were silent on the way home. When Noodles told Yoshio he could fall asleep in the passenger seat my brother said "No, it wouldn't be worth it." The time together would be wasted. Instead he opted for coffee at the next drive-through.

Sitting in the backseat with Mr. Mesmer, I felt happy listening to them talk. It had been some time since I had felt so peaceful. I wanted to thank god for keeping alive those people who made it possible for me to feel that way again. So when an enormous truck with the words FALLING STAR written on the side zoomed past us with its twinkling lights shining, passing with a tremendous swoosh, I opened my mouth and whispered a small prayer.

Please don't let anyone here have any more unpleasant memories, throughout the rest of time.

The night continued to be unforgiving, cutting away the few precious moments we had left to be together. Before long, the neon signs along the highway in Tokyo came into view, along with the other familiar lights. Noodles slowed down the car as we turned onto the sharp bend that would take us into the city.

"When are you leaving?" Noodles asked Mr. Mesmer.

"Day after tomorrow," he answered.

We told him to give us a call once he was there so he could give us his new address.

"I want you to know I have forgiven you for tossing me aside," Mr. Mesmer said to Noodles. She burst out laughing.

"You liar!" she screamed. "I was the one who was tossed aside. But what does it matter? We've split up. From here on out we're just friends."

"Yes," Mr. Mesmer said, "we are."

"As long as you have friends, there's no need to worry about what's going to happen, because everything will be okay. Your power to protect others will always be strong, right along with your will to stop doing things that would make you embarrassed in front of others."

"Yes," he said, "you're right."

~

"I had so much fun!" Yoshio said as we parted in front of the train station in Tokyo. "I'll never forget how much I hated to see it end."

"Feel free to visit me in California anytime," Mr. Mesmer said. "Because if you still feel uncomfortable living in Japan once you're grown up, there's no law that says you have to stay here."

"Uh-huh," my brother replied.

"And the two of you are also welcome," Mr. Mesmer said as he looked up at me and Noodles. Then he turned around and began to stroll away. As I watched his saddened, weak image from behind fade into the darkness, I couldn't help but think he was the starving Cinderella wandering through the night.

Noodles rode with us on the train to our stop, saying "Bye-bye!" with a smile. My brother and I returned to our house, where my mother and Mikiko were waiting. When I called home from the train station in Shibuya, my mother told me to bring Yoshio back home with me that night because Mikiko had picked up a truckload of sweets and goodies. We didn't need a thing. It was all there waiting for us.

At that point, a small portion of the sadness I had carried with me disappeared along with the same amount of my memories of the ocean . . .

. . . even though my arms were still flushed red with sunlight

. . . even though my shoes were still soggy with sand from a wonderful beach

. . . and even though I could close my eyes at that very moment and recall the smile in her eyes and hear the sound of the waves echoing softly in my heart. I felt like a small child who'd just gone to visit her relatives in a faraway town, the one who bawled her eyes out on the train ride home. I remembered that feeling, and for a short moment I tasted a hot sensation that was greater than anything I had felt thus far in my life.

∾

On the same day that Mr. Mesmer left for the States, I stayed at Ryūichirō's apartment for the night. For some reason we found ourselves completely absorbed in a video he had capriciously picked up, *Gone With the Wind,* even though Ryūichirō said he was interested only in hearing the background music. In the end we didn't get to bed until four o'clock in the morning, and even then we weren't together. Ryūichirō slept on his bed and I crawled into a futon on the floor next to him. There was quite a difference between us.

"I'm tired."

"Why did we stay up and watch the whole entire thing? Hadn't you seen it before?"

"Yeah. Three times."

"I should've known."

"I'm too tired to even have sex tonight."

"I was afraid of that happening to us. We have fallen into the trap of all sexless couples."

"No we're not, we're just getting old."

"No, just tired."

"But why *Gone With the Wind*? I wonder if that movie is all it's cracked up to be."

"Well, it came from a wonderful book."

Somewhere amid the conversation rolling from our mouths, I found myself falling fast asleep.

Looking around I saw that I was in a place that resembled a hotel lobby. The entire room was pouring with sunlight. An enormous ceiling miles above me was covered completely in glass, showing me a clear view of the blue sky. The sun cast an even glow on everyone around me, causing their fair skin and blond hair to shine vividly in the light.

How beautiful, I thought to myself.

Golden hair swaying gently over their shoulders. The tone set by the sound of English all around me, echoing like the whisper of beautiful music, filling every inch of the lobby.

I glanced down to see I was in my sundress, sitting next to a large wooden table covered in wisteria. The top of the table was glass and the red flowers bloomed nicely from a crystal vase in the center.

I wondered what was sparkling on the other side of the room. After squinting my eyes at the brightness, I saw that there were doors leading outside, and beyond that was a terrace. Even beyond the terrace was a beach and an enormous sparkling ocean. At first I wasn't aware that the brightness of the light, so strong I couldn't look into it directly, was really the light reflecting from the water.

Suddenly a feeling came over me.

How cruel it is that something would be brought so close to me, only to be taken away.

As I wondered where my feelings came from, I noticed a sunburned man walk nimbly from the other side of the room. He was tall and lanky, and there was something sober about his appearance. Just as I thought to myself, *I know you,* he had quickened his step and approached me with a smile. Mr. Mesmer.

"Mesmer," I asked. "Where are we?"

Gazing around the lobby, Mesmer turned back to me and said, "Somewhere in your head. It's a place you've created in your imagination by combining what you think of airports, California, and all other foreign lands." He continued to smile as he sat down across from me at the table.

"You look so healthy," I said. "So I suppose you were right. You really don't get along well in Japan."

"Exactly," he replied with a grin. "There's not enough sun."

"I had such a wonderful time with you the other day. Thank you so much for everything."

A group of children in their bathing suits rushed past me, looking as though they were headed for the ocean. A server also strolled by with some kind of wonderful drink on his silver tray.

We were silent for a few moments, and within that silence I looked out again over the ocean. It looked so bright, as if it were made of silver and gold. Another large mass of sparkling light.

"What about Noodles?" I asked. "Would you like me to pass anything on to her?"

Mr. Mesmer shook his head.

"No, it's over. We had a wonderful time together, but now we are done. I really do love her, and her youthful way of looking at life. I'm impressed by subtle things about her as well. Even if we were together, the relationship would be in her hands now. But we're not, and I'm going to take it hard when she finds someone else to be with, even if that new person is only close enough to see the crease in her skirt. Noodles is like a flower. She's hope and light. She's everything that's weak, and everything that's strong. And without a doubt, she will soon belong to someone else, along with everything that comes with her—her smile, and the warmth of the palms of her hands.

"Life can really be cruel sometimes. I'd better face the realization that someday Noodles will be together with somebody else. Right now the pain of her leaving me still resonates in my heart like beautiful gospel music, a beauty that comes with the flow of time, and the cruelty that came along with it. Even if I let her go now I'll still have something to call beauty, only it will manifest itself in a different form. So that's the way I have to go on living, redeeming myself with true friends."

"I see," I replied, as an image of Noodles floated up in my mind. She was standing across from me with the usual smile in her eyes, and she wore a long skirt.

"Thank you," Mr. Mesmer said. "Thank you very, very much. Regardless of how far away our separate paths might lead, I'll always love you forever."

~

My eyes opened. The room around me was dark, the middle of the night. I felt a sharp twinge of pain when I realized Mr. Mesmer had come to bid me farewell. The desire to write down every inch of that dream, from start to stop, top to bottom, welled up inside me. I wanted to put it in an envelope and have the entire package tightly sealed, never to forget it.

Something was different somehow.

There was a beauty that gradually came into my arms, slowly moving away. It would be wrong to hold on too tightly to the memories of the ocean, and to the memories of my friends' smiles as they drifted far away.

Peering up at Ryūichirō still lying in bed, I saw that his eyes were wide open, and he was staring down at me.

"What's the matter?" I asked with surprise. "Didn't you say you were tired?"

"Yeah, but for some reason I just opened my eyes," he replied. "Tell me, did you just have a beautiful dream?"

"Yes," I said. "Why? Did I look beautiful as I was sleeping?" I batted my eyelids.

"No," he said, shaking his head.

"So I talked in my sleep."

"No," Ryūichirō replied. "I just had this bizarre sensation that the room filled with light. That's why I woke up. Then I looked down, and you were asleep. As I watched you an image of an enormous hotel lobby with lots of light, someplace near an ocean, came over you."

"Wow. Now you're clairvoyant, too."

"No," he replied. "I'm just a writer. And your boyfriend."

"Is that so?" I said, secretly agreeing.

Since I was up, I decided to have coffee with crackers. Just about the time the sun began to filter its way through the curtains, I began to feel tired again. I drifted back to sleep. After that, the only other thing that made an appearance to me that night was a sleep so sound it made me feel like I'd been dropped in thick, wet mud.

No one else paid me a visit in my dreams.

Chapter 22

One day while I was waiting around for Ryūichirō to come back to his apartment, I found I had absolutely nothing to do. Suddenly I had the urge to jot down all the major events that had happened to me over the past few years of my life. With the TV blaring in front of me, I formulated the following list:

1. Mayu dies
2. I fall and hit my head, concussion, surgery
3. Memory lost
4. Yoshio turns into "the clairvoyant kid"—hears and sees strange things
5. I get involved with Ryūichirō
6. Trip to Kochi
7. Trip to Saipan
8. Berries closes down
9. I find a new job
10. Memory returns
11. Yoshio goes off to the center for special children
12. Junko runs away
13. A new friendship with Noodles and Mr. Mesmer

When I was finished, I put my pen down and looked at what I'd written. It seemed odd to see it all there before me as though a limitless expanse of time had brightly unfolded, something firmly etched in stone. At the same time it was evidence of the insignificant days that had governed my life.

I walked over and placed the list on top of the table. To say that it was nothing more than a scrap of square white paper would not be stretching the truth. Even if I had wadded up the list and thrown it in the wastebasket, its meaning would have stayed the same. Still, I felt attached to that piece of paper.

It reminded me of a precious piece of microfilm filled with information of the past. As events flowed, they seemed to color the years. My heart reflected in that little piece of paper. I'd spent several years wandering through those images and at some point in time I'd managed to wind up here—on top of the table in my boyfriend's apartment.

But who knows? My journey had not been reliable. Tomorrow this place could become the den of an enemy, or this dear paper recording my history could be lost and I would no longer have any way of remembering what had happened to me. Tomorrow I could be run over by a car and the curtain of my life would come crashing down, an end to my existence. Or maybe all the people who I had had no problem meeting and talking to ten minutes ago would fade away into faraway distances.

As of now, no one had informed me of where I would be this same time next year.

I can't help but be impressed by those who are able to move forward, despite knowing what lies ahead.

People are so adept at fading and slipping away. They face whatever is in front of them. They laugh, cry, and bear grudges against one another. They fool one another as well.

Each of us will die someday, but that doesn't matter. We simply move forward, trying not to break under all the pressure

Quietly I found myself covered in the soft veil of memory. All I could do was look up into the rays of the shining sun through the branches of the trees that had thrived for thousands of years. I gazed across a neverending mountain range reflecting the light of an evening sun, and at the facade of a wooden structure that people of the past devoted their entire lives to build, only to find peace.

Surely I'd awake the next morning, somewhere.

I wasn't exactly sure where.

I would continue to live, that much was clear. The next day would bring a new feeling about life to me—something inside would be happily content. I would rise in the same form of that sleeping spirit curled up somewhere near my heart, the one who was with me in my dreams.

Life is just that way. There are times when I get tired of it all, and feel like I just want to die. But there are also times when everything is so amusing I want to go on living forever. It's like the scene in cartoons when a little angel is standing on your right shoulder and a little devil on the left, and they're fighting over who will win. My will to live and my desire to die were the same as the angel and the devil—it was a fifty-fifty tug-of-war raging in my soul. Gravity seemed to be the only thing holding me down.

~

Dear Family:

After doing such a thing I thought it would be best not for me to get in touch with you, but for some reason I felt the need to write this letter. Now I sit with pen and paper in hand.

Right now I'm with my daughter at my mother's house.

I promise to return the money I borrowed.

It was such a joy living with all of you. But my heart was often troubled because I often thought that if I was having so much fun with you, people who were not even of my own flesh and blood, how much more fun I could be having with my daughter.

Now that I see things as they really are, I realize not everything will be ideal. Since my daughter and I have spent so much time away from each other, I am still unable to talk to her freely. It makes me realize how much I love each and every one of you—Yoshio, Saku-chan, Mikiko-chan.

How wonderful it would have been if I could have just stayed in the house, Yukiko as husband and me as wife. The happiness would have gone on forever. In the end I had to deny myself that desire. I had to get on with my own life, and running away was the only way to do it. I apologize for any misunderstanding. It has been very painful.

However, now I am with my own mother and daughter, and I hope to continue the joy in this home that I experienced so vividly in yours.

Please, continue to be happy. I promise to see you all again.

I pray you all grow strong and healthy.

With love,
Junko

I hardly ever cry in front of others, and my mother, well known for her saying "No use crying over spilt milk," was even worse. At least that's the way she made it seem. But when my mother and I read Junko's letter together, we broke down in tears. I suppose that's what people mean when they talk about parents who proverbially cry over their little ones.

Junko's letter arrived on the same day my brother checked out of the children's center. That morning was hot—the sun beat down brightly. I went with my mother to pick up Yoshio. As we approached the receptionist behind the counter she smiled and said, "I don't think I've ever seen a child leave this place as much as Yoshio. But one thing is certain, we're going to miss him." While she was talking I saw Yoshio walk toward us down the hallway with a suitcase in his right hand. He had a young girl with him. She smiled as she clung tightly to his free arm.

The receptionist leaned over to us and said, "Yoshio's the first person in the world that little girl has talked to."

She was obviously not alone. As soon as word was out that Yoshio was leaving the center, dozens of children came barreling out of their rooms to bid him farewell. Some of them could not speak. Others were still wearing diapers, despite their age. Some looked troubled, with dark rings around their eyes; others were so thin you could fit your entire hand around their forearms. Still others were extremely large.

All the children were crying, and nothing would remove their eyes from my brother. They stood with clenched fists, showing their sadness the best way they knew. Before long Yoshio was completely surrounded by the children. Each of them had small letters and notes, or small trinkets they'd made themselves. The presents just kept coming one right after another. In the end my brother seemed rather jarred.

He didn't cry. He just returned their greetings by saying, "I'll be sure to write you all a letter," or "I'll come back and play," and "Next time we'll go fishing."

"He looks like those pictures you see of Christ," my mother joked.

Since the children seemed like they didn't want to let my brother go, a teacher came out of one of the classrooms and announced classes were about to begin, which didn't seem to have much effect on the children. They remained standing around him with tears in their eyes, not wanting to let him go. I realized at that point how much I loved my brother.

All of the things that had happened since Yoshio arrived at that center came rushing by me at an extremely fast pace, not as memories, but simply as a fresh breeze filled with a peculiar light radiated at the center. The air that filled the hallway that day was ten thousand times more painful than any of the memories or images of the center that my brother might have remembered. I'm sure that's what brought tears to their eyes.

Eventually my brother broke down and started crying, too. We took him over to the elevator as he wiped moisture from his eyes, and we jostled our way through the door with all the other children. Yoshio's friends acted as if they wanted to stay with him forever.

Finally away from the center, and away from the other students, my mother turned to my brother and said with a stuffed-up nose, "What did you do there? Start a new religion?"

"No," my brother replied. "They were just my friends, just like in Saipan, and in the park with Noodles. I found myself with kids I could be really sociable with, something I never experienced at school. So now I want to go on being friends with them, forever, and from here on out I want to help out a lot more people like them."

"That would be wonderful," my mother said. "Friends are so important."

Yoshio and I were silent. Even now I can bring to mind a vivid picture of my mother and Junko sitting around the kitchen table talking through the night. Whenever I pulled myself out of bed to go to the bathroom or to get a drink, I'd walk down the hall and hear my mother and Junko talking and laughing like two girls in high school about the things that concerned them in life.

~

Dearest Saku-chan:

Forgive me for being so formal, writing a letter and all.

But I had to say thanks for the other day.

I had a glorious time.

It was really, really fun. It made me feel glad to be alive.

In all honesty, I've always felt proud that I have a special talent for seeing things and helping other people, and for spending the time in California that I did. However, there have been times when half of me really hated knowing it, yet the other side of me has always been full of pride.

Things changed back then and I began to lose my ability. It hurt to be at the institution. On top of that, things between Mesmer and me were bad (because he was so devoted to the lifestyle back there). But now that I am here in Japan and have broken things off with him, I have a chance to think about why I'm alive. I've also thought a lot about why I went back to California.

When we were together at Kamakura I saw the ocean and the blue sky. Everything was warm. I was with my former lover and a couple of beautiful new friends. It was wonderful. Now I realize that it is possible to have something happen to me in life, free of problems.

It was a first for me.

I didn't make any mistakes.

Thank you.

Being surrounded by friends like you, I feel like I can spend the rest of my life rushing down a path filled with happiness. Eventually I'm sure I'll just trip, fall over, and die. That might be too blunt to write in a letter, but it's bound to happen.

It won't matter, though, thanks to you and the day we spent together.

It was a first for me.

I hope it happens again soon.

With love,
Kaname

∾

"I feel like I've been here before," I said to Ryūichirō.

"You mean another memory just popped into your head?" he replied.

We'd walked into a cafe, just back from a trip to buy Ryūichirō a new bookcase for his apartment. The building was a huge greenhouse, and strong rays from the summer sun poured themselves all over the green plants. Outside the wind was so strong it blew the hair and skirts of people walking back and forth on the street, and I could see that trees along the side of the road were swaying heavily in the wind.

As I told Ryūichirō about the similar kind of wind that blew through our neighborhood the day my brother left the house, and as I mentioned how he was now home with a whole new host of friends and a tremendous amount of self-esteem along with it, I had the impression that I'd been in that building before. The feeling came upon me so quickly I hardly knew what was going on.

Half of the building opened up to the outside, and the floor was made of concrete. I'd been sitting with someone around a circular table. . . but who? The memory was too far away. I was drinking orange juice, the other person was having beer.

As I pondered on my memory Ryūichirō suddenly said, "Are you sure it wasn't with your old boyfriend?" Once again he looked dejected.

"How could I have come all the way out here, just to forget about it?" I asked. "I mean, I think this is the first time I've ever gotten off at that train station. . . ."

"Then maybe you saw a picture of this place in a magazine," Ryūichirō replied. "It has been around for ages, and you see it a lot in travel books and the like."

"I've got it!" I exclaimed.

Little by little, the memory evolved in my mind. Concentrating closely on the images that came bubbling up, I slowly pictured my father's face. He was smiling.

"I came here with my father," I said. "The one who died?"

"Yeah," I replied.

"Now I remember."

"So how old were you?"

"About ten, maybe . . ."

"Wow," Ryūichirō said. "Were you ever really that young?" He leaned over the table and squinted his eyes as though imagining what I looked like when I was ten.

Meanwhile, I wondered why it was just my father and me on the trip that day. Why had Mayu and my mother stayed behind?

Oh, yes. My father had gone for the results of a medical exam at a hospital not so far from here. I'm sure his medical reports were already threatening him with a shadow of death, clearly recording signs of his high blood pressure and overwork. I wondered if his daughter, still so young, thought that calm Sunday afternoons like that one with Dad would just continue to go on forever. There was no way of ever knowing for sure.

I remembered my father had already put on an unusual amount of weight. Everything was crazy at his job. He'd stayed the night there a few times. But he sipped golden beer from a large glass mug that afternoon, as if nothing was wrong in the world. Even though I was only a child, I remember thinking how delicious his beer looked to me back then.

It was the same cafe, only years later. And . . .

. . . it seemed like there was something else. Something important.

"There are only couples here today," my father said. Then he laughed. "I guess you could say that about us, too."

"Yuck!" I said. "I would never date you, Daddy." Since I was so little it was only natural for me to object.

"I really can't picture it," my father said, looking me in the eyes. (His expression was exactly like Ryūichirō's, although he was looking at me when I was ten and trying to imagine an adult, not the other way around.) "The thought of you and Mayu growing big and taking the place of one of those young women sitting over there. To think one day you'll be moving in with boyfriends, getting married, and so on. But even more than trying to fathom you as older, I think it's harder for me to see myself being there when it happens."

The statement faded into a whisper as if he were having a dream.

He looked lonely, an expression that was different than usual.

Tell me where you'll be!

I wanted to say it, but I couldn't. It hurt just thinking about it. I got a lump in my throat and I suddenly felt like crying, even though I couldn't bring tears to my eyes.

Just tell me when you've gone so far away.

My father said, almost in response to my question, "I really don't think I'll be here when you and Mayu grow older."

"NO!" I screamed. Then I stopped and said, "Daddy, will you take me back to that store we passed and buy me the doll in the window?" I really didn't want it; I was only trying to fool him. Perhaps I was trying to fool myself. I just had to say something to get it out of my mind—that terrifying thought of him leaving.

"You're hopeless," my father said, standing up and grabbing me by the arm. His face was red and he walked with a wobble. "We'd better pick another one up for Mayu. She'll start hollering if she doesn't get a doll, too."

∾

"I'm starting my new novel," Ryūichirō said.

Taken in by all the sudden memories, I'd told him that I'd treat us to some beer. He made his announcement right after we'd placed our order.

"Oh?" I said. "So you're leaving the country again to collect materials? If that's the case, you've got to let me live in your apartment while you're gone."

"Why do you always think I have to go away to write books? I'm staying right here."

"So you'll write your book in Japan? What is it about? Will it sell? Will you make lots of money? Are you going to be rich? What are you going to buy me?" Questions poured from my mouth.

"Hmm . . ." Ryūichirō paused for a moment. "I'm not sure how it will do."

Just like in the past, the server brought over two huge glass mugs filled with golden beer. We clinked our glasses together and took a foamy sip. The sun filtered through the windows in the cafe with the same exactness as it did on the street and trees outside. Our chairs, glasses, trays, and the mirrors, all reflecting the sun's brilliance.

"I'm paying you money for your story," Ryūichirō said.

"Who?" I asked. "Me?"

"Yeah. You're the model for my main character. It's going to be a story about a woman who loses her memory and then gets it back."

Oh no, I thought. It would never sell.

"Don't worry. The character won't be exactly like you. It will just be a few of the things I've thought about you over all this time. I saved the list you wrote on that scrap of paper in my apartment. Do you remember leaving it behind—that list of all the things that have happened to you over the years? After looking at that I decided it would make a good story, because something about it really touched me. I mean, even within such a simple list there's so much to write about. I'm shocked to see how much you've been through. I could never come up with that stuff on my own."

"I suppose you'll call the novel *The Story of a Beautiful Woman*?"

"No," Ryūichirō said, not going along with the joke. "I'm calling it *Amrita*."

Now it was certain. The book would never sell.

"You'll never sell a book with a title like that!" I screamed.

"Do you really think so?" he asked.

"Of course I do," I replied. "What does it mean, anyway?"

"It comes from the old Sanskrit word *amrta*. You know, a divine nectar, something the gods indulged in by guzzling the stuff down. They say that when you let the liquid gush through you, you've actually achieved life, because what happens to the flowing water is similar to what happens to people. At least that's the way I see it, don't ask me why. But don't you think it will make a good title for a novel? Sure, it might not sell, but that's beside the point."

"If it comes down to it we always have my paychecks from the bakery." I sighed.

Letting water gush through your body . . . At some point in time I'd heard the story from someone else before . . .

. . . or so I thought as I listened to Ryūichirō go on.

She was someone beautiful, with a natural smile and a wonderfully sweet voice. I heard the story told in a world where light shone gracefully down in slender rays. She was in my heart from the beginning, and although she was no longer around, I loved her deeply.

I want to see her now.

That beautiful child I grew up with.

Dear Sakumi:

How are you? Kozumi and I are fine.

I was so thrilled to get a call from you the other day, but when it was just about a prank someone played on you by sending you a tape, I was a little bit disappointed. I would have enjoyed talking to you more about a whole lot of different things.

Kozumi and I were also disappointed that someone had beat us to such a clever trick. We decided to send you a funny tape, too. So the night you called we went through every record and CD in the house, trying to find something that would be just right for you. After listening to records and tapes for a few hours, it turned into a twisted version of "Name That Tune."

We weren't able to come up with one song in particular for you, but we had a glorious time singing and dancing to the music until dawn. After that neither of us could sleep.

We took a long stroll along the beach that morning.

The ocean seemed spread out forever in front of us. It was radiant blue. The sky was a pale purple. In the distance I could see a sliver of pink, until finally a single ray of light came shining brilliantly over the ocean. The day had finally started, and yesterday was over. Didn't we often stay up all night playing, when you and Ryūichirō were here in Saipan, along with your cute brother? Those were the days. I often think about how wonderful it would be to see you again.

I really wanted to stop you when you left and say, "Hey! Don't go! Stay here and live with us forever. We'll spend the rest of our lives playing." Because I had so much fun being with you.

Every day seemed like an exciting adventure when you were here. It was like I was suddenly living life in color.

If only you'd said you would stay with me forever, even if you really didn't mean it!

But I suppose you're still too young to realize why Kozumi and I chose to find our own peace on this island. You haven't been through as many hardships yet, either.

Life on the island is like living a dream. Time really doesn't exist here. Things that haunted Kozumi and me all our lives haven't followed us here, but everything else has. Since time does not exist, we really have all the time in the world. We have space and freedom, and of course we're surrounded by people. Some are alive, others are dead. Some passed away only yesterday, others passed away in the distant past. There are Japanese and there are foreigners. Everyone is here. We have the ocean and the town and bars for karaoke. Mountains and songs are intermixed with sandwiches. It's a dream, and in the dream if I suddenly have the urge to eat a piece of cake—boom!, there it is right in front of me. When I have the urge to say hello to my mother who passed away, it's the very same thing. It's a wonderful existence.

Maybe both of us went through too much early on in life. We've lived a hundred times more than most, so we made the decision to spend the rest of our lives here where the only requirement is to float. Here we are, waiting for others to join us. Our arms are always open to welcome you.

You know you have an open invitation to come back.

Always.

Which brings me to the real reason I'm writing you this letter. This morning as I took my usual walk along the ocean, I noticed a beautiful young woman who I hadn't seen before. She was collecting shells on the beach. I remained silent as I slowly made my way around her, watching her the entire time.

Her hair was pulled back in two soft braids, and she wasn't wearing any makeup. She was beautiful. Her skin was so white I could have melted into it.

When she looked up at me, she smiled.

I returned the smile, and then moved past her. When I looked back to view her against the light of the morning sun she was gone.

Things like that happen a lot around here.

Apparently the woman was your sister.

Kozumi told me later.

He told me she had come to be with us because she saw how much we longed to be with you, Sakumi.

I agreed.

She was beautiful! So thin I wanted to wrap both of my arms around her.

I don't know if it's good or bad, but Saipan is that kind of place. You could think of it as a distant shore, or a place where all goals are realized.

Lately I've been asking myself, "Who is Sakumi?"

I think about it all the time.

Do you just exist because you're alive, or are you alive because you exist? When I look out and see you there, all of a sudden I feel like crying. My tears don't stem from sadness, instead they come from joy. Isn't that strange?

I can't help but think about how I was able to meet you, and about the time when we came together, even though I really don't care about such things anyway. Now I always feel like I am with you.

I think about the things you're thinking. I know how you are feeling. It thrills me to have access to such knowledge. How you are doing, how you slip out of place, and even how you get angry sometimes. I can't predict what you will do, but somehow I am aware of you, and that's why I feel alive.

I couldn't ask for a better present in this world.

Were you just a dream? I find that I question myself as I lie down in bed to take an afternoon nap. When my eyes open I see curtains swaying in the breeze and I look beyond at the ocean outside my window. Everything is filled with light.

All the things we did together—were they just a dream?

Laughing together on the beach until our sides hurt. Holding each other tightly.

Falling asleep under the afternoon sun.

Was it real? Or just a dream?

I think about it all the time. There couldn't be a better fantasy.

I really think so.

And when I close my eyes I can see your smiling face and everything spreads out in front of me, a face filled with strong destiny.

Your white double tooth. Your eyebrows curved perfectly like half-moons. The sparkling brown in your eyes. Your eyelashes. Your legs so long and straight. Your hands surprisingly strong. The thick ring you wore on your finger. The worn-out leather of your bag. And the steady contour of your profile—the straight way you held yourself.

I remember it all.

Once again I think how wonderful it would be to see you again.

The time we spent together was special. We talked about so many precious things, even if they did come slowly like drops of water spilling over a large glass. You showed me that sun and water, and everything else along with it, would only be with us for a day. You taught me to take in as much as possible rather than being stingy with it.

Even if I was just walking along the beach. I wondered if I had fallen in love.

Maybe I was just trying to say thanks.

Since I've had more than my share of Kozumi's hard-rock music over the past few days, I've spent the past few nights going through some of my favorite music to try and come up with something I could send. I've made a copy of one of the songs most dear to me, and I'll enclose it with this letter. Then I'll be off to sleep.

I apologize that I can't be there in person to give this to you. My words simply don't seem to be enough.

With love,
Saseko

∾

On a clear afternoon a few days later, I discovered in our old rusty mailbox the small package sent from Saipan. The beautiful letter and a black cassette tape were inside. As I removed the tape from the envelope, a gush of air came pouring out, bringing with it the wonderful fragrance of a room filled with sunlight. I felt a sharp tug at my heart.

I put the tape in my stereo, and soon every inch of my entire room was filled with a beautiful melody. The lyrics went something like this:

You're a distance light-years away, in a place very close to my heart
I always feel your gaze
I include with this letter a dream I had of you
My words will cross the ocean and reach you in seven days

I cry out for you now, as I stand on this distant shore
I'm calling to send you word
that from my heart which has sprouted wings,
comes love from a far eastern world

It happened again. Time secretly came to a standstill. With intense speed and force, I was suddenly rushed back to the quiet evenings of Saipan. My entire world seemed drenched by Saseko's lovely voice, her quiet mannerisms, and the frame of her small body glowing against the evening sun. Everything poured from her song with such fine radiance it seemed to stretch on forever.

The grace of those moments in life when I knew I was truly alive.

Looking up into a cloudless sky and feeling the drops of rain from a welcome shower.

Water filled with glory.

Without a doubt it had happened to me before, at some point in time. Certainly the feelings wouldn't end there, because they weren't concerned with future or memories. It was simply a faraway dream that looked deep into the heart of the chromosomes that determined who I was, and what I would become.

. . . or so the words of the song came over me.

It had always been out there, shining brightly. I just hadn't reached out to touch it. But every now and then I felt surrounded by its presence. From right to left, from here to there, like water flowing downstream. A limitless amount of sweet oxygen. The more I took in, the greater the supply.

Like a saint in the legends who reached out and took jewels from the sky, I had the same kind of talent for gathering miracles in my life. There was no doubt about it. Those feelings had always been with me.

You know, banging my head on the stairway wasn't such a bad thing after all. . . .

And that's how I see it.

Epilogue

"When I think back to those days when my life was so messed up . . ."

Not long ago, on a night when my mother was out of the house on a date, I had dinner with my brother. It had been ages since we talked. After slurping up a couple of bowls of thick udon soup, we sat around drinking tea and munching potato chips. That's when Yoshio started to speak.

"You know, back when you and I were running around the beaches of Kochi and Saipan, I was really happy."

"You're the last person in the world I'd want to hear that from!" I exclaimed. Having gone through so much with my little brother, I couldn't just sit back and take a comment like that lightly. And I let him know how I felt about it, too. But, actually, deep down I knew what Yoshio was trying to say.

Even now as I look back over the different things we encountered, all those incidents too numerous to mention here, it feels like time has just steadily moved forward. Despite everything that went on, I never felt pressed or hurried. The people we met, the places we visited, those who stayed with us each step of the way—they all seem tightly connected somehow. And as I think about it, I can't help but wonder if that was my turning point in life, a new maturation of sorts, something that came far too late in my own life, and much too early for Yoshio.

"I can't help it," he continued. "It seems like every day brought with it some kind of new challenge."

I looked over to him. "So how's life treating you now?"

Yoshio had just started middle school and oddly enough he'd developed an interest in baseball. Ever since he'd joined the school team, the energy he used to radiate like some supernatural power started to slowly leave him. Then his body started changing as well. If I were to put a label on it, I'd say he was becoming a jock, and the athletics were shaping him in a way his special powers never could. I mean, he looked like a model out of the pages of a fitness textbook. It was that simple. I laugh about it now as I realize this mechanism we call our bodies is put together more modestly than we'd care to admit. Things get complicated only when our emotions separate from our physical bodies, scattering in a thousand different directions, as our hearts pound wildly with excitement. At that point the gap between our physical selves and emotional selves becomes visible, a gap filled with a darkness so fearful you never want to taste it again and a beauty far greater than anything in this world. Even when you have grasped this knowledge that still doesn't mean you'll be happy, or sad for that matter. But to take a stab at it, I'd say that happiness is the end result, more often than not.

Yoshio piped up. "I don't use my mind as much as I used to. I mean, before something was always going on in my head. Almost like I had a fever."

Well, my head wasn't exactly cool then either, I thought to myself. My own feelings allowed me to empathize with my brother. In those days our troubles had come from the exhausting effort we put into protecting each other, but when I recalled the foolish way we behaved, jumping from one place to another, I couldn't help but remember the wonderful, fun times, too.

We were like young buddies huddled close in front of a fire together, warming our cheeks on a frosty winter night. After throwing on some CDs, we'd pass the night away eating candies and drinking beer, occasionally falling deep into serious conversations only to laugh our way out of them.

So much had been upset in our lives, with everyone rushing in opposite directions—back and forth, left and right—that when the light began to shine through the distant waters I knew something had happened. I knew I was saved.

~

Eventually I gave up my job at the bakery. My manager, however, was so taken with me that I went back regularly for a while, to help out when they needed an extra hand, or just to buy baguettes. Once he even invited me to spend some time at his villa in Nice, an offer I gladly accepted.

The French city was wonderful—the atmosphere of a truly provincial town still lingered in the air, amid the streets and alleys. That's what gave the place its charm, and the sea that bordered its edges looked like something out of a movie. The colors in the sky and around town burst with dynamic energy. Dogs of all kinds ran freely through the streets. Retired couples strolled here and there, too. On top of it all, I got to visit the nearby Matisse Museum for free.

That's what surprised me the most. In the first place, I couldn't imagine something that wonderful being open free of charge in Tokyo. Then I saw the rainbow of color that filled that silent space and felt like a piece of Matisse had forever imprinted itself onto my mind and soul.

~

By the time I got home my boss from Berries had come back to Tokyo with the wild idea of opening a "reggae" version of Berries, but in a new location. Unlike the old bar where we'd put on music in tune with our moods, the new bar was exclusively reggae. Perhaps it won't be long before my boss finds a new hobby and changes the place to suit his latest craze—but I try not thinking about that. As a member of the opening staff I was involved with even the smallest details of the new bar, from the menu all the way to the decor. I really don't get into reggae, and I've never been to Jamaica, but before I realized it I was practically a pro in the field. I couldn't help but be pleased with my own strategy for learning; but at the same time I was often turned off by the trendy young people who would clamor in the bar, and my boss, the pseudo-Jamaican. Then there was the never-ending rattle of their meaningless conversations, not to mention the spicy Caribbean food that was served even when the season outside our windows made me crave pounded rice cakes and hot pot. I suppose I easily got tired of it all, because the thought of quitting crossed my mind several times.

But something amusing always seemed to pop up, and I found myself sticking with the job. One day, for example, I jumped into a cab, thinking nothing of it since the driver was your run-of-the-mill Japanese taxi driver—gray pants and white shirt, oily hair parted thickly to one side—but the minute he discovered I was working at the bar, he announced:

"I'm proud to say that a member of Aswad, you know, the reggae band, has ridden in this cab before."

And our conversation took off from there. Surprised to hear a cab driver drop a name like that, I replied by saying, "My, I'm amazed you were able to recognize someone from Aswad."

"Don't be," he said. "It was during Japansplash, and I'd heard they were in town with Janet Kay." His matter-of-fact way of talking continued to astonish me. After that he rambled on about how much he was into Bob Marley, and about the wonders of the music. By the time we arrived at my destination I'd forgotten all about quitting my job.

To this day I think of that driver as an angel sent to me by the goddess of reggae.

~

I'm still with Ryūichirō. I guess you could say we're practically living with each other. Luckily, royalties from his novel have continued to flow in, allowing us to travel back to Saipan and have a few other luxuries in our lives as well. The retired young couple living on the island is doing fine; that special languor that comes over those living in foreign countries continues to cover their faces. I still see their lives sparkling with color; and whether that image conjures up soft winds or bright sun rays in my mind, or whether it creates a ravishing landscape or the darkness of night, I figure it clearly comes from a place in their souls that exists in a special world, a place where time evolves differently than it does in Japan.

It's been about a year now since Ryūichirō cheated on me. Around the time he was expected home from one of his many jaunts overseas, I discovered that he'd been staying with another woman in Spain. I'd become aware of this through a telephone call she'd made to our apartment.

The next time I spoke with Ryūichirō I informed him that his lover had called. He stopped talking, then hung up. One week passed, and then I heard his footsteps outside the door.

Stunned to see him carry his luggage into the room, I asked him where he'd found the courage to come crawling back to me like that. Rather than give me a direct answer, he simply replied, "Why are you giving up on the two of us so fast?" Apparently we were both surprised by the way the other had acted.

He apologized by saying that he's a pushover for young, angelic faces, rather than people with crabby dispositions like mine. It was an absurd excuse, but hearing him talk about angelic faces made me recall Mayu, and before I knew it I was thoroughly depressed. "But that doesn't matter," he stated, "because I enjoy being with unpredictable types like you. You're the best kind of person to be with. I rushed home hoping you wouldn't feel uncomfortable with the situation. I didn't want to give you the wrong idea."

His sincerity amused me, and even though I hesitate to say that I'm in love with the man in Ryūichirō, I can say that he's the one person on earth I could never grow weary of. With that, I made up my mind to reconcile our differences.

Now, even though things have been like this for a while, funny enough, there's still more to the story. About two weeks after Ryūichirō got back, I was strolling along a small street in front of the nearby train station when I came across a small flower shop. It just so happens that they were displaying exotic flowers from faraway lands in miniature bouquets, and the entire front of the store was alive with them. All the neighborhood shops—meat market, pharmacy, and vegetable stands—were in a confused jumble of shopping housewives and high school kids hanging out. The lights streaming from the shop windows danced across the sidewalk.

There, amid the bustle of all those people with warm homes to go back to, I purchased some of the flowers, not really thinking much about it, and then made my way to Ryūichirō's. After placing the bouquet in a vase and staring at the blossoms for a while, I grabbed something sweet and plopped down in front of the TV. Then I allowed my mind to wander for a few minutes. How long would it take before I, too, would generate the same kind of warmth that a small bundle of flowers brings to a simple story? Before long I felt a sharp pain in my heart, and for the first time since shortly after Mayu passed away, I felt the bitter heat of tears streaming down my cheeks.

All of us have within ourselves a weak spot somewhere near our hearts that needs to be nourished. Every now and then it's not such a bad idea to expose that part of ourselves, by allowing the tears to flow. I'm convinced it's the best way to show you care.

After I shared these thoughts with Ryūichirō, he sat silently for a moment, reflecting. At that point I, too, just sat thinking, glancing down into the darkness of the road beyond the window. It occurred to me that at some point in time I might have the desire to take someone by the hand and step out into that darkness. Then again, maybe I'm already out there. But rather than let it all get to me, I just kept to my own silence—after all, Ryūichirō was kind enough to ponder my thoughts with me, and before I knew it, he'd even started doing the dishes.

So that's how it would be. Regardless of what might happen, things will never change. I'll continue to flow endlessly through life. . . .

And nothing will get in my way.

Afterword to the American Edition

Now as I read over this novel I realize how naive it is, and I feel my face turning red. Then again, when I think that I might not ever write another book as lengthy as this one, it becomes a cherished item to me.

The theme of this book is simple. I want to express the idea that, regardless of all the amazing events that happen to each of us, there will always be the neverending cycle of daily life.

I give my deepest thanks to the one who translated this book, so random and disjointed, with such thoughtful care—Mr. Russell F. Wasden. I also reach out over the distance in time and water to thank all of you, my readers abroad.

You will always have a special place in my heart.

Banana Yoshimoto
Early spring, 1997